D0893980

DISCARD

# PRAISE FOR ABBY JIMENEZ

## LIFE'S TOO SHORT

"This is the kind of novel that leaves you a little better than when it found you. Jimenez is a true talent."
—Emily Henry, *New York Times* bestselling author of *Beach Read*

"Abby Jimenez's knack for tackling heavy subjects with humor and care shines through in this exquisitely written story about love, difficult family relationships, and living life to its fullest."
—Farrah Rochon, *USA Today* bestselling author of *The Boyfriend Project*

"With refreshingly real characters and compulsively readable prose, Abby Jimenez captures the thrill of falling in love without shying away from deeper themes. Clear your schedule because you won't be able to put this delicious book down!"
—Katherine St. John, author of *The Siren*

"Jimenez masterfully blends heavy issues and humor."
—*Publishers Weekly*

## THE HAPPY EVER AFTER PLAYLIST

"Sparking wit and vulnerable characters bring this story to life. Jimenez tackles deep emotions without ever losing sight of fun."
—*Publishers Weekly*, starred review

"A perfect blend of smart, heart-wrenching, and fun."

*—Kirkus*

"*The Happy Ever After Playlist* tackles love after loss with fierce humor and fiercer heart." —Casey McQuiston, *New York Times* bestselling author of *Red, White & Royal Blue*

"*The Happy Ever After Playlist* shines."

*—Entertainment Weekly*

"A powerfully life-affirming love story...and a dangerously addictive sense of humor." *—Booklist*, starred review

"Sweet and achingly romantic—a truly wonderful love story." —Beth O'Leary, author of *The Flatshare*

"Delightfully adorable." *—Library Journal*

"Emotional and exceptionally swoon-worthy. You won't be able to stop grinning and gushing as you read this master-piece." —SheReads.com

"Sweet and funny, yet with vulnerable depths, *The Happy Ever After Playlist* is a delightful romance." —Shelf Awareness

## THE FRIEND ZONE

"*The Friend Zone* is that rare beach read with tons of heart that will make you laugh and cry in equal parts." —PopSugar

"A brilliantly written romantic comedy."

—*Booklist*, starred review

"Jimenez manages to fulfill all expectations for a romantic comedy while refusing to sacrifice nuance. Biting wit and laugh-out-loud moments take priority, but the novel remains subtle in its sentimentality and sneaks up on the reader with unanticipated depth.... Deeply relatable."

—*Publishers Weekly*, starred review

"An excellent debut that combines wit, humor, and emotional intensity."                                            —*Kirkus*

"Zingy dialog, laugh-out-loud humor, and plenty of sass temper the heartbreak of infertility in this modern, well-grounded debut that is sure to satisfy."       —*Library Journal*

"A deliciously hot, sweet debut full of banter I couldn't get enough of. This book is an absolute treat."

—L. J. Shen, *USA Today* bestselling author

"A zippy, instantly recognizable voice and fresh, funny characters."                           —*Entertainment Weekly*

"This novel doesn't shy away from anything—it's fiercely loving all the way to the HEA."                        —NPR

ALSO BY ABBY JIMENEZ

*The Happy Ever After Playlist*
*The Friend Zone*

# LIFE'S TOO SHORT

# ABBY JIMENEZ

FOREVER

*New York  Boston*

Copyright © 2021 by Abby Jimenez
Reading group guide copyright © 2021 by Abby Jimenez and Hachette Book Group, Inc.

Cover design by Sarah Congdon
Cover copyright © 2021 by Hachette Book Group, Inc.

Forever
Hachette Book Group
1290 Avenue of the Americas, New York, NY 10104
read-forever.com
twitter.com/readforeverpub

First Edition: April 2021

Forever is an imprint of Grand Central Publishing. The Forever name and logo are trademarks of Hachette Book Group, Inc.

The publisher is not responsible for websites (or their content) that are not owned by the publisher.

The Hachette Speakers Bureau provides a wide range of authors for speaking events. To find out more, go to www.hachettespeakersbureau.com or call (866) 376-6591.

Library of Congress Cataloging-in-Publication Data
Names: Jimenez, Abby, author.
Title: Life's too short / Abby Jimenez.
Description: New York ; Boston Forever, [2021]
Identifiers: LCCN 2020053569 | ISBN 9781538715666 (trade paperback) | ISBN 9781538715680 (ebook)
Classification: LCC PS3610.I47 L54 2021 | DDC 813/.6—dc23
LC record available at https://lccn.loc.gov/2020053569

ISBN: 978-1-5387-1566-6 (trade paperback), 978-1-5387-1568-0 (ebook)

Printed in the United States of America

LSC-C

Printing 1, 2021

*To my grandma, who was
the picture of a life well lived.
I wish you were still here
to hold this book in your hands.*

clickbait (noun)

click·bait | \ 'klik-ˌbāt \

Definition of *clickbait*: something (such as a headline) designed to make readers want to click on a hyperlink especially when the link leads to content of dubious value or interest

—Dictionary by Merriam-Webster

# CHAPTER 1

# HEARD CRYING FROM NEXT DOOR, WHAT I FOUND WAS SHOCKING!

## ADRIAN

W ailing.

Banshee, demon-baby wailing from the apartment next to mine for the millionth hour straight. I lay in bed, looking at the ceiling in the dark.

Rachel groaned from beside me. "You have to do something. Go over there."

I scoffed. "I'm not going over there. I don't know her."

I think I'd seen my neighbor in the lobby getting her mail once, but she was on the phone and she didn't make eye contact with me, so I didn't say hi. Now I wished I'd at least gotten to know her well enough to be able to text her and ask her to please move to a room that didn't share a wall with my bedroom.

Rachel let out a frustrated breath, and I rolled over and hugged her back to my chest.

She tensed up. She'd been tensing up since she got here three days ago, actually.

"What's wrong?"

She spoke over her shoulder at me. "Nothing. I'm just tired. I'm two seconds from getting a hotel room so I can sleep. Without *you*," she teased.

I chuckled tiredly. She knew how to poke me, that was for damn sure.

I only got one weekend a month with my girlfriend. Losing the last night with her to a hotel before she went back to Seattle was a price I was not willing to pay for my neighbor *or* her baby.

*Fuck.*

I begrudgingly climbed out of bed, put on a T-shirt and slippers, and let myself out into the hallway of my apartment building.

No idea if she'd answer the door. It was 4:00 in the morning, and I was a stranger. Rachel probably would have called the police if she'd seen a man she didn't know knocking on her apartment in the middle of the night.

"Who is it?" a woman's voice called over the wailing.

"Your neighbor."

The chain raked from the other side and the door opened.

Yup, the woman from the mailbox. She looked like hell. Baggy faded black T-shirt with a hole at a seam on the shoulder and some drawstring sweatpants with stains on them. Dark circles under her eyes, wild frizzy hair.

"What?" she said, looking at me over the tiny, loud bundle she had pressed to her chest.

I'd never seen a baby that small. I had bricks of cheese in my fridge bigger than this kid. It didn't even look real.

It sounded real though.

She eyeballed me impatiently. "Yeah?"

"I have a deposition in four hours. Is there any way you can—"

"Any way I can *what*?" She glared at me.

"Any way you could maybe move to another side of the apartment? So I might be able to sleep?"

"There *is* no other side of this apartment. It's a studio."

Right. I knew that. "Okay…Well, can you—"

"Can I what? Make it stop?" She cocked her head. "Maybe put her in a closet? Because I'd be lying if I said I hadn't considered it."

"I—"

"This isn't a trumpet I'm playing in here. It's not a TV I have turned up too loud. It's a tiny human being. It can't be reasoned with, and it's not responding to negotiation attempts so I don't know what to tell you." She bounced the shrieking infant, and it cried on. "She's fed, and clean, and dry. She doesn't have a fever. She's too young for teething. I've given her Tylenol and gas drops for colic. I've bounced her and rocked her and I'm coming to the conclusion that she's simply playing out some cosmic karma-based retribution for crimes I committed in a past life because I *cannot* for the life of me understand what I'm doing wrong." Her chin started to quiver. "So no, I can't make it stop. I can't help *you*, or *me* or *her*, and I am truly sorry if my own personal hell is inconvenient for you. Get earplugs."

She slammed the door in my face.

I stood there, blinking at her peephole.

Great. Now *I* was the asshole.

I dragged a hand down my beard and let out a long, tired breath and knocked again. I knew she was peeking through the peephole because the wailing was pressed right to the door. She opened it. "What?" She had tears running down her face.

I made a give-it-here motion with my hand. "Give me the baby."

She stared at me.

"Go take a shower. I'll hold her."

She blinked at me. "Are you kidding me?"

"No, I'm not. You obviously need a break. Maybe it will help."

Continuing to do the same thing was going to yield the same results. What she was doing wasn't working, and it was clear that this situation wasn't going to resolve itself without outside intervention.

She looked at me like I'd gone mad. "I'm not giving you my baby."

"Why? Are you afraid I might piss her off?" As if she intended to illustrate my point, the wails went up an octave. "I'm going to hold her until you're done. If neither of us are sleeping, it makes no sense for both of us to suffer. And you have vomit in your hair."

She looked down on the hair gathered over her shoulder and saw the white goop. She rolled her eyes like it didn't surprise her and came back up to me. "Look, I appreciate what you're trying to do, but this isn't your problem."

I rubbed my forehead tiredly. "Well, I beg to differ. As long as we're sharing a wall, we're in this together. Sometimes a change of circumstances can change behavior. Someone new to hold her while you go and lower your anxiety might make the difference."

She bounced the baby uselessly and it kept crying. I could see the frustration around the woman's eyes. She looked exhausted. "I don't know you," she said.

"My name is Adrian Copeland. I live in apartment 307, next door to you, and I own this building. I'm thirty-two years old, no criminal history, I'm a partner at Beaker and Copeland in St. Paul. I'm harmless and I'm standing here in the hallway at"—I looked at my watch—"4:07 in the morning, trying to help you. Let me in and let me hold her."

I watched the deliberation on her face. She was going to crack. I could read people. She was that deadlocked juror who was going to fold—and she did.

She pulled open the door and let me in. I stepped inside.

Fuck, her apartment was a disaster.

It looked like the place used to be nice. It had that Pottery Barn thing going on. But the studio was small and completely cluttered with baby paraphernalia. A car seat, a crib by the king-size bed at the back of the apartment, a swing. Bottles were piled on the kitchen countertops and the place smelled faintly like shit. Actual shit. Dirty-diaper shit.

She eyed me. "Just so you know, I have my little stabby thingy so don't try anything stupid."

I arched an eyebrow. "Your stabby thingy?"

She jutted her chin up. "Yeah. You know, the keychain thingy? I've got cameras too. Tons of them. And a gun," she added. "I also have a gun."

I crossed my arms. "Okay. And do you know how to use this gun you have?"

"No," she said matter-of-factly. "Which makes me more dangerous."

I snorted.

She stood there, still holding the baby like she'd decided to let me in but hadn't yet committed to actually letting me help her. I put my hands out, but she shook her head. "You need to wash your hands first."

Right. I'd heard that before. Babies had weaker immune systems. I went to her kitchen and washed my hands over the stack of dirty dishes. "You weren't pregnant," I said, over my shoulder, raising my voice so she could hear me above the screaming. "Where'd you get her?"

"Target," she deadpanned. "She was on sale and you know how you can never leave with just one thing," she mumbled.

The corners of my lips quirked.

The paper towel roll was empty and based on the state of the rest of the place, I didn't trust the towel hanging off the stove. There was a rogue Chipotle napkin by an empty fruit bowl, so I dried my hands with that. It disintegrated into spitballs, and I dropped them into the overflowing trash can.

"I'm fostering her," she said over the crying, answering my question. She eyeballed me as I cleared the space between us and put my hands out again to take the baby. She turned her body sideways away from me. "Have you ever held a baby before?"

"No. But I can't imagine there's much to it."

"You have to support her neck. Like this." She showed me her hand on the back of the little kiwi-looking head.

"Okay. Got it."

"And you need to bounce her. She likes that."

"As evidenced by the earth-shattering wailing," I said dryly. She narrowed her brown eyes at me.

"I'm kidding. I'm very capable of this, I promise you."

She still didn't move. I waited patiently.

She finally nodded. "Okay." She got closer to hand the baby over. Close enough that I could smell her hair as she leaned in to put the baby in my arms. Vanilla—and a touch of spoiled milk.

I cradled the tiny angry bundle. She was red faced and furious. She couldn't be more than ten, eleven pounds, tops.

"Are you sure about this?" she asked, eyeing me.

"Go. I got this. And take your time."

She paused for another moment. "I'll be right on the other side of that door if you need anything."

"Okay."

"That's Grace. My name is Vanessa."

"Nice to meet you, Vanessa. Now go. Take. A *shower*."

She stood another few beats, then finally turned and rummaged clothes from the dresser and headed to the bathroom. She closed the door slowly, looking at me through the crack until it shut.

A higher-pitched cry came from the wiggling pink blanket in my arms. I peered down again at the baby.

Not much made me nervous. Actually, outside of flying, nothing made me nervous. I was a criminal defense attorney.

I looked pure evil in the eye daily. But it surprised me when a sudden sense of—I don't know what it was. Anxiety?— overcame me looking down at that little person. She was so fragile. Thinner than the forearm she nestled in.

It felt safer to sit than stand, so I moved to the couch.

The screaming continued as the water turned on in the shower. It was amazing how long something so small could cry.

"What's wrong with you?" I mumbled.

I tried to think of what might be causing this distress. There was a finite number of issues that could be bothering someone who didn't yet know about things like taxes and existential dread.

Vanessa had said she'd fed her, so she wasn't hungry. She was dry. No gas, no pain. She had to be tired, but something was keeping her from sleeping.

What kept *me* from sleeping?

And then I had a thought.

I laid her down on the couch cushion, opened the blanket, and started to feel around her little footie pajamas. I ran my fingers along the seams and about mid-belly I found it. A clear T-shaped plastic tag fastener, still stuck to the outfit. Totally invisible.

"No wonder you're pissed. I'd be pissed too," I said. I looked around for scissors. Didn't see any. So I leaned down and pulled the thing off with my teeth. Then I unzipped her little pj's and took out the rest of the offending object and rubbed the red spot on her belly with a knuckle. "Shhhhhhh . . ."

She stopped crying almost immediately.

## CHAPTER 2

# HOT GUY TAMES MY BABY!

## VANESSA

I wasn't entirely truthful when I said I didn't know him. Adrian Copeland was the hottest guy in my building, so of course I knew him. Or, rather, I knew *of* him. Everyone did. He was sort of this bachelor legend around here.

He probably didn't know me. And when I finally met him, it was 4:00 in the morning, my poor parenting skills had woken him up, and I had barf in my hair—because of course I did.

I was honestly too tired to care. This had been the worst night of the worst two weeks of my entire year. I'd been thrust into instant motherhood, I'd gotten into a huge fight with my sister, and now Grace was having some sort of epic meltdown that I couldn't figure out.

I just didn't understand it. Grace was a mythically good

baby. Like, *ridiculously* good. If I was going to have a surprise infant dropped on my doorstep, I couldn't have asked for an easier one. She wasn't a crier, she slept well, we'd gotten our routine down over the last two weeks— and then all of a sudden right after her bath she lost her ever-loving shit.

I'd tried it all. I even did a video call with her pediatrician who seemed wholly unconcerned and suggested I bring her in tomorrow if she was still "fussy."

Adrian's offer was too good to refuse.

One, his reasoning made sense. What I was doing—or *not* doing—was not working. And I was extremely open to suggestions at this point. I would have tried an exorcism if the person who had knocked had been a priest instead of a hotshot attorney.

Two, the man had too much to lose to do something stupid. This was a guy who made it into the *Star Tribune* at least once a month for his legal prowess. I knew this because every time he did, Yoga Lady in 303 sent me a link along with twenty heart-eye emojis. I think she had a Google Alert set up. She was practically his stalker.

Adrian was like me. He had a reputation and a public persona to safeguard. Murdering Grace and me would be highly out of character and really bad for business. Plus, he thought he was in an apartment full of cameras—which he wasn't—but he didn't know that.

And lastly? Nobody was coming to rescue me. No one else was banging my door down to help me in my seventh level of hell. And I needed that shower. *Bad.* I just needed to wash off the barf and the sweat and change out of pants that didn't have baby pee on them. And Grace needed someone to hold her while I did it. Every time I tried putting her down she started crying so hard she looked like she was going to explode.

All I needed was five minutes. Just five short minutes. Maybe it would help—and if it didn't, at least I'd be in a better headspace to keep dealing with the screaming because as it stood, I was two seconds away from a complete mental breakdown.

I stripped and washed myself like I was being timed for speed. Approximately four minutes after I'd gotten in the shower—which was by far the best, if not the shortest, one of my life—I turned off the water to get out, and I was met by eerie, cold *silence*.

My heart plummeted.

Oh my God.

Something was wrong.

I wrapped a towel around me so fast I almost slid on the tile.

What had I been thinking? I didn't know this man. I mean I *did*, but I didn't. What if he kidnapped her? Dropped her off the balcony? What if he was a perfectly normal guy who had been on the verge of a psychotic break and the crying had pushed him over the edge and now he'd shaken her to death? I was so stupid!

I threw the bathroom door open, braced for Lord knows what, and froze.

Adrian was lying across the sofa in my dim living room, head on a throw pillow with a finger pressed to his lips. Grace was nestled in the crook of his arm on her back, and she was *sleeping*.

I just stood there gawking at him. I couldn't even believe it. I had to tiptoe over to them dripping wet to see it close up.

What *was* this sorcery? How did he do it? The man was like a baby whisperer or something. Grace cooed softly in her sleep, and I had to clutch a hand over my heart.

There must be a primal internal switch that flips when you see a man take care of a child, because I swear I fell a little bit in love right there. I mean, the guy was gorgeous without this witchcraft, but now? Holy shit.

I was sopping wet, just staring at him. When I didn't move to go, he blinked at me and made a small shooing motion. I blushed, forcing myself to go back to the bathroom to get dressed.

When I returned, working my hair into a damp braid, Grace hadn't moved. I stood next to the sofa twisting an elastic around my hair.

"All done?" he whispered.

I nodded and leaned down to pick her up.

God, he smelled good. Something sleepy and warm and masculine rolled off him. Clean cotton and testosterone.

I lifted Grace into my arms and prayed that she wouldn't wake up and start crying again when I put her in her crib.

She didn't.

When I turned back to Adrian to thank him, he was already walking to the door. He stopped and wrestled my garbage from the kitchen trash can, carried it with him, and without another word, he was gone.

I pushed the bangs off my forehead with a palm. Oh. My. *God.*

I needed to make a video. *Now.*

The last two weeks had been a content desert. My YouTube channel had gone completely dark. I'd had to lay off my entire production team for this hiatus. Only my cameraman, Malcolm, was still on the payroll. Not only was I not making any money, I was also letting down my subscribers on top of it all. But I'd had nothing to talk about.

Being a stay-at-home mommy isn't exactly exciting. I'd had a video chat with Malcolm yesterday to discuss segments I could do from home. They were all pretty lame. Mostly beauty tutorials. Me trying crazy mud masks and dying my hair random colors. A vlog of me opening fan mail. Boring.

But this...

I grabbed my laptop and tiptoed to the bathroom. I sat on the toilet seat and titled the video "Hot Guy Tames My Baby." I didn't bother to blow out my hair or do my makeup. I liked my content to be authentic. I took a deep breath and hit Record.

"Hi, all! Look, I'm alive!" I gave the screen a wave. "Well, it's been an interesting two weeks here. I've been getting your concerned emails. Thank you for worrying about me, guys. And yes, I bailed on the L.A. conference last week. I know a lot of you were disappointed and I'm so, so sorry. If you bought a ticket to see me, send a picture of it and your address to Malcolm at the email here." I put my finger up above my head where Malcolm would make an email address pop up. "And I'll have him send you a signed picture of me. I know it's not quite as good as the real thing, but I promise you I had a good reason.

"I'm sure you're all wondering where I went. As you can

see from the title of my entry, I have a baby! Surprise! Are you surprised? Because I know I was." I tilted my head and gave the camera crazy eyes.

"Somebody I care about was expecting. Three weeks ago, she had a healthy baby girl. Then two weeks ago she dropped the baby off with me so she could run to the store for something, and she never came back.

"Grace's mom is unfortunately not in the best place right now. Grace's dad isn't in the picture, so I am now the temporary guardian of a newborn I have no idea how to take care of. Needless to say, the trip I planned to Mexico for my Christmas segment in three weeks is now canceled and instead we'll all be exploring the exciting eight hundred square feet of my studio apartment for a while."

I sat there for a heartbeat before continuing to let this all settle in.

"Now, I'm sure you're all wondering how the hot guy comes into it. So it's just after four in the morning here and I was up with my little angel. We were on about a million hours straight of unabridged crying. Both of us," I added. "And my next-door neighbor knocked on my door to ask if I needed help.

"Let me tell you a little about my next-door neighbor. This is the hottest guy in my building. Maybe the hottest guy on my block. He is so attractive that if he rolled up on me in an alley in a windowless white van, wearing rubber gloves and waving duct tape, claiming he has candy—I'd get in. Not only is he a prominent, single professional, but he also pulls off a really magnificent beard. When I moved in here back in September, he was going for all these runs with his shirt off and the man has Jesus's abs. In fact, that's what we're gonna call him. Jesus's Abs.

"So he comes in like some kind of knight in shining pajama bottoms. I have barf in my hair, and not in a fun, too-many-tequilas-in-Cancun kind of way. In a tiny-human-vomited-in-my-hair kind of way. He offers to hold the baby while I go take a shower. I let him. Please don't judge me. It was a very quick shower. And when I come out, he has baby whispered this child. They're both lying on my sofa together. It was quite honestly the sexiest thing I've ever seen in my life. He looked like one of those staged photos Instagram models post of themselves doing casual stuff around the house while looking effortlessly sexy. Nobody looks this good lounging in real life. Seriously.

"As you guys know, I'm a sucker for hot bearded men. It's my weakness. But honestly, after this last week? I'm starting to find dad bods attractive. Like, I'm at the point where I see a man at Target with a beer belly, a receding hairline, and a kid strapped to him in a BabyBjörn and I'm checking him out like 'I bet that guy could change diapers allllll night.' So seeing this man with my cranky baby on his chest—I maybe fell in love just a little bit.

"'Are you ready for love?' you ask." I cocked my head to the side and let my braid fall over my shoulder. "No. My position on dating has not changed, Jesus's Abs aside. So don't get excited. Also, even if the attraction *was* mutual and this is a guy willing to overlook my many, major shortcomings—oh, and *this*—" I got up, opened my bathroom door, and turned the camera to scan the disaster that was my apartment. I shut the door and came back to me. "Yes, those are actual diapers full of human waste, on my coffee table. This is what it looked like when he came over. How could he not fall in love, right? Anyway, I am still not on the market for the foreseeable future, for reasons previously and frequently discussed. But a girl can still window-shop."

I yawned into the back of my hand. "Time for bed. A couple of things before I go. If you enjoyed this video, make sure you subscribe to my channel. And, as always, any donations to my favorite charity are deeply appreciated. Together we can find a cure."

I ended the video and sent it to Malcolm. He would insert links, add hashtags, and within the next two hours have the video uploaded to my YouTube channel, where my subscribers, who probably thought I was dead after not posting anything for almost two weeks, would likely descend on it like rabid bears.

From there I had only a rough idea how this would all go. I was a travel vlogger. My videos were almost always filmed on location. I had never made a video from inside my apartment. This was a far cry from my norm, and I might even lose subscribers for this. I honestly didn't know.

I had loyal fans who would stick with me no matter what. But most of the Internet had very short attention spans. If I wasn't consistently giving them something entertaining, they'd leave.

If I lost my ability to make money...

I tried not to think about it.

I mean, I sorta knew what would happen with the video. All the usual stuff would go down in the comments. Some people would be supportive, some people would not, and the supportive ones would attack those hating on me. Probably more than a few would harp on my judgment for letting a stranger hold my baby. A few others would shit-talk the state of my living space. There would be the standard hateful comments about my appearance.

Most of it would roll off my back. After being the focus of this type of attention for more than two years now, nothing could hurt me. Also, I had a little thing called perspective, in higher doses than most people, and I don't sweat the small stuff.

Ever.

And most things were, in the grand scheme of things, very, very small...

Especially when you might only have a year left to live.

# CHAPTER 3

# CHEATER GETS BUSTED!

## ADRIAN

I ran the trash from Vanessa's down to the dumpster. When I got back to my apartment, the light was on in my room. Rachel was out of bed and whirling around the bedroom, tossing things into her carry-on.

I stood blinking at her in the doorway. "What are you doing?"

"Packing."

I drew my brows down. "What? You're leaving? I thought your flight wasn't until three. We were supposed to have lunch."

She didn't answer me. She went into the bathroom, and I could hear her moving around, drawers opening and closing, the click of the medicine cabinet. She came back in and put her makeup bag into her luggage and zipped it, extending the handle.

"Rachel…"

"I'm getting the seven fifteen flight," she said without making eye contact. "We're training a new recruit and I need to be there."

"You need to be there? You just decided this at four in the morning?"

She paused for a moment, looking at the floor before her eyes came up to mine. "Adrian, I think we need to take a break."

I froze where I stood. "What? *Why?*"

She peered at me from across the room and her chin trembled. "I shouldn't be here. I have responsibilities and commitments, and I shouldn't be halfway across the country—"

I nodded. "Okay. You're right, it shouldn't always be you coming here. Let me come to you for a while. I'll drive out, take a week off."

She shook her head. "No. This isn't working for me. This isn't what I signed up for. I didn't expect things with us to get so serious. I can't let myself get further into this, not with my circumstances…"

I shook my head at her. "What circumstances?"

"Adrian, I'm married."

The words hit me like a smack. "*What?*" I breathed.

Her chin quivered. "I'm married," she said again.

I stood there staring at her for a solid thirty seconds.

"I didn't mean to hurt you," she whispered. "I planned on leaving him, and then I didn't and… This was supposed to be a one-night thing with you and it just… *wasn't*. And I wasn't ready for how I'd feel about you and…"

I dragged a hand down my mouth and sat on the edge of the bed in shock.

I went through an onslaught of rapid-fire emotions. Surprise, betrayal, hurt, confusion. We'd been together for eight months. Eight fucking months. And she was *married*???

I let out a steadying breath and looked up at her where she stood by the door.

She swiped at her cheeks. "I'm sorry. I don't even know what else to say."

She swung her laptop bag over her shoulder, then paused for a long beat. "I'll miss you."

She gave me one more apologetic look and then let herself out.

~~~

Ten hours later, my paralegal dropped a file on my desk, and I leaned back in my chair and rubbed my eyes.

"What's your deal today?" Becky asked unceremoniously.

She was chewing gum. Loudly. *Again.*

I liked my paralegal/assistant. She did a good job. She was driven and competent. She'd started as an intern and done such a good job that I'd hired her full-time. But as much as I liked her, sometimes it was a little like having a high schooler working for me instead of a paid professional. Becky had zero filter. She did not give a *shit*. Not only would she tell me I had coffee on my tie, she'd tell me she thought the tie was ugly too.

"Lose the gum, please," I muttered, opening the file. "I didn't get much sleep."

She plucked the gum out of her mouth and stood there holding it, as I flipped through pages. "Yeah, you're, like, more emo than usual today."

I took a deep breath. "I think I might cut out early."

She blinked at me. "Okay, you're not gonna, like, go home and start writing depressing haikus, are you? Because that would be really unfair for me to have to read that stuff."

I scoffed. "No, I am not going to go home and start writing haikus."

"Good. Though you should know that your horoscope today said your life is about to change drastically."

I arched an eyebrow at her. "You read my horoscope?"

"We're both Capricorns?" she said impatiently, like this was something I should know.

She put a hand on her hip. "You never go home early. You've been super off for like two months now. You haven't been going to the gym—"

"How do you know I haven't been going to the gym?" I mumbled, talking to the file I was flipping through.

"Because my boyfriend goes to that Life Time Fitness and he says you would go like every day and now you don't go at all. You barely finish your lunches, you're all mopey. What's your deal?"

I puffed my cheeks and looked away from the paperwork in front of me. "I don't know. I'm not having the best year. And Rachel and I broke up."

"Good, I hated her."

I scoffed, looking at her. "Excuse me?"

She shrugged unapologetically. "Never liked her. And her Instagram looks like a sock puppet account."

I wrinkled my forehead at her. "A what?"

She made a frustrated noise. "Oh my God, you are such a boomer! A sock. Puppet. *Account?*" she said, slower, like that would somehow convey the meaning. "A fake?"

I pressed my lips together with a tight nod. "Well, that makes sense," I said. "And it would have been nice if you would have pointed that out sooner." I closed my file. "I just need to take a personal day today."

Becky made a resigned noise. "Fine. I'll clear your schedule. But I swear to God, Adrian, you'd better get out of this funk. Why don't you, like, adopt a dog or something?"

My mom had said the same thing a few weeks ago. Apparently dogs are the answer to all life's problems.

"Don't get a cat," she went on. "It'll walk around pushing your drinks off the coffee table. You're not emotionally strong enough for that."

I snorted. "Thanks for the tip. I'll keep that in mind."

"I have a friend who runs an animal rescue. They need people to foster dogs. Want me to get you one? If you like it, you can adopt it and if you don't, someone else will."

A dog wasn't a horrible idea. I guess I could bring it to the office or something. Make Becky walk it while I was at court. I *did* miss feeling like I had a purpose.

I spent a lot of time with Mom and Grandma, but they'd moved to Nebraska with Mom's new husband in October.

This was the event that had started me on the downward spiral Becky was picking up on. I was going to be alone for the holidays.

They'd invited me to join them, but I didn't care for Mom's husband, Richard. I hadn't gone to their wedding in August, and I refused to join them for Thanksgiving and Christmas.

Rachel's visits had been the only thing I'd had to look forward to.

The sudden gaping black hole in my personal life was the nail in the coffin of my mood.

Our junior associate, Lenny, poked his head into the office and looked around Becky, who was still standing in front of my desk on her phone. "Hey, Becky just texted me and said you and Rachel broke up. Sucks, man."

"Yeah, thanks." I put the files I was taking home into my briefcase.

He leaned in my doorway with his arms crossed. "Hey, want to grab lunch this week? You got time?"

"He's got time," Becky said without glancing up from her phone.

I gave her a look before replying to Lenny. "Just tell me when."

He tapped a knuckle on the door frame, gave me finger guns, and left.

Becky still stood in front of my desk, texting into her phone. She'd put the gum back in her mouth.

I sat there, waiting for her to notice that I was staring at her. "Becky…" I said, looking up at her, irritated.

She popped a bubble. "I think I found a dog for you."

"Great. Wonderful. Please continue to find it at your own desk. And try to refrain from telling anyone else my personal business on your way there."

She smirked, unfazed as usual, and turned for the exit.

Five minutes later, Marcus strolled in. "Hey, buddy."

Marcus Beaker was the founder of my firm and my counterpart. He was fifty-two, bald, slightly overweight, and sharp as a tack. Married, and not happily, to a doctor wife who could barely stand him and liked to take long vacations without him.

We made a good team. I was a good front man for high-profile cases—rarely caught off guard and a favorite with the media. Marcus had a reputation for being a bulldog and was the only person I'd ever met who could match my work ethic.

He dropped into the chair in front of my desk. "I hear you're cutting out early," he said.

I knew why he was here. My going home before 5:00 was tantamount to an emergency siren wailing around the office. A prized racehorse limping around the track.

He didn't have anything to worry about. I funneled my stress and unhappiness into work. I always had. Even in high school. The more shit I was dealing with, the more productive I became. It's why I'd graduated early at the top of my class and coasted into college scholarships. My depressing personal life was currently driving this firm into the top five in Minnesota. I didn't fault Marcus for checking on me though. I liked that he was shrewd.

"I've got two ex partes on Wednesday," I said. "I can do the paperwork from home. I think I'm getting a migraine," I lied.

Telling him my real reason would only add to his concern.

"I could always put someone else on the Keller case," he said, talking to his tie as he smoothed it down.

I kept my expression neutral.

He did this to poke me. He was letting me know that

whatever my problem was, he expected me to wrap it up quickly and get back to my job.

Again, I *did* like that he was shrewd.

I didn't look up as I keyed in an email to Becky. "I don't think anyone else could handle what I have going on." I hit Send with a final tap and leveled my eyes on him.

Marcus leaned back in his chair, his fingers threaded across his belly. "Keller and Garcia? What have those two idiots done now?"

"Garcia violated his custody order and took his daughter over state lines to visit his mother last week. They're asking for full loss of his parental rights until the conclusion of the trial."

He bobbed his head. "The guy's being indicted for tax evasion. It's not a violent crime. They won't grant it."

"I know. Maybe a slap on the wrist."

"And Keller?"

I scoffed. "His ex-wife caught him jerking off outside her window at two in the morning in violation of her restraining order."

"Ouch," he chuckled.

"She is also asking for loss of custody."

He looked at his watch. "And she'll get it. That guy cannot keep his dick in his pants. This isn't going to help his assault case."

"No, it is not." And I wouldn't trust anyone else but me to deal with it—and neither would he.

Marcus nodded for a moment. "Well, have a good night, then." He got up, then paused with a hand on the back of the chair. "Hey, why don't you come up to the cabin with us for Christmas next month? Jessica's just put a hot tub on the deck."

I shook my head. "I think I might head out to Nebraska. Mom's been asking me to see the work they've done on the house."

Another lie.

I didn't like spending Christmas alone, but spending it with Marcus, hanging out with his cranky wife and watching their loveless marriage, was my idea of hell. Marcus's career was a monument to hard work and dedication, but his personal life was a cautionary tale.

I wrapped up things at the office and left by 3:00.

Mom called while I was driving home.

I stared at the notification on my car's Bluetooth. I was not in the right headspace for her, but I didn't like sending her to voicemail in case something was wrong—which was highly likely given her circumstances.

I let out a long breath and hit the Answer Call button, mustering more enthusiasm than I felt. "Hey, Mom."

"Adrian. I'm just calling to see how your Thanksgiving was."

Of course.

She was calling to browbeat me into coming for Christmas. Hoping I'd learned my lesson after spending Thanksgiving alone and was now ready to play nice.

No.

"Thanksgiving was fine," I said flatly.

It wasn't fine. I'd spent the day by myself eating Chinese takeout and reading transcripts.

She let out a sigh. "It doesn't have to be like this, you know. We *want* you here. Please come for Christmas."

My jaw ticked. "No."

I could almost feel her pinning me with her disapproving stare. "You know, you're not just hurting Richard with this boycott. You're hurting me, and you're hurting your grandmother. She doesn't understand why you're not there. She gets more confused by the day, and I don't know how much more time you'll have with her. Are you really willing to sacrifice that for this…this *petty* disagreement?"

I barked out an incredulous laugh. "Petty disagreement? Is that a joke?"

I could picture her throwing up her hands. "He made a mistake. And no matter how you feel about that, Richard is my husband now and he wants to get to know you—"

"I have absolutely no desire to allow him to do any such thing. He's not good enough for you. You should have never married him after what he did."

She paused for a long beat.

"Maybe one day you'll need forgiveness, Adrian. And someone will give it to *you*."

We fell into a silence.

She was crying. I could hear her sniffling on the other end of the line. I pulled into my space in the parking garage under my building and put the car in park.

I'd been close to my mom before this. Before *him*. I took care of her—I'd *always* taken care of her. I'd done it since I was fifteen years old and my piece-of-shit dad walked out on us. Normally I was over there every Sunday for dinner with her and Grandma. I paid for repairs on the house, drove Grandma to the doctor.

Then Mom had her whirlwind romance.

That was already bad enough, but then he moved them to fucking Nebraska.

The situation was getting progressively worse and since it didn't look like Richard was bailing or Mom was gearing up to leave him, apparently *I* had to be the one to be flexible. Either that or I could kiss my family goodbye. These were the choices.

And they were impossible.

She blew her nose.

I squeezed my eyes shut. "Can we just talk about something else?"

"Adrian, I know this has been hard. Maybe you should see someone—"

"No. Me spending two hundred dollars an hour on a therapist isn't going to make me feel any different about this."

She sniffed. "Well then. I guess we don't have anything left to discuss. You call me when you've decided what's important to you."

She hung up on me.

I sat in the car, pinching the bridge of my nose for a solid minute before I dragged myself out.

When I got back to my building, I collected my mail in the lobby and took the stairs up. I was one staircase from my floor when I heard the screaming.

A woman.

I paused on the landing, trying to determine if it was coming from up or down.

Up.

*My* floor.

I took the steps two at a time and pushed out into the hallway.

A bored-looking young man in a peacoat and scarf stood scrolling through his phone next to a short blond woman in a gray hoodie. A second man was wedged halfway into Vanessa's apartment.

"Let go!" Vanessa screamed, from inside. "I'm calling the cops!"

"Hey!" I shouted.

Everyone froze. I walked purposefully toward them, and the man let go of the knob and took a step back. He was older. Probably fifties. White, salt-and-pepper hair, bushy eyebrows, argyle sweater under a blazer.

The woman was high. Pupils the size of marbles.

Vanessa peered out into the hallway from the crack in the door. Her lip was bleeding.

My jaw flexed. "Is there something I can help you with?" I asked, glowering down at the older man.

He looked me up and down. "This is none of your business, fancy hall cop. We don't need your assistance. Stay out of it." He looked back at Vanessa. "We have every right to see her!" he said, jabbing a finger at her.

Vanessa jutted up her chin. "Uh, *no*. You actually don't. I've been awarded temporary guardianship. If Annabel wants to see her daughter, bring her back when she's clean."

The younger man let out an impatient huff. "Okay, Vanessa? I'm just here for that Gucci backpack you promised me? If you hand it through the door, I can be one less person in this hallway."

"Fuck off, Brent!"

His mouth dropped open. "Why are you mad at *me*? I only came with them for the ride!"

"You shouldn't have let them come at all!" Vanessa snapped.

He crossed his arms. "Are you pissed because I'm not helping with the baby? Is that what it is? I have a *very* sensitive gag reflex, Vanessa, I *cannot* do poopy diapers. Remember that time you ordered that Greek salad at Nico's and the feta made me throw up in that planter?"

Vanessa gave him crazy eyes. "Brent, take. Them. *Home.*"

"He will do no such thing! Not until we see Grace!" the older man barked. "This is kidnapping!"

Brent scoffed. "Um, but it's actually not?" He crossed his arms. "Can we just go? This is *so* not dignified."

The older man looked like he was about to make for the door again. I took another step to put myself between him and Vanessa, and he shrank away from me. I was in a suit and tie, but I was still six-two and well aware of how intimidating I could look if I didn't smile. "If you're a noncustodial parent, any visitation needs to be scheduled with the court."

The older man puffed his chest. "We're not going until we see the baby, and that's final!" he said, glowering up at me.

"Okay. Let's get the police over here to work this out." I nodded at the woman. "She's clearly under the influence. And I'll make sure to mention that I saw *you* trying to forcefully make your way into the apartment. Vanessa's bleeding, so I'm assuming an assault and battery has taken place, at which point I'd advise she press charges and get a restraining order. And she *will* get it. Then your visitation, which you likely won't be awarded, will be supervised and will have to take place at the sheriff's station." I looked at him sternly. "Something tells me the two of you wouldn't do well in a sheriff's station."

He stood there looking up at me defiantly, and the blond woman looked like she wasn't even processing what was going on.

Brent was smiling at me like he'd just fully acknowledged that I was here. He put a hand on the side of his mouth. "Are you seeing this? How hot this is?" he stage-whispered to Vanessa, who was still peeking through the door. "And that's a *really* expensive Armani suit."

I ignored him.

The older man straightened and tugged the bottom of his jacket down indignantly. "Fine." He shot a look back at Vanessa. "We know where we're not wanted."

He didn't look me in the eye as he edged down the hall dragging the blond woman by the sleeve. Brent paused a moment before following them. "Love the tie."

Then he was gone too.

I turned back to Vanessa. She blinked at me with wide eyes for a second—then slammed the door in my face.

I was still standing there looking at her apartment number when she opened the door. "Thank you," she said quickly.

And then she slammed it again.

Okay…

I waited a few moments to make sure whoever the hell those people were didn't come back.

They didn't.

It was almost 5:00 and I was sitting at the bar in the kitchen going over case work when someone knocked on my door. I opened it to find Becky.

With a *dog*.

"I called you like seven million times," she said. "I thought you were dead. You always answer your phone."

"Can we not talk about me being dead?" I asked, standing in the doorway. "What the hell is this?"

"It's your dog?" She picked up its paw and waved it at me. "The one I told you I was getting you?"

I shook my head. "That's not my dog."

It was a—I don't know what it was. A Chihuahua maybe? But it was ancient. It had short brown fur with a random bald spot on its chest, cloudy, bulging, watery eyes, and a tongue that hung an inch out of the side of its mouth. It looked like a caricature of itself.

"Uh, yeah. It *is* your dog," she said, smacking her gum.

I crossed my arms. "No, *my* dog is a dog I can take running. *My* dog is a dog too big for me to carry."

She scoffed. "You're a hermit now, remember? I bring you a Weimaraner or something, you don't take him out, and he destroys your apartment. Then you go deeper down your rabbit hole and I have to visit you in the psych ward and smuggle a cell phone to you in my underwear so you can keep working because heaven forbid you take a mental health day." She blew a bubble. "This dog is a lifestyle match."

I narrowed my eyes at her.

"You're meticulous with time management and routine, he's got three medications a day. You want to stay home, so does he. You have a fancy apartment, he's not destructive. He doesn't shed, his poop is the size of a Tootsie Roll. He uses pee pads so you don't even have to walk him if you don't feel like leaving the house. He's perfect. If you don't love him, bring him to work tomorrow and I'll take him back or something."

I let out a long sigh and looked at the little thing. "Does he even have teeth?"

"Nope. Which is good because he bites."

I snorted.

She picked up her bag from the floor. "Let me in so I can show you his stuff." She squeezed past me, and I closed the door behind her. "Hold him." She held out the shivering dog. When I didn't take him, she gave me crazy eyes and pushed him gently into my chest.

He growled.

She plunged her hands into the bag she had with her. "Okay, so he's got arthritis and allergies and a skin infection, so he gets one of these every morning and this last one at night too." She shook three bottles. "Put them in cream cheese. He'll just swallow it. He can't have dry food because of the no-teeth thing, so he's got wet food here. He needs a medicated bath once a week for his dry skin. Here are his diapers—"

"Diapers?" I said. "It's *incontinent*?"

She paused with her hands in the bag to scowl up at me. "He's *fourteen*. That's like a million years old in people years. Also, he has worms."

"*What?*"

She rolled her eyes. "They already treated him for it. He's

just gonna poop them out or something, so don't freak out if you see a tapeworm in there. Only freak out if it's moving. Then you need to take him back to the vet."

"Jesus Christ, Becky." I pinched the bridge of my nose. "You're asking me to be a damn dog nurse."

"Yup." She stood and handed me the bag.

I let out a resigned puff of air. "What's his name?" I mumbled, looking reluctantly at him.

"Harry Puppins."

"Oh God."

"You'll be fine."

"Even though my horoscope today says my life is about to change drastically?"

She shrugged. "Well, the way I see it, it can only change for the better."

She popped her gum one more time and left.

# CHAPTER 4

# THIS STARTLING VIDEO WILL HAVE YOU COVERING YOUR EYES!

## VANESSA

I was dabbing Carmex on the split in my lip when I heard talking in the hallway. I leaned on my fingertips to peer through the peephole. Adrian, with some girl who was holding a Chihuahua.

I could barely see him from that angle, but I had a full view of her.

She was pretty, which I guess wasn't surprising. The man was a ten. He could probably date supermodels if he wanted to.

Adrian got closer to her to look at the dog, and he shifted into my line of sight. He was still in his suit from earlier, only he'd lost the jacket and tie. The top two buttons of his light-blue work shirt were undone and his sleeves were rolled up to the elbow.

God, he was sexy. You could make a calendar of the many

looks of Adrian Copeland and raise enough money to fund the cure for cancer. Adrian, jogging shirtless. Adrian in a suit. Adrian, with my cranky niece on his chest.

He looked annoyed. He had his arms crossed. I couldn't really hear what they were talking about.

My laptop chimed with an incoming Skype call.

*Drake.*

I left my post and sat down and answered.

Drake Lawless's tan face popped up onto my screen. Judging by the palm trees behind him, he was someplace tropical. I was already jealous.

He had on his shark-tooth necklace, no shirt as usual, and his blond hair was wild. I could practically smell the coconut sunblock and ocean through my computer.

"'Sup, gorgeous." He gave me one of his dazzling smiles. "Sooo...Jesus's Abs?"

I snorted. "You have no idea. The man is God's gift to all of us," I said, poking around my desk for a nail file. "It was like Jesus's Abs take the wheel over here."

*Too bad I'll probably never see him again unless I look through a peephole.*

Drake didn't get a chance to reply because Laird walked naked across the back of the screen.

"Laird!" I shrieked, turning hard to the left. Both men laughed from my laptop.

"Hey, Nessa," Laird called.

I huffed indignantly at my floor. "Laird, I'm still not speaking to you."

"Oh, come on." I could hear the smile in his voice. "He made me an offer I couldn't refuse."

I peeked up at the screen. Laird stood grinning at me over Drake's shoulder, a direct view of his crotch mercifully covered by Drake's body.

I crossed my arms. "First you leave me for Drake and make me scramble to find a new cameraman, and now you've made me see your balls. Just when I thought my week couldn't get worse."

Both men laughed again and Laird walked off screen, penis swinging. I looked back at Drake. "Please buy your employee some pants, or give him a fig leaf or a loincloth or something?"

He chuckled good-naturedly.

Typical Drake. *Zero* decorum. Camp Lawless was like a hippie commune. Naked yoga and going on about chakras. I wouldn't be surprised if a goat wearing a lei with a chicken riding its back wandered through next.

Drake tipped his head. "You need anything, butterfly? How's motherhood?"

"Good. Great. It's amazing how much it changes you. I find myself saying things like, 'It's just baby pee.' Like that's okay, like it's superior to the regular kind so I should be fine that it's on my goose-down comforter."

He laughed.

I let out a long breath. "I have no idea how I'm going to keep stretching content out of this situation."

"No change with Annabel? Do you have any idea where she is?"

I scoffed. "I know *exactly* where she is. She's at my dad's. And speaking of Dad, he showed up here with her earlier demanding that I let them see Grace. She was completely high.

And then Dad accidently pushed the door into my mouth." I put my tongue to the scab. "Jesus's Abs came home and ran them off—because it wasn't enough that I only seem crazy in front of him once."

He managed to appear concerned and amused at the same time. "How did she look?"

I glanced away from him. "Not good. Maybe the worst I've ever seen her," I admitted.

Drake was well aware of my family issues. I didn't need to regale him with the details. He knew all about the day Annabel dropped off Grace and never came back.

She used my bathroom before she left. Stole a whole bottle of hydrocodone and drank all my cough medicine with codeine and then filled the bottle up with water so I wouldn't notice—I noticed.

"I'm trying to get her into rehab, but she won't go," I said.

"Can you talk to your dad?"

I huffed. "Yeah. Dad can't even help himself," I said bitterly. I rubbed at my forehead. His eyes followed my hand up and focused on the brace I wore. For the first time, maybe ever, I saw the humor drop away and a frown touch the corners of his mouth. Drake *always* smiled. I'd seen him smile being carried off on a stretcher with third-degree burns. The man's happy didn't have an off switch.

I put my arm off camera. "It's just for typing," I lied.

He went quiet for a moment. "Are you going to have it looked at?" he asked, his voice low.

I pressed my lips into a line. "There's no point in spending months at the hospital getting poked and prodded for a diagnosis that won't change the outcome. I'm not living my life like the Cyclops, giving up an eye to know the future of how and when I'll die. My grandma had it. My sister Melanie had it. My aunt Linda had it. My mom had it too. All women, all dead by thirty. There's a fifty percent chance I inherited the gene and based on the female line, I'd say it's higher than that. I want to be blissfully ignorant until it's painfully obvious how this ends. This is *my* choice. I have to live with it, sort of like everyone else's shitty choices that I *also* have to live with."

I couldn't even do genetic testing to see if I was a carrier. Doctors couldn't identify the mutated gene that ran in my family. If I *was* born with it, I wouldn't know until it started to kill me.

He studied me quietly. "Are there any new clinical trials? It can't hurt to try."

I shook my head. Drake knew my position on this too.

Melanie had gone the Hail Mary route when she got sick. Tried it all. I promised myself if I ever got it, I wasn't going to put myself through that. There was no point.

"It's probably nothing. I'll be okay. And hey, it could be worse," I said. "I could have the gene that makes cilantro taste like soap."

This drew a crooked smile.

Seeing that I wasn't going to further the discussion, Drake took mercy on me and changed the subject. "If you're looking for content, you and I could always get back together."

I rolled my eyes. "Oh ha ha."

He grinned. "We were great together, butterfly. I miss you. And if you came here, I'd give you Laird back."

"Keep him. I've seen enough of him for a lifetime."

He chuckled.

"Anyway, I can't take the baby out of the country. I'm trapped in my apartment, dealing with Child Protective Services, and getting an emergency injunction for guardianship over an abandoned infant because once again my family dumped their responsibilities on me."

"Want me to send you my herbalist?"

I laughed a little. "No, it's fine. I'll manage. I always do."

Well, I would as long as I *could*. Until I wouldn't be around anymore to do it.

And that day might come sooner than I thought.

## CHAPTER 5

# MAN RESCUES DOG BUT WAIT UNTIL YOU SEE WHAT IT DID TO HIS APARTMENT!

## ADRIAN

The dog was shitting everywhere.

I'd had the thing less than three hours, and I was already counting down the seconds until I got to hand him back to Becky.

The diapers wrapped around his belly and stopped only the urine from getting everywhere—which I suppose I should have been grateful for. But it did nothing for the pudding-like stool he was shitting all over my apartment. Luckily, he'd done this only on the hardwood so cleanup had been minimal, but it was far from pleasant.

I'd called Becky about it and she said it was probably just the dewormer upsetting his stomach and it would pass.

I knew nothing about dogs. We never had them growing up. My introduction so far was not going well.

On top of the messes, I was pretty sure the dog was not only deaf but also blind. He ran into walls and the legs of chairs. He growled every time I picked him up, but mostly because he didn't see me coming and I think I was startling him.

I'd decided to try my luck at getting him to go outside, but in the freezing late November weather, he just stood on the sidewalk shivering and looking miserable until I took pity on him and put him in my jacket to go back upstairs.

I was making my way down the hall, pulling out my keys, when I glanced at Vanessa's apartment door as I walked by.

I stopped.

What if that guy had come back after I'd gone inside?

*I should check on her.*

I knocked.

When Vanessa opened the door, she was in considerably better shape than earlier. Her split lip was almost invisible now that the blood was gone. Her long hair was in a neat braid over one shoulder—no vomit—and the pink tank top she was wearing was clean and showed off a nice figure I hadn't noticed before.

"Hey, my hero." She gave me a smile.

I fiddled with my keys. "I just wanted to make sure you're okay—and to see if you needed your trash run down. I imagine it's probably hard to take it out with the baby."

"Yes. I would love that service, thank you." She tilted her head. "Wow, you just never stop giving, do you?"

"I figure your cockroaches are my cockroaches," I mumbled, looking away from her down the hall and back again.

She grinned. "I didn't know you had a dog."

I looked down at Harry's head poking out of my jacket.

His tongue was hanging out, and he was shivering. "I don't. I'm fostering him."

"Oh. So we're both fostering. Cool. It can be very rewarding, you know."

I grunted noncommittally. "Well, right now it's just shitting everywhere."

She laughed. "Yeah, mine too."

"Hey, we should probably exchange numbers," I said. "So we know how to get in touch in case we need to." I put a hand up. "I'm not hitting on you," I added.

She scoffed. "Well, thank God for that because you are *hideous*."

I snorted.

She leaned on the door frame. "Hey, I was about to order a pizza. You want to join me? You can bring your dog. And just so you know, I'm not hitting on you either," she said. "I don't date. This is purely in the spirit of saying thank you and wanting to hang out with someone old enough to drive."

I paused a moment, debating her offer. I didn't feel like being social—even though I knew I probably *should*. Sitting around feeling sorry for myself wasn't good for me. I could practically hear Mom's voice in my head telling me to get out and do something.

I heard Becky's voice too. It was more annoying but saying the same thing.

"Well?" Vanessa cocked her head.

"Yeah. Sure." Why not. "But no pizza. It's famine food. I'll pick us up something."

Her eyes got big. "Like what? Like *real* food? From a restaurant? One that doesn't do DoorDash?"

"That's what I'm thinking."

She put a hand to her chest. "Oh my God. I haven't had anything exciting to eat in weeks."

I smiled a little. "Do you like Muffoletto's?"

"Yes," she breathed. "Chicken marsala and... and a cannoli. Wait, no. Tiramisu. And spaghetti and meatballs and—"

I chuckled dryly and pulled out my phone. "Here, give me your number. Then just text me what you want. I could be back in forty-five, if that's okay?"

"It's so okay. And I'll pay you back," she added quickly.

"No, it's fine. It'll be my treat. I think maybe you've had a worse day than me." If that was even possible.

She gave me her number and sent me her order. She didn't ask for the cannoli, but I got it anyway. Then I wandered into their deli and grabbed a few of their prepared meals for her. Chicken piccata, a lasagna, and another chicken marsala.

I stopped, looking at the row of wine.

I liked a nice white with Italian food, but it felt a little too much like a date if I brought wine.

Eh, screw it. We'd both been pretty clear that wasn't what this was. And I could use the drink. I picked a chardonnay I liked and made it back to her apartment with five minutes to spare.

She pulled open the door and let me inside. She'd thrown on a dark-green belted sweater. Open in the front. And she'd put on a little makeup. She looked nice.

Vanessa was a good-looking woman. She reminded me of that actress—what was her name? Jennifer Lawrence. Irony aside, she had that girl-next-door thing about her.

She held the door while I came in with the bags. "Ta-da!

Clean!" she declared, putting a hand out proudly to show me the apartment. "It's much easier to do when you don't have to hold a screaming infant."

The studio was spotless. It didn't even look like the same space.

"Thank God," I said, putting the bag down on the small table next to her kitchen. "I was worried we'd have to clear diapers to use the table."

She laughed.

Grace was sleeping in a little swing next to the couch, rocking back and forth, a green pacifier in her mouth.

I'd left Harry Puppins at my apartment, locked in the bathroom with pee pads. I figured letting him shit all over Vanessa's place probably wouldn't be the best way to be a good house guest.

He'd bitten me before I left.

I began pulling out the food. "I got a few extra meals for you. Okay if I put them in the freezer?" I did it without waiting for her reply. "I got you a cannoli too."

She eyed me suspiciously. "Are you sure you're not hitting on me?" she asked, crossing her arms. "Because I gotta be honest, I could be into this." She spied the bottle of wine and gasped, picking it up. "Oh, I *love* this one! It's been months since I've had a Chateau Montelena chardonnay."

I arched an eyebrow as I closed the freezer. "You know your wines."

"I *adore* wine. Once I had a whole bottle of Château Margaux Margaux on the rooftop of my hotel in Paris." She grabbed a wine opener from the drawer. "I'll never forget the hangover the next day, but it was *so* worth it."

"Pricey bottle." About twelve hundred. More if the hotel sold it. She must make decent money.

"You only live once," she sang. "God, I know I've only been doing this baby thing a few weeks, but it feels like a lifetime. You're not supposed to take newborns out too much because their immune system isn't strong enough yet, so I feel like a prisoner." She handed me the bottle opener. "Would you mind?"

Grace had woken up and she watched us now with large blue eyes, like she was following the conversation. A cute baby.

I opened the wine bottle and handed it to Vanessa. "Why did you decide to foster?"

She poured us two glasses. "I kinda didn't. She's my sister's baby. The girl in the hallway from earlier. Annabel."

She set my wineglass in front of one of the chairs at the table and grabbed some plates from the cabinet. "She's nineteen. No idea who the father is. Gave the mom thing about a week and then came over, dropped Grace off to run an errand, and never came back." She paused. "She struggles with some addiction issues."

"I'm sorry to hear that," I said, taking a seat in one of the chairs.

She set down napkins and silverware. "Thankfully she didn't use while she was pregnant. She was doing really well. She'd been in recovery for almost two years before this relapse."

They'd given us butter for the bread, but Vanessa pulled out two plates and poured olive oil on them. Then she drizzled them with balsamic, ground fresh pepper over it, and tore open two Parmesan packets and sprinkled it on top.

I rummaged our to-go containers from the bag and served

her marsala onto her plate and set it down in front of her seat. "So who were the other two?"

"My half brother, Brent. And my dad."

I stopped and looked at her. "That was your dad?"

She shrugged. "He wants to see his granddaughter. I don't really blame him—but I'm not letting Annabel in here when she's high. He didn't mean to bump my lip, by the way. He sorta fell into the door and it hit my mouth. Anyway, I have no idea what I'm doing with this baby. Half the time I think I'm just messing everything up." She sat down and scooted in her chair.

"Well, you should know that the reason she was crying this morning was because there was a plastic tag fastener stuck to her pajamas. It had nothing to do with you or your lack of parenting skills."

She stared at me. "Are you freaking serious?"

I opened the lid on my ravioli and served it onto my plate. "I never lie about plastic tag fasteners."

Vanessa burst into laughter. A sparkling smile lit her face. "Oh my God." She shook her head. "Poor Grace."

"I only thought to look because I can't stand tags on my clothes. I figured that might be it. It was easy to miss."

"Well, I'm grateful you showed up." She hovered her fork over her food. "You know, you're kind of a legend around here."

I cut a ravioli in half. "Really. Why's that?"

"You're the sexy single guy in this building. And you're all brooding and aloof. You have that whole smoldering alpha male thing going on. You came over here all like 'give me the baby,'" she said with a hard face in a fake male voice.

I snorted. I was neither aloof *nor* brooding. At least I didn't *think* I was. But then when I thought about it, I didn't really talk to anyone in this building. Not because I wanted to be rude. I just left early and came home late and was usually in a hurry.

I made a silent vow to smile more in the hallways.

She took a bite of mushroom, chewed, and swallowed. "They're not going to *believe* I'm actually hanging out with you."

"Who's they?" I asked, picking up my wineglass.

"The ladies."

I raised an eyebrow. "The ladies?"

"Yeah. There's the yoga lady in 303. There's the super-early-morning jogger lady in 309. And the two lesbian ladies in 302—who by the way want to see if they can have some of your sperm."

I started to choke.

"They're family planning," she said, going on. "They told me to ask you if you'd be open to it if I ever met you, seeing as how we're next-door neighbors and all. But don't worry, I told them it was a long shot. I mean, you can't just come at a complete stranger like, 'Can I have some sperm?' I was like, 'Come on, guys, at least buy the man dinner first,'" she said out of the side of her mouth.

I coughed into my fist, my eyes watering. "Thanks?"

"You're welcome. I mean, I don't blame them. If I was in the market for sperm, I'd probably want to ask you too. You're obviously intelligent. Good bone structure, and green eyes are very nice."

I cleared my throat and took a large swallow of wine. Well, at least I had *that* going for me.

She grinned. "So, tell me about yourself. *Are* you the sexy single guy in this building? Or are you dating someone? We should put this rumor to rest."

I wiped my mouth with a napkin. "I did have a girlfriend. Rachel."

"Did? What happened?"

Normally I wouldn't volunteer the details of my love life. Especially to a stranger. But I don't know what it was, I just didn't feel like filtering. Maybe because Vanessa didn't seem to feel like filtering.

"We met on a dating app eight months ago. She lives in Seattle. She's also married. I found out this morning."

She sucked air through her teeth. "Ouch. That sucks." She looked genuinely sorry to hear this news. "So was it serious with you guys?"

"It was the most serious relationship I've had in a while," I said honestly.

"Are you gonna get back out there? Fire up the dating app?"

I laughed dryly. "No. I'm officially done dating for the foreseeable future."

I'd had enough. At least for now. I was completely and utterly drained. I wouldn't say I was heartbroken—we hadn't been together long enough for that. But I was hurt and disappointed and seriously questioning my ability to trust people. To say I was emotionally unavailable at this point would be an understatement.

She changed the subject. "So you own the building?"

"I do. A management company runs it for me. I don't deal with any of the tenants. Actually, I offered your apartment to my assistant, Becky, before you rented it."

"Was that the woman who brought you the dog?"

"You saw her?" I asked.

"I heard talking. I looked through the peephole. She's pretty. You guys ever date?"

I shook my head. "No, we're just colleagues."

"Why? Does she have a boyfriend or something?"

I scoffed. "Sometimes."

"She never wanted to date you?"

"Not that I'm aware. And the feeling was mutual."

"Well, she must have some Herculean self-control." She waved her fork over my chest. "I mean, you're not exactly a hard sell. This body looks like you just got out of prison."

I snorted. She just said whatever popped into her head, didn't she?

"What about you?" I asked. "You said you don't date."

She sighed dramatically. "Well, the women in my family have a tendency to die young. I figure it's not really fair to make someone bury me, so single it is."

I arched an eyebrow. "Would you like to elaborate on that?"

She shook her head. "Nope, not really."

"Okay. So what do you do?"

"I'm a YouTuber."

I drew my brows down. "A what?"

"A video blogger? I have a travel channel. Basically I go places and I make videos about it."

She started cutting her chicken. I noticed she was having a hard time with the knife. Her right hand didn't seem to be gripping properly. She was getting the job done though so I didn't ask if she needed help.

"And how do you get paid for that?" I asked, looking away, not wanting to be rude. "Sponsors?"

"Yup. That and people pay to run ads during my videos. I also do appearances at cons and stuff. I get a percentage from products I sell on my Instagram and a lot of resorts invite me out for free in exchange for vlogging my experience."

"Huh. So where have you been?"

She shrugged. "Everywhere. I've traveled the world. I've been on a safari in Uganda and on a gondola in Venice. I've climbed volcanos and ridden a donkey up a mountain in Greece. You name it, I've done it." She skewered her chicken and took a bite.

"Wow. How'd you get into that?"

She chewed and swallowed. "Well, my sister Melanie got sick when she was twenty-seven. She died less than two years later. Afterward, I decided that starting on my twenty-sixth birthday, I was going to travel the world like I had one good year left to do it. So I started a GoFundMe, liquidated my meager 401(k), and got ready to go. And right before I left, I made a video about what I planned to do and that went viral. The rest is history."

"Can I check out your channel?" I asked.

"Sure. It's called Social Butterfly."

I'd never heard of it. But then I also couldn't remember the last time I'd been on YouTube.

"And what did you do before that?"

She shook her head. "I don't tell anyone that."

I arched an eyebrow. "And why's that?"

"I make people earn it." She smiled. "It's too good to just give away."

"I'll have to keep that in mind." I poked at my food. "You must enjoy your current job. I've always wanted to do more traveling."

She gave a one-shoulder shrug. "Do it. What's stopping you?"

I laughed mirthlessly. "Well, I don't fly, for one. And life."

"Life is no excuse," she said. "You should always have an adventure lined up. Having something to look forward to is tantamount to happiness."

I cut another ravioli in half. "Oh yeah?"

She looked at me matter-of-factly. "Yeah. Even if you have no money or time or the weather is bad, you can still live an exciting life if you try."

"Okay," I said. "How? Give me an example."

She set her fork down. "All right. Today, for example. The weather's bad, so play hide-and-seek in this building. Or poke around in all its nooks and crannies."

I gave her an amused look.

"What? I'm serious. This building is *so* cool. I mean, I know you own it, but have you actually ever explored it?"

"Of course. It was a flour company in the late 1800s. There was a loading dock for the train where the lobby is now. It's one of the things I loved about this property. They put flooring over the railroad tracks in the public areas, but if you go into the boiler room, it's still there."

She beamed. "I looove this building. Did you know the broom closet in the lobby by the mailboxes has the original brick where the workers for the mill graffitied their names?"

I hadn't known that…

"You can pick a name and google him. See how he lived."

She went back to eating. "You can always figure out a way to have fun. Even if you can't go anywhere."

Huh.

I bet she was good at her job. She had this bottomless-energy thing about her. Something perky and shiny, the thing news anchors pretend to have on air.

"So that's why I don't really see you around," I said. "You're gone a lot."

"Oh, I'm around." She gave me a wry smile. "You probably just weren't looking."

Grace started making noises from her swing. Vanessa got up and grabbed a bottle from the dishwasher. I watched her as she had her back to me. She had a nice ass. A nice everything, actually.

I tore my eyes away from Vanessa leaning against the counter to get formula from a cabinet. "How old are you?" I asked, looking for something to talk about.

"Twenty-eight." She measured formula with a scoop. "How tall are you?"

"Six-two."

"So tall," she said, filling the bottle with water. She twisted her lips into a smile. "If I need something from a high cabinet, can I text you to come grab it for me? Or would that be abusing my new phone number privileges?"

I chuckled. "Sure."

"And I have a hard time with jar lids. Weak hands." She wiggled her fingers. "Can I count on you for that too?"

"Why not."

"Sweeeet," she said, scooping formula into the bottle. "I'm going to do that, you know."

I wiped my mouth with my napkin and nodded at the swing. "I'll feed her. You eat."

She shook the bottle with her finger over the tip. "Really?"

"Yeah." I got up to wash my hands and joined her by the sink. "You just have to show me how to do it."

"You've never fed a baby?" she asked, looking up at me.

I dried my hands on a paper towel. "I've never done anything with a baby. This is the first baby I've ever held."

"Really? Well, you're a natural."

I walked to the swing, leaned down, picked up Grace the way Vanessa had showed me this morning, and sat back at the table.

Vanessa crouched next to me. "It's pretty easy." She put the bottle in Grace's mouth and the baby sucked on it hungrily, making little cooing noises. "Just keep it angled like this so she doesn't get bubbles in her stomach."

Vanessa's head was just a few inches under my nose as she leaned over Grace with the bottle and again I thought about how good her hair smelled. It was better without the vomit.

I took the bottle, and Vanessa sat back down to her food.

"Hey, do you wanna watch a movie?" she asked. "Here? After we eat? I feel like I'm in solitary confinement. I am bored out of my *mind*, and I just wanna hang out with somebody."

Now that I'd torn off the Band-Aid and come over, I realized I wouldn't mind staying. I'd officially had about all I could handle of the Keller transcripts for one day. And frankly I didn't love the idea that I'd be going back to my empty apartment in a few minutes to sit around dwelling on the

Rachel/Mom/Richard situation until I got tired enough to go to sleep. Why not.

"Sure," I said, looking at Grace but talking to Vanessa.

"Yay! So what do you want to watch?"

"Whatever you want is fine," I said, smiling down at Grace. She was falling asleep while she ate, nodding off with milk pooling around the sides of her little mouth.

She was so small. Trusting.

I'd never really been sure I wanted kids. I'd always been worried I'd screw it up. That I'd somehow fail them. I hadn't really had a good childhood myself. My parents had a tumultuous marriage. Then Dad left, and I'd practically raised myself from that point on. I hadn't exactly been shown a good example.

I rubbed Grace's tiny pink cheek with a knuckle.

But maybe being a father was like this. Just being there and doing what needed to be done, one small task at a time until they added up to something good.

Maybe if you started at the beginning and stuck around…

Vanessa picked up the remote. "I know exactly what we should watch. You cannot go wrong with *The Office*, even though you've probably seen it a million times."

"I've never seen it," I said.

She blanched. "You've never— Are you *serious*?" She looked at me like I was crazy. "Where have you been? How do you understand memes?"

"Memes are not really a large part of my day-to-day operations."

She blinked at me. "Oh my God. This is…Okay, you know what?" She waved a hand. "We're gonna set this right.

We're going to start now so that starting tomorrow you won't
have to walk around and tell people you've never seen *The
Office* like some kind of lunatic."

I laughed. Again.

~

Three hours later, I was standing to stretch. The TV was
asking us if we were still watching, and I hoped we were. I
liked the show—and Vanessa was easy to be around. She was
one of those people who just sort of rolled with things. The
kind you didn't have to work at hanging out with.

Grace spit out her pacifier, and I leaned down over her
swing and put it back in her mouth.

I'd changed my first diaper today. I was here, might as well
help give Vanessa a break. She showed me how to do it, and I
took the next changing off her hands.

Vanessa was holding Harry Puppins.

About an hour into the show my conscience got the better
of me and I went to go get him. I figured as long as someone
was holding him, he wouldn't have any accidents. Vanessa had
been more than happy to do it. Apparently she loved dogs.

He bit her when she picked him up.

He didn't have any teeth. It didn't hurt, but it was the
thought that counts. I was worried it would put her off, but
she couldn't stop laughing. She said he was like an angry
potato with legs.

"So is this your bedroom?" she asked, pointing to the wall
at the head of her bed.

"Yup."

The headboard of my bed was pushed up against the same wall. We were separated at night by only about a foot of bricks and plaster. It was a little weird to think about.

I had a retroactive twinge of relief that Vanessa hadn't heard me having sex with Rachel through the wall. I didn't realize they were so thin.

Vanessa had been renting this unit for only three months. When Rachel came out in September and October, we'd stayed in the hotel her company put her up in. And this trip she was on her period and didn't want to have sex. That was her preference, not mine. *I* couldn't care less what time of the month it was. But now I wondered if she'd been honest about that excuse. Probably not. She must have come out here knowing she wanted to break up with me and she was trying to make some space between us.

We hadn't slept with each other since early October. It was almost December.

I should have known something was wrong.

I couldn't stop looking for all the signs. Scouring the last few months for red flags or things I should have picked up on. We were both busy. She was a software engineer and just like me she worked long days and irregular hours, so not being able to reach her wasn't exactly eyebrow raising. But it was hard not to be angry at myself for not noticing something wasn't right.

I had to shake it off and try to focus on something else before I let it drag my mood back down.

I looked around Vanessa's studio. She had a wall of art. "That's a nice photograph," I said, nodding at a framed picture. It was a copper-colored dog on the shore of a lake. Looked like up north.

She closed the space between us to stand next to me. "It's not a photograph. It's a painting."

I raised my eyebrows. "Really."

"Yeah. I got it at a MADD fund-raiser. I had to pledge a fortune for it. It's a Sloan Monroe."

"Oh, Jaxon Waters's wife. I know her," I said, studying it.

"You *know* her?" she said to the side of my face. "*How?*"

"My cousin Josh is married to her best friend. He lives next door to them in Ely. And I went on a date with her once."

"Bullshit."

I looked at her and her eyes were wide. I pulled out my cell phone and went to Instagram. I found Sloan's private page and handed her the phone.

"Oh my God," she breathed, scrolling through the pictures of Sloan and Jaxon, my cousin and his family intermingled in the feed, sitting around a campfire, at the table for Thanksgiving, playing with each other's kids.

"This is so cool! You just got cooler by association," she said, smiling up at me. "I'm a total fangirl. I *love* her—she is *so* talented. There's like a three-year waiting list for one of these."

"I can see why," I said, looking back at the artwork. This couldn't have been cheap. She must make pretty good money doing this vlogger thing to afford fine wines and a Sloan Monroe.

I moved down the wall to look at the next piece. It was made out of real butterfly wings, arranged in a colorful, intricate design. "They're all so different."

"I surround myself with things that make me happy. That's sort of a rule I have. I got that one in Costa Rica."

"And this one?" I pointed to a black-and-white pencil drawing of a half-naked woman draped in a sheet. Her head was tipped, and her hair covered one eye.

"An artist in Sicily. That's me, by the way."

I arched an eyebrow at her.

She laughed. "Antonio is about seventy-five years old and very professional. I wanted someone to paint me like one of Jack's French girls before I die."

I looked back at the drawing. It was tastefully done. But she was nude from the navel up. "You could have given the old guy a heart attack."

She laughed again. "He painted Sophia Loren topless. My boobs didn't stand a chance of doing him in."

I begged to differ on that.

She'd hung it, so she must be okay with people looking at it, but I wasn't really appreciating the art—I was appreciating the *view*, and that wasn't the same thing. I went on to the next one, just so I wasn't staring at her naked.

It was a photo of a graffitied brick wall with a woman dressed like the Statue of Liberty painted on it holding up a globe. "Why does this look familiar?"

"That one's a Banksy," she said.

I narrowed my eyes at the woman's face. "Is that you too?" I looked back at her.

She shrugged. "Yeah. I met him at a water park in Shanghai."

"You met Banksy, the famous anonymous street artist, at a water park in Shanghai," I deadpanned.

She shrugged again. "I mean, I didn't *know* it was him.

We talked for like twenty minutes by the kiddie pool. And
then like two days later this photo gets delivered to my hotel
room—which was super weird because I didn't tell him where
I was staying. He wrote on the back 'From the guy you talked
to by the kiddie pool—Banksy.' "

I blinked at her.

"He authenticated it on his website. It's supposed to
represent global unity through traveling and embracing other
cultures or something? I don't know, it's sorta confusing. They
sell prints of it."

I shook my head. "What did he look like?"

"I don't know. A normal guy? Not as handsome as you."

I snorted.

She looked up at me. "So what kind of law do you practice,
Adrian?"

"I'm a criminal defender."

"Huh. Why?" She tilted her head.

I looked back at the Banksy. "I like the challenge of it."

"Are a lot of your clients guilty?"

I scoffed. "*Most* of my clients are guilty."

"And that doesn't bother you, trying to get people off when
you know they deserve to go to prison?"

"Everyone deserves a defense," I said.

She went quiet next to me for a moment. "You know,
somebody like you could really change the world if you
wanted to."

I turned back to her. "And do what?"

"Fight for something that needs fighting for. Like disability rights."

"Disability rights. That's specific."

"My sister was a wheelchair user before she died. You wouldn't *believe* what it's like for the disabled." She ticked off on her fingers. "Discrimination, lack of resources, lack of basic accessibility. I mean, housing alone. Do you know how hard it is to find accessible, affordable housing for the disabled? It's why so many disabled people end up in institutions or living in substandard or unsafe living conditions."

I crossed my arms over my chest. "And you think the cause could use another good lawyer?"

"Oh yeah." Her lips twisted into a grin. "Especially one who likes a challenge."

I gave her a small smile and looked at my watch. "I should probably let you get to sleep. It's almost midnight."

I couldn't be sure, but I thought I saw a flicker of disappointment on her face. She handed me Harry. "Thanks for hanging out."

"Thanks for having me over."

Half an hour later, I was lying in bed and Vanessa knocked on the wall of my bedroom over my headboard.

I smiled and knocked back.

## CHAPTER 6

# IF YOU HAVE THIS SYMPTOM, YOU MIGHT BE DYING!

## VANESSA

The numbness was back in my right hand.
    I'd woken up this morning and fumbled my phone with fingers that felt dead.

It was 6:34 a.m. Saturday morning. I was sitting in the dark in my room wrapped in a blanket, my legs crossed on my bed, trying to do the in-through-the-nose, out-through-the-mouth breathing Yoga Lady had taught me to calm myself down. But the terror rolled through me like waves. It got bigger and bigger until it burst from my lips in a choking sob.

I didn't want to wake Grace, so I stumbled to the bathroom with a hand over my mouth. I put the lid to the toilet down to sit and swiped open my phone to read the article on WebMD again, squeezing my right hand into a fist, feeling certain that I'd lost grip strength.

ALS can start off with something as simple as a
weak feeling in your hands or feet. It's a disease
that attacks the brain cells that control a lot of your
muscle movement.

ALS Association:

Gradual onset, generally painless, progressive muscle weakness is the most common initial symptom
in ALS. Other early symptoms vary but can include
tripping, dropping things, abnormal fatigue of the
arms and/or legs, slurred speech, muscle cramps
and twitches.

Mayo Clinic:

Hand weakness or clumsiness...

I don't know why I needed to keep reading this. I knew
*exactly* what this disease looked like.

I bit the inside of my cheek so hard I tasted blood.

At first I'd hoped it was just carpal tunnel. But I'd gone in
for testing, and it was negative. They'd wanted to send me for
more study and I'd refused.

There was no test for ALS. They diagnosed it by excluding
other diseases that mimic it and monitoring the progression
of your deterioration. It could take up to a year of invasive
procedures and poking and prodding before they slapped ALS
on what was happening to me—and when they did, there was
nothing to be done anyway. It was 100 percent fatal.

And now maybe the countdown had finally begun.

My life might officially be going from living to dying.

An average three-year life expectancy from the onset of symptoms—less if my family history was any indication. Melanie had lived only nineteen months after her voice started to slur, and she took the medications—which I would not.

I figured I had about a year. My muscles would continue to waste away, a little at a time. Then I wouldn't be able to walk, feed myself, move. I was going to die unable to swallow, unable to speak, like Melanie had. Entombed in the prison of my own body, fully aware, until it paralyzed my lungs and I suffocated to death.

I put my phone facedown on the bathroom sink and sobbed into my hands.

# CHAPTER 7

# THINGS YOU CAN DO TO MAKE YOURSELF HAPPY (YOU WON'T BELIEVE #4!)

## ADRIAN

I woke up to knocking on my door. I glanced at my phone. It was 7:03 in the morning. It was Saturday, so I didn't have to work and I'd been planning on sleeping in. Damn. Probably Becky.

She'd texted me a few times last night to check in on the dog, and I hadn't texted her back. She was probably here on her suicide watch.

Harry Puppins growled from the pillow next to mine as I threw off the covers and put on slippers. I'd started letting him sleep in the bed. I couldn't stand the frail, confused way he looked at me when I'd put him in the laundry room at night.

He still bit me every chance he got.

I opened the door expecting my assistant, but it was

Vanessa standing there. She had Grace strapped to her front in a baby sling. "Hey." She beamed up at me.

I hadn't seen her since Monday, five days ago, when we'd done dinner and *The Office* at her place. I'd worked late every night this week, and I hadn't knocked to take her trash out again because I didn't want to wake her up when I got home.

She'd been randomly sending me *Office* memes. It was like a tiny little smile that popped up on my phone once in a while to surprise me. I liked it—though I was too busy to respond most of the time.

I smiled at her. "Hey. Good morning."

Her eyes were a little red. Maybe she hadn't slept well last night.

She bounced the baby. "Sorry I didn't text. This is sort of an impulse visit. I was on a walk around the building. I get stir-crazy in there. I passed by your door and the next thing I knew, I was knocking."

She was very perky for 7:00 in the morning. I felt my smile reach my eyes.

She was in pajamas. Fleece bottoms with the Grinch on them. I couldn't see the gray shirt under the baby sling, but it was baggy. Her hair was piled in a messy bun on top of her head and she had on unicorn slippers. She was a hot mess and it was oddly attractive.

I wondered what the real reason was that she didn't date. She certainly *was* datable. Good-looking, intelligent, fun to be around. Inherently likable. I'd really enjoyed hanging out with her the other night.

I hadn't had a chance to check out her channel yet. I'd been slammed at work. I was in the middle of a jury trial. But now I wished I'd taken a few minutes to look at it.

She cradled Grace's bottom in the sling. "Anyway, I was wondering if you'd like to…" She wrinkled her forehead and peered past me. "Are those crime-scene photos?"

I looked over my shoulder. "Oh, yeah. I was working from home last night."

She edged past me without being invited in and made her way to my dining room table. She scanned the photos with her back to me. "You know, without the lawyer thing for context, this makes you look like a serial killer. Like you might as well have a necklace made of teeth or something."

I chuckled. "And yet you're not afraid to be alone here with me?"

She looked back at me and shook her head. "This is not how I die. Believe me, I know."

She was wearing a brace on her right hand. I nodded at it. "Did you hurt yourself?" I asked.

"No. Carpal tunnel." She cocked her head. "Is your tetanus shot up to date?"

I wrinkled my forehead at her. "What?"

"There's a thing I thought you might want to do with me. Do you have time?"

I smiled. I actually did have time.

The weekends were hard these days. It's when my personal life, or lack thereof, really glared. No more dinner every Sunday with Mom and Grandma. I'd had Rachel to look forward to every few weeks, but now that was over. I wasn't training for anything at the moment, no marathons or fun runs, and it was winter, my least favorite time of the year to be outside. If Vanessa hadn't shown up, I think I would have opened my eyes to an instant gloom. I appreciated the distraction.

"I have time," I said. "What's the thing?"

"You'll see. We can do it at my place, or here, since you have the floor space." She looked around with her hands on her hips. "Why is your apartment so big? I feel like mine used to be a file room or something."

"This used to be two units. I took them both and knocked down the wall. Put in the bigger kitchen."

"Do you cook?"

"Not really. Kitchens equal resale value," I said, crossing my arms.

"Okay. But you obviously make coffee," she said, nodding at the $2,000 espresso maker I had on my counter. "That thing is vulgar."

I glanced into the kitchen. "I like good coffee. I get the beans locally roasted." I looked back at her. "Do you want one?"

"Well, I'm not gonna say no to that. But I need to eat before I caffeinate. I'll go have cereal real quick and I'll be back in ten minutes?"

"I could make us eggs," I offered.

She grinned. "I thought you said you didn't cook?"

"I'm perfectly capable of eggs," I assured her.

"All right. If you say so. I do need to go get the thing we're doing, though, so I'll be right back. Can you take Grace?"

I held the baby while Vanessa made two trips back to her place. One to get Grace's swing and a diaper bag, and the other for the mystery activity she had planned. In between I brushed my teeth and washed my face as best I could while holding a baby. I didn't change. I was in house slippers, a white T-shirt, and gray pajama bottoms.

I didn't usually let myself be dressed down like this in front of anyone. But since Vanessa didn't have the sling on her chest anymore, I saw that not only was she wearing a Schrute Farms shirt with a picture of a beet on the front—an *Office* reference that I now understood—but she also wasn't wearing a bra. Changing might make her uncomfortable, like she was underdressed.

And I liked it. I *liked* that she didn't feel the need to impress me and I didn't feel the need to impress her. There was something comforting about it, about just being you in whatever state you happened to be in.

Vanessa came back lugging an enormous canvas bag behind her. The sack was so full it jammed in the doorway and I had to put Grace down and run to help her.

"What the hell's in here?" I asked, setting it in the middle of the living room floor.

She was panting from the effort, leaning forward with her hands on her hips to catch her breath. "Adventure and excitement. It's fan mail—sure to be both thrilling and horrifying in equal measures."

"You get this much mail?" I asked, eyeing the sack.

She shrugged. "Sure. It comes from all over the world, so…" She crouched down and grabbed the bottom of the bag, then lifted it and spilled the contents onto the carpet. Letters fanned and boxes tumbled out.

"Jesus, how many months' worth is this?"

"About two weeks," she said, kneeling back and looking it over.

I blanched. "Two wee— How many people follow you?" She shrugged again. "A lot."

I made cappuccinos while Vanessa sorted the envelopes and boxes into piles. Then I went to the fridge and started to rummage. I didn't have much. I ate most of my meals out. But between some cheeses, the sauce from some leftover chicken cacciatore I'd brought home a few days earlier and some crème fraîche, leftover Italian bread, and a container of Chipotle guac Vanessa ran to get in her apartment, I managed to make us some pretty decent Spanish omelets.

We sat on the floor of the living room to eat them in our laps so we could start to open mail.

"This tastes *amazing*," she said, licking some sauce off her thumb. "You seriously undersold your egg-making abilities."

Grace was napping in her swing next to us and Harry was snuggled up against Vanessa's thigh, sleeping. She put a hand on his head.

He growled.

She set her plate on her knees. "Okay, some fan mail disclaimers."

I took a sip of my coffee and set the mug back down on the carpet. "Shoot."

"All right. I don't know what's waiting for us in this pile. Most of my fans are perfectly normal and nice. But it *is* the Internet. I'm not saying there's a severed ear in here, but there might be a severed ear. General rule of thumb, if it's dripping, smells bad, or vibrating, I don't open it."

I put my plate in my lap and spread the crème over my omelet. "Why? Because it could be a bomb?"

"No, because it's probably a vibrator."

I almost choked on my laugh. Jesus, she cracked me up.

"There's going to be nudes. Hopefully for your sake, you only open up the female ones."

I was still chuckling. "Women send you nudes?"

She looked me dead in the eye. "All. The. *Time.* And I don't eat anything anyone sends me."

"Even if it's untampered with?"

"Yup. Somebody might have rubbed their balls on it or something. It does not go in my mouth. Also, I don't touch anything from Monett, Missouri. We'll need to set it on fire. Don't ask."

She reached into the diaper bag she'd brought over for Grace and pulled out hand sanitizer and baby wipes and set them off to the side between us. "We'll need this. Are you ready?"

"Ready," I said.

She gave me a mock serious look. "You're a brave man for doing this, Adrian Copeland. Braver than most."

I smiled as I grabbed the first box and tore the tape off it.

An hour later we were sitting in a pile of empty envelopes and cardboard, wearing an assortment of paraphernalia from the fan mail. Both of us were covered in glow sticks. Vanessa wore a necklace strung with Froot Loops. She'd made me put on an extra-large shirt from a fan in Maryland that said I HAVE CRABS on it, and we both had stickers on our arms.

It was ridiculous. Normally I'd never do something this juvenile, but I had to admit I was having fun.

Vanessa did all the cards and I did all the packages, since she had a hard time with her hand. This meant she got the majority of the dick pics.

"We got another one," she announced, putting a picture upside down in the dick pic pile.

I shook my head with a smile. "This is some job you have here."

Vanessa scoffed. "I just don't understand why men think we want to see that. It looks like a wrinkled elbow or something. It is not cute. Send me a picture of a puppy or cookies or something." She ripped open an envelope. "If some guy sent me a picture of a cake at two a.m. like, 'Hey, gurl, you up?' I'd be like, 'Hell yeah I'm up, come over.'"

I snorted. "Is it really that common? Do women get pictures of strange men's dicks often?"

She tore open a pink envelope. "Most of being a woman is running a gauntlet chock-full of penises," she mumbled. "I hope you don't send them."

I picked up the next box. "I've never sent a dick pic. I prefer the shock and awe of letting them see it in person."

She practically cackled, and I smiled at the victory of making her laugh that hard. "Just for the record," she said, "I soooo do not believe you."

I gave her an amused look. "You don't believe I don't send dick pics?"

She shook her head, still giggling. "Nope. Men like you *always* send dick pics."

I smirked, looking at the contents of my box. A large, squishy poop emoji. "Men like me, huh? And exactly what kind of men is that?" I held up the brown spiral and Vanessa nodded to the donate pile.

"The super-confident, self-assured, brooding alpha male kind."

I chuckled. "Well, I hate to disappoint you, but, as far as I am aware, my penis has never been photographed."

She put her hand out. "Let me see your phone."

I squinted at her. "What?"

She looked at me, dead serious. "Let me see it. You don't have any dick pics. What's the problem?"

I grinned. "Okay. Let me see yours."

She shrugged. "Fine. Whatever. But no deleting anything first. We hand them over and whatever's in there is in there. No filter."

"Okay." I unlocked my screen and handed it to her.

She grabbed at it excitedly. But then she froze and clutched it to her chest. "Wait, why aren't you nervous?"

I cocked an eyebrow. "Because there's nothing in there you can't see."

She narrowed her eyes. "This feels suspicious. Is this your burner phone?"

I laughed. "No. What kind of guys do you date that you think I need a burner phone?"

"I told you, I don't date. I just find it awfully odd that you're not sweating bullets right now."

"Because there are no dick pics in there. Like I *said*." I put my hand out for her phone.

She gave me a long, hard, playful glare and then slapped her cell into my palm.

We both went quiet looking at each other's phones.

Vanessa's cell was like the digital version of her. Nothing but fun. It was bejazzled in pink rhinestones with a sparkly PopSocket on the back. Her home screen was a picture of Grace wearing a little beanie with teddy bear ears.

Mine was the opposite. Black, functional, and with a stock lock screen. And I meant what I said. There was nothing in there she couldn't see.

Her home screen had a music app, Uber, Lyft, Tripadvisor, Audible, Instagram, iFunny, and a couple of games.

I tapped on her photo icon and started to scroll through. Everything in her gallery was excitement and color. Pictures of resorts. The bed in the hotel room, an elephant made of towels on the comforter. A snowy small town with a huge mountain range in the backdrop. Her, laughing in a bikini at a swim-up bar in a pool. There were pictures of her holding a sangria on a cobblestone street. A cruise ship on blue water somewhere.

My gallery was boring in comparison. I almost felt sorry for her getting the short end of the stick. It was mostly legal documents and several dozen shots of the sign in the parking garage downtown by the courthouse so I'd remember where I parked. A picture of a light bulb I needed to pick up at the store, the claim ticket on a dry-cleaning order.

"Wow," she said, looking at my screen. "You sure do park a lot."

I chuckled and scrolled on. There was a picture of Vanessa dressed in a milk maid's costume of some sort under a large tent. She had an enormous stein of beer, bigger than she was. I turned the phone to her. "Where was this?"

She looked up from my phone. "Oktoberfest. Germany. Where are your pictures of Rachel?"

"I don't think I have any," I admitted.

She laughed. "So you had a girlfriend, but she doesn't go to this school?"

I smirked. "You don't think I had a girlfriend?"

She shrugged. "I'm just sayin'."

I nodded at my phone. "Look for her on Instagram. Her account's private, but if you search on my phone you can see it. Her name is Rachel Dunham."

I watched her punch the icon and scroll through my phone and my smile fell a little. I should probably unfollow Rachel and her fake account. I made a mental note to do that as soon as I got my cell back. I looked back at the picture of Vanessa, trying to distract myself.

In the Oktoberfest photo her chest was pushed up almost to her chin by a bodice of some sort. Her hair was in an intricate braid that wrapped around her head and she was smiling. She looked beautiful in it.

Her cell phone vibrated in my hand and a number popped up at the top of the screen. It was *mine*.

"What are you sending to your phone?" I asked.

She didn't look up. "Pictures of you. I told you, the ladies aren't going to believe I'm hanging out with you. I'm gonna need proof."

I tapped on the message and a text from my phone filled the screen. She'd sent herself three pictures of me from my gallery. One was me with Mom and Grandma at Mom's birthday back in June. Another was a shot of me shaking hands with Marcus, at a fund-raiser. And the last one was my finisher picture for the last marathon I'd run, six months ago.

"You know, just because you have pictures of me doesn't prove anything," I said. "The ladies might say you just took them off my Instagram."

She narrowed her eyes. "Good point, lawyer. I *am* a known cyber stalker. What do you have in mind?"

"We could take a selfie," I suggested.

She brightened. "Good idea! Let's put the baby and the dog in it for a time stamp."

She picked up Grace and handed her to me. Then she grabbed the dog and crawled through the pile of trash between us, scooted over, and leaned into me, her shoulder pressing into my biceps.

The contact sent a warm ripple through me. It surprised me, gave me an impulse to turn my head to her.

I kept my face straight.

She angled my phone, we smiled, and she took the picture. Then she took Grace from me and moved back to her side of the pile with the baby in her lap.

The spot Vanessa had touched felt vacant.

We spent another few minutes going through each other's phones. We both played the first song in each other's favorite playlist.

Hers was "Redemption" by Lola Simone. Mine was "Back Down" by Bob Moses. I liked running to it.

"So," she said, returning my phone. "Tell me, Adrian, how much time do you spend at the gym? Why are you so chiseled?"

I laughed. "Chiseled?"

"Yeah." She cradled Grace and kissed her cheek. "I read a lot of romance novels and this is definitely chiseling that you have going on."

"I try to stay in shape. I do triathlons sometimes."

She blanched. "For *fun*?"

I peeled the tape off a box. "What, you don't think running, biking, and swimming are fun?"

"I think walks on the beach, leisurely bike rides, and floating are fun. I don't run unless I'm being chased. So, do you drink anything other than wine?"

"Bourbon sometimes. You?"

"Gin, socially. What are your vices?"

I wrinkled my forehead. "I drive too fast. And I like good restaurants. I spend too much money on food."

"Me too! The restaurant thing, not the driving thing. What's your favorite restaurant?"

"Oh, that's a tough one." I pulled a tissue-wrapped snow globe out of the box I was opening, dipped it so that the snow flew, and showed it to her. She nodded to the keep pile. "I can't say I have a favorite restaurant. Just favorite dishes."

She looked at a postcard with a crayon drawing on it. "Even better. Which ones?"

"Well, let's see. I like the cavatelli with braised rabbit at Lucrezia's."

She was nodding. "Their gnocchi is in my top ten."

"Yes. And for steaks I like Cl—"

"Clove and Cleaver," she said, finishing my sentence without looking up.

I smiled. "I love their jalapeno poppers."

"And the fried green tomatoes."

I laughed. "Yes."

She put the postcard in the keep pile. "I am a *huge* foodie. I almost fainted once in Rome after a PA wanted to eat at McDonald's. If someone invites me to lunch, and they take me to Taco Bell or something, it's no longer an outing, it's a kidnapping. Small business, all the way—except Chipotle," she added. "I do like Chipotle."

I chuckled, because I was the same way. Every time I took Mom out to eat and she wanted to go to Perkins, I died a little inside. I preferred supporting small businesses too. And why would you get something mass produced when you could try someplace unique? There are a finite amount of meals in this life and wasting one on something mundane when you have the means to have anything different is a travesty.

"Have you ever been to Badger Den?" Vanessa asked. "In L.A.?"

I had to stare at her for a second. "You know about Badger Den?"

She looked at the front of an envelope, holding Grace against her chest. "I've been on their waiting list for two years."

I blinked at her. I couldn't *believe* I was sitting here talking to somebody who knew what Badger Den was. In Los Angeles, sure. But in Minnesota? The exclusive, invite-only, secret-location pop-up dinner had been on my bucket list for as long as I could remember. "I'm on their waiting list too, but I haven't gotten in."

She smiled. "How about we make a pact. If either of us gets into Badger Den, we'll take the other as our plus-one."

"You have a deal," I said, a little too quickly.

"Of course, you'll have to fly there. They only give you a few days' notice."

"I drive very, *very* fast."

She laughed, setting Grace back in her swing. Then she grabbed a yellow manilla envelope and pulled out a package of sponges. She squealed. "Yeeeees! Yes yes YES!"

I cocked an eyebrow. "Sponges?"

She smiled down on them in her hand. "I did this segment on small things you can do to make you happy. Clean sheets, warm towels out of the dryer, fresh flowers in your bedroom. A new sponge." She looked up at me. "It is *amazing* how restorative a new sponge is." She got up. "I'm giving you one."

"A sponge?" I asked, twisting to watch her walk to the kitchen.

"Yup. It's going to change your life." She unwrapped it and set it on the sink, tossing the old one. "It's like a spiritual cleansing. A cosmic reset."

"A sponge…" I deadpanned, giving her an amused look.

She looked like she was about to reply, but someone started pounding loudly on a door in the hallway. Vanessa peered up past me toward the banging. "That sounds like my door, doesn't it?" She walked from the kitchen, undid the bolt lock, and poked her head outside. Then she looked back in at me, her face etched in worry.

"I have to go. The police are here."

# CHAPTER 8

# THE POLICE SHOWED UP AND WHAT HAPPENED NEXT WILL BLOW YOUR MIND!

## VANESSA

"Can I help you?" I asked, leaning halfway out of Adrian's apartment.

The officer looked over at me. "I'm looking for a Vanessa Price."

"I'm Vanessa."

He glanced at a clipboard. "Do you own a white 2018 Kia Rio?"

*Shit.*

My heart launched into rapid fire. "Yes, is everything okay?" I swallowed.

Adrian came up behind me and peered out into the hall. "Officer Sanchez," he said, over my shoulder. "How are you?"

Recognition crossed the cop's face and he broke into a smile. "Copeland! You live here?"

"Going on five years," Adrian said. "How's the wife?"

He laughed. "Pregnant again. Haven't seen you at the gym lately."

"Been busy. In the middle of a jury trial. What seems to be the problem?"

Officer Sanchez looked back at me, still smiling. "Yeah, we found your car wrapped around a tree over by the fairgrounds this morning, Ms. Price. Nobody in it. Do you know anything about that?"

His posture had gone casual the moment Adrian popped out. There was nothing accusatory about the question. But I could feel my pulse thrumming in my throat anyway. "No," I said, hoping I sounded normal.

"Did you give the vehicle to anyone to drive?"

Adrian squeezed my elbow discreetly from behind. "Sounds like it was stolen. Probably a joy ride," he said.

Officer Sanchez looked over my head at Adrian. "The keys were in it. It wasn't hot-wired."

Adrian's breath tickled my ear as he spoke to me. "Didn't you say you lost your keys, Vanessa?"

He was coaching me. And standing sooo close. Ridiculously close. It was on purpose. He wanted the officer to think we were together.

He was lending me his credibility.

He'd known me less than a week, he knew nothing about what was going on, and he was stepping in to defend me, giving me the benefit of the doubt and protecting me from whatever repercussions there could be from this. I didn't know why he was doing it, but I couldn't be more grateful. I was freaking out.

I nodded. "Yeah, actually. I lost the keys a few weeks ago," I lied. "I've been using the spare."

Officer Sanchez nodded, but his eyes felt like they were studying me all of a sudden. "Where were you last night at around three a.m.?"

Adrian laughed. "Where do you *think* she was?"

Officer Sanchez looked back and forth between us. Then he chuckled a little. "All right, buddy. I'll write it up as a stolen vehicle." He looked back at me. "It's in the impound. Here's the info." He handed me a card.

I cleared my throat. "I'm sorry, um...was there any blood or anything? Do you think anyone got hurt?"

Officer Sanchez shook his head. "Hard to tell. The airbag deployed, but we canvassed the immediate area. Nobody dead in a ditch. I think they ran off on their own two feet." He nodded up to Adrian. "Hey, you need to get back to the gym to spot me."

Adrian's laugh practically rumbled against my back. "Will do. Have a good day. And tell Karla I said hi."

As soon as we stepped back inside the apartment and the door closed behind me, I darted for my phone.

I dialed Dad. It went right to voicemail. Then Annabel. Voicemail too. Brent would have answered, but he blocked me after I told him he could have my Gucci backpack when he got a job. Arg!

"Shit. Shit shit shit shit shit. I have to go."

I started grabbing things, shoving wipes and hand sanitizer in the diaper bag, running to the kitchen to get the bottle I'd left drying on his sink. I had to collect Grace and her swing. My fan mail was all over the floor. I was so panicked and flustered I couldn't organize myself.

Adrian crossed his arms, watching me spin in circles around his apartment. "Who was driving the car?" he asked.

The hospital. I needed to call hospitals.

"My dad. I bought him a car to use. He's on probation, he probably got scared."

"Probation for what?" he asked.

"Health code violations. Stuff in the yard." I stopped in the middle of the room, panting, the diaper bag swinging off my elbow. "Do you think your friend knew you were lying?"

He shrugged. "Doesn't matter. There were no injuries, no property damage. Unless he has video footage, he can't prove anything and he knows it. It's not worth his time. I relieved you of any liability and saved him the paperwork and a trip to your dad's house. And I knew it wasn't you. I could hear you up with the baby at three a.m."

I nodded, too freaked out to feel bad that Adrian was awake with us in the middle of the night, and I dove past him to grab Grace's BabyBjörn off his table.

"Hey." He put his hands on my shoulders to stop me as I whizzed by him. "Breathe for a second." He dipped his head and looked at me with those deep green eyes. "What do you *need*?"

I swallowed. "I need...I need you to watch Grace," I said quickly.

It came out before I even had time to think about it. But I did. I couldn't take her on my scavenger hunt across hospitals and jail cells. And I *definitely* couldn't take her to Dad's.

Adrian nodded and took the diaper bag off my arm. "Of course. I got it. Go do what you need to do."

"Are you sure?" I asked breathlessly. "You can handle it?"

He looked me in the eye. "I'm very sure. Go. She'll be fine with me."

He had this strong, steady, take-charge thing about him. The air of someone who was used to being depended upon. He was so capable and I wondered offhandedly if this is what other people's dads were like.

I nodded at him and practically tripped over my feet getting out of the apartment. I ran home to change—but after getting almost all the way to the elevator I realized I didn't have my purse or car keys and I was in unicorn slippers and a Froot Loops necklace.

I drove the twenty minutes to Eagan. I'd called all the local hospitals on the way. Dad wasn't at any of them. He also wasn't in the Ramsey County jail system. I asked about Annabel too, just in case she'd been with him during the crash and she was hurt, but her name didn't ping either.

By the time I banged on Dad's door, my panic had moved into anger.

I mean, what the actual fuck? He crashes the car and he doesn't think I'm going to find out about it? He doesn't bother to call me and give me a heads-up, tell me he's okay?

When he answered, the smells of mildewy shower and festering garbage rolled out of the house at me.

"Dad," I said dryly as he stood there, red-eyed and disheveled. He didn't *look* like someone who'd been in a car crash, but who knew.

He squinted at me. "Melanie?"

It hit me like a punch to the gut. I had to take a moment to compose myself to answer. "Dad, it's *Vanessa*."

He blinked at me, and the light faded a little from his eyes. He pulled the door open and let me in, walking stiffly back to the sofa, where he lay down with a grimace.

I closed the door behind me.

God, the place was gross. Dad had always been a pack rat, but this was bad, even for him.

I wrinkled my nose at a bag of rotting trash by the front door that someone had pulled from the kitchen but never run to the curb. It was leaking from the bottom and sat in a putrid brown puddle. As usual there were stacks of random stuff everywhere. Shit he saw on the curb destined for the dump that he'd brought home with the grandiose plan of fixing it or using it somehow. It was ridiculous.

Normally I took off my shoes when I came into a house, but I wasn't walking barefoot in here. "So, I see you're shooting for a new personal best," I said, stepping over a dirty, torn dog bed—which was interesting because Dad didn't have any pets.

He spoke from the sofa like he was in pain. "Vanessa, I'm in an exceptional amount of discomfort. Your sister has relieved me of all my Percocet, and my back is killing me. I didn't sleep a wink last night. If you're going to give me a hard time, I'll thank you to let yourself out."

He'd injured his back last week tripping over something in the house. I told him to lock up the pills, which of course he didn't do. I also told him to clean this place up, and he didn't do that either.

I walked to the sofa and stood over him with my

arms crossed. "Are you wondering why I'm here today?" I asked. When he didn't bother to open his eyes or answer, I went on. "The police stopped by my apartment. Apparently they found your car wrapped around a tree this morning? Empty? Do you happen to know anything about that?"

He groaned and put an arm over his face.

"Are you injured?" I asked, irritated. "Do I need to take you to the hospital?"

"Fit as a fiddle," he muttered.

"So you what? Just crashed it and ran?"

He didn't answer me, and I kicked the footboard of the sofa. "Dad!"

He sat up slowly, wincing. "All right, all right. You have my attention. Happy?"

I glared at him.

"It wasn't me," he said. "It was Annabel. I wasn't even there."

I dropped my arms. "You lent her the *car*?" I stood there, my mouth agape. "Why the hell would you give it to her? She was probably high! And her license is suspended!"

"You don't need that government-issued nonsense to drive," he said, waving me off. "That's just Big Brother's way of making money off us for something a ten-year-old could do. What's next? Mandatory GPS trackers in our brains that we'll have the privilege of paying yearly fees for? Human barcodes? No thank you."

I stared at him. "Please tell me you're kidding."

"Why would I be kidding? And I didn't give her the car," he said, rubbing his lower back. "She took it."

"Without *permission*?"

He squinted up at me. "She's a grown woman, Vanessa. She hardly needs *my* permission to leave the house—"

I gawked at him. "Wow. Just *wow.*" I shook my head, incredulous. "You know what? I'm *done.* You're getting your shit together, Brent's getting a job, and she's going into rehab and not living here anymore until she does, do you understand me?" I jabbed a thumb into my chest. "I pay this mortgage. *I* make the payments on that car she just crashed. It's registered under *my* name. I pay the insurance on it and the maintenance and now the repairs. And I do it so that *you* can get your life together and maybe Brent can have a way to get to a job if he ever decides to get one, not so Annabel can use it to endanger the general public. If you three think I'm going to enable this…this *bullshit* by continuing to fund it, you've lost your minds."

I started snatching empty soda bottles off the coffee table and clutching them to my stomach. "She could have *killed* someone," I said, fuming, bottles clinking against one another. "You're lucky all she did was wrap it around a tree." I stopped and glared at him. "Did she take money? And don't lie to me."

He looked indignant. "You cut her off. How else is she supposed to eat?"

"How much?" I demanded.

He waved a dismissive hand around. "Maybe a few twenties. And my phone," he added. He bobbed his head. "And…"

I waited.

"Your mother's wedding ring."

Fucking fucking UGH!

I threw up my arm and stomped to the kitchen. I wanted

to destroy something. Break a plate. Take a baseball bat to this whole fucking disgusting house.

He followed me as I dumped the bottles in the trash. "You know, it wouldn't hurt you to have a little compassion for your sister," he said to my back. "Addiction is a disease. And a mother deserves to see her child."

I whirled on him. "I *have* compassion. That's why *I'm* doing everything in my power to get her into treatment. And if you loved her, you'd be helping. She needs boundaries, Dad. There have to be consequences. And if you don't give them to her, then you're part of the problem."

His scruffy jaw set.

I gave him my back and started to rage-wash dishes. "You know, just *once* I want to be the one to fall apart. I'm so tired of cleaning up everyone else's mess."

The garage door off the kitchen opened. Brent came in.

He lived with his boyfriend, Joel, and his family in the house across the street. He probably saw my car in the driveway and he needed something, as usual. God knows neither of us ever came to this hellhole just because.

"So, the princess has returned," he quipped.

I shot him a look. "You're on thin ice, Brent. Do not test me. And you have a lot of nerve blocking me from a phone *I* pay for, by the way."

He scowled around the kitchen and balled a sweater-covered hand over his nose. "Ugh, this place smells *so bad*. Anyway, I wanted to talk to you—"

I scoffed. "Of course you do. What pyramid scheme do you want money for this time?"

He made an indignant huffing noise. "First of all, it is

*not* a pyramid scheme. It's an actual business and I get to be my own boss. I just need an initial investment to build my inventory."

"Great. Another MLM. Even *better*." I slammed a plate into the drying rack. "I'm not giving you a dime, Brent. You have a business degree. Get. A. JOB. A *real* one."

"I am not cut out for the traditional workforce, Vanessa, you know this! I hate everyone, food service is gross, and I'm not built for manual labor," he whined.

Dad stood somewhere behind me. "Your brother is a budding entrepreneur, and all he's asking for is a little start-up money."

"Oh yeah? Then *you* give it to him."

"This family takes care of each other," Dad said, going on unfazed. "It's what we *do*. I took care of you and your sister when your mother died. Annabel and you took care of Melanie, and now you're taking care of us. It's the Price way. If we don't have each other, what else do we have?"

"You took care of us?" I laughed indignantly. "Is that what you call it?"

"Look at you. You turned out great!" he bellowed from behind me.

I slammed another plate angrily into the drying rack. "How dare you call your 'fend for yourself' parenting anything other than what it was. No money, our clothes smelling like mildew so we got bullied at school, nothing but expired food in the pantry. You bringing home some moldy sofa you found on the curb so we got bedbugs in the house and we got to spend Easter at Joel's parents' while you fumigated—"

Brent looked at his nails. "That sofa *was* pretty gross . . ."

"That was almost fifteen years ago," Dad said. "How long are you two going to bring up that sofa—which was a gorgeous Victorian that just needed a little reupholstering, if you want to know. And expiration dates are myths. They just want you buying food you don't need."

"Who's 'they'? Big Grocery?" Brent said sarcastically.

I snorted.

"I taught you resourcefulness," Dad continued. "It's an indispensable life skill, and you're welcome for that, by the way. You owe everything you have to the way I raised you and you have me driving around in a used *Kia*. It's an insult. And frankly it makes you look bad. The father of a famous Internet personality should be in something distinguished. Maybe a Lexus. Or that new C-Class..."

I scoffed. "The car is *done*. You can Uber where you need to go from now on. And you clean this house and change the locks, or I'm done paying the bills. You can figure it out on your own."

And then my chin started to quiver because how the hell was this family going to go on when I was gone?

I was the duct tape. The only thing that held this shitty piece-of-crap unit together.

If I went, Dad would have to step up and take care of Grace, and I had only the barest faith that he would come through for that baby. I wouldn't even bring her over here to visit, let alone live. He was such a mess he'd probably die under a garbage avalanche in the den, and they wouldn't find his body until the neighbors complained about the smell. Annabel would end up overdosing trying to chase her high, and she'd never come back for Grace at all, and Brent would spend his inheritance on some get-rich-quick scheme and be broke and starving before my body was cold.

I figured I had about a year. One more year if my hand meant what I thought it meant. And then I'd be gone and buried, and this shit show would continue without me with no one to curb it and they would all suffer horribly until the day they died.

A sob burst from my mouth and I turned and slid down the dishwasher until I was sitting on the filthy floor, crying into my hands. And the worst part of all was I couldn't feel the tips of my fingers as I was doing it.

I could hear Dad coming to console me because the linoleum was so sticky his shoes were making Scotch tape noises as he stepped, and it just made me cry harder.

It was like the whole Price family was headed for extinction. Faulty genes, predisposed conditions, and Murphy's fucking Law.

And poor Grace. An addict mother, a narcissistic granddad, a deluded uncle, and a dying guardian.

I wailed, completely losing it, and Dad put an arm around me. "Why are you crying, pumpkin? Life is good! Annabel will be fine, and Grace has you to take care of her."

I wailed louder.

I couldn't tell him about my hand. I couldn't tell any of them. Dad would completely unravel—if only to make it about himself. Brent would go full drama mode and who knows what it would do to my sister.

God. Somebody should just adopt Grace. Closed adoption and run away with her. A nice couple who would spoil her silly, put her in fun sleepaway camps, and buy her a pony, and she'd grow up never knowing the dumpster fire of a family that she sprang from because none of this was *ever* going to change.

Brent stage-whispered over from where he still stood by the garage door. "Okay, so, like, you know I want to comfort you, right? But I am *not* sitting on that floor."

I did a laugh-cry.

I wiped my eyes on the sleeve of my shirt, drawing in a shuddering breath, willing myself to calm down. As usual *I* couldn't afford the luxury of a proper breakdown.

I would probably benefit from some therapy. Maybe another online support group at the very least. But what was the point in trying to fix myself when I probably wouldn't even exist in twelve months?

"So where do you think she is?" I muttered, putting my palms to my eyelids.

"She texted me this morning," Brent said like it annoyed him. "She's fine."

"You know Annabel," Dad said dismissively. "She always lands on her feet."

Brent scoffed. "She's more like a cockroach than a cat," he mumbled.

I felt Dad turn to look at him. "That is your *sister*, young man."

"What? I'm not being mean! I'm just saying she's indestructible. A nuclear bomb could go off and there'd be Annabel, scurrying around in the ruins unscathed, still wearing the Burberry scarf she stole from me, while insisting that she hasn't seen it." He crossed his arms. "I *miss* that scarf," he added.

I let out a long, tired sigh. "I reported the car stolen. Lucky for me, I happened to be hanging out with a criminal defense attorney when the cops showed up." I wiped at my eyes with my palm. "You know, this stuff is public record, Dad. It can hurt my image. You have to be more careful."

"Is that the hot guy from the hallway?" Brent asked.

I nodded wearily.

"Good-looking guy," Dad said. "Good job too. Lawyers make money," he added. "It would be nice to have a lawyer in the family."

I snorted quietly. *How convenient.*

Dad and I didn't have the kind of relationship where his opinion of the men I dated mattered one ounce to me. Not that I was dating Adrian or ever would. That man wanted nothing to do with my hot mess. And that just made me want to cry too.

I liked him. He was sooo my type. If things were different, if he was even remotely interested and I wasn't staring down my expiration date, I'd jump on that body like a trampoline.

The very idea of what Adrian probably thought of all this made me cringe. It was like every single day something humiliating had to happen to me in front of him, just because the universe needed a good chuckle. I did another choking laugh-cry and put my forehead to my knees.

I had to get this family independent. I *had* to. I couldn't enable any more of this irresponsibility. Soon I wouldn't be here to help them clean it up. But I didn't know what to do. I couldn't help Annabel unless she wanted to help herself. Brent was dead set on chasing rainbows. And Dad...

I'd hoped the city's intervention would have been a wake-up call. He was fined and placed on six months' probation for the cluttered state of the yard. I know he was humiliated by it. But he wouldn't stop collecting things. It had moved on from some sort of deep frugality to something else. He was saving trash. Some of the stuff he hung on to was literally garbage. And he was bringing it in faster than I could take it out.

I sniffed and put my forehead into my hand. "Go take a shower. We're going to a Nar-Anon meeting. Brent, you too."

They didn't argue. Probably because they knew if they wanted me to keep paying for things they'd have to at least appear to be cooperating.

I followed Dad to the living room and gave him two Aleve from my purse. We'd have to get another prescription—and a safe to put it in. He'd need a new phone too.

When the water in the shower started, I did a quick clean of the house. Made Brent run the vacuum while I mopped. Threw a load of laundry into the washer. It wasn't even one-hundredth of what needed to be done, but it was a start.

A half hour later, Dad got out of the shower and came down the hallway dressed and clean as I was turning on the dishwasher.

"Can we go to Perkins for lunch?" he asked, pushing up the sleeves of his sweater.

I sighed. Dad was a good-looking man. He wore a white button-down shirt under his V-neck vest and he'd shaved. He had his glasses on. He looked like the kind of guy who lounged in a leather chair by a fire, thumbing through a novel. He looked like an educated, sophisticated gentleman who was ridiculously smart and too charming for his own good—which in reality, he *was*.

Sometimes I thought Dad's intelligence was why he was the way he was. He was too smart to be blissfully ignorant, hyperaware of everything around him, absorbing the world like a sponge. He could have been anything. A doctor. A scientist. An accountant, like he used to be.

Instead he was *this*.

I couldn't think of anywhere I'd rather eat at less than Perkins.

And I took him there anyway.

⁓

I was gone for almost five hours. It was 2:00 when I got back. I'd checked in on Grace half a dozen times while I was out. Adrian kept assuring me he was fine and not to rush. When I finally got back to his apartment, I knocked on the door, and Adrian called from inside for me to come in.

He was at the sink in the kitchen, running the water. He had his briefcase open on the kitchen table and some paperwork strewn about like he was trying to get some work done. I felt even worse now for stealing half his day off with my bullshit. He probably had things to do.

"Hey," I said, closing the door behind me. "How was she?" I glanced at Grace's swing, but it was empty.

"Good, until about twenty minutes ago," he said, looking down at whatever he was washing. "She had a pretty bad diaper."

I came around the kitchen counter and saw that he had Grace in the sink.

He was giving her a bath.

My heart *melted*.

He had a rolled-up towel in the sink to support her and a wet washcloth was balled up on the counter. He was rinsing her with a cup. He'd taken the travel-size baby shampoo from the diaper bag, and it was half empty.

He wiped his forehead with the back of his hand. "It went right up her back. It was even in her hair. I didn't know they could do that. I almost threw the whole baby away and started over."

A laugh burst from my mouth, and I covered it with my hand. "I'm sorry, it's not funny. I shouldn't be laughing."

He smiled over the sink. "It's okay. You *did* promise me adventure and excitement today." He nodded at a trash bag on the floor. "Her dirty pajamas are in there. I was going to wash them."

I moved next to him and rolled my sleeves up. "Let me help you. She can be really slippery when she's wet." My arm pressed into his as I leaned over the sink with him.

He smelled good. *Really* good.

I thought about how he'd stood so close to me earlier in front of Officer Sanchez and my heart fluttered a little.

It had been way too long since I'd had sex. I didn't date, but I didn't object to the occasional one-night stand now and then. But as I got more famous, that got harder for me to do. I'd meet men and they'd know who I was and then it just made things weird. I was afraid they'd tell some torrid sex story about me online or take pictures of me while I was sleeping and sell them. Nothing sucks the romance out of a situation like an NDA.

My fame was isolating. It was almost as isolating as my own reasons for being alone.

And then it occurred to me that maybe the last time I'd had sex was the last time I'd have sex.

I let out a puff of air as this realization washed over me. If I was really sick, a lot of the things I was doing, I might be doing for the last time. Maybe I'd just had my last Thanksgiving. This would be my last Christmas. Then my last New Year's. This might even be the last time I stood shoulder to shoulder with an attractive man.

I forced myself to stop thinking about it. To do what I always did—find gratitude in what I'd gotten instead of dwelling on what I'd lost.

Adrian had distracted me and helped me when I needed it. He'd given me that one video, content for my channel so I could keep earning money for ALS research. And now I had the chance to know him, something I never imagined I'd ever get to do. A few days ago we'd been strangers. All things I could be thankful for.

But I felt myself sinking deeper anyway.

Maybe it was everything hitting me at once and I just couldn't rebound from it like I usually did. My hand acting up and what it probably meant. Dad, Brent, Annabel. Exhaustion, Mom's ring.

There was something terrifying in thinking that I might be losing my resiliency. That I might finally be hitting my limit on how much tragedy and despair I could handle.

Rebounding quickly was my coping mechanism. I recovered in record time from devastation. I was a glass-half-full optimist. An inherently positive person. It was my thing. I lived life to the fullest, lived every day like it was my last.

But today? Today took something from me. And the weird

thing was I think it had more to do with Adrian than anything else.

I was used to Annabel's instability and Dad's and Brent's
bullshit. I was even used to the idea that I'd be dead by thirty.
But I wasn't used to *this*.

Him.

Adrian was one of those milestones I'd never reach. Maybe
not him exactly. He was uninterested and unavailable. But
the *idea* of him. A man I could fall in love with.

I'd never have a husband. I'd never have a family of my
own. Hell, I'd never even have a boyfriend again.

ALS took this from me, like it had taken so many
other things. It was more than just a thief of life. It stole
hope. Dignity. Dreams. And it would take until there was
nothing left.

Not even me.

My breath came out shaky. "For someone who's never
washed a baby before, you did it right," I said, trying to push
down the dark feeling I got being so close to him.

"I had to call my mom. I didn't even know where to begin."

I laughed again, but it didn't reach my eyes.

He poured a final cup of water over Grace's shoulders, and
I lifted her out with the towel.

He pulled the plug out of the drain as I snuggled my wet
baby, kissing her cheek. A surge of protectiveness washed over
me. Because for all intents and purposes, right now she really
was *my* baby.

Kids had never been in my plan. I'd had my tubes tied a
few years ago. Since they didn't know what gene caused ALS
in my family, I couldn't do selective IVF to rule it out. And

while *I* was very glad I'd been born, even with my risks, and many people in my situation chose to have children anyway, I refused to play gene Russian roulette with my own kids on principle.

I wouldn't give ALS one more victim. It had taken enough from the Price family. I didn't need to lay another possible sacrifice at its feet.

There were other options. An egg donor or adoption. But I'd never considered those because I couldn't be sure I'd be there to raise a child. And that was the same situation I was facing now. I couldn't raise Grace either.

Even if I wanted to.

I wanted to believe that everything would be okay. That Annabel would get clean, like she got clean once before. That she'd come back for her daughter. But I didn't have time for faith. Not anymore. I couldn't afford to bet on this and lose.

I needed a long-term plan for this little girl, and I needed to execute it now, while I still could.

"Do you know of a good lawyer who specializes in adoptions?" I asked.

Adrian leaned on the kitchen counter, drying his hands on a towel. "I know someone. Are you thinking of adopting her?"

I couldn't tell him the truth. He didn't need to know it. *I* didn't even want to know it, that I was going to have to give her up, find her a different family. The pain in my heart bubbled up and I swallowed it. "I just think she needs stability, you know?"

"Will your sister sign over her rights?"

I shook my head. "I don't know."

Adrian dropped the towel on the counter. "If she won't sign over her rights, you could always throw money at it. Offer her an incentive. That usually works." He crossed his arms. "Did you get everything straightened out with your family?"

I let out a long breath. "Sort of. Annabel crashed the car. Stole it, so good news, you didn't perjure yourself to the police. She stole my dad's phone and money and my mom's wedding rin—" I choked on the last word. I couldn't help it. I didn't see it coming and I couldn't hold it back. I bit my lip and turned for the living room. "I'm sorry," I managed. "It's still setting in."

I had a rule. I didn't dwell on things. It wasn't allowed, no matter what it was. Life was too short. But this one hurt.

Mom's ring was one of the few family heirlooms I cared about. I had so little of my mother left.

And now that was gone too.

"Did you file a police report?" he asked from behind me.

I nodded, laying Grace down on the sofa to put a diaper on her. I swallowed hard before speaking. I didn't want to cry in front of him. "I did, but the diamond is small. The whole thing comes to less than a thousand dollars. They won't look very hard. It's got a *kismet* inscription, so I guess it's not totally impossible, but they'll probably never find it." I sniffed. "It is what it is. It's fine. It was just sentimental is all."

He came up behind me and handed me the little outfit he had picked for Grace. I took it without looking at him.

"Did you lose your mom?"

I nodded. "Yes. When I was six. Car accident." I slipped the pajamas over Grace's head.

"Your sister's nine years younger than you. A half sister?"

"With my dad's second wife. That's Brent's mom too."

"And where is she?"

I finished buttoning the outfit and picked up Grace. "As far away from *us* as humanly possible. And I don't even blame her," I mumbled. I turned to him and wiped at my eyes. "I'm sorry I took so much of your day. Thanks for watching her. I'll be out of your hair in a minute."

"Do you want to join me for dinner?"

The question took me so by surprise I had to stop and stare at him. He was sitting on a chair. He had his elbows on his knees, hands clasped, gazing at me.

"You want to have dinner with me?" I asked, blinking at him.

"Yes."

"You're not sick of my shit yet? Or her shit?" I nodded at Grace.

He chuckled. "No, I am not."

He wasn't hitting on me. This was totally platonic. But I liked him and letting myself spend more time with someone I could develop feelings for wasn't in my best interest—or his. He had no idea what he was getting himself into. My life was like a warehouse with one of those THIS MANY DAYS SINCE THE LAST ACCIDENT signs, and the number was always at zero.

I licked my lips. "Getting close to somebody right now isn't a good idea for me."

"Why?" he asked.

I let out a sigh. "Adrian, my life is a mess. It's a *mess*. You have no idea. My whole world is like a muddy hill of shit, and if you get too close, you'll be sliding down it with me."

"Because you have family problems? There's no such thing as a perfect family. There are just families that do better PR than yours."

The corner of my lip twitched.

"I like hanging out with you," he said. "And I need to watch more of *The Office*. I'm still not hitting on you, if that's what you're worried about."

Well, at least there was that. *God.*

My fucking life. Imagine the hot, smart, incredible guy *not* hitting on you being the preferred scenario.

"I'll make lamb shanks," he said.

I wrinkled my forehead. "I thought you said you don't cook."

"I may have misstated that a bit. I don't like to cook just for myself. It's not worth it. But I do very much enjoy cooking for someone else. Especially someone who will appreciate it."

I bit my lip. "I don't know. I have to do laundry, and if I eat with you, I won't get to it until tonight. The laundry room is crowded after eight."

He shrugged. "Do it here. I have a washer and dryer."

I arched an eyebrow. "You do? Really?"

"My apartment's a lot bigger than yours, remember? Do as many loads as you want."

"Are you sure?"

"I'm sure."

I smiled. "You're making this very hard to say no."

"That's what she said."

I snorted. "Ha! *Office* humor. I've already changed you for the better. All right. Let me go take a shower. I just cleaned a house that should have been condemned," I said, looking down at my clothes.

He stood and reached for Grace. "I'll take her."

I tilted my head. "Really?"

He smiled at Grace in a way that made my heart hurt. "Yeah, I don't mind. I'll leave the door unlocked. Let yourself back in when you're ready."

~

I got ready. I got more ready than he'd ever seen me. Not because this was a date, obviously, but because having somewhere to go and getting dressed up was a luxury I hadn't been afforded in weeks. I was usually just different versions of rolling out of bed these days. Plus, my personal presentation had to be equal to the dish. The man was making lamb shanks.

I put on a slouchy pink sweater and jeans, curled my hair, and did my makeup. When I let myself into his apartment an hour later, classical music was playing. Harry Puppins was curled up in his diaper, sleeping on his dog bed by the sofa. Grace was sitting in her swing at the mouth of the kitchen, where Adrian could see her.

Adrian had a fire going and he stood in the kitchen with a spatula over a copper frying pan, a black kitchen towel draped over his shoulder. He was wearing jeans, a white apron, and a burgundy sweater with the sleeves rolled up. The whole thing looked like a page in a damn Williams-Sonoma catalog.

There had to be an imbalance in the universe. Some poor guy probably got shorted so Adrian Copeland could get his disproportionate share of good looks.

"Hey," I said, bringing in a basket of laundry and a bottle of wine.

All my fan mail was by the door, carefully organized and in banker's boxes.

"I had Becky take the donations to the Salvation Army for you," Adrian said over his shoulder. "I hope you're hungry."

"Starving."

The place smelled *amazing*.

He nodded to the hallway. "The laundry room's the second door on the left."

"Thanks," I said. "Can I help you with anything first?"

He looked up at me for the first time since I'd walked in and paused a second. "No. I've got it." His eyes lingered another moment and then he went back to his cooking.

I smiled to myself. *He just checked me out.*

It was nice to know maybe the attraction wasn't one-sided. Not for any practical purposes, of course. Nothing was going to happen between us. But it did wonders for my self-esteem.

I stopped and checked on Grace. She was watching Adrian cook with her pacifier in her mouth, eyes wide. I tucked her blanket around her, then took my basket and wandered down the hall.

The apartment was a three-bedroom. The master was to the right of the living room where it shared my wall. That door was closed.

Then there was the kitchen, a nice open dining room in the middle with a table that seated six, and the hallway I was wandering down to the left. I peeked into rooms as I went.

One spare room was a lawyerly-looking office with a floor-to-ceiling cherrywood bookshelf behind the desk. He'd turned the other room into an impressive home gym. There was a full bathroom between them, and then finally a decent-size laundry room.

The whole apartment was immaculate. Nothing was out of place. He was meticulous. Even the laundry room was organized and spotless. All his detergents and fabric softener were lined up in a perfect row on top of the washer.

The walls in the apartment were cool grays with white trim. He had dark hardwood floors, except for in the bathroom. That was some sort of slate-type stone. It was all very cold and masculine.

He needed plants and candles.

I started a load and came back into the kitchen. "God, your apartment is palatial."

I peeked over his arm to look at what he was cooking. He was braising potatoes with some rosemary in a pan. It smelled so good my stomach growled.

"Why not get a bigger unit?" he asked. "Seems like you could afford it. You're obviously very successful."

I put my back to the counter next to the stove and leaned. "I donate most of my money. That's why I live small. I keep only what I need—plus a little so I can have fun. And wine," I added.

He poured a splash of merlot over his pan with a sizzle. "Right, I read that on your Wikipedia. You donate to ALS research."

So he'd been looking into me.

Which meant he *knew*.

He could watch any one of my videos and get the general gist of what I was about. I talked openly about all of it:

my 50 percent chance of having the mutated genes that cause ALS. My inability to test for them. My desire not to seek treatment if I was sick. It was all in there. Maybe not dumped into a single episode, but sprinkled pretty generously around. Not to mention all the articles about me and my Wikipedia page. If he did even the barest of lawyerly due diligence, which it sounds like he had, he'd get a crystal-clear picture of what my life was.

And now I could see where this conversation was going, and I needed it to stop. I didn't want to get into a casual discussion about my possible terminal diagnosis. I wanted to enjoy this dinner.

I wanted to forget the death creeping into my hand.

I tucked my hair behind my ear. "Can I ask you a favor?"

He gazed over at me. Warm, green gorgeous eyes.

"I don't want to talk about...anything that you learned on my channel. *Ever*. It's just...being around you feels like a break. Like, you're not my crazy family, and you're not part of the YouTuber world or ALS side of my life either, and I like that."

He held my eyes a moment. "Sure," he said. "This has been a bit of an escape from reality for me too. I get it." He did an impressive flip of his potatoes. "So what wine did you bring?" he asked.

I smiled and got the bottle and held it out for him to see.

"Nice," he said, grinning at the label. "Were you saving it? That's a great year."

"I never save anything," I said, grabbing the bottle opener on the counter. "I enjoy things as soon as possible. I burn the expensive candle, I use the fancy rose-shaped soap, and I drink the wine, even if the only thing I'm celebrating is the fact that it's Tuesday."

He turned down his burner. "Well, I'm glad for my sake that you do that. I'll definitely appreciate it. Here, let me." He took the bottle opener from me, which I was fumbling, and opened the wine. Then he took two glasses from a cabinet, poured, and handed me one.

"Thanks." I swirled the liquid and put my nose into the glass and breathed in. "If you like wine so much, you should visit Tuscany. Have you ever been?" I looked around his apartment for frames. "Where are your vacation photos? Are they on your laptop or something?" I put a thumb over my shoulder. "Because if you have a backup photo album, I'm gonna need to see it to look for dick pics."

He snorted. "I don't have a backup album. I don't take vacations."

I blinked at him. "*Ever?*"

"I drove out to L.A. for a week a few years ago, but I was there for a work conference."

"So that's all you do? Work?"

"Pretty much."

I stared at him a moment. "*Why?*"

He shrugged, leaning against the counter. "It's not easy for me to take time off. The firm needs me. I'm a partner. And I don't mind the work. The money's good."

"Do you need it?" I asked.

"What?"

"The money. Do you need it. Like, is there some goal you're working toward? Pay off your student loans, get out of debt? Saving up for something big?"

He shook his head. "No. I don't have any loans. Mom paid for my college. And the income from this building is decent. I just work to work, I guess."

There was something a little tight about the way he said it.

"What?" I asked.

He looked away from me. "I don't know…"

"What? Tell me."

His eyes came back to mine. "I like what I do. It's fulfilling. And rewarding. It's just not…" He shook his head and pressed his lips into a line. "I just can't shake the feeling that something is missing. Maybe because I just broke up with someone." He rubbed his forehead. "It's probably that."

I tipped my wineglass at him. "You suffer from One Day Syndrome."

He wrinkled his brows. "What?"

"One Day Syndrome. You live your life like there'll always be one day to do all the things you put off. One day you'll take the trip. One day you'll have the family. One day you'll try the thing. You're all work and not enough play. Money can't make you happy unless you know what you want, Adrian. So what do you want?"

He shook his head at me like he'd never considered the question before. "I don't know."

"You should try to figure it out. You know, you're really lucky. Most people don't have the means to live differently, or to make drastic changes in their lifestyle, pack up and take six months off work and still be able to pay their bills. But you do." I shrugged. "So do it."

He looked amused. "Just do it? Just pack up and go."

"Or stay. But make time for other things that aren't work. Find balance. Find *joy*. You are the kind of man who can't see the shapes in the clouds. And it's not because you lack imagination. It's because you're too busy to look up."

He blinked at me a moment. Something I couldn't read moved across his face. Then he cleared his throat and pushed off the counter. "Well, Italy might be a stretch," he said, reaching for the potatoes. "I don't fly, remember?"

Grace started to fuss and I unclipped her from the swing and picked her up. "You're really serious about that no-flying thing, huh?" I said, bouncing her.

He slid the contents of his frying pan into a waiting dish. "I get panic attacks."

I frowned. "Well *that* sucks. Have you tried Xanax?"

He put the pan in the sink and ran water over it with a sizzle. "I've tried everything."

"Therapy?"

He shook his head. "I get enough psychoanalysis from my mom. She thinks it's because I'm not in control of the situation. I'd probably be fine if I was the one flying the plane." He took the towel from his shoulder and dried his hands. "She says I have abandonment issues." He looked amused. "My dad left us when I was young. She says this grew into a deep-seated need to always be in control."

"Huh. Is your mom a psychologist?"

He chuckled. "No. Though she's probably been to enough of them to know."

"So how do your abandonment issues mess with your relationships?" I asked, putting Grace's pacifier in her mouth.

He opened the oven and peeked in. "What do you mean?"

"Your childhood damage *always* messes with your relationships. I think it's a rule."

I knew this rule because I was completely bound by it. And in my case, it meant I didn't *have* relationships.

I was taught early on that love was always needy. It was a responsibility. An obligation. Love bleeds you dry and takes advantage of you. Asks you for money, crashes your car, drops a baby on your doorstep.

It leaves you.

It dies.

I didn't want to do that to anyone else. I didn't want anyone to fall in love with me only for them to watch me waste away and then leave them behind. And anyway, I wasn't worth all that. Not at this point. The payout was too small. I probably had too little time left.

He lowered the temperature on the oven. "Other than making it hard to get to Seattle to see her, I don't think my issues had any bearing on Rachel."

"So did you have any serious relationships before her?" I asked.

Adrian folded his kitchen towel into a perfect square and set it on the counter. "A few. I dated someone in college for a couple of years. Dated people on and off. My job makes it hard to make time. She was the first girlfriend I had in... three years?"

I pulled my face back. "Wow. She must have been pretty special."

He blew a breath out, but he didn't answer.

I felt my face go soft. "Are you okay? Finding out someone's married is a really shitty way to break up."

He nodded. "I'm okay. Or I will be. Eventually. Having someone to hang out with helps."

I smiled and kissed the top of Grace's head. "We should toast." I picked up my wineglass and raised it. "To just friends."

He gave me a crooked smile. "To just friends."

We clinked our glasses.

# CHAPTER 9

# MAN TRAPPED IN GRUESOME AVALANCHE! YOU WON'T BELIEVE WHAT BURIED HIM!

## ADRIAN

I woke up thinking about Vanessa.

It was incredible to me that I didn't know her before this. That I didn't realize someone so vibrant lived right next door. It seemed like the kind of thing that would have been self-evident. A warmth that I felt through the wall.

Last night she'd brought over a 2013 Far Niente cabernet. It was exquisite. We ate dinner and started watching *The Office*, but we ended up talking so much we paused it and never got back to it.

I'd done some digging around on her while she was dealing with her dad and his "stolen vehicle." I searched "Vanessa Price" and clicked on the video with the most views. It was with some other YouTuber named Willow Shea and the video was the two of them eating ghost peppers. It was hilarious.

Then I'd checked her Wikipedia. It was brief. She was a staunch advocate for disability rights and had a charity committed to raising funds for the cure of ALS—and she was famous, a fact I'd gleaned from the amount of fan mail she had and the five million views on the ghost pepper video I'd watched.

I was hoping I'd see what her old job used to be, but the Wikipedia page was sparse.

She'd said she didn't date because the women in her family die young.

Her mom had died in a car accident and her sister died of ALS. I'd done a quick Google search of it. It was a progressive neurodegenerative disease that affects nerve cells in the brain and the spinal cord. Causes muscle atrophy and eventually leads to death. Raising money for ALS had spawned that Ice Bucket Challenge from a few years ago. Stephen Hawking had had a slowly advancing version of it.

It was very awful and *very* rare. Ninety-five percent of all cases were random, which meant it probably wasn't hereditary for her. Her dad was alive and well and while her mother had died when Vanessa was young, it wasn't ALS that killed her. Wikipedia didn't list any other of her relatives that had had it. Shit luck that her sister developed it, but it didn't sound like anything Vanessa had to worry about.

With two untimely deaths in the same family and a sister hell-bent on self-destruction, Vanessa probably thought she was living out some real-life *Final Destination* movie.

Of course, that was ridiculous and something I think she'd eventually get over. Something I *hoped* she'd get over. She was too incredible to be lonely forever.

And she'd been right. I'd underestimated the restorative nature of a new sink sponge.

I was standing in the kitchen making a cappuccino. It was barely 8:15. I had no plans today and was thinking of hitting the treadmill when my phone rang.

The house phone at Richard's.

My good mood immediately evaporated.

When I'd called Mom yesterday to ask her how to clean up Grace after her diaper fiasco, she'd thought I was calling to tell her I was coming for Christmas. She was surprised that I was watching someone's baby. She was less surprised that I was still sticking to my guns and refusing to be anywhere in Richard's presence.

I picked up, thinking it was going to be another guilt-trip phone call from her.

It was worse. It was Grandma.

"Adrian?" she said, in her small, frail voice. "What time are you taking me to lunch today?"

I drew my brows down. "Grandma, I'm not coming to see you today."

"But it's Tuesday! You always take me to Perkins on Tuesday."

It wasn't Tuesday. It was Sunday. And I never took her to lunch. Dinner was our tradition.

She was confused again.

I rubbed my forehead tiredly. "Grandma, you're in Nebraska now, remember?"

She went quiet and I knew she was doing that thing she did when her mind got turned around, drawing down her thin eyebrows and searching the floor with her eyes.

It was more difficult to connect with her on the phone.

She was less disoriented in person. I hadn't really talked to her since the move. Every time I'd call, she'd lose her train of thought or forget who she was talking to and set the receiver down and wander off.

It made me that much angrier that Mom had moved her away from everything familiar, and my hatred for Richard went up a notch.

I heard someone in the background. "Who are you talking to?" Shuffling, and then Mom got on the phone. "Who is this?"

"Mom, it's me," I said wearily.

"Adrian? I didn't hear the phone ring."

"She called me."

Now she went quiet on me too.

"She's been asking about you," she said after a moment.

I squeezed my temples.

"She doesn't understand why you're not here," she said. "And I can't explain it to her."

"Well, maybe you shouldn't have moved her out of state," I said, my tone more clipped than I'd intended.

"I have a life, Adrian. Even if you don't want to be a part of it."

Any truce we'd committed to on the phone yesterday when I called to ask how to wash Grace was officially over.

"I'm handing the phone back to Audrey so you can say goodbye," she said curtly, obviously done with me.

There was more shuffling and then Grandma was back on the call. "Adrian?"

"Grandma, I love you. I have to go, okay?" My voice was getting thick.

"Okay. You stay out of trouble. I'll see you soon. Bye bye."

I hung up and squeezed my eyes shut, blowing out a long breath.

I was clearly in the throes of a custody battle and the only way I was getting visitation was if I agreed to make peace with Richard and go down there—which I would never do.

I felt instantly exhausted and like I was being punished for having principles.

I went back to making my coffee. The phone rang again and I looked down at it, half expecting it to be Grandma. This time it was Vanessa. I smiled at the screen and swiped the Answer Call button. "Hey—"

"Adrian, I need help. It's an emergency."

I set my coffee cup down and immediately started for the door. "What's going on?"

"I need you to come with me to my dad's."

I paused with my hand on the doorknob. "Your dad's?"

"Like, it's not a call-the-police thing, but it's definitely urgent, and I need someone strong to help me. My hand is too weak, no one's home at Brent's house, and I don't know anyone else."

"Okay. Let me get dressed," I said, making a beeline for my room.

"Don't wear anything you'll be sad to douse in gasoline and set on fire later."

Vanessa left Grace with Yoga Lady—whose real name was Dawn. I drove.

"What happened?" I asked, getting onto the freeway.

She was wringing her hands. "Some stuff fell over and he's trapped."

I jerked to look at her. "Trapped? As in *under* it?"

She nodded. "Yeah, but it's just his legs. He was able to call me. He's not in any immediate danger. I don't think he's hurt or anything. He just can't get out by himself."

I shook my head. "And you didn't want to call 911? They would have gotten there faster."

"I can't call the police to that house. They'll red tag it."

I drew my eyebrows down. "Red tag it? What's wrong with it?"

She let out a long breath. "Remember I told you about the muddy hill of shit yesterday? And you were all cavalier and wanted to be my friend anyway?"

I changed lanes. "Yes…"

"Well, this is the slide."

Fifteen minutes later we pulled up to a two-story house in Eagan. Vanessa jumped out and ran up the walkway and went inside without waiting for me. When I came up behind her, I stopped dead in the doorway.

The smell hit me like a wall.

I came slowly into the entry breathing into my elbow. I'd never seen anything like it. Not in real life.

Floor-to-ceiling stacks as far as the eye could see. Shit literally everywhere. Every standing surface had a pile on it.

The love seat in the living room was completely covered with some sort of magazine/newspaper collection piled so high it blocked the light from the window. There was a broken blender on the credenza filled with bottle caps next to a rotting gourd with fruit flies buzzing around it. Bins everywhere, lining the walls with God knows what in them, the rim to a tire, a box filled with broken picture frames,

one of those white wicker baskets used for flowers at wed-
dings in the 1980s with a dented pink helium tank sitting
in it—

There was a chaotic method to some of the madness. Certain things seemed to be grouped together. A stack of board
games piled on a chair, a CD collection. But all around it
was garbage and decaying food. Broken, useless trinkets and
appliances.

Vanessa called me from somewhere deeper in the house and
I picked my way over the clutter on the floor to a hallway that
was so crowded with stuff I had to turn sideways to squeeze
through it. Vanessa stood in a room at the end trying to lift a
fallen armoire off a pile of clothes.

"I got it," I said, heaving it up and leaning it against the
wall. Only after I had it moved did I realize there was a man
under it.

Vanessa was already digging her dad out from under
shirts and pants. "Dad, you okay?" she asked, pulling him
to his feet.

He brushed his sweater down, a sock still draped over his
shoulder. "Fine, fine, pumpkin. I put some laundry on an
open drawer and it must have been too top-heavy. Toppled it
onto me. Had a nice little cushion for the fall though."

Vanessa looked back at me, a tired expression on her face.
"Thanks for helping."

Her dad gave me a broad used-car-salesman smile. "We
haven't been formally introduced," he said, extending a hand.
"Gerald Price."

I was feeling nauseous. My eyes were starting to water.
"Adrian Copeland," I managed, shaking it.

Gerald put his hands in his pockets and rocked jovially back on his heels. "So, Vanessa tells me you're a lawyer."

He smiled up at me like nothing was wrong. Like I hadn't just lifted a dresser off him and we were running into each other in a Panera or something.

I couldn't make small talk with him here, standing in this garbage pile. I was having a hard time breathing. Not just because of the smell, but because the room was so crowded with junk it was giving me anxiety. The floor under my feet was uneven. I was standing on blankets and balled-up socks and my head was too close to the ceiling. I felt claustrophobic.

"I'm sorry, excuse me. I need to step out."

I left them standing there. I didn't stop moving until I was outside again on the porch, gulping fresh air.

How the *fuck* had Vanessa grown up in this? I wouldn't say my own childhood was without trauma, but this made me feel like calling my mom and thanking her.

Three minutes later I was still on the front porch when Vanessa came out and plopped down next to me on the weathered bench I'd retreated to by the screen door.

I shook my head. "Wow."

She scoffed. "I prefer a four-letter word, but sure."

I looked over at her. "I'm sorry, I didn't mean to be rude back there. I just needed to get some air."

She sighed. "It's overwhelming, I know. Especially when you're not used to it."

"You're used to this?"

"I'm used to a lot of shit." She laughed a little mirthlessly. "I found a raccoon living in one of the closets one time. Once you realize you're one open window and a hoarded bathroom away from living with trash pandas, the whole second half of your life begins."

I laughed, even though it wasn't funny.

She nudged my arm. "So, you still believe that whole 'other families just do better PR' thing?"

I snorted and shook my head at the yard. "Has he always been this way?"

She took a deep breath and blew it out in the cold air. "Pretty much. But this is honestly the worst it's ever been," she admitted. "It gets worse every time something big happens. Mom, Melanie. Annabel. I think it's his way of dealing with it."

She dug into the neck of her shirt and pulled out a yellow tube of Carmex.

I squinted at her. "Did you just pull that out of your bra?" I asked, watching her put it on.

"Yeah. Leggings don't have pockets. Plus it gets cold and won't squeeze from the tube unless I keep it somewhere warm. I call it my boob stick." She smacked her lips. "Want some?" She held it out.

"No. I don't like the way that stuff tastes."

"Yeah, it's kinda gross. But it makes your lips super soft." She pressed her lips together again and put the tube back in her bra.

I dropped my eyes to her mouth for a flicker of a second. Her lips *did* look soft...

I looked away from her.

A car pulled into the driveway of the house across the street.

"Oh, so *now* he's home," she mumbled.

"Who?"

She rubbed her hands on her arms. "Brent. He lives there with his boyfriend, Joel."

"How old's your brother?"

"Twenty-one. Joel is too. They're high school sweethearts. He's been living over there since he was fifteen."

I arched an eyebrow. "Your dad let him?"

She shrugged. "He was over there all the time anyway. It was just across the street. And Dad still made him come home for dinner every night and holidays. It was sort of a win-win. Brent got out of this house, and Dad got to put shit in his room." She laughed dryly. "Joel's family is nice. Brent's in a good place over there. He's got the most potential of all of us to end up somewhat unscathed by this fucked-up family," she muttered.

We watched Brent get out of the passenger side. He stopped and looked at us for a second before waving. Then he went around to the trunk and grabbed some grocery bags and went into the house with another young man.

"So what does he do for a living?" I asked.

She scoffed. "Lose money? He was a student. He went to college for business, but he graduated last spring. Absolutely refuses to get a job. He's always got some disastrous side hustle he's super into."

"Like what?"

"Oh God, herbal supplements, skin-care products—you name it. To be fair, I *did* like the leggings though." She blew into her hands. "Right now he's trying to get me to invest in some business he wants to start. Not interested."

"Why doesn't he just go to a bank? Get a loan?"

She pressed her lips into a line. "Can't. His credit is

fucked. All our credit is fucked. When Melanie got sick, we almost lost everything. The medical bills were astronomical, and insurance didn't cover even half of it. Dad had to file for bankruptcy. We were living on credit cards at the end."

She stood up. "You want to wait for me in the car? It's trash day the day after tomorrow. I figure since I pay for the service, I might as well fill the bin. I realize it's an effort in futility at this point, but at least it's something."

I pushed up on my knees. "I'll help you."

She paused by the door. "You sure? There's probably at least one of the hepatitises in there."

"If you're getting one of the heps, I'll get it too," I mumbled.

She laughed and it made her eyes twinkle and I felt instantly glad I offered.

I didn't want to go back in there—but neither did she. And I wanted to help her. Even if the thing we were doing was pointless, making her feel less alone in it wasn't.

Gerald was standing in the kitchen when we came back inside, blowing on a mug of soup. "He returns," he muttered.

Vanessa gave him a look as she pulled some trash bags from under the sink. She shoved one into his chest. "*Help.*"

He eyed her. "Help with what? What, pray tell, do you think you're throwing away, Daughter?"

"Trash," she said. "And you are too."

"There is no trash here. Everything in this house has a purpose."

She picked up a broken vase. "Oh yeah? And what's the purpose of this?" She jiggled it.

"As soon as I find the missing shards, I'm gluing it back together," he said, completely straight-faced.

She let out a slow, patient breath and set the vase on the counter with a clink. "Dad? This house is seriously not okay. I understand this is difficult, but I need you to work with me. We've got three bags. These bags are going to get filled up and taken out. You can do this."

He frowned. Then he turned to me. "What are your intentions with my daughter?"

"Dad! Focus!" Vanessa snapped.

I put my hands up. "I'm just here to help."

He narrowed his eyes at me and Vanessa huffed. "Three bags. You do the upstairs," she said, pushing the trash bag into his chest again.

Gerald gave me one last narrow-eyed look and set his mug down. Then he snatched the bag and wandered off up the staircase, muttering to himself.

Vanessa watched him go and then turned to me, blowing air through pursed lips. "So, you wanna see something?" She smiled.

I shrugged. "Sure."

She led me back down the narrow hallway and opened a door. The room was full of bikes. *Full.* They were piled on top of one another in some sort of macabre bicycle graveyard. Mountain bikes with bent rims, fat-tire bikes with flats, rusted children's bikes with the training wheels still on them.

"This was my room," she said. "I used to sleep over there under the one with the tassels and the basket. Before the bikes," she added.

She didn't say it with any sort of regret in her tone. She was just showing me. Like she could separate what it was now versus what it used to be without it making her sad.

I think this was one of the most impressive things about her. Especially now that I saw the other side of it. She didn't let anything get her down. She took things like a blow to a punching bag. She got knocked back, but then she was up again. So resilient.

I wasn't like that. I couldn't let things go.

I crossed my arms and leaned in the doorway. "Did Child Protective Services ever get involved?"

Vanessa shook her head, leaning her back on the door frame. "I mean, they were called. But the few times they came out, he'd pull off some eleventh-hour save, get the house livable again, and we'd get to stay. It was the only time I ever really saw him bust his ass." She looked back at me. "Dad screwed up a lot of things, but he always managed to keep this family together. Family is the most important thing to him. Even if he has a weird way of showing it," she mumbled.

I looked back into the room. I was getting nose blind to the smell of the house, thank God.

There were things of hers still on the walls, half covered by the rising mound of bikes. Evidence of an abandoned life. Pussycat Dolls posters, the mirror of a vanity with photos stuck to it, a blue first-place ribbon.

I wondered what it must have been like to grow up in a place like this. It couldn't have been easy. Vanessa must have risen from the ashes like a phoenix.

"We should get started," she said. She turned back for the kitchen and I followed her. She began tossing garbage on her way. "Just so you know, he's going to fight me on every single thing. He'll go through the bags, so make sure your trash is legit."

"Legit trash. Got it." I grabbed a crumpled chip bag and a greasy Chinese takeout container. "There's some mail here," I said, nodding at the end table. "Should we make a pile? Looks like these are for your sister."

She was looking at a toaster with a frayed wire. "Yeah. Thanks." She shoved it in her bag.

The toaster was concerning. This place was a huge fire hazard. Exits were blocked, the stove had crap all around it. I bet the smoke alarms didn't work, and there was no way he'd ever find an extinguisher in this mess. This was dangerous. I didn't like the thought of Grace being here. At *all*.

"Did Annabel live here with the baby?"

Vanessa shook her head. "No, never with the baby. She had some roommates at a house in Hopkins. When she started using again, they kicked her out and she stayed here for a few weeks. I have no idea where she slept. *Her* old room is full of car parts."

I wandered the living room, leaving things so obviously garbage it made me cringe. I found more mail and added it to the pile. Then more. And more. It looked like he'd grab it from the mailbox and then set it down somewhere in the living room and forget it. "There's a lot of mail here. You said you pay the bills, right?"

"Yeah. I get all the important stuff sent to my apartment." She made a face at a plastic fish tank with a rotting tomato in it. She looked up at me over it. "I bet when you woke up this morning you couldn't imagine how many times you'd be muttering 'What the fuck?' by ten a.m."

I snorted.

She scanned the living room and sighed. "You know, I'm

not usually humiliated this frequently in front of the same person. This is a new personal best for me."

"You shouldn't be embarrassed about this. It's not your fault," I said.

"Where's the mail pile?" Vanessa asked, waving a white envelope. "I found another one."

I nodded to the end table by the sofa and she walked to it. She stood over the stack I'd already begun and picked up the top letter. The corners of her lips fell. Then she tore it open and stood there reading it, her frown deepening.

"What is it?" I asked.

She shook her head and looked from the page to the pile of letters. "Oh my God..." she breathed. "It's so much worse than I thought."

I set my trash bag down. "What?" I cleared the space between us and took the paper from her hand.

It was a bill for Annabel for an emergency room visit.

I looked at the stack and picked up half of the envelopes and flipped through them. There had to be twenty, twenty-five different bills here. Clinics, urgent cares, hospitals.

Vanessa looked at me, her face white. "She was drug seeking. Faking injuries to get prescription meds." She paused. "And she was doing it while she was pregnant."

~

Vanessa was quiet the whole way home. When we pulled into the parking garage and I turned off the engine, she sat there a moment, staring straight through the windshield.

"Look," I said. "There was only one clinic visit while she

was pregnant. And we don't know if she took the pills they prescribed her."

She shook her head. "I don't understand how a doctor could give a pregnant woman a narcotic."

"Liability. Doctors can't prove or disprove pain. If they deny her pain control, they can be sued."

She took a deep breath and then pivoted to face me in the seat. "Do you want to go to Duluth today?"

I wrinkled my forehead. "What?"

"Duluth. You know, two hours up north? We could go see the Christmas lights at Bentleyville and do the lake walk."

I sucked air through my teeth. "I don't know..."

"What?"

"Why don't we just stay here? I can make us lunch."

She smiled. "Oh, I see. You *do* want to hang out with me, but you don't do spontaneity."

"I can be spontaneous," I said defensively.

She smirked. "Oh yeah? When's the last time you did something that wasn't thoroughly planned? And stuff inside your apartment building doesn't count. That's still your safe space."

"Well, I saved a man from an avalanche today."

She laughed. It was good to see the humor return to her face.

"Doesn't count," she said, still smiling. "You're a fixer, so today's emergency was totally in your wheelhouse. I'm talking about a genuine, spur-of-the-moment, seat-of-your-pants *fun* thing."

I had nothing.

How did this woman have my card so thoroughly pulled?

When I didn't answer, she cocked her head. "That's what I

thought. You thrive on predictability." She narrowed her eyes. "I bet that's why you like the job you have."

"How do you mean?"

"You like being in control. And what better way to feel like the master of destiny than to beat all the odds with everything stacked against you? Make innocent men out of the guilty."

I mulled this over. "I never thought of it that way."

"You're not that hard to figure out, Adrian Copeland. Even your *hobbies* are planned. You run races that you train for for months, you work, work, work—you are a creature of habit. A total control freak. Your dang junk drawer is organized."

I arched an eyebrow. "You looked in my junk drawer?"

"I was looking for a spoon for my coffee. I was *not* prepared to see that. Your paper clips were all color coordinated, and you had a little caddy for your loose batteries—" She shuddered. "I can't even talk about it. It really freaked me out."

I snorted.

"I promise you, you will not implode if you do something you didn't plan on today." She grinned at me. "Come with me. It'll be an adventure. And there's this Italian restaurant on Lake Superior and I swear to God, it's the best Italian food in Minnesota."

Coming from her, this was high praise.

"I can't remember the last time I went up north," I said somewhat distantly. "Dad used to take me, but I haven't been in ages."

"You're missing out. The North Shore is ridiculously gorgeous. So. Duluth. Are we going?"

She waited for me to answer like a puppy wagging its tail.

"Okay. But *I'm* driving."

She clapped her hands excitedly. "Yay!"

I smiled. I realized that doing what she wanted gave me a little high. She was some kind of mood booster for me—even when all we were doing was picking up trash in a hoarded house.

I liked her.

And that gave me a little high too.

# CHAPTER 10

# HOW TO FIND WHAT YOU'RE MISSING USING THIS ONE WEIRD TRICK!

## ADRIAN

I walked into my office after a court visit on Monday morning feeling like my two-day weekend had been a six-month vacation from life. Despite the amount of actual shit I now dealt with on an hourly basis, I was smiling.

I'd spent the whole weekend hanging out with Vanessa. We hadn't gotten home from Duluth until almost midnight last night.

We'd bundled up the baby and walked through the Christmas lights at Bentleyville, an outdoor village completely decked out for the holiday. Got hot chocolate, had dinner at the place on Lake Superior—and Vanessa was right. It was the best Italian food in Minnesota.

I'd had a good time. A *great* time. I couldn't remember

when I'd ever enjoyed a date so much—not that it had been a date. It wasn't, of course. But I couldn't help acknowledging that I hadn't had that much fun with someone in ages.

Vanessa made me laugh. She made me *forget.* About everything other than what we were doing in that moment. It felt like a rest for my soul. I'd been living under the constant pressure of work and Mom and Richard and now this breakup with Rachel, and suddenly I was distracted and having fun and all those stressors got shut off. Now they were duller somehow. They mattered less. And I wondered if this is what Vanessa meant about always having something to look forward to. Only, the thing I seemed to be looking forward to was *her.*

Not in any inappropriate way. I just wanted to see what she'd do next. It was like I'd found some cool new restaurant and the menu was never the same and I wanted to keep going back to see what they were serving.

Becky stood at the door of my office waiting for me like she did every morning, holding my coffee and wearing that searching look on her face that she gave me these days, trying to discern my mood.

"Did you, like, go tanning or something?" she said, handing me my cappuccino. "You look brighter."

I walked around my desk, sat, and unbuckled my briefcase to pull out the Keller file. "I didn't," I said, ignoring her narrowed eyes. "What's on my schedule for the day?"

"You have a consultation at ten, lunch with Marcus at eleven fifteen to go over the Keller case, and the rest of your day is free." She looked around. "Um, where's the dog? You *do* remember you have one, right?"

"With all the shitting it does? How could I forget." I logged on to my desktop.

"You just left him at home? He can't be in the apartment all day by himself, he'll be lonely."

"He's got the demon he's possessed with to keep him company."

She scowled at me.

I tried not to let her see my smile. "He's with a friend. I'm keeping him until he gets adopted." I didn't look up to see the triumphant grin I knew she was giving me.

Vanessa liked Harry. She'd asked to dog-sit him while I was at work and I'd happily agreed.

I signed in to my email. "I need you to call Sonja Duggar to see if she's available. I might have a full-time job for her. And don't put anything on my schedule after lunch. I'm leaving early again. I'll finish listening to the Buller tapes from home."

Becky didn't speak to give me her opinion on this like she usually would. A silent Becky was cause for concern, and I was forced to look up to make sure she hadn't died where she stood.

She stared at me, slack jawed. "You're going home early? *Again?*"

My cell phone pinged, and I pulled it out. It was a video from Vanessa. Harry in a diaper, growling at a chair leg. I laughed.

When she'd had my phone the other day, she'd changed my lock screen to the selfie of us. I didn't notice it until a few hours later.

I hadn't changed it back.

She was wearing that stupid cereal necklace in it and I had on that Maryland crab shirt and a glow stick bracelet. Her arm was peppered with stickers. The baby was smiling and the dog had his tongue out. It was this colorful, fun slap of happy right in the middle of my black, serious phone—and it made me smile every time I looked at it.

"What is going on?" Becky demanded. "Are you on drugs?"

I squinted up at her. "No, I am not on drugs." I looked back at my computer. "I just had a good weekend."

"Is it a *girl*?" She gasped into her hands. "Oh my God, if it's a girl, it's serious. Your horoscope today said your soul mate is in your midst!"

I scoffed. We had the same sign, and the idiot Becky was dating was definitely not anyone's soul mate, let alone hers.

I waited a moment before replying, just to torture her.

Becky was practically gyrating.

"She's a neighbor," I said. "Her name is Vanessa, and we're just friends."

She squealed, obviously ignoring the just-friends part. "Oh my God! Okay, tell me everything. What does she do? Is she pretty?" Then she stopped bouncing and went serious. "You're not acting all gloomy and *Interview with the Vampire* around her, right?"

I gave her a look as my cell phone rang. It was my PI returning my message.

"She's a YouTuber. She's beautiful. And again, we're just friends," I said, swiping the Answer Call button and putting the phone to my ear. "This is Adrian."

"Tom Hillbrand here. Got your message."

I swiveled my chair to give Becky my back. "Thanks for

returning my call so quickly. The ring was stolen on Friday. A police report was filed with the Eagan police department by a Vanessa Price. Can you get access to that?"

Wind came through the phone like he was outside. "Shouldn't be a problem. Any identifying features?"

"She said it's got an inscription inside. 'Kismet.'"

"Good. Makes it easier to know what I'm looking for. How hard do you want to hit this? I can get my guys over to the pawn shops easy enough, but if it's not there, hunting this thing down could get expensive."

I smoothed my tie down. "Whatever it takes. It has sentimental value. Just find it."

"You got it. I'll keep you posted."

I hung up the call.

I didn't tell Vanessa what I was trying to do. I didn't want to get her hopes up. But if anyone could find this thing, it was Tom.

I swiveled back around to find Becky standing there like a marble statue. Her face had gone white. "You're Jesus's Abs," she breathed.

I leaned over my desk for a pen. "What?"

"Jesus's Abs," she whispered. "Windowless white van guy. I can't believe this is happening…"

"You can't believe *what* is happening?" I asked, clicking the pen.

"This is the greatest day of my life. I'm in the presence of a hero."

I hovered over a legal pad. "Becky, I'm going to give you five seconds to explain to me what you're talking about, and then I'm going to need you to go," I said.

"The girl you're seeing is Vanessa *Price*? She talks about you. In her videos. Your abs are famous!"

I froze. "What?"

She was already pulling out her cell and then frantically typing into her screen. She held her phone out in front of me. "LOOK."

The video was Vanessa, sitting in her bathroom, the morning I'd met her by the outfit she had on.

I watched it with wide eyes.

And then she was talking about *me*.

# CHAPTER 11

# TAKE THIS QUIZ TO SEE WHICH *OFFICE* CHARACTER YOU ARE!

## VANESSA

It was 2:30 on Monday. Harry Puppins was sleeping in his diaper on his doggy bed in my bathroom. I had Grace's stroller and was just grabbing my keys to run to the store when someone knocked on my door. I opened it to Adrian standing there with a cocked eyebrow, leaning an arm on the door frame in his suit, his tie loosened. "Jesus's *Abs*?" He grinned.

He was watching more of my videos.

I beamed at him and put my hands up in a shrug. "I'm a teller of truths."

He laughed. He was thoroughly amused by this. Thank *God*.

Even though I hadn't given revealing information about him, I didn't know if being fodder for my channel might bother him. It clearly didn't.

And it was a good thing that he wasn't weirded out by me talking about him, because my viewers *loved* him.

Sight unseen and mentioned once, Adrian was, by far, the most requested topic I'd ever had, short of my brief romance with Drake Lawless. They were begging for updates.

I was going to have to do another vlog, and soon.

He peered past me at Grace in her car seat. "Were you leaving?"

I looked over my shoulder and came back to him. "Yeah. I was going to go get a Christmas tree." I paused. "Well, sort of. I can't lug a whole tree up here by myself so I was going to Whole Foods to see if they had a little one in a pot or something." I tilted my head. "Why don't you have a tree? It's December."

"I don't need a tree. It's just me."

I laughed. "So? It's *Christmas*." I tugged on the end of his tie. "Want to come with me?"

He glanced down the hallway and then came back with a smile that reached his eyes. "Well, I was going to go get an oil change for the windowless white van today, but I think I could fit this in."

I snorted. "You'd better not let this thing go to your head. I have to talk about my life in my videos, and you're ridiculously attractive. I don't know what you want me to do about it."

He smiled and pushed off the doorway. "Give me five minutes to get changed."

Adrian insisted that he drive again. His car was an itty-bitty slate-blue BMW coupe. We couldn't fit the car seat in the back, let alone a Christmas tree. Not even one in a pot. So we took my GMC Acadia.

Despite his warnings that he drove too fast, he was being very careful and considerate with the baby in the car.

He smelled really good. His cologne or whatever he used was super fresh and it lingered in the car. I was breathing through my nose on purpose.

"Do you always get out of work this early?" I asked, as we idled at a red light. "You got out early last week too."

"No," he said, talking to the road. "I usually work late. I don't get home until midnight sometimes. I'll leave early if I need to take my grandma to the doctor, but that's about it."

"You go with your grandma to the doctor?"

"I used to. Up until October when she still lived here."

*Gah.*

This man was amazing. Like, in every single way. Unless he had a micropenis he was self-conscious about, I couldn't see why he wasn't all over Tinder letting women climb him like a ladder. I'd climb this man no matter what he had in his pants.

Maybe he *did* have a micropenis…

Maybe that's why he didn't send dick pics…

Maybe that's what he meant by shock and awe…

I gasped quietly and slid my eyes over to his lap.

"My assistant is obsessed with you," he said, breaking into my thoughts.

I darted my gaze away from his crotch. "She's not from Monett, Missouri, is she?"

He laughed.

He was different this afternoon. Lighter somehow. More Mr. Bingley and less Mr. Darcy.

"You're almost not brooding at all today," I said. "I don't know what to make of it."

He smiled at the road. "I think it's the sponge."

I pulled my legs up and crossed them under me on the seat. "You know, I have a lot of good ideas."

He turned into the Whole Foods parking lot. "Like what?"

"Like, I think you need some throw pillows, a fleece blanket, and a plant in your living room. Your apartment's a little *American Psycho*. Every time I'm in there I feel like you're going to start talking to me about Phil Collins."

"'Invisible Touch' was the group's undisputed masterpiece," he said, giving me a line from the movie.

I laughed so hard I started choking on my spit.

He turned into a parking space with a grin. "I'm not letting you decorate my apartment."

I wiped at my eyes. "I'm not trying to decorate your apartment," I said, putting my fingers in quotes. "I'm trying to enhance your quality of life. Your surroundings affect your mood." I nodded through the windshield. "There's a Pottery Barn, right there. I say we go."

He chuckled, putting the car in park. "Okay. I'll make a deal with you. I will let you enhance my quality of life with homewares on the condition that you tell me what you used to do before you were a YouTuber."

I pivoted in my seat to look at him full-on. "Four throw pillows, two throw blankets, a Christmas tree, and I get to pick a centerpiece for the dining room table."

Something lawyerly flickered across his face. "*Two* throw pillows, *one* blanket, a poinsettia, and we agree on the centerpiece."

I narrowed my eyes. "No. Not good enough." I got unbuckled and got out of the car.

"That is an extremely generous offer my client is making you," he said, as we both leaned into the back seat on our respective sides to grab Grace at the same time. I let him take her and I picked up the diaper bag instead.

We met around the back as I pulled the stroller from the trunk in the nippy winter air. "What I used to do for a living is epically ironic. You will *love* it. I'm not wasting it on some half-assed attempt at placating me." I pulled out the stroller and he clipped the car seat onto it. I started pushing Grace toward the shops.

"Placating you?" he said, chirping on the car alarm and jogging next to me with a grin.

"Poinsettias are poisonous. You have a dog and a baby that comes over," I argued.

"I'll get a fake one."

I blanched and he laughed.

"A fake—that is so not even the point of this exercise. My God, you're Scrooge," I said, navigating the sidewalk. "I need you to smell *pine* when you come home. It's part of the thing."

He opened the door of Pottery Barn for me to a whoosh of warm cinnamon-scented air. I went in, then turned to face him in the entryway. "I can be agreeable to two throw pillows and one blanket," I said. "But *I* pick the centerpiece, and you get a Christmas tree. A live one."

He put a hand to his chin like he was thinking about it. He paused in his fake musing. "Are you having dinner with me at my place tonight? Because I'm not setting any of this up on my own. You come over and help or we don't have a deal."

I scoffed. "I mean, yeah, totally. Of course I'm coming over. What kind of question is that?" I didn't let him see it, but I seriously liked that he'd asked it.

I was officially in crush territory. There was no more denying it. I liked him. A *lot*.

I couldn't do anything about it. My dating rules were my rules. Plus, my good days were likely numbered now—and the number was low—and it wasn't like he was available anyway. He wasn't dating, so it probably wouldn't have made one difference even if I *could* have pursued him. But I was crushing on him just the same.

He smiled. "Okay. We have a deal."

I smirked, walking into the store.

"I'm waiting," he said from behind me.

I stopped at a sleek leather recliner and picked up a pillow with Rudolph on the front that I knew he'd hate. He had a red bell for the nose. "I like this one," I said, wiggling it so it jingled. "What do you think?"

He took it from my hand and set it back on the chair I got it from. "Your part of the bargain first." He crossed his arms.

I twisted my lips and smiled. "I was a receptionist for a paper company."

His arms dropped. "Oh, come *on*. Like Pam Beesly from *The Office*? Here I was, ready to buy a damn Christmas tree—"

I looked him in the eye. "I am dead serious. I *was*."

He walked away from me toward tablewares.

I followed him, pushing the stroller. "I'm not making this up," I said to his back.

"Deal's off," he said over his shoulder.

"I have prooooof," I sang.

He stopped at a table with a Christmas dinner setup and pretended to look at a napkin ring, but I could tell he was waiting for me. I punched into my phone and then waved it at him. He glanced up and arched a playful eyebrow at me.

"They used to call me Van Beesly," I said.

He snorted. "Fine. I will momentarily entertain this farce." He put his hand out.

I smacked my phone into his palm. "That's me, three years ago." I'd pulled up the album called Work Christmas Party. "It's called Paper Waits Cards. We sold cards, invitations, envelopes, and craft paper. I worked at their home office in Edina."

He flipped through the pictures of me dressed in office casual. Then raised his eyes to mine. "Van Beesly?"

"Yes. And you'd better not call me that if you want me to answer."

He looked like he didn't believe me.

"Okay, you need more proof. Fine." I took my phone from him. "I will call an old coworker. I'm willing to make the ultimate sacrifice because I think you need a Christmas tree in your life and I'm a giver. I give. It's what I do." I scrolled through my contacts, found the number, hit Send, and put the call on speaker. I held the phone between us as it rang, staring at Adrian's face. Someone picked up and a man's voice came through the line. "Van Beesly!"

I hung up. "There. Now do you believe me?"

Adrian nodded at the phone. "Who was that?"

"Not my Jim Halpert, I'll tell you that." The phone was already ringing in my hand as he called me back. "He was obsessed with me the whole time I worked there and he *just* stopped trying to slide into my DMs like six months ago. I just shook the hornet's nest. For *you*. You see how committed I am to this project?"

He laughed. "Okay. Which pillows do you want?"

I smiled triumphantly.

I didn't torture him too much. I chose two very tasteful, sophisticated Christmas pillows that said MERRY CHRISTMAS and HAPPY HOLIDAYS on them and a red fleece throw blanket with a faux fur trim. We agreed on a pine-and-berry center-piece. *And*, he let me pick a wreath for the inside of his door. But only because I was watching his dog for free, he said.

I think he secretly liked it.

We grabbed him some ornaments, a star, a few strands of lights, and a tree skirt.

We bought it all, put the third row down in the trunk of my car, and loaded it in, and then wandered over to Whole Foods for groceries.

"So what do you want for dinner?" he asked as we walked in through the automatic doors.

"Soup," I said, pushing the stroller. "We can throw it all in a pot and simmer it while we set up your tree."

"Soup it is," he said, grabbing a cart. "What kind?"

"Um . . . chicken and wild rice? It's filling enough for dinner."

He smiled. "Agreed. We'll get some bread bowls to put it in."

I bounced. "Let's get a gingerbread house for dessert! We can decorate it and then eat the roof."

He grinned, walking into the produce section. "Does anyone ever tell you no?"

I pretended to think about it. "Never."

"Oh, I forgot to tell you," he said, stopping by the oranges to pull a business card out of his jacket. "I thought you might be interested in this for your dad." He handed it to me. "Her name is Sonja Duggar. She's a sober companion and life coach."

"A what?" I asked, taking the paper.

"A sober companion and life coach. We use them to keep clients out of trouble while they're on trial. She's particularly good at cases where the client needs to look reformed in front of the judge at their next appearance. She's good. He'll like her."

I looked up at him. "What does she do exactly?"

"Whatever needs to be done. If alcohol or addiction is the issue, she'll get the client clean and sober and keep them there. She drives them to AA meetings and therapy sessions and supervises visitation. Makes sure they're not in any violations of their court order. Ensures that medications are taken, they hold down their job, and show up to court on time. She used to be a therapist. She's retired now and she does this on the side."

I scoffed. "A babysitter. And it's sad because he actually needs one," I mumbled.

We started walking toward the onions. "She'll be expensive," he said. "Insurance won't cover it. But it'll free you up so you're not worrying about him when you're not there.

She'll get the house taken care of, and she'll help him deal with the underlying reasons that got it there in the first place."

Oh God, that would be incredible. There wasn't enough of me to go around. I was spread too thin as it was.

I smiled over at him. "This is amazing. I didn't even know this was a thing."

"It's a thing. It might be difficult to get him onboard. The stakes are higher for my clients, so it's not that hard of a sell when *I* pitch it."

I snorted. "Oh, the stakes are high here too. If he doesn't get his shit together, I'm cutting him off."

He smiled and grabbed a bag for the onions. "She'll even live there if he has a spare room and he doesn't mind her cat—though it'll cost more."

I didn't care about the cost. I needed results. And Dad was always so lonely he'd probably love someone staying with him who wasn't as fucked up as he was.

Speaking of Annabel...

My sister hadn't surfaced since the car accident. She was still posting her digital art pics on Instagram, so I knew she was alive. Probably crashing on someone's sofa if I had to guess, completely oblivious to the chaos she'd caused, as usual. I was beyond pissed at her. Between destroying the car and finding out she was maybe using while she was pregnant, I was *done*. I'd officially gone full tough love on her ass. I'd already cut off the money, and she wasn't allowed back at Dad's. But yesterday I'd had her cell phone shut off too. I wasn't contributing one dime to enabling this bullshit. Let her hit rock bottom faster.

"I'll call Sonja today," I said. "Thank you for this."

He smiled at me. "You got it."

Picking out groceries with Adrian was one of the most fun things I'd done all year. He was exactly like me when it came to produce. He inspected everything, picked out all the best ingredients. He went with fresh herbs instead of dried stuff, organic heavy cream and chicken broth for the base, Plugrá butter for the roux.

Then we went crazy and bought like seventeen different cheeses. People were staring at us. We were dangerous together. I couldn't even imagine us in France. We'd go broke on the wine alone.

Somewhere along the way, dinner for tomorrow came up and suddenly we were shopping for that too: chicken cordon bleu, with horseradish mashed potatoes and glazed carrots. But at my place this time instead.

When it came time to wander out to the tree tent in the parking lot, Adrian paused with the shopping cart at the sliding doors.

"What?" I asked.

He had a weird look on his face, like he wasn't sure he should say what he was thinking. "What if we went and cut one down?"

My face lit up. "Like at a tree farm or something?" I started bouncing. "Will you wear a flannel? Will you have an ax?"

He snorted. "I do not own a flannel. And if memory serves, they give you a handsaw."

I bit my lip and squealed excitedly.

He smiled. "My dad used to take us to a tree farm every year. He'd cut one down. It was a tradition."

Ahhh. Now I understood the hesitation. *And* the reason he never had a tree.

My face went soft and I peered up at him. "Was the last time you got a Christmas tree back when your dad was around?"

He paused a moment. "Yes."

"So when your dad left, it was the end of your childhood," I said.

He drew in a long breath. "I guess that's one way of looking at it."

I smiled up at him. "But look! Now you're the grown-up and you get to cut down a tree for Grace's first Christmas and give that experience to her like someone gave it to you once."

His eyes went soft and he looked at Grace in her stroller. "I hadn't thought of it like that. Though she's probably too small to remember it."

I shook my head. "You don't know what she's going to remember. There are things that will happen to her while she's a baby that will form who she is for the rest of her life. She might be a hundred years old and still feel a sense of calm when she smells someone who smells like you."

He wrinkled his forehead at me. "What?"

"Yeah. You don't notice it? How she calms down faster when you pick her up? She already associates you with feeling safe because you saved her that night. She's imprinting, right now. Little synapses are connecting and telling her that you're good. She might be drawn to bearded men with kind green eyes and marry one one day, just because she knew you once. And she'll never even know why."

He blinked at me and something I couldn't read moved across his face.

"Anyway," I said, pushing the stroller toward the exit, "I think we've made real progress here today. Even if there's not going to be an ax and flannel."

He smiled and pushed the cart, following me out into the parking lot.

⁓

Half an hour later, we pulled into the tree lot. A woman in a heavy winter coat and a Santa hat approached the car and gave us a site map and a saw. The saw smelled like pine.

"You smell that?" I smiled. He rolled up the window as we crept down the snowy road toward the different plots.

He smiled back. "I do."

I looked at the map. "So what kind of tree do you want?"

"Balsam fir," he said without skipping a beat.

"Right answer." I nodded to a lot on the left. "Those are balsams."

He pulled into a parking space and we got out. I took Grace from her car seat and did a quick diaper change. Then I bundled her up, and we set out between the rows of pines.

It was a beautiful day. Sunny and around thirty degrees— a Minnesota heat wave for December. We crunched through the snow, looking at the selection.

"Isn't this better than being at work?" I asked, closing my eyes and breathing in the crisp air.

"I have to admit this does beat depositions," he said, holding the saw.

"So you're a partner, right?" I asked, looking over at him. "What does that mean exactly? You're the boss?"

"I am one of the bosses, yes."

"But not the big boss?"

"The big boss is Marcus. He's the owner and founder of the firm."

"And what's he like?"

He bobbed his head. "Serious. Shrewd."

"So how does that work exactly? He's the owner and you're what? Like if this was a retail setting, what position would you have?"

He stopped to look a tree up and down. "Well, I guess if this was retail, I'd be the store manager. Marcus and I agree on what cases we take and who we hire. I consult with him if I need to, but he defers to my judgment for most things."

"And how many lawyers are there?"

"We have nine right now. Plus three paralegals and a couple of administrative assistants."

A soft wind blew and I tucked Grace's blanket around her face, kissing her warm forehead. "So do you get all the best clients?"

We kept walking. "Technically clients belong to the firm. Any of us can show up to represent them. But I usually head up the bigger cases."

"Ahhh. I see. And do you like Marcus?"

"I *respect* Marcus. Liking him isn't really necessary."

I stopped at a large tree. "What about this one?" I nodded to it.

Adrian examined it. "For me or you?"

"You. I'll need something a little smaller. I don't have as much room as you do."

He nodded. "This works for me."

He got down in the snow and tucked under the boughs of the tree and started to saw.

"So what's Annabel like?" he asked, the tree shaking back and forth.

"Angry."

He stopped sawing and poked his head out to look at me. "Angry?"

"Angry. Like a pissed-off, grounded, petulant high schooler."

"Why?" He went back under.

I scoffed. "Why not?"

Annabel was mad at the world. Mad that Mel died. Mad that her mom left. Mad that a condom broke and she got pregnant by some rando in Punta Cana on her grad trip—that *I* paid for, by the way. I thought gifting her with my love of travel would help her love her life a little more.

*That* backfired.

At least she'd never have to worry about dying of ALS. She and Brent had a different mom from Melanie and me—which meant Grace was safe too. That alone should be enough to be thankful for. But Annabel didn't really *do* gratitude.

The tree shook one more time and fell sideways with a small crack.

Adrian got up and brushed snow off his jacket and I grinned at him. "You did it. You've come full circle."

He looked down at it with a smile. "Let's go get yours."

Three hours later we were back at his apartment. Both trees were erected in their respective living rooms. I'd decorate mine later. His was the one that was critical.

The fireplace was on, Christmas music was playing, his tree was decorated, and we were eating soup out of bread bowls on his sofa. He'd made hot toddys, and I had his new throw blanket on my lap with Harry Puppins snuggled up next to me. He growled in his sleep.

I loved that insane little dog. He was like some curmudgeonly old man, chasing people off his lawn. When we got back with the tree, Harry attacked Adrian's pant leg. Adrian was trying to put the tree into the stand so his hands were busy and he couldn't get Harry off him. I was laughing so hard I couldn't even help. I almost peed my pants.

"Don't you wish you'd gotten two blankets now?" I asked, nudging Adrian's thigh with my knee. "I'm so comfortable and you're over there all cold and sticking to the leather."

He laughed, scraping his spoon down the side of his bread bowl. "I run hot."

I smiled, gazing around his apartment. It was actually homey now. "Tell me you don't feel better," I said, looking back at him.

He smiled. "I do feel better. You were right."

I put my mug on the floor. "You know, I think it was fate that you met me. You definitely needed me in your life."

He slid his bread bowl onto the coffee table. "While I'm very glad that I met you, I don't believe in fate."

I shook my head at him. "How can you not believe in fate?"

"I don't think things are preordained or written in the stars. I believe we make our own destiny."

"Ah, spoken like a true control freak." I put out my palm. "Give me your hand."

He eyed me suspiciously.

"Give it to me," I said, waiting.

He smiled and put it out in front of him. The second I picked it up, warm electricity shot through me.

God, I bet this man knew what to do with his hands...

Adrian didn't really strike me as the kind of person to half-ass sex. He didn't fail. At *anything*. I bet he could teach a master class in giving women orgasms.

I liked men with a little experience—since I didn't have time for training.

I cleared my throat. "I'm going to read your palm," I said, flipping his hand over.

He looked amused. "Where'd you learn to do that?"

"A fortune teller in a little village in Spain."

"No wonder Becky likes you."

I ran a finger along his love line and smiled. "Why?"

"She's into astrology," he said, leaning into me to watch what I was doing. His face was a little close to mine. It made my heart flutter. "She's always reading me my horoscope," he said.

"And you don't ever feel like there's truth to it?" I asked, studying the creases in his palm.

"Nope. So what's my palm telling you?"

I smiled a little. "You see this?" I dragged a line at the base of his fingers. "This is your love line. You've got a break in your heart line, right here. That means something traumatic happened to you. That's probably the thing with your dad leaving. But look. Look how long and steady it is after that. The whole rest of your life is one solid, happy line."

I smiled at his palm. He had featherlike creases at the start of his line. Passionate. And it stopped right before his index finger, which was good. It meant he could have a healthy love life.

I tipped his hand toward him. "You see how your heart line forks at the end? Turns down a little? That means you're willing to sacrifice everything for love. You're a romantic."

When I looked up at him, he wasn't looking at his hand. He was looking at me.

"And yours?" he asked, holding my eyes. He turned his hand over and flipped mine and held it between us. "What does yours say?"

The way we were leaning into each other, I could feel his breath just tickling my face. It was *so* close.

"Um...it's a lot like yours, actually. Only my hand shape is a fire sign. I have a long palm and shorter fingers. It means—"

"Let me guess." He gave me a small smile. "Energetic. Enthusiastic. Outgoing."

I was having a hard time breathing normally while he was touching me like this. "Pretty much," I managed. "Yours is air. It means you're an intellect and logical. A good communicator."

He ran a thumb along my palm. "Fire and air." He looked back up at me. "And what about the rest of it? Will you have a long life?"

My smile fell and I pulled my hand away, pretending I needed to pick up my drink all of a sudden. I sat back into my corner of the sofa, putting the ocean back between us. "Lifelines show well-being," I said. "Life changes. They don't actually tell you how long you're going to live."

It was the numbness in my fingers that usually did that.

# CHAPTER 12

# THIS MAN CUT HIS WORK HOURS IN HALF AND THE RESULTS ARE STAGGERING!

## ADRIAN

Becky and I sat in the conference room working. It was noon on Friday and we were waist deep in backlogged paperwork. The Bueller trial was amping up, and I wasn't prepared.

I hadn't looked at the bodycam footage or the toxicology report yet, and Marcus had been giving me side-eye because I missed a filing deadline last week after leaving early to take Grace to the pediatrician with Vanessa.

I hadn't planned on going to the doctor with her. Vanessa didn't even invite me. But I'd mentioned the baby's appointment to Lenny and he said that his kids cried so hard when they got their shots they were inconsolable. Then he said Vanessa should have given Grace Tylenol before she got there, which I wasn't sure she had. I'd texted her but she didn't reply.

I'd sat there in a conference call, bouncing my foot and checking my phone, until finally I'd said fuck it and walked out and driven to the doctor's office.

Vanessa couldn't bring Grace back from that kind of upset like I could. Vanessa was right when she said Grace was calmer with me. She liked it when I held her when she was fussy—she actually preferred me over Vanessa when she was really worked up. It would be better if I held her while she got her shots—and anyway, I wanted to meet this doctor. Run a background check for malpractice and at the very least check his ratings on WebMD.

The nurses kept calling me "dad." Vanessa giggled every time they did it.

I was gone only an hour, but the disruption had messed up my whole day. I'd spaced on the filing and was ten minutes late to a consultation. Lenny had taken notes for me for the rest of the conference call, but I'd missed my opportunity to ask questions while everyone was on the phone so I'd had to send emails to get up to speed.

In addition to this midday walkout, I hadn't pulled more than an eight-hour shift in almost two weeks. The time I usually gave to my cases, I was now giving to Vanessa.

I'd started delegating.

I never handed off work. *Ever.* I always did everything myself. There were fewer mistakes that way. But I'd given Lenny the Garcia case because I knew if I didn't, I'd either have to sacrifice the quality of my representation or I'd have to sacrifice Vanessa. And for the first time in my life, work wasn't my priority. These days when 5:00 hit, I left. I didn't like losing any time with her. It had gotten to the point where I even hated the end of the night because I knew she'd go home and take Grace with her and leave my apartment hollow and lifeless again.

I was behind on everything. *Everything.* I was trying to get caught up, so I was working through lunch. I had to, because today was a short day for everyone. We all were leaving early for the annual Children's Hospital gala.

I wasn't looking forward to it.

I liked the gala. The food and the entertainment were always good, and it was nice to spend time with the rest of the team outside of work. But I'd only bought one seat because Rachel hadn't been planning on coming out this weekend. I tried to get another ticket for Vanessa last minute, but the event was sold-out.

She wouldn't be there.

Suddenly an evening of eating steak and lobster and listening to a live band sounded like the last thing I wanted to do with my night.

I'd been hanging out with Vanessa every day for two weeks straight. We had dinner every night. Spent last weekend snowed in, wandering the first floor, googling names we found scrawled on the walls, watching *The Office,* and going back and forth between each other's apartments.

Our lives had fused together without seams. I found baby socks in my sofa cushions, and there was a bottle warmer on the bar next to my decanter of Basil Hayden's bourbon. I'd bought my own playpen and swing so we didn't have to keep lugging them back and forth.

Vanessa gave me a spare key, and I didn't even lock my door anymore when I was home. She came and went as she felt like it. Didn't even knock. Came right in talking like we were always in some ongoing conversation, did laundry, used my espresso maker, took Harry Puppins home with her when I was at work and left Grace with me while she took showers or ran errands. Yesterday she sat on my weight bench in her pajamas, talking to me and eating a frittata I made her while I ran six miles on my treadmill. They were always there. *She* was always there. I liked it. I liked *her*.

A *lot*.

I was having a hard time knowing how that made me feel because there wasn't much I could do about it.

A core part of our relationship was us *not* hitting on each other. She flirted with me, yes. But that was just who she was. There'd been times she'd told me how hot I was and reiterated that she didn't date in the same sentence. It didn't mean anything. She had been very clear that she was uninterested in dating. That's probably why she felt so comfortable spending so much time with me—because I wasn't trying to sleep with her.

I was painfully aware that if I brought it up, tried to talk to her about the way I was feeling, I'd run the risk of losing the friendship. Even the conversation about crossing the line was crossing a line. Afterward there would always be the knowledge that I wanted more, even if we never acted on it. It would change things—and I was terrified of changing things. I couldn't lose this.

Becky moved her stack of papers into a neat pile and leaned forward on her elbows. "So what's it like hanging out with Vanessa?" She grinned. "Do you guys get VIP treatment? Is it the coolest thing ever? Does she get mobbed when you go places and you have to be her bodyguard and peel strange men off her?"

I shook my head. "She signs autographs now and then. I don't really see that side of her. We do normal things. She's just like everyone else," I said, slipping a paper clip over my stack of corrections.

Becky gawked at me from across the table. "Okay, but she's *totally* not. People *love* her. They pay money at cons just to be able to take, like, *one* picture with her, and you just get to hang out with her all willy-nilly and you're not even freaking out about it?!"

"I very much appreciate that I get to hang out with her. Willy-nilly." I circled a typo.

She gave me crazy eyes.

I loved messing with Becky.

She blinked at me. "You don't get this, do you? Your neighbor is America's sweetheart and I feel like you're not fully appreciating this. She was a judge on a panel with Tom Hanks once and they called *her* 'the nice one.' She had a cameo on that one Gordon Ramsay cooking show and he refused to yell at her—Post Malone has her name tattooed on the inside of his lip!"

I looked up at her. "She's met Tom Hanks?"

She stared back at me, horrified. "Why don't you know *any* of the things?!"

I stifled a grin. I didn't know about Tom Hanks—or the Gordon Ramsay show, come to think of it. And I didn't know what the hell a Post Malone was either.

I was fully aware that Vanessa was a celebrity. But to me she was just… *Vanessa*. She was grounded and normal. Most

of the time I forgot what she did for a living entirely—
something I think she preferred. She didn't like to talk about
her channel.

Admittedly, there *were* times when we were out that I
noticed she was being recognized. Even if people didn't
approach her, I could tell they knew who she was.

I could never be on camera like that, my life so exposed, no
anonymity. I don't think she particularly enjoyed that aspect
of it, but for her, raising money for ALS trumped privacy. I
guess if you found something important to you like that, it
would be worth it.

"I don't need you to tell me how lucky I am or how
incredible Vanessa is," I said. "I am well aware."

Becky was shaking her head at me, rendered mute by
how totally uncool and uninformed I was. She let out a disappointed sigh at my unwillingness to gossip about this and
went back to her subpoenas.

The occasional celebrity surprises aside, it occurred to me
that I officially knew more about Vanessa and her family in
two short weeks than I had known about Rachel and hers
after eight months.

I'd had a lot of time to think about that relationship
since it ended, and I was coming to conclusions that I wasn't
thrilled about.

Part of me knew that Rachel had probably been purposely
cagey about her real life, and that's why I didn't know her
better or catch on to what she was doing. But the other part
of me was starting to wonder how much of a role *I* had played
in that. Because the reality was I didn't care enough to dig.

I made no effort to meet her friends and family or to visit

her in Seattle. If she didn't text me for a few days or answer my calls, I barely noticed because I didn't have time to talk to her anyway.

I wasn't blaming myself for what Rachel did. But Vanessa was right about what she said all those weeks ago. I didn't have balance. My life only allowed for a once-a-month girlfriend who was a stranger to me after almost a year of dating because that's all I'd made room for. And that I *did* have to take ownership over.

And there was something else. A small but niggling voice that told me that maybe I *liked* it this way. That maybe Rachel was another manifestation of the control I seemed to need, a symptom of a bigger problem. That making work my number one focus was a way to protect myself from getting too close to someone who might end up hurting me. Leaving me, like Dad had. And the funny thing was Rachel *did* end up leaving me. But the more I really thought about it, the more I realized that I didn't care.

I was indignant and angry about it, but on principle, not because I'd been in love with her, or even close to it. Did I choose her by design? Because I knew somewhere buried in my subconscious that she couldn't get near enough to my heart to damage it?

I couldn't shake the thought. I didn't like this. At *all*.

Vanessa said that childhood trauma always messes with your relationships. And I was starting to think she was right.

She was right about a lot of things.

Vanessa made me different. *Better.* She made me see the world through a new lens—or a lens that I'd forgotten existed.

It was like I was a kid again. We played like children. Had squirt gun fights in her living room, played the floor is lava. When it was negative five outside, we boiled water and threw it off the balcony to make fog. We blew bubbles to watch them freeze, made snow angels on the roof, had snowball fights that made me want to fall into a snow drift in our coats and kiss her.

I laughed until my stomach hurt, noticed the beauty around me, and marveled at the fact that I'd stopped seeing it in the first place. I felt like I'd been half-dead and I didn't even know it, walking through my life in a sleepy fog until she'd woken me up.

Vanessa had said once that money can't make you happy unless you know what you want. And it was becoming clearer and clearer to me by the moment what that was. With every day that I spent with Vanessa and Grace, I became more sure of it. But the thing that I wanted couldn't be bought. I had to earn it.

I just didn't know if I *could*.

I was still in the conference room scanning the Bueller police report when Becky made a shrieking noise from across the table. Becky being dramatic wasn't usually cause for me to look up from what I was doing, so I didn't see Vanessa come in with Grace in her stroller until she cleared her throat in the doorway.

"You must be Becky?" she said, smiling at my hypnotized paralegal over my shoulder.

My heart skipped at the unexpected sight of her.

She was beautiful. She was *always* beautiful, but I hadn't been braced to see her.

She had on a purple sweater I'd never seen her wear before, and her hair was down and curled. It gave me a twinge of pride that this woman had just walked through my office to see *me*.

I got up, grinning. "Hey, I didn't know you were coming."

"Since I'm not hanging out with you tonight, I thought I'd come down to surprise you and bring you lunch." She held up a paper bag.

I stood there, just smiling at her like an idiot until Becky made a whimpering noise from behind me. "I'm gonna go have lunch at my desk," she squeaked.

She clutched a jumbled pile of paperwork to her chest and grinned at Vanessa like a lunatic as she edged past her and closed the door.

Vanessa beamed at me. "You know, you're even hotter in your office."

I laughed.

Grace smiled at me from her stroller. She'd been doing that now for the last few days. Every time she had her pacifier in and I made her smile, it popped out and she'd beam up at me, all gums and twinkling eyes. And if I tickled her, she giggled. I couldn't get enough of it. I loved playing with her.

I reached down to scoop her into my arms and nuzzled her with my nose. She had on a tiny blue fleece onesie with snowflakes on it and she smelled like baby powder and Vanessa's perfume.

She smelled like home.

She put a fat little hand up, and I bit her fingers with my lips and she made happy giggling noises. I couldn't stop smiling.

I suddenly understood what it felt like to have family come see you at work, like a wife and kids. I'd never had that jolt of happiness at seeing someone I cared about when I wasn't expecting it. I wanted to hold Grace while I walked Vanessa around to show her my desk. Introduce her to Marcus. Revive Becky and formally introduce her too.

"What are we eating?" I asked, looking up at Vanessa.

She was watching me holding Grace. I couldn't make out her expression, but there was something distant about it.

I nodded over to the table. "Come sit with me." I moved some files with my free hand and cleared a spot for her.

"I got us Thai food," she said, setting down the bag she'd brought. "Oh, and before I forget to tell you, I can't hang out on Monday. I just found out." She looked at me and put her bottom lip into a pout.

I felt my face fall. "Why not?"

"A work thing came up," she said, reaching into the bag and pulling out to-go containers.

I had to force down my disappointment. That was two nights that I wasn't seeing her.

"Do you want me to watch Grace?" I asked, hoping she couldn't hear the letdown in my tone.

She opened a container of fried rice and scooped it onto a plate. "You don't have to. I was going to ask Yoga Lady."

"I can do it," I said, putting Grace down in her stroller and taking the chair next to Vanessa's.

She shrugged. "All right. If you want to. I didn't want to assume." She finished serving my food and slid it over to me.

I looked at her while she was making her own plate. She wasn't paying attention.

She'd dyed the ends of her hair last week for a video. They were blue and purple to match her sweater. It looked exotic. She had a little dimple on her cheek that came out when she smiled. Soft freckles along the bridge of her nose, long lashes.

Beautiful.

I felt that thing happening, that urge to keep looking at her for longer than was appropriate. It was something that I'd been dealing with almost constantly for the last week or so.

I felt like a teenage boy panting over some girl in my gym class. I wanted to touch her. All the time. When she sat next to me on the couch, I wanted to put an arm around her. I wanted to hold her hand at the grocery store, pull her onto my lap when she'd come see what I was working on at my desk at home. It was ridiculous how strong the impulse was.

I knew I was probably just projecting my own shit onto this situation, but the space between us always felt unnatural. Like we were both pretending that we wanted it there and it was an effort for both of us to maintain it.

Vanessa made videos about me. I didn't watch them—I didn't have time to. And Becky regaled me with the dramatic recap every time one posted anyway. Mostly Vanessa talking about what we did that day and gushing about how attractive I was—not that any of this mattered. Besides being flattering, it didn't change anything. We were still just friends and that's how it was going to stay for the foreseeable future.

I forced my eyes away from her and back to my food.

"So what am I supposed to wear on Sunday?" she asked, picking up her soda.

I was taking her out for her birthday. I had something pretty big planned.

She bit the end of her straw while she waited for my reply.

"Just wear something nice. Maybe the gray sweater dress," I suggested, taking a bite of my noodles. I liked that dress on her.

I liked everything on her.

"Thanks for taking me out. I'd probably just be sitting at home if you didn't."

I found *that* very hard to believe. "What about your other friends? There's nobody else who would have done anything?"

She shrugged. "Nobody local. I've got plenty of friends. It's only exes I'm short on. I'm so single I don't even have someone to drunk text," she mumbled.

I smiled. "You can drunk text me."

She snorted. "Good. It's only a matter of time. Nice to have permission. I hope you like typos and crying emojis."

I laughed.

"You know, you could have a boyfriend if you wanted one," I said. "I still don't understand why you don't date."

She scoffed. "Nobody wants to get involved with my kind of baggage. Trust me."

"Your baggage is not as bad as you think it is," I said, wiping my mouth with a napkin. "Any man would be lucky to have you."

*I'd have you . . .*

She pointed her fork at me. "See, that's exactly the kind of stuff people say to make you feel good, but isn't it funny how the people who insist you're a catch are never the ones who actually want to date you?"

There was something clipped about her tone.

She looked away from me and brushed her hair off her forehead in that way she did when she was frustrated.

I stared at the side of her face. "What's wrong?" I asked.

She wouldn't look at me.

I studied her. Her chin did the slightest quiver. I swiveled my chair until our knees touched, and I put a hand on her arm. "Hey, look at me."

The second her eyes met mine, she burst into tears.

I leaned forward and pulled her into a hug. "What happened?" I smoothed her hair down. "Hey, shhhhhhh. Tell me."

She just cried. Vanessa *never* cried—even in situations when she *should*.

A helplessness tore through me, an instant impulse to fix whatever was wrong.

"Vanessa, what *is* it?"

*Tell me so I can make it better.*

She shook her head. "Sometimes I feel like I'm spinning. Like I'm in a tornado and I can't ever stop moving and the only time I feel still is when I'm with you."

The comment took me so by surprise I didn't know what to say.

She let me hold her for another moment. Then she pulled away, sniffed, and brushed at the tears on her cheeks. "Hey, let's read our fortune cookies. If you say, 'while in bed' and then read it, it's always funny." She forced a smile at me.

Like a projector changing reels, one scene to the next in a split second.

I shook my head. "Don't do that."

Her forced grin got bigger, and she smiled at me with tears still in her eyes. "Do what?"

"*That.* That thing you do where you pretend to be happy. You change the subject and go do something distracting. It's okay to be upset sometimes. You don't have to fake it with me."

She looked at me and she was suddenly so sad again I almost hated that I called her out on it.

"Adrian, if I don't laugh, I'll spend the rest of my life crying," she whispered.

My eyes moved back and forth between hers. I reached out and gathered up her hands. Our knees were still touching. I could feel energy transferring between us like I was absorbing her sadness, making her calm down. I *wanted* to absorb it. I'd take all of it if it meant taking it from her. "What's wrong?"

She looked at me for a long moment like she was debating whether to continue. "Adrian, I'm worried my hand isn't just carpal tunnel."

I drew my brows down. "What do you think it is?"

She pulled her face back and looked at me, tears in her eyes. "What do you *think* I think it is?"

I shook my head at her. "Listen to me, you are not dying. Okay? And it's normal for you to be afraid of that. Especially after losing Melanie. But that's not what that is."

Her eyes searched mine. "And what if it is?"

I gazed back at her steadily. "It's *not*. And if you're that worried, let's go have it looked at—"

She shook her head quickly.

I could see the fear in her eyes.

I couldn't imagine what it must have been like to watch her sister die the way she did. Having something random like that happen to someone you love must make it difficult to ever feel safe again. And her birthday was Sunday. Her sister and her mom hadn't made it to thirty. Vanessa was turning twenty-nine. That had to be frightening.

I squeezed her hands tighter. "You'll just have to take my word for it, then. You're a beautiful, healthy young woman and you're going to live for a very long time, Vanessa." I put a hand on her cheek. "Everything is going to be okay," I said gently.

Her sad eyes canvassed my face, almost as if they were searching me for the truth. She turned her cheek a little into my palm, like she was chasing the warmth from it, and her lips accidentally grazed my skin.

I wanted to kiss her.

The urge was so intense I had to physically restrain myself from leaning in.

What would it be like? To lean down and kiss away whatever was going on in that beautiful, brilliant head?

But she didn't want me kissing her. She didn't want *anyone* kissing her.

At least there was that.

She reached for her napkin and pressed it under her eyes, and I let my hand fall away from her face, disappointed that the excuse to touch her was over.

"I'm sorry to dump all this on you at work." She sniffed. "You don't like me like this. You like me when I'm fun."

"I like it when you're *happy*," I said honestly. "Fun is just the lucky by-product."

She changed the subject. "Are you ready for my dad's tomorrow?" She wiped under her eyes. "You don't have to go if you don't want to."

"Of course I'm going."

"Are you sure? I know the house really grossed you out."

I wasn't particularly excited to spend more time at Vanessa's dad's house—or with Vanessa's dad. The apple had fallen in a completely different orchard with that one. But I wanted to check in and make sure Sonja was doing her job.

And the other thing.

I wouldn't give up a night with Vanessa. Not for anything.

She was a light that I saw behind my eyelids now, long after I'd stopped looking at it—and I wanted to keep looking at it. All the time. And if that meant I had to have dinner in a hoarded house tomorrow night, then that's what I was doing.

Vanessa peered at me from where she sat. She was calmer now.

I realized that she'd come here today because showing up to have lunch with me was one of her distractions. One of the things she did to keep her mind off whatever was bothering her.

I wondered how often she did this. How many times she showed up to hang out with me as her way of cheering herself up instead of succumbing to whatever sadness she was battling. She came here because I made her feel better or because she wanted to talk to me about it.

*Because she was spinning in a tornado and the only time she feels still is when she's with me.*

And then it occurred to me.

I was her person. Me.

I couldn't adequately put into words the way this made me feel.

It wasn't in her DNA to let someone else take care of her. I knew because it wasn't in mine either. We were the rocks in our family, always putting the needs of everyone else before our own, so I knew what it meant that she let me be there for her.

It was a privilege I didn't take lightly. An honor to be the one she ran to when she needed someone to catch her. By some random stroke of luck, some geographical coincidence, *I* got to know her and *be* something to her.

And I'd be lying if I said being something to her wasn't suddenly all I felt like doing.

## CHAPTER 13

# HE LAUGHED AT MY BODY WHEN WE WENT TO SECOND BASE!

## VANESSA

Adrian looked up at me, pure amusement on his face. "And you thought this was advisable why?"

I did my best to look indignant, which was hard with my head stuck the way it was. "You know what? I don't need your judgment right now. Not all of us are giants, some people need to use ladders."

"The ladder part I get. It's the ceiling fan proximity I have questions about." He was laughing now. "It's a good thing you gave me a key."

He was in a tuxedo.

I thought Adrian had maxed out his ability to look attractive, but my imagination had failed me once again.

He had that gala tonight. I'd called him with my little

emergency hoping I'd catch him before he left. I hadn't. He was already at the venue. When I tried to hang up with him, he insisted I tell him what was wrong. I did and he immediately walked out to come rescue me—or to see it for himself. It was a crapshoot.

He started to climb the ladder to help me, and I braced myself against the wobble.

"What were you doing up here?" he asked.

"Something. I'll show you later."

The something was glow-in-the-dark stars I was sticking to my ceiling. I was putting some in the spot above the fan and I somehow managed to get my hair stuck in one of the votive lamps. I could not figure out how to undo it, and one of my hands was half-numb, which wasn't helping. I finally gave up and sat on top of the ladder to wait for Adrian to get home, which mercifully was only fifteen minutes into my captivity.

There was no room on this ladder for two grown adults. He stopped when my knees hit his chest. "I can't get up there unless..."

*Unless I spread my legs and let him climb the last two steps between them.*

Oh my *God*.

I'd been about to get into the shower when the maintenance guy showed up with the ladder I called for this morning. He wanted it back before he went home for the day, so I decided to blitz the project. So that meant I was in a dark-blue, thigh-high silk robe. No bra, no underwear. Just me and a thin slip of fabric with my head attached to a light fixture. Fuck my life.

I tucked my robe between my legs and opened my knees, wishing for the floor to open up and swallow me.

To his credit, Adrian didn't glance down.

He climbed two more rungs and his zipper pressed directly into my crotch. I almost fell backward.

He put a hand between my shoulder blades and caught me. "Maybe you should hang on to me," he said. "I don't want you falling."

*GOD.*

I wrapped my arms around his waist and died a little inside.

"You okay?" he asked, his chest practically rumbling against my cheek.

I nodded.

No, I was *not* okay. I hadn't been okay all day.

I'd been to see the adoption attorney this morning.

It wasn't certain I'd need to use her. Annabel could still get her life together. But knowing adoption was still something I had to seriously consider was enough to hurl me into a spiral. I'd stifled tears the whole way to Adrian's office earlier. Then when I got there, I'd broken down and ruined his tie sobbing into it. Afterward, I'd gone home and gotten my hair stuck in a ceiling fan and my stupid tingling fingers couldn't get their shit together to get me out. And now I was straddling Adrian, which was one part a complete turn-on and the other part just sad since he was perfect and therefore not into me.

My position on dating had shifted a bit in light of Mr. Copeland. I didn't feel like it was fair to date someone if I might be sick. But if he *knew* I might be sick, like Adrian did, and wanted me anyway? Who was I to tell the man what to do? It's why I told him about my hand earlier. It's also why I'd strategically stopped mentioning that I was glad he didn't hit on me. I couldn't bring myself to come right out and tell him I liked him. I was too afraid of what his reply to that might be. And how does one even broach that subject? Hey, I like you. I know you just went through a really crappy breakup, we're supposed to be friends, and I might be dead in a year, but you think you could be into that? UGH.

He tolerated my shameless flirting well enough, but he never flirted back—which I suppose was to be expected. But if he ever did make a move on me, I'd climb into his suit while he was still wearing it. He'd have to scatter expensive truffles on the floor to get me off him and then make a run for it because I'd never let him go.

He reached up and put his hands over my head. "How did you *do* this?"

His chest was right in my face. It had been in my face earlier too when I was crying into it, and just like earlier he smelled good and heat was coming off him and I was reminded that I'd probably go to my grave with cobwebs on my vagina.

"Um, I don't know? You know, I bet Sloan Monroe gets her hair stuck in ceiling fans all the time."

"Uh, no. I can guarantee you that Sloan has *never* had her hair stuck in a ceiling fan. She's not really a hair-stuck-in-a-ceiling-fan type."

"Oh, so there's a type now?"

He fiddled around a bit. "Well, if the fan blade fits..."

I stifled a smile.

I felt it the second he released me, and I breathed a sigh of relief.

"There," he said over me. "You're free."

I rubbed my head, and he stepped down until his eyes were level with mine. "Do you always get in this much trouble?" He was grinning.

His face was really close, and he was still standing between my open legs.

Sometimes I looked at Adrian and felt like I couldn't breathe.

At his office earlier when he'd been holding Grace, I thought about how he'd be such a good dad and how proud I was of him, seeing him in his element. He was so intelligent and capable, and over the last few weeks, I'd found myself completely and utterly losing myself in him...and the more I did, the worse my hand got. It was like one thing was connected to the other. Like my growing feelings for Adrian came at a price.

I tucked my hair behind my ear. "You should get going. You're missing your gala."

He waited another moment. Almost like he *liked* standing there. Then he looked away from me, jumped down, and helped me off the ladder.

He didn't make a move to leave.

He stopped at Grace's swing and crouched to say hi to her. She beamed at him and her pacifier popped out of her mouth. He tickled her belly and then put her paci back in. Then, instead of leaving, he picked up Harry Puppins from his dog bed and leaned against my dresser, petting him and smiling at me.

Okay...

I wrapped my robe tighter around me. "So I guess I'll just

see you tomorrow?" I said, feeling like I had to fill the silence with something. "Dad's going to embarrass me. I hope you know that."

He just stood there. "You'll be fine."

When I said this to myself, I called bullshit. When *he* said it, I sort of believed him. Maybe because Adrian had a way of making things fine. Or making me forget if they weren't...

Dad wanted me to see the progress he was making on the house. I hadn't been over there since the armoire avalanche.

Sonja and I had talked often since she started two weeks ago. Dad *really* liked her. She'd asked to bring in a professional organizer and a cleaning crew that specialized in biohazards. I gave her anything she wanted. Threw money at it with complete abandon. I either spent it now and maybe put Dad in a better place, or he'd end up spending the money on junk after I was dead—I'd rather spend it now.

She also recommended a therapist who could treat obsessive compulsive disorder, which I guess she thought he had. Dad had been seeing her twice a week.

Dad seemed pretty excited about his progress, but I was skeptical. Since I couldn't even toss a bag of garbage without him picking through it, I couldn't imagine Sonja was making much of a dent.

Anyway, the only problem now was I wasn't making enough videos to earn enough money to keep supporting it all. Not for what I needed to accomplish over the next twelve months.

I'd done three vlogs since my Jesus's Abs one. The first one was me dying my hair and not mentioning a word about Adrian. I know it was crazy just based on how much everyone wanted to hear about him. But honestly, I wanted that side of my life to just be *mine*.

Adrian wasn't some anecdote to me. He was real. What I was feeling for him was real. It felt like I was cheapening it to invite millions of strangers to join in on it for their entertainment. But the hair-dying video tanked. My viewers were *pissed*. People were so thirsty to hear about Jesus's Abs I was afraid I was going to lose subscribers if I didn't fold, and I couldn't afford to not make money. So the next two videos were just me recapping my days with Adrian, acting all starry-eyed and in puppy love—which to be honest wasn't even acting. Those had some of the highest views since me and Drake. So as little as I liked sharing the private side of my life, it was a necessary evil.

I had something pretty earth-shattering planned for Monday's post and it couldn't come a moment too soon. I needed the money. I had enough for my day-to-day living—and Dad's and Brent's. And for years I'd been setting aside enough to cover my medical care in the event I got sick. But I needed to think further into the future than that.

I wanted to be able to provide my family with a modest income to live on for the rest of their lives. I'd been to my accountant yesterday to set up a trust for Grace, Brent, Dad, and Annabel—with stipulations that she pass a monthly drug test to qualify for the funds, and she check in to rehab if she didn't. It wasn't foolproof, but at least she'd have some accountability.

I had a stipend arranged to keep Sonja on staff after I passed, and I designated a large lump sum to my charity.

I made sure I was registered as an organ donor. My DNA defects didn't rule my organs out for transplant. They could take the whole lot of it—and I hoped they did.

I still needed to make my funeral arrangements, but I wasn't quite ready for that one yet. I'd pay that off too though. I wouldn't leave any of the details for anyone else to have to deal with when I went.

I'd been executing this depressing end-of-life checklist every day for the last two weeks while Adrian was at work. And then at night, I'd let it all go. I'd have dinner with him, and he'd make me forget everything. He made my shitty world blur around me until there was nothing but him and those gorgeous green eyes and I didn't even want to go home at night. I just wanted to stay with him and keep feeling what he made me feel. I wanted to be still.

He pushed off the dresser and put Harry Puppins back in his bed. "You want me to give Grace a bottle while you get dressed?" he asked, folding up the ladder and leaning it against the wall.

I shook my head. "You have to get back. You'll miss—"

And then I saw it.

I hadn't expected Adrian to come over. I hadn't picked up my place yet—which meant the pair of dirty grandma underwear I'd dropped when I'd changed out of my clothes was still lying sunny-side up between us on the carpet.

I sucked in a horrified gulp of air and looked at Adrian just in time to see that his gaze had followed mine down to the floor.

A hot, red blush seared up my neck. I stared at him in wide-eyed mortification for a split second, and then I dove to snatch my underwear. But when I bent over, I stepped on the wizard sleeve of my robe and a boob popped out. I shrieked and grabbed the rogue breast, but it was too late. He'd seen it. He'd seen *all* of it.

I stood like a statue clutching my robe closed, a hand over my breast like it might escape again of its own free will. "No," I breathed. "No no no. This isn't happening."

"It's okay," he said quickly. "It's not a big deal." The corners of his lips twitched.

I blinked at him. "My life's a damn rom-com..." I whispered. "You're here in a tuxedo and my boobs are loose, just flying around."

He was grinning now and looking *very* amused.

I shook my head at him. "This isn't funny! We just went to second base!"

That did it. He burst out laughing.

I did my best to look indignant, but his laughing was sort of making *me* laugh. I crossed my arms over my chest. "You better forget *everything* you just saw."

He shook his head. "Oh, I don't think that's going to be possible."

"Adrian, I will *kill* you. I am not afraid to go to prison."

He was howling now. "Kill me with what? The gun or the stabby thingy?"

"Adrian!" Gah! "Get out!"

I wrangled him out the door and I could hear him laughing all the way down the hall, back to his gala.

I probably needed at least a full month to be able to face him again.

He gave me about five minutes.

Someone knocked on my door and when I went to look through the peephole, there was a finger over it.

"Who is it?" I asked, already suspecting the answer.

"Room service," he called through the door in a ridiculous falsetto.

I rolled my eyes as I raked the chain off the lock.

He was leaning with his forearm on my door frame, still in his tux.

I crossed my arms. "What? If you're here to laugh at my boob, you can just go back to your thing."

He gave me one of his dazzling grins. "I'm not going back. I brought you something. Let me in and close your eyes."

I wrinkled my forehead. "What? You're not going back?"

"Close. Your. *Eyes.*"

I gave him a look, but I pulled the door open and closed my eyes. I heard him come in, then the sound of my sliding glass door opening. "What are you doing?" I asked, feeling a blast of cold air.

"Don't peek," he said from what sounded like outside.

I heard the door close, and the sound of my curtains yanking shut. When he spoke again, he was standing in front of me. "Okay. You can look."

I opened my eyes to find him smiling down at me like he found me amusing. The whole front of his tuxedo was wet.

"Why are you wet?"

"Go sit on the couch."

"For what?"

He shook his head with a smile. "Go on."

I eyed him, but I went to the sofa and flopped down onto a cushion.

He went into the hallway and brought in a large plastic takeout bag. He took off his tuxedo jacket and draped it over the back of one of my kitchen table chairs. Then he undid his bow tie and unbuttoned his wet shirt and peeled that off too. When he sat down next to me on the sofa, he was in nothing but a white T-shirt and trousers. He leaned over the coffee table, pulling out containers. Then he opened one and held up a humongous orange lobster and waggled it. "Lobster?"

I snorted. "You brought me a lobster?"

"And caviar, prawns, baklava, petit fours—I even brought the garnish for you. Look." He plunged his arms into the bag and pulled out a halved watermelon with the name of the fund-raiser carved into it and held it proudly.

I laughed. "Oh my God, they're never going to let you back into the Depot."

He set it in the middle of my coffee table like an out-of-place centerpiece.

He was *still* smiling.

"You better stop," I said, giving him side-eye.

"What? I'm just thinking of something funny Lenny said."

"You are such a liar."

Maybe I should start doing a Kegel every time I embarrass myself in front of him, get something out of all this humiliation. Two weeks and I'll be able to snap a man in half with my pelvic floor.

"You know, I've seen you topless before. In the painting." He nodded to the wall.

"Okay, that is *not* the same thing. That's a drawing and he t liberties—"

"No, he didn't. Frankly, he didn't do you justice." He glanced at me. "At least not on the side I saw." He grinned and finished emptying the bag.

I had to hide my smile in my hand.

"So what do you feel like eating?" he asked.

"Uh, all of it? But you're sure you don't need to go back?"

He took the lid off a to-go cup of drawn butter. "I think the fund-raiser can carry on without me."

"Are you just trying to make me feel better that you had to leave to make sure I didn't die attached to a ceiling fixture?"

He laughed.

I drew my eyebrows down. "How did you get here so fast?" I looked over all the stuff he brought. "I called you and you came in, like, ten minutes. How'd you get all this ready and steal a garnish and still make it to rescue me in under an hour?"

He cleared his throat and talked to the food he was setting out. "I was already on my way with it."

I pulled my face back. "You were on your way home when I called you? Your thing started at six thirty. It's seven fifteen. Did you just show up with a bag and start pillaging? You weren't planning on staying?"

"I guess not."

I watched him opening more containers. "*Why?*"

He didn't answer me for a long moment. "I just figured you had a rough day and might want to watch TV with someone."

I blinked at him.

Those tickets were $200 apiece. I *checked*. I wanted one so I could go with him—not that he'd invited me to. But I would have shamelessly crashed the place if the thing hadn't been sold-out.

There was a silent auction and a raffle, live music and dancing. The event ran until midnight. He rented a tux. And he just... *left*? To watch TV with *me*?

Either he really hated hanging out with Marcus or he *really* liked *The Office*.

Or hey, maybe he has a massive crush on me, can't stand to be away from me, had to get back to me as soon as possible.

Ha *ha*.

"Do you want to see my surprise?" he asked.

"This isn't it?"

He smiled and got up. I watched him draw the curtain back on my sliding glass door.

My hands flew to my mouth.

There, on the tiny snow-covered bistro table on my balcony, was an ice sculpture of a swan.

"Came right off the dessert buffet." He put a hand up. "Don't worry, I didn't steal it. I donated a couple hundred bucks for it. They were more than happy to let me have it."

I shook my head. "You carried that up here?" I breathed.

"It'll be there until spring. Every time you see it, I want you to remember that I put that dripping ice cube in my coupe for you."

My heart tugged. It reached out for him uselessly like arms trying to stretch across an ocean.

He was perfect. He was perfect in every single way.

All I ever wanted was to live. To grow old and have more time. And now I had something else I wanted as much as that.

I wanted *him*.

And neither one was probably ever going to be mine.

## CHAPTER 14

# THESE PEOPLE ARE EATING DINNER IN A DUMP AND YOU'LL NEVER BELIEVE WHY!

## VANESSA

We pulled into Dad's driveway. It was 6:30 on Saturday night. We'd left Grace with Yoga Lady. I didn't want her to breathe the black mold and dust mites that Adrian and I had signed up to endure for the next two hours.

Adrian put the car in park and looked up at the house. "Are we really eating dinner in there?" he asked grimly.

I looked over at him. "I thought you said you were willing to get one of the heps with me?"

He snorted.

I pulled my Carmex out of my bra. "I don't trust Dad to cook food that won't kill us, but I trust Sonja," I said, applying the lip balm and putting the cap back before tucking it back into my shirt. "I think it'll be okay."

I peered back through the windshield. The Christmas lights

were on. I'd like to say this was Dad being festive, but this was actually Dad being festive like four years ago and they never came down. For just one month of the year, Dad's house *didn't* piss off the neighbors.

"What does your dad do for a living?" he asked.

I shook my head. "Now? Nothing. Not really. He used to be an accountant. He's really smart. Then he found out that he could sell all the random stuff he liked to collect, so he quit his job to hawk things on eBay and Craigslist full-time. Dad's not very handy, though, and most of what he tried to sell was junk, so he never made enough. That's when the whole clutter thing went from bad to worse, because everything became something that could be 'fixed and sold.'" I put my fingers in quotes. "He'd bring anything home. A toilet sitting on the curb. Broken luggage, someone's old ice skates."

"Bikes."

I scoffed. "Soooo many bikes."

I sighed. "I know I give him a lot of shit, but I think he did the best he could." I paused. "It wasn't easy living through the things he did. I think enough tragedy can unravel anyone."

Adrian turned to me. "I think it depends on who you are. You know, you've been through all the same things he has and you're not unraveled."

I smiled softly at him. "Yeah. Well, I think that stuff tends to get worse the older you get. Let's just hope I live long enough for it to really hit me. Turn me into that eccentric aunt who wraps things from her house to give away as gifts at Christmas."

He laughed.

I nudged him. "Hey, so when do I get to meet your crazy

family?" I asked. "It doesn't seem fair that mine gets all the attention."

"My whole family's in Nebraska now. My mom moved there with her husband and my grandma in October. Richard and Mom invited me down for Christmas, but I'm not going."

"How come?"

He shook his head. "I don't feel comfortable. I don't like Richard."

"Oh yeah? Why not? Is he a dick?"

He laughed a little at my joke. Then he paused for a moment before letting out a long breath. "Richard is my dad."

My mouth fell open. "What? Like... the dad who took off and left the family? *That* dad?"

He nodded. "That dad. They got back together a year ago. They're remarried now."

I blinked at him. "Oh my God," I breathed.

He scoffed. "Yeah."

"I mean... *why*? What was his reason for leaving in the first place?"

He shook his head at the windshield. "He had an affair with some woman he worked with. Left us for her. It didn't last."

I sat back in my seat. "Wow."

"Yeah. Mom was a mess. For *years*. In and out of depression. I had to do everything for her. Pay the bills, clean the house. I couldn't even go to college out of state. I couldn't leave her."

I shook my head. "Did he pay support?"

He nodded. "He did. I'll give him that. Paid child support and alimony—kept paying even when he didn't have to.

Tried to keep up a relationship with me, but I had zero interest in it."

I blew air through pursed lips. "Yeah, I can see that." I peered up at him. "It's kind of romantic though. That they circled back to each other."

He stared at me.

"What?"

His jaw twitched. "You sound like Mom."

I shrugged. "Well, it's true. People fuck up. And it sounds like he realized it. Maybe they were soul mates and neither of them ever found that same happiness with anyone else."

"I don't *believe* in soul mates," he said, his tone clipped.

I scoffed. "Well, Dad doesn't believe in expiration dates, but that doesn't mean they don't exist."

He barked out a dry laugh.

"Is your mom happy?" I asked.

He looked at the windshield and nodded reluctantly. "Yes. I guess she is."

I shrugged again. "Good. You should forgive him."

His head snapped back to me. "*What?*"

"Why not? I mean, you don't have to *like* him. You don't have to trust him or forget what he did or follow him on Facebook. But he's in your mom's life now and holding on to this vendetta is only going to hurt her and your grandmother. I mean, you won't even go see them for Christmas? Why? Because *he's* there? Fuck him. Go see your family."

He blinked at me.

I shook my head. "Wow. Somebody in this car never had to ignore their drunk misogynistic uncle at Thanksgiving, and it really shows." I pivoted in my seat to look at him head-on.

"Adrian. Hate is exhausting. Life is too short to hate. Let it go. And while you're at it, it might help you to try to see him as a whole person who isn't all black or white. You know, he can be your dad who loves you and your mom, *and* someone who did something really crappy to hurt you guys once. He *can* be both."

I watched some sort of internal struggle move across his face. "So just…what? Show up for Christmas?"

"Yeah. Why not? I'll go with you if you want. If it sucks, we'll leave."

He wrinkled his forehead. "You'll come?"

I shrugged. "Sure."

He nodded at the house. "What about your dad? Won't he be alone for Christmas if you're not here?"

I waved him off. "Let Brent tap in. I'll go see him Christmas Eve. I'll take him to Denny's or something for breakfast. He'll be thrilled. We can leave after that and make it to Nebraska for dinner."

"You wouldn't mind spending Christmas with me?"

"I was gonna spend it with you anyway."

The corner of his lip twitched.

He peered at me for a long moment. "Okay." He nodded. "All right. I'll go, I'll try it."

There was something instantly softer about his face. Like deep inside he wanted permission to let this go, but he couldn't give it to himself.

Adrian didn't change gears very quickly, I realized. That was part of what made him great. His devotion to the people he cared about was unwavering. It made him steady and reliable. But it also made him inflexible and prone to hang on to things that weren't good for him for much longer than he should.

"You know, maybe you should talk to someone," I said. "A good therapist could help you work through some of this stuff."

He shook his head. "Mom went to therapy for years, and it never seemed to make anything better."

"How do *you* know it never made anything better? Maybe without it she would have been a million times worse."

He didn't answer.

"Anyway, this'll be fun," I said. "We should pick out an audiobook to listen to on the ride. Stop at the gas station and get, like, a million snacks."

He smiled at me.

I was actually *excited* to go to *Nebraska*. I was over here hoping his mom's house only had one guest bed and we'd have to share.

Then the corners of my lips fell the slightest bit.

He wouldn't always be single. And when he wasn't, I wouldn't be going with him anywhere. Probably ever. He'd have a girlfriend for that.

*What if he started dating again?*

This thought killed me. What if he went full man-whore in a delayed Rachel-induced breakup death spiral? Would I be there in my dinky apartment listening to him bang other women through the wall?

The thought broke my heart a little. It was so dumb, but I felt betrayed even thinking about it. It felt like cheating.

I couldn't imagine him being someone else's. I knew technically he wasn't mine. But in practice he was. Not in all the ways that mattered. Not in enough ways to be enough. But he *was* mine.

At least for now.

"What's wrong?" he asked, looking slightly worried. "Your face just got serious."

"If I'm still alive and you're single on my thirtieth birthday, will you marry me?"

He laughed. "What?"

"Will you enter into a marriage pact with me? One year from now, you and I tie the knot if you're single and I'm still alive. We can be one of those Pinterest couples who wears matching flannels and goes to a pumpkin patch to take that engagement photo where we both jump at the same time."

He looked amused. "First of all, you *will* be alive. Second of all, we both know you don't jump."

I twisted my lips. "Right. Good point. And you don't own a flannel. How about the one where it's just our legs and a chalkboard that says, 'she said yes'? Only we could change it to 'he took pity on me'?"

He laughed. "And you're sure that I'm the man for this job?"

"Totally. I'm not explaining my crazy family to someone new. It's way too much work."

He laughed again. "Don't you want to marry for love?"

*Yes. That's why I asked* you.

I took a deep breath and changed the subject. "Hey, sorry about your office yesterday."

He gazed at me with those gorgeous green eyes, and I remembered how he'd gathered my hands in his and my heart had done a somersault.

Adrian never touched me. I mean, of course he didn't, we

were just friends. But it had calmed me down like a gentle whisper for my screaming soul.

I understood why Grace preferred him. His arms were everything safe and whole. And I hated that the only time I got to be in them was when I was breaking my own rules and mourning my own fate.

"Do you want to talk about it?" he asked.

I paused a moment and looked out the window at the snowy lawn.

"You know how when you ask someone what they'd do if the sun was headed for Earth and they had twenty-four hours left to live? And everyone always says they'd be with family, eat their favorite food, go someplace they've always wanted to go? Nobody ever says they'd spend the last day curled up in bed crying—because they wouldn't. That's not what anyone wants to do with their final hours." I looked back at him. "I mean, yeah, you'd cry. And you'd be scared because you're gonna die. And you'd find yourself looking at the sky throughout the day, knowing what's coming because that's just human nature. But for the most part, you'd just enjoy the time you had left. Especially because there's nothing you could do about it. There's no escape, nowhere to hide. So why bother? Obsessing over the end is pointless." I held his gaze. "If you spend your life dwelling on the worst possible thing, when it finally happens, you've lived it twice. I don't want to live the worst things twice. I try *really* hard not to think about the bad stuff. But every once in a while I'm human and I look up." I studied him quietly. "Yesterday was just one of those days that I looked at the sun."

He peered at me, something gentle on his face. "You

are a remarkable woman, Vanessa Price, you know that?" he said quietly.

I smiled a little. "We should probably go inside," I said. "Dad's waiting." I grabbed my purse. "Remember, it's easier if you breathe through your mouth."

Adrian gave me a reassuring smile and got out of the car.

We stood on the front porch while I knocked and the door opened a few seconds later.

Dad beamed at us with a smiling Sonja right behind him. "Welcome to my humble abode," Dad said with a flourish. "Please, enter."

He moved from the mouth of the doorway, and my jaw fell open.

The first thing that hit me was the light. Dad's house was always dim. It reminded me of the Upside Down in *Stranger Things*, all eerie and gray. But the entry was lit. Warm. And when I stepped inside, I saw why.

The house was *spotless*. The cleanest I'd ever seen it. I peered around the living room from the entry in total shock. "Dad..." I breathed.

The piles were gone. All the trash and clutter were gone. I could see carpet—and it was *clean*. New, actually. I think he'd even painted. The flat-screen TV that had been propped against a wall had been mounted. Someone had framed and hung a painting that Melanie had done in grade school that used to be stuck to the wall with a thumbtack. There was a new-looking playpen next to the sofa with a crocheted baby blanket carefully folded and draped over the side. And the smell—there wasn't one. Not a bad one anyway. The house smelled like simmering tomato sauce.

I grabbed Adrian's arm and clutched it like my legs might give out.

Dad stood rocking back on his heels, beaming at the house.

Sonja smiled at me. "We talked a lot about goals. And do you want to know what your dad's number one goal is, Vanessa?"

I looked at Dad, so overwhelmed I felt out of breath.

He nodded at the playpen. "I want Grace to have sleepovers at her grandpappy's house."

I started to laugh. And then, just as quickly, I started to cry.

I don't think I ever really believed that my family was capable of being okay. In any sense. It's the thing that terrified me most about being sick, the thing that kept me from being at peace with dying. But maybe Dad *could* change. And if he could change, maybe Annabel and Brent could too. And if they were okay, Grace would be okay. Then I could go. I could focus on me and what time I had left, if that's what was happening, and ALS would take one less thing. It would take my life, but maybe it wouldn't take my family with me when I went.

Adrian leaned down and whispered in my ear. "I thought you said this place was a shithole..."

I did a laugh-cry, and he gave me a sideways hug.

Dad hung up my purse. "I made goulash for dinner, just like old times."

I blinked at my dad through the tears, standing there in his clean house. And then I cleared the space between us and hugged him.

We weren't really an affectionate family. I didn't see the hug coming and neither did he. But we were both happy to be in it and for a flicker of a second, I was a little girl again.

I broke away from him, wiping under my eyes as Brent came around the corner with Joel, holding a martini. "Oh my God. Oh my GOD." Brent gestured dramatically to the house. "I mean, I saw the dump trucks outside, but I thought they were bringing things *in.*"

I laughed.

Brent put a hand up. "Dad, you should be *very* proud of yourself."

Dad beamed, looking a little misty-eyed. "I have a special surprise. To the living room, chop-chop." He clapped his hands.

He herded us over to the sofa and when I saw what he was leading us to, I gasped.

On the coffee table were our family photo albums. The ones Dad said he couldn't find. The ones I was worried were lost in the hoard, never to be seen again.

"You found them?" I breathed, picking one up.

"I did," Dad said proudly. "With the help of this lovely lady, of course."

Sonja smiled, sitting on a chair that used to be stacked with board games. "He's the one who put in the work. I've been very impressed with him."

Dad practically glowed.

Dad was always a hundred times prouder of himself than he should be. Delusions of grandeur abounded. But this time he deserved to be proud.

I sat on the sofa and opened a photo album with reverence. This was the one with pictures of Mom. My eyes started to tear up again as I flipped through the pages. Mom sitting in a lawn chair, and me and Mel playing in a kiddie pool on the grass. Halloween, Mom dressed like a biker chick, smiling with a jack-o'-lantern. Birthdays with the Baskin-Robbins ice cream cakes she always liked to get us. The house was clean back then too.

There were pictures of Dad, twenty-five years younger. He had sideburns and clear eyes.

He wasn't broken yet.

I wondered how long the ripple effect lasted after someone died. Maybe until everyone who knew them was dead too? Or was it something that went on for generation after generation because the damage was handed down, touching each new person and changing them, even if they don't know why?

Something told me it was that one.

Grace would never know her aunt Melanie, but the loss of her would ruin her just the same—because that loss ruined her mother.

Annabel used drugs to dull the memory of what she witnessed at the hands of ALS. She couldn't do what I did— live a good life in spite of it. She needed something to take the edge off the pain and devastation she'd endured. And so her loss was now Grace's loss too. Grace would ride the ripple of it her whole life unless Annabel got clean—or unless I took Grace out of the pool. Got her adopted by another family who didn't share this tragedy.

I shook it off.

There was no point in thinking about it. I'd spent enough time dwelling on things I couldn't change today. I didn't want to look at the sun again.

Adrian sat down next to me, so close his thigh pressed into mine. He peered down at the album. "She looks just like you," he said.

I nodded. "Yeah. She did," I said quietly.

And just like me, her disease was invisible—but it was there, lying in wait inside of her, ready to spring its trap.

Mom had been a dancer. She taught at an academy. Losing her ability to do the one thing she'd loved the most, one muscle-withering day at a time, would have been extra cruel. It was a reminder that some things are worse than death—losing the things worth living for are worse than death.

Traveling was what *I* loved.

I never saved anything for the long run. I didn't go to college. I couldn't afford it back then anyway, and why waste my life sitting in a room working on a degree when I'd die before I'd get to use it?

I didn't watch my cholesterol or exercise. I didn't worry about where I'd be in ten years. I made long-term plans for my family, not myself. But I did plan for *this*.

Back when I'd started my quest to travel the globe, I'd researched all the best cities in the world for wheelchair users. And in all my journeys, I didn't visit a single one. Barcelona, Vienna, Singapore, Sydney, Berlin—these were my things to look forward to. To keep living a life worth living and having new adventures for as long as possible. I'd squeeze every drop of happiness from my time on this Earth. I'd cherish every second.

Especially now that the seconds were likely running out.

Dinner was amazing. For the first time in longer than I could recall, I didn't feel worried or angry or resentful toward my dad. I just got to enjoy him. I got to hear him tell his funny stories and laugh and remember how charming he could be. And the best thing of all was that Adrian saw it too. I could tell. Dad would say something witty and Adrian would look over at me and I'd see it in his eyes. It was like taking someone to a magical place from your childhood and having them see all the same wonder that you did once, even though it didn't hold the same power over them. And I couldn't explain how precious this was to me.

I wanted to be proud of Dad. And there was nobody in the world that I wanted to feel that way in front of more than Adrian.

He was so normal and grounded and had all his shit together, and I was like one five-alarm fire after another. Debris in a cyclone of chaos. I knew he liked to hang out with me because I was fun—and I *really* tried to stay fun in front of him. But the more time he spent with me, the more he saw. And most of what he saw was just sad. To share and celebrate some normality felt like a gift.

After dinner Adrian stood shoulder to shoulder with me, helping with dishes. Dad and Sonja had cooked, so we cleaned. They were in the living room with Joel and Brent— who didn't do anything to earn the right to relax, but that was typical.

Adrian looked over at me. "You should be really proud of what he's done here," he said quietly.

I nodded. "I am."

It wasn't the whole house. My old room was still home

to half a dozen bikes that Dad had insisted he keep and sell. And the upstairs hadn't been touched yet. But the progress was beyond encouraging.

Sonja had explained to us that the process of cleaning the house was bigger than just getting rid of things. It was helping Dad understand why he felt like he had to acquire them in the first place. Her plan of attack wasn't just to clean up. It was for him to relearn behaviors and find other ways to cope with the stresses that caused the compulsion to begin with. And one of the core aspects of that was him finding a different job. One that didn't require him to collect things for a living. She didn't have to tell *me* that was a slippery slope, I'd seen it with my own eyes. Dad was looking for accounting work again. He had an interview on Monday.

I dried a plate and set it on the counter. "You know, this wouldn't have happened if you hadn't recommended Sonja."

She had clearly been the catalyst for this life-altering change in Dad. But Adrian was the reason Sonja was here.

He made me feel like I had a partner. Like I didn't have to be the one to always figure things out and know what to do—and I *always* had to be the one to figure things out and know what to do. Even with Grace he'd picked up the load. It was like she belonged to both of us now. We coparented her, and it all just happened so naturally and effortlessly.

I'd meant what I said yesterday at his office: I had lots of friends. But they didn't know me like Adrian did. Nobody did. Drake knew the stories I told him. I was always honest with him and we talked about everything. But it was different from living them alongside me like Adrian did. Telling someone about Dad's house was different from going there with me to rescue him from under an armoire.

There was something eternally endearing about a person who could see what Adrian had seen and not run or judge you. It made me feel safe and stable. Like I'd been drifting in the wind and I'd found a strong, deep-rooted tree to perch on and take sanctuary in. I felt like I could be any level of fucked up or crazy and he'd still be there, holding me.

We finished the dishes and headed into the living room. Adrian excused himself and went to the bathroom. The second we were alone, Dad started in on me. "So, how's it going with the lawyer?" He bounced his bushy eyebrows.

Of course. It was only a matter of time.

I shook my head. "We're just friends, Dad," I said quietly.

He barked out a laugh. "You're kidding me, right?" He leaned forward conspiratorially. "The man is besotted. *Look* at him," he whispered.

Sonja smiled into her coffee cup and Joel nodded.

"He can't keep his eyes off you," Brent whispered. "It's been like watching a tennis match all night—his head going this way, that way, watching you walk around."

I scoffed. "He is *not* watching me."

Dad shook his head. "You'd have to be blind to not see it. Please tell me that I didn't raise a daughter this obtuse."

I narrowed my eyes at him, but I didn't have a chance to reply because Adrian came back down the hall.

Dad smiled theatrically. "We should probably wrap up tonight's activities. I'm sure this strapping young gentleman has a romantic evening planned."

I rolled my eyes and shared a look with Adrian. He just smiled.

"We probably should get going. I don't want to leave Grace longer than we need to," I said, pulling my vibrating cell phone out of my pocket. I didn't recognize the number, but it was local so I swiped up to answer the call. "Hello?"

I sat there listening to what I was being told on the other end of the line.

My heart sank.

It was a police officer calling from a hospital.

My sister was in surgery.

She'd been shot.

## CHAPTER 15

# THE DOCTOR COMES OUT AND EVERYONE IS STUNNED!

## ADRIAN

We were in the waiting room at Royaume Northwestern Hospital. It was 10:00 and we'd been here two hours.

The information had been choppy. Apparently, Annabel had been trespassing, climbing into a window, and the resident of the property shot her. The bullet had gone into her shoulder and the injury wasn't life-threatening. She was in surgery to close the wound and then Vanessa, Brent, and Gerald could see her.

Besides the quick info dump that Vanessa had gotten from the officer who called her, no one had been out to talk to us. As far as I knew, no charges had been brought—yet. In addition to the B and E, they'd found Annabel with several bottles of narcotics in her possession. None was in her name. Where she'd gotten them was anyone's guess, but if she was breaking into this house, she might have broken into others.

Gerald and Sonja were talking quietly. Brent and Joel were on their phones. Vanessa was curled up next to me, sitting in a chair with her head on my shoulder. I had an arm around her and my jacket draped over her. I had to fight the urge to kiss the top of her head.

I had to fight the urge to do a lot of things.

I'd like to say that I'd rather be home in my bed, but if Vanessa wasn't going to be there with me, I was perfectly happy to sit in this chair and hold her here instead.

She'd come to me and not her dad.

She'd retreated into my arms like I was the only safe haven in the world—and I wanted to be that. I realized today that I *always* wanted to be there to receive her. I wanted every opportunity to be useful to her. I craved it. Waited for it. Watched her to see when she might need me to catch her. See her beautiful eyes search a room and zero in on me, a sign to pluck her from her whirling tornado and keep her still.

I was glad to see Gerald was getting his shit together. I was glad for Vanessa's sake. But the thing I realized tonight was that even if he didn't, there was no amount of crazy that she or her family could throw at me to make me change my mind about her.

The doors opened and the doctor came out. As soon as she saw him, Vanessa bolted to her feet and the family crowded him.

The doctor made it brief. "I'm Dr. Rasmussen. She's in recovery. She's stable," he said, his tone flat. "I don't think we'll need to keep her more than a day."

Vanessa looked relieved. "Can we see her?"

He looked down at Vanessa like the question irritated him. "No, you cannot. She's under arrest."

Vanessa's face fell. "What?" she breathed.

Gerald blanched next to me. "Arrested? On what grounds?"

The doctor ignored him. "No visitors, and she'll be released into the Hennepin County jail system," he said, not even trying to hide his disapproval.

My jaw flexed. I didn't like his tone—and I knew *exactly* why he had it.

To him, Annabel was a criminal and a drug addict. And neither thing was his damn business. She was Vanessa's sister and Grace's mother, and he'd better pray to God his prejudices didn't translate into poor care because I'd drag his ass through a malpractice suit the likes of which he'd never seen.

"I'm her attorney," I said, my voice clipped. "She has a Sixth Amendment right to counsel. I'll need to speak with her." I looked at him levelly. "And I sincerely hope when I do, I find she's receiving nothing but *exemplary* medical care."

I watched his eyes narrow.

I'd seen it all. Every sort of subtle cruelty subjected on criminal patients. Making them wait on pain meds, using the largest needle possible for blood draws so they hurt more, treating and streeting them—discharging them early and to the patient's detriment just to get them off their floor. I knew all the shit they pulled.

And now he knew I knew.

"Fine," the doctor said stiffly. "Show your ID at the nurses' station. Give her another twenty minutes to come out of anesthesia or she won't be much of a conversationalist," he added. And then he left.

Vanessa looked up at me. She was starting to cry.

I put my hands on her shoulders. "Hey, don't do that."

Her bottom lip trembled. "This is my fault. I turned off her phone. She was probably cold and hungry. She went back to her old house to climb into a window because it was negative five outside and she couldn't even call me for help, and now she's going to prison with a bullet wound."

Brent cleared his throat. "Actually, this is *my* fault." He sucked air through his teeth. "She was sorta staying with me and Joel after you said she couldn't be at Dad's. I kicked her out this morning after my Tiffany bracelet went missing."

Vanessa blinked at him. "She's been with *you* this whole time?"

"She called me after she crashed the car." He made a face.

Vanessa's jaw dropped open. "Why didn't you tell me?!"

"You know how you get! And anyway, I gave her very firm boundaries and enforced them when she fucked up—and you know what? No." He crossed his arms. "This isn't my fault. It's not your fault or Dad's fault. She's a hot fucking mess and that's on her. Maybe her dumb ass needs to go to prison."

"Brent!" Vanessa blanched. "She needs help! Not to be incarcerated!"

I put my hand up. "And she'll get help. She's not going to prison. I'll make sure of it."

Vanessa looked back at me with a sniffle. "How?"

"The house she was breaking into—you said she lived there once? It was her old house?"

She nodded.

"Did they evict her? Or did she just leave?"

Vanessa shook her head. "I think she just left."

"How long ago?"

She wiped under her eyes. "Three? Maybe four weeks?"

"Okay. Then she's still a resident of the property and she had a legal right to be on the premises. She wasn't trespassing—in fact, I'd venture to say the shooter has more to worry about than she does. She'll be the one dropping charges."

"But what about the pills? She had all those stolen pills on her. Won't they say she was selling or something? Say she was a dealer?"

"If anything else sticks, I have a favor I can call in. I'll get the prosecution to agree on a treatment program in lieu of time. I'll have her arraigned bedside. She'll never step foot in a police station, I promise you. She's in the best place for her right now. She's safe, and she's going to get help. I'll take care of this. You don't have to worry about it."

I saw the stress drain away from her beautiful expression. The relief.

She trusted me. She believed me when I said I'd make things okay—and I would.

I was good at my job. But seeing that she knew I was capable of what I said I would do made me prouder of my law degree than any court case I'd ever won, or any article ever written about it. Her opinion of me meant more to me than anything. And her advice did too.

I'd never in a million years have agreed to Christmas at Mom and Richard's if it weren't because Vanessa said I should. I trusted her implicitly. Especially when it came to things that would make me happy. I was beginning to realize that I couldn't even think outside of my own limited world views to know what those things *were*.

I was unmovable. I didn't like change. I didn't like to adapt. It was easier to decide to hate something or someone and stick with it, because the other option would be to expose myself to the unknown or open myself up to be hurt. And she was right. Why hate Richard? What was the point? It was making everyone unhappy. Including me. And I don't think I ever would have landed on this realization if she hadn't taken me there.

She peered up at me with wet eyes, and I put a hand on her smooth cheek and brushed a tear off her face with my thumb. "I'll go speak with Annabel, wrap this up so we can get you home."

Gerald looked pleased with himself. "I told you it was nice to have a lawyer in the family—"

"Dad!" Vanessa glared at him.

"It's ridiculous," he said, going on unfazed. "Trying to lock up an innocent nineteen-year-old girl, shot for climbing into a window in her *own* house. This government has nothing better to do than mess with tax-paying citizens simply living their lives. I'm going to write the governor a strongly worded letter and tell him where he can shove it."

Brent sighed dramatically. "Of course. Great idea. Right up there with cutting your own bangs. Well, I'll be in the parking lot smoking stray cigarette butts if anyone needs me." He hoisted his backpack, grabbed Joel by the hand, and left.

Vanessa looked back at me, exasperated, and I smiled at her.

I liked Brent. And his flaws and eccentricities aside, Gerald was starting to grow on me too.

He loved his family. He loved his daughters and he loved Grace, and I found it very hard to dislike him, no matter how off the wall his opinions were—at dinner he had announced that the moon landing was a hoax.

I gave Vanessa's arm a squeeze and headed to the nurses' station.

This was the second time I'd met Annabel, and even after half an hour of getting her groggy side of the story, I *still* hadn't met her. She was coming out of anesthesia and she was drugged up—either by her own hand, or by the hospital. Either way, I think she barely registered the encounter. I was glad Vanessa didn't get to see her. It would have upset her. Her sister was handcuffed to the bed.

I spoke with the head nurse and informed her that the patient had a high tolerance to narcotics, which should be taken into account when managing her pain. I also made it *very* clear that I expected her to be made comfortable and that I would be closely monitoring her care.

After I was done, I drove Vanessa home. Gerald and Sonja had their own car and left with Joel and Brent when we did. Vanessa looked spent. We got Grace from Yoga Lady and I carried her to Vanessa's place and came inside on the premise that I'd help put the baby down for the night, but the truth was I didn't want to leave her.

I hated the walls between us. The physical ones and ones you couldn't see.

I wanted to ask Vanessa to stay the night at my place—which was ridiculous because I didn't have a guest bedroom. But I wanted to ask her. And I knew if I did, she would. She was always about distraction and fun. She'd probably squeal about sleepovers and accept my invitation and make me paint my nails and do mud masks—and I didn't even care. I'd do it. I'd put her in my bedroom with Grace and I'd take the couch…

But it was a bad idea for me.

This wasn't a woman I was just friends with—even if she was just friends with *me*. Everything with Vanessa meant something. And every time she gave me more of herself, I found it difficult to give it back. If I got to wake up tomorrow morning and see her there, every day that I couldn't would be that much emptier than before.

That's why I couldn't ask her to stay over. It would just make this harder on me, blur lines. Lines that she'd placed there for a reason. Lines she'd made clear she didn't want moved.

Vanessa went to the bathroom to get into her pajamas while I changed Grace's diaper. When she came out, she'd pulled her hair into a ponytail and washed her face. She had on a maroon Vance Refrigeration shirt and some polka-dot pajama pants, and she smelled like toothpaste and some sort of flowery soap or lotion.

It felt like I should be getting changed too. Getting ready to go to bed with her. The feeling was so casual and natural I almost had to remind myself that I didn't live here—even if it felt like I did.

I wondered what it would be like to be with her in the middle of the night. To sleep next to her, even if we never touched. Waking up with Grace to let Vanessa sleep, hearing Vanessa softly breathing and being able to see her as I opened my eyes, tuck a blanket around her. Know that she and Grace were safe and protected because I would never let anything happen to them…

Those late hours were forbidden to me. They were as forbidden to me as kissing her. And I wanted them. I wanted the privilege of them.

I was starting to feel a building desperation. Like I knew in my soul we were supposed to be more than this and I didn't know how to make her know it too.

The longing was beginning to feel all consuming. And it was only going to get worse, because every day I spent with her it already did.

I laid Grace down in her crib and Vanessa came up beside me and sighed quietly. "You know, most people who see a train wreck a mile ahead have the sense to get off the train," she said tiredly. "Not you. Now you have a Price for a client."

"I don't mind helping," I said, straightening and turning to her.

She peered up at me. "I wish there was something I could do to thank you for everything you've done for me."

"I *like* doing things for you."

Her face went a little soft. "Because you're a fixer. It's your way of being in control. But you know, not everything can be fixed. You can't always make everything better, Adrian."

When I didn't reply, she changed the subject. "How was she? When you saw her. Was Annabel okay?"

I crossed my arms. "Disoriented. A little scared maybe. But she'll be fine."

She shook her head. "Will she? What if this wasn't the wake-up call we're hoping it is? What if being shot isn't actually her rock bottom?"

"There's nothing you can do to get her there. Just take care of Grace and focus on you."

She bit her lip and paused for a long moment. "I saw the adoption attorney yesterday morning."

I smiled. "Oh yeah? What did she say?"

She looked away from me. "She said if I can get Annabel to sign over her rights, I could have Grace placed with a family in the next few months."

This news hit me like a slug to the chest.

"What?" I breathed. "I thought *you* were adopting her."

She shook her head and turned back to me. "Adrian, I might not be around in a year." Her chin quivered again. "I *can't* be her mommy." She choked on the last word.

I looked down at Grace and felt an ache in my heart that I had no right feeling.

When my eyes came back to Vanessa's, they were anguished. "Adrian, I have to give her the best chance at stability. I hope Annabel gets clean. I hope she *stays* clean. But if she can't...my life isn't conducive to motherhood. Especially single motherhood. I have to do what's best for her."

I never thought about what being a parent might mean for Vanessa's career. She'd have to get back to the road eventually. I knew what she was doing wasn't sustainable, and it wasn't realistic to drag an infant all over the globe while Vanessa made videos. It was hard enough taking the baby to the *store*. I couldn't imagine putting Grace on international flights and trying to keep her on a routine while Vanessa traveled. But give her up?

I dragged a hand down my mouth.

What could I even say? I wasn't a member of the family. I wasn't Grace's dad. I wasn't even Vanessa's boyfriend. I was just the neighbor—some guy she'd met a few weeks ago who babysat sometimes. This was none of my business.

So why did it feel like something was being taken from me without my permission?

She wiped at the tears on her face and I saw the switch coming. The effort to redirect and think or do something that didn't make her sad.

Looking away from the sun.

"Hey," she said. "What do you think of a sleepover?"

I drew my brows down. "What?"

"Here. Tonight. My sofa has a pullout bed. It could be fun. We could stay up late watching *The Office* and do mud masks."

I almost had to laugh at the irony.

I shook my head. "I wish I could. But that really wouldn't be appropriate."

Her face fell. "Oh. Right." She tucked a strand of hair behind her ear. "I get it."

We stood there a moment, a weird heaviness between us. It lingered like steam from a shower.

I didn't want to go home. But being in her apartment with the lights dimmed and her barefoot and braless and asking me to stay the night was dangerous ground.

I was keenly aware of the potential to get hurt here. I knew I was falling for a woman who didn't want to be pursued. And continuing to put myself in intimate situations that made me wish she *did* wasn't good for me. But at the same time, I didn't want to leave. I didn't want to miss anything. She made me never want to close my eyes around her. I didn't even want to blink. I realized it at my office and on that ladder yesterday, her perfume dancing around me like lightning bugs flickering in the summer. I realized it laughing with her after her robe malfunction and sitting there next to her at her dad's where I could feel her there like a raging bonfire, she was so warm.

She looked up at me with those big, vulnerable brown eyes and I thought again about kissing her. A part of me wanted to say fuck it and just do it, take the risk, break the rules, forget about the consequences, the possibility of losing her, and just lean in.

I let my gaze fall to her mouth. Her lips looked soft and warm. I could imagine running my hands up her shirt, around her waist, pulling her into me. I wanted to put my nose into her neck, rake fingers in her hair, taste her mouth. I wanted her to touch me.

I stared for only a second before looking anywhere but at her.

She had no idea the power she had over me—and I don't think even *I* realized it until tonight. It was almost comical, Gerald declaring they had a lawyer in the family—because they *did*. I'd do anything she needed. She'd wrapped me around her little finger without even trying.

I'd had clients go to prison for doing something stupid at the behest of some woman and I always shook my head at their gullibility. But now I understood it. I had a feeling Vanessa could call me and ask me to help her move a body and I'd show up five minutes later with rubber gloves and bleach.

I cleared my throat. "I should go."

I grabbed my jacket and let myself out before I said, or worse, *did*, something stupid.

At midnight I lay in my own bed, a foot away from where she was probably lying in hers. It was officially her birthday.

I sent her a text I'd had ready all day. A picture of a salted caramel Nadia Cakes torte that I'd gotten her with a candle in it and a text that read "Hey girl, you up?"

I heard her laugh through the wall.

She texted me, "Fuck yeah, I'm up. Come over."

I sat up and stared at the plaster and brick between us. I wanted to come over. I wanted her to really want me to. And not for a sleepover either.

I replied with a laughing emoji. Then I rolled over and spent the next hour tossing and turning, missing her, trying to fall asleep in the wrong bed.

# CHAPTER 16

# I SHOWED UP TO MY BIRTHDAY PARTY AND YOU'LL NEVER GUESS WHO WAS THERE!

## VANESSA

I spent the morning of my birthday with Dad and Brent. Another Nar-Anon meeting and then out to eat. A meeting wasn't really my idea of a good time, but I wasn't above using my birthday as leverage to make them go. Adrian watched Grace.

He'd wanted to come out with us.

First he offered to make me breakfast. Then when I told him where I was going, he asked me if I wanted him to take me. I said no. There was only so much bullshit I could in good conscience allow him to endure. Dad twice in less than twelve hours, a Nar-Anon meeting, *and* Perkins would probably be the end of this friendship.

I'd gotten back around 11:00 a.m., but Adrian told me he'd keep Grace so I could have a few hours of alone time. He always watched Grace for me while I showered, but I never drew it out. I didn't want to take advantage. A few hours of alone time was probably the best birthday gift I'd ever gotten. I was so freaking excited. I was going to take the world's longest bubble bath.

On top of this, I'd come home to flowers in my apartment. He'd cleaned too. There were vacuum lines on the carpet. He'd made my bed and done all the dishes. He'd even cleaned the bathroom.

I can't tell you the strength it took to keep me from running back to his apartment and tearing off his clothes.

Last night I'd asked him to stay over—I wasn't planning anything scandalous, but if *he'd* initiated something scandalous, I wasn't gonna say no. Instead he'd politely declined before fleeing back to his place as quickly as humanly possible. Then he'd texted me at midnight with a picture of a cake and I'd told him to come over. I wasn't kidding.

He'd sent me a laughing emoji.

It was fucking depressing. I was falling in love with a man who was totally uninterested, because of course I was.

I took my bath and a long nap. Then I got ready and met Adrian at his apartment at 6:00. He'd enlisted Becky to watch Harry Puppins and Grace over at his place while he took me out for my birthday tonight. He assured me Becky was perfectly capable and had plenty of babysitting experience. I think she would have assured me too, but she still couldn't speak around me.

Adrian drove us to Summit Avenue, an upscale neighborhood in St. Paul. The street was peppered with historic mansions, the residences of the railroad magnates and lumber barons of the 1800s. We pulled up to an enormous house, built in 1881 according to the historic landmark plaque on the front.

"Where *are* we?" I asked, peering up through the windshield as he pulled the car into the driveway.

He was grinning. "I'm not going to ruin it."

The door was open, and Adrian let himself in. Unfamiliar voices drifted into the foyer from an adjoining room. The house smelled like something incredible was cooking.

Adrian set my birthday cake down on the credenza and helped me out of my jacket and hung it up. "Hello," he called, shrugging out of his own coat. "We're here."

The first person to clear the corner was the last person I'd expected. It was Malcolm. And he was *filming*.

"Happy birthday, Vanessa!" he said from behind his lens.

I laughed. "Oh my God. What is going *on*?"

"I hope you don't mind that I called him," Adrian said. "I know you're having trouble getting content for your channel, and I figured tonight might be video worthy. I got permission from everyone here. You don't have to use the footage unless you want to. It's up to you."

A second later I understood why he thought I might want it.

A woman came around the corner to greet us.

It was Sloan Monroe.

I actually shrieked.

"Hi!" She gave me a warm hug. "Happy birthday! It's so nice to meet you."

She turned to my companion. "Adrian, it's good to see you again."

He kissed her on the cheek.

I'd seen the pictures of her. The magazine covers and the black-and-white photo on the front of *Sloan In-Between*, the album her husband had dedicated to her. But Sloan was even prettier in person. She had long blond hair and an arm of colorful tattoos. She'd used some sort of shimmery eye shadow that made her brown eyes pop. I didn't get a chance to ask her what it was because the rest of the guests were funneling out behind her. Adrian's cousin Josh, his wife, Kristen, and Sloan's husband, Jason, aka famous Grammy Award–winning musician Jaxon Waters.

I was breathing into my hands. "I can't believe you did this," I whispered.

Adrian smiled at me. "Sloan's making you dinner. Her osso buco recipe from her cookbook. They all came down from Ely just for you. I got the house for the night. A client owes me a favor."

I looked up at him, and tears filled my eyes.

This might be my last birthday. In fact, if family history was any indication, it probably was.

And he'd gone and made it the best one of my life.

Three hours later we'd had dinner and cake and I was sitting in the living room in front of an enormous crackling wood-burning fireplace with Kristen and Sloan. The guys were standing over by the bar talking. I'd sent Malcolm home after they sang happy birthday to me. I appreciated that Adrian had thought to have him here, but I wouldn't be sharing the video.

Adrian had told me once after I had to take a picture with someone at Trader Joe's a few days ago that he didn't know how I dealt with all the lack of anonymity. I dealt with it because it's what made my fight against ALS possible. But Adrian had no such skin in the game.

My following was no small thing. If I shared that video, he would be instantly famous. He'd never be anonymous again. It was one thing for me to talk about a man named Jesus's Abs, but it was something else entirely to put a face on him. He'd be recognized in public, viewers would hunt him down online, they might even show up at his work. Everyone else here was probably used to that. Sloan and Jason for sure, and Josh and Kristen by association. But Adrian still had his privacy. When I explained this to him, he said he was still fine with me sharing the video—but I could tell he'd rather I not. So it was a not. But I loved that Malcolm had gotten the footage. That way I could always remember this day.

I *loved* Adrian's friends. I loved that they came here simply because he asked them to. I loved that they were all so grounded and nice and went completely out of their way to make today special for me. It sort of made me jealous that they were so normal and he had to deal with the shit show that was my posse.

I was slightly drunk. Jason had been making martinis.

Sloan ate the olive out of her drink. "God, it's been so long since I had one of these. I'm still nursing."

"A boy or a girl?" I asked.

She smiled. "Girl. Emma. She's a year now."

I looked at Kristen. "And you guys have, like, what? Four?"

"Yup. Oliver is five. Kimmie and Sarah are ten and twelve, and the baby's one."

I tucked a leg under me. "Wow, who's watching all of them?"

Kristen snorted. "Jason's mom. The woman's a saint." She put her drink on the coffee table and leaned in. "Okay, you have to tell me. How's the penis? Is it big?"

Sloan groaned and sat back in her chair. "Oh God, the penis thing again."

I looked back and forth between them. "What? What's the penis thing?"

Sloan shook her head at her best friend. "They're just friends. She hasn't seen it. Leave her alone."

I put up a hand. "Uh, no, wait, I'm here for this. What's the penis thing?"

"She's here for it, Sloan. Stay out of it." Kristen smiled, sitting on the edge of the sofa.

Sloan rolled her eyes at her.

"Josh has this enormous penis and I have a theory it's hereditary," Kristen said.

My eyes darted to Adrian across the room. "*Really?*" I whispered.

Kristen nodded. "Yup." Then she made a space between her hands to show me, and Sloan started choking on her drink.

Sloan shook her head at her best friend, coughing. "This is so not appropriate."

Kristen blinked at her. "This is important research, Sloan."

I nodded quickly. "I agree, further study is needed."

Kristen laughed, and Sloan looked slightly horrified. I got the feeling flustering Sloan was one of Kristen's hobbies. She seemed very good at it.

I sat back against the sofa. "I would *love* to explore the possibility of Adrian's magic peen. But unfortunately he's not into me."

Kristen and Sloan shared a look.

I glanced back and forth between them. "What?"

Kristen leveled her eyes on me. "I don't know what he tells you, but that dude's whipped."

Sloan was giving me a slow, wide-eyed nod.

I scrunched my forehead. "What? No."

Kristen looked up over me. "He's literally staring at the back of your head right now. He's been staring at you all night."

I looked sideways, but I didn't turn around. "Is it like he's watching a tennis match?" I whispered. "Like, his head goes this way and that way watching me walk around?"

Sloan nodded. "It's *exactly* like he's watching a tennis match. That's really accurate, actually."

"He talked about you for thirty minutes straight on the phone with Josh when he called to ask us to come," Kristen said. "Josh hung up and was all 'Daaaaamn, I've never seen him like that.'"

My heart fluttered a little. And then it remembered it had no reason to.

I let out a sigh. "I really don't think he's interested."

Sloan drew her eyebrows together. "Why?"

*Impending death?*

"My lifestyle isn't conducive to relationships," I said instead.

Kristen nodded. "Oh yeah, the fame thing. That shit sucks. You try dating and you end up with some dude who's obsessed with your dryer lint."

Sloan nodded. "It was hard for Jason too. He didn't even tell me who he was until two weeks after we met. It's not easy."

"Yeah, it's not really that," I said. "Just some stuff I'd rather not talk about."

Sloan smiled gently in a way that told me she followed my channel. "Well, just remember, the universe doesn't give you more than you can handle."

Kristen scoffed. "Yeah it does. It does *all* the time. The universe doesn't give a shit, it's a total asshole."

# CHAPTER 17

# WILL YOUR CRUSH EVER NOTICE YOU? TAKE THIS QUIZ!

## ADRIAN

I watched the women huddled together in the living room. "What do you think they're talking about?"

Jason took a swallow of his drink. "Well, looks like Kristen has activated my wife's nervous eye twitch, so I'm going to say it's something inappropriate."

Kristen threw her hands up. "It's science, Sloan!"

Vanessa laughed and peered over at me, her pretty eyes twinkling.

I grinned at her. "What are you ladies doing?" I called.

Vanessa twisted to smile at me over the back of the couch. "Summoning the devil to Eastwick. Don't come over here."

Josh chuckled and handed me an old-fashioned.

"Just one," I said, taking it. "I'm driving."

"I'm glad you called," Josh said. "We should get together more often. Come up to Ely and see the new house." He nodded at the girls. "Bring Vanessa."

I looked over at her and smiled. I'd like to bring her. I'd like to bring Vanessa anywhere. She made me proud to know her. She was exactly what her YouTube channel said she was—a social butterfly. A woman you could put in any situation and she'd charm the pants off whoever she was with.

Vanessa was effervescent. I'd never met a person that I could describe that way, but it was true. She glowed. Energy came off her and illuminated everything and everyone around her.

It wasn't until I noticed that Jason was talking to the side of my face that I realized I was staring at her. "I'm sorry, what?" I asked, looking back at him.

"I was just saying I'm glad you didn't pull out all these stops on your date with Sloan or my wife might have married you instead of me."

I chuckled. "I never stood a chance. To this day, I have never had a woman run out of a date faster."

Jason laughed. His wife looked up at the sound, and he winked at her.

"How long have you two been dating?" Jason asked.

"We're not," I said, talking into my tumbler. "We're just friends."

Josh snorted. "Are you sure?"

"Vanessa's not interested in dating," I said.

Josh laughed. "My wife told me the same thing once." He nodded to the vestibule. "Hey, I think there's some mistletoe hanging by the front door." He bounced his eyebrows.

I didn't want Vanessa to kiss me just because we were

standing under mistletoe. I didn't want her to kiss me because it was midnight on New Year's. I didn't want a one-night stand or to be friends with benefits. I wanted all of her. I wanted it the right way.

I wanted her to want me back.

# CHAPTER 18

# HOW TO LOSE A GUY BY MAKING THIS ONE BIG MISTAKE!

## VANESSA

Adrian pulled into the garage under our apartment building. It was around 10:00 p.m. and I was still pretty buzzed. I lolled my head on the seat to look at him. "So what'd you guys talk about over by the bar?"

He put the car in park. "Diaper cream, mostly. Jason and Sloan's daughter has a rash."

I put my lip out in a pout. "I know, poor baby Emma."

He turned off the ignition. "What did *you* guys talk about?"

I gave a shrug. "Your penis mostly."

He blanched. "*What?*"

"Josh's too," I said defensively. "But mostly yours."

He looked amused. "And what exactly did any of you have to say about my penis? None of you have seen it."

I threw up my hands. "I know! It was a lot of conspiracy

theories mostly." I unbuckled myself and turned to him with my knees on the seat. "There's a rumor that it's huge. You don't have to tell me—blink once if it's true—but you don't have to tell me."

He laughed and got out of the car. I watched him come around and open my door. I practically tumbled out.

"All right, come on," he said, gathering me to my feet. "Can you walk?"

I shrugged. "If I trip, I'll just turn it into a sexy dance."

He was grinning. "I'm keeping Grace for an extra few hours until you sober up. Can you hang on to me if I carry you?"

I rubbed my nose. "Yup."

He turned around, and I jumped up onto his back.

He carried me into the building and took the stairs. At a *jog*.

Three flights up and he wasn't even out of breath. I could only imagine the endurance this man would have in bed—seriously, I could only imagine it. I'd never been with someone with a body like his.

I giggled as Adrian piggybacked me down the hall. "Hey, can we go to my apartment before we go to your place to get Grace? I wanna show you something."

"Sure." He stopped at my door and dug for his keys while I hung off him like a monkey.

I loved that he had a key to my apartment. Not just so he could come in and save me from the ceiling fan or do unannounced birthday cleanings, but because I loved that there were no closed doors between us. Not really. Not physically or otherwise. He knew everything there was to know about me. He knew about my shitty family—he even knew I was worried I might be sick. And here he was anyway.

When he got the door open, he carried me to the sofa, turned, and set me down.

"All right," he said. "What do you want to show me?"

"Sit," I commanded, tugging at the pocket of his pants.

He smiled and sat next to me, and I reached for the lamp to turn off the lights. A hundred glowing stars beamed down on us from the ceiling.

"Wow," he breathed.

"I know, right?" I turned to him in the dark. "Did you ever have these growing up?"

He laughed a little. "Yeah. I think they were still up there in my old room at my mom's house right up until they sold it."

"Why do grown-ups stop doing things like this?" I asked, lolling my head to look back at the ceiling. "Why do we forget?"

"It's not very sophisticated. I think I'd have some explaining to do if I brought a woman home and this was the ceiling in my bedroom."

"Oh my God. I would *love* if a man brought me home and this was the ceiling in his bedroom. I'd be way more excited to have sex with him."

I could feel him look at me. "Really? You think these are available on Amazon Prime?"

I giggled. "Just so you know, I'm not having sex with you just because I come over and you have glow-in-the-dark stars on your ceiling."

"Is there anything you will have sex with me for? I'd like to get started on it."

I laughed. Well, *that* was flirty. Not his usual MO. He never said stuff like this to me.

He was kidding, of course.

I wished he weren't.

He looked back to the stars. "If this view had a soundtrack, what do you think it would be?" he asked.

"I don't know, but I feel like there'd probably be a pretty epic saxophone solo. A little jazz break in the middle?"

He laughed. "Where do you come up with this stuff?"

I shrugged. "My inner monologue is like a hundred open tabs. You should hear the things I *don't* say." Then a mischievous smile crept across my face. "Adrian?"

"Yes?"

"Can I touch your six-pack?"

He snorted. "What?"

I turned on the light and blinked at him innocently. "I'm serious. I've never touched one before and yours is really nice. It's sorta on my bucket list."

He laughed. "Sure?"

I clapped excitedly and he lifted the bottom of his shirt and sat back into the sofa. I tucked my legs under me and bit my lip, looking down at his body.

A trail of hair descended down into the top of his pants. I don't know why, but this was even hotter than the abs.

I held my breath as I started brushing my fingers over his stomach, tracing along the ridges of his muscles. Then I flattened my palm and ran it over his warm skin. I practically shuddered from the contact.

I'd never been this attracted to someone. *Ever*. And it wasn't just physical—it was everything. I loved his steadiness and confidence, his gentleness with Grace. He was generous and kind and protective of the people he cared about. He was intelligent and funny and loyal—and he made me want to do things to him.

I wanted to plunge my hands into his pants, straddle his lap, and kiss him. Feel him go hard underneath me, let him take my clothes off. I could picture him pushing me onto my back on this sofa, sliding over me. I could almost feel the weight of him between my legs...

The tip of my pinky finger slipped under the waist of his pants as I canvassed his skin and he cleared his throat. "Okay, we're going to have to stop that here or we're gonna have problems." He sat up and tugged his shirt over his stomach.

I swallowed hard, trying to play off how out of breath I was. "What *kind* of problems?"

"You *know* what kind of problems."

I blushed, sitting back down next to him, feeling somewhat triumphant. I don't think sober me would have had the wherewithal to look so pleased with herself for almost giving my neighbor a boner, but drunk me was thrilled.

"Hey," I said, tucking my hair behind my ear. "Thank you for tonight. You gave me the perfect day today. It was *perfect*. Jaxon *Waters* sang happy birthday to me. How did you know what I'd like?"

He studied me quietly for a moment. "Because I know you. I know what's important to you," he said, holding my eyes. "Content for your channel so you can keep raising money for ALS research. Good food. Once-in-a-lifetime experiences."

I smiled at him gently.

"I'm so lucky I know you," I said quietly.

He paused for a moment. "I feel the same way. Like my life was a stuffy room, and you're the breeze that came in when the window opened."

We peered at each other...then he slid a warm hand over the one I had on the sofa between us. It zinged through me like lightning.

He was touching me!

Adrian almost never touched me—and when he did, it wasn't like this.

I dropped my eyes to our hands and when I looked back up, his gaze had moved to my lips.

Oh my God...

Oh my God, he wanted to kiss me!

I immediately thought about how much he'd had to drink. Not a lot, right? Because I couldn't even wrap my brain around the idea that he wanted me, in any way, unless there was something screwing with his decision making. But he *did* look like he was thinking about it.

How much had *I* had to drink? Was I misreading this?

My heart was pounding. His thumb started to move back and forth across the top of my hand like a reminder that it was there on purpose. I felt an invisible tug toward him, like there was a rope between us that both of us were pulling in.

I stared at him for one more moment. Then I sat up, leaned in, and kissed him.

Aaaand he didn't kiss me back.

I think I would have registered this much faster if I hadn't been buzzed. Sober me would have realized it wasn't going well. But since I was drunk, I let it go on about three seconds longer than I should have. Just pressing my lips to an unresponsive mouth.

He pushed me gently off him. "Vanessa, no..."

Instant humiliation washed over me. "I'm sorry I don't know what—"

He shook his head. "It's—"

I waved him off. "You know what? It's fine. I wouldn't kiss me either," I said, getting up quickly.

He stood and took a step toward me and put a hand out. "That's not it—"

I couldn't even look at him. I was so embarrassed. What the hell was I thinking? "You should go. I'll just see you tomorrow."

"Vanessa, I think we should talk about this—"

I laughed dryly. "I *really* don't want to. I made a mistake. I was just caught up in the moment and I'm drunk—it didn't mean anything, honestly. I wish I didn't do it. I'm sorry," I said, looking him in the eye.

Something flashed on his face.

"Please," I said. "Just have Becky bring Grace home. Thank you for today and let's just forget about this."

"Vanessa—"

"Adrian, go!"

He waited a moment, just looking at me before he set his jaw, walked past me, and left. I closed the door behind him and slid down to the floor, instantly sober—and wishing I weren't.

# CHAPTER 19

# 10 THINGS GUARANTEED TO MAKE YOU SAY WTF

## ADRIAN

My phone had been deafeningly silent since last night. Nothing from Vanessa. Becky and I had some work stuff to go over so we did that until midnight while I gave Vanessa some time to sober up. Then I had her drop off Grace since Vanessa clearly didn't want to see *me*.

It wouldn't have been right for me to kiss her. I suspected she wasn't sober enough to know what she was doing. She was too drunk to walk, for God's sake.

*It didn't mean anything. I wish I didn't do it.*

Was she just upset? Or did she really feel that way?

Maybe both.

Maybe she was upset with me for rejecting her *and* she meant it. Maybe she was just drunk and did something spontaneous and the whole thing never meant anything at all.

The thought that kissing me was just some foggy-headed, alcohol-induced mistake made me feel physically ill. And now I worried more than anything that instead of *me* fucking things up and changing our friendship by telling her how I felt, she'd accidentally done it by kissing me for no other reason than she'd had too much to drink.

My stomach was in knots. I couldn't sleep last night. I wanted to talk to her, but I didn't even know what to say after what she'd said to me. In the morning before I left for the office, I texted her.

**Me:** Can we talk later?

She didn't reply for almost ten minutes. This was eight years in Vanessa time. She always replied immediately. This wasn't a good sign.

**Vanessa:** I guess.
**Me:** Do you still want me to watch Grace tonight?

Another four-minute wait.

**Vanessa:** You don't have to.
**Me:** I want to.
**Vanessa:** K. Do you want me to get Harry?

I thought this one over. She always watched him for me, but it would be weird if I saw her and we didn't talk, and I didn't have time to do it before work. I didn't want to be rushed, especially considering what we needed to discuss.

**Me:** I'll take him to work.
**Vanessa:** K

That was it. She didn't say anything else.

Harry was crabbier than usual, like we were sharing our mood. He bit Becky three times by noon. Oddly enough he didn't bite *me*, which made me feel like maybe we were on the same team for once. He slept in my lap while I worked at my desk and didn't even growl at me when I moved him to get up to use the bathroom.

Work dragged. I kept checking my phone to see if Vanessa had messaged me, which she didn't. I left work early to knock on Vanessa's door thirty minutes before she'd asked me to come so I could talk to her. I figured if she really regretted kissing me, the best I could hope for was for us to get over any weirdness and stay friends. But I guessed by her silence that the chances of that were probably low.

I felt a gnawing anxiety at the uncertainty of it. A panic at the possibility that this was all over.

I heard her chain rake across the lock, and I braced myself for our first encounter since last night. But when the door opened, it wasn't Vanessa who answered it. It was...some guy?

He stood in the doorway holding Grace. He was shorter than me but muscular. Shaggy blond hair, tan skin. He was wearing a clunky faux fur jacket that came to his knees. It was open and he had no shirt on. A shark-tooth necklace hung around his neck.

"Hey," he said. "You must be the babysitter. Come in."
He spoke over his shoulder. "Hey, butterfly, your sitter's
here."

I was frozen where I stood. Rendered completely mute.

"She just had a bottle," he said, handing me the baby. "I
changed her diaper. She should be good for a bit."

I let him put Grace in my arms right there, still standing
in the doorway.

She was swaddled. It wasn't Vanessa's handiwork. The
blanket was twisted into some weird intricate knot. He saw
me looking at it and he nodded at her. "It's an old Aboriginal
wrapping method. A medicine woman taught me."

An Aboriginal wrapping—

Who the fuck was this? What the hell was going on?

And then Vanessa came up behind him and the whole
thing went from bad to worse.

She took the breath right out of my lungs. Her makeup
was done and she wore a fitted burgundy dress and heels. Her
hair was down and curled. She was stunning.

She was going-on-a-date stunning.

"Hey, come on in," she said distractedly, fiddling with an
earring she was putting in—or trying to. Her fingers were
fumbling. She nodded at the guy. "This is Drake. Drake,
Adrian." She dropped the diamond stud and made an impatient huffing noise as she knelt to pick it up.

"Here, let me help you," Drake said, putting his hand out.

She handed the earring to him and stood still while he got
closer to put it in, tipping her head to the side.

"You look nice, butterfly," he said, his voice low.

She gave him a flirty sideways smile. "Thanks. So do you."

Hot, thick jealousy ripped through me. There was something familiar about the way he touched her. Like he'd done it before.

As soon as he was done with her earring, she pivoted to grab a small purse.

"Hey, I know we're supposed to talk, but can we do it after?" she said to me, putting on her coat. "Drake and I need to get going. We'll be at Vermilion."

I wrinkled my forehead. "Vermilion? They're not open on Mondays—"

"He bought out the restaurant."

He bought out the—

???

"Hey, thanks for watching Grace," she said. "She'll probably sleep for a bit. I'll be home by eight."

Then she edged past me out the door with Drake trailing behind her and was gone.

He never put on a shirt.

What. The. FUCK.

Who the fuck was Drake? And why was he taking her to Vermilion? *I* wanted to take her to Vermilion!

I looked around her apartment, holding the baby, feeling whiplashed.

The room still smelled like Vanessa's perfume. There were dresses on her bed. Lots of them. And shoes all over the floor. It looked like she'd tried on her whole damn closet. It was a studio. Did she try them on with him sitting there watching? What the hell?

I pulled out my phone and called Becky. She answered on the first ring. "'Sup, boss?" She popped a bubble in my ear.

"Do you know somebody named Drake? Does Vanessa ever talk about him?"

The line went silent, and I thought I lost the call. "Why?" she said ominously.

"Vanessa's out with him—"

"You let her go out with *Drake*? Oh my God. Oh. My. *God.*" She let out a shaky breath. "Okay, this is going to be okay. Adrian, this is very important. When you saw him was he wearing a shirt?"

"What?"

"A shirt! Did he have a shirt on?!"

"No. Just some fake fur jacket, open in the front—"

"Noooooo! Oh God!" she wailed. "It's worse than I thought. He's pulling out all the stops! She's totally helpless around his pec muscles. He might as well have brought a hypnotist with him! Did you know his chest is insured for over two million dollars? Did you? Almost as much as his biceps. Not as much as his glutes."

She gasped for air. "I should have known. I should. Have. *Known.* Mercury's in retrograde. Your horoscope today said you were getting an unexpected visitor. This is so fucked up. I wanted you guys to get married and have a million babies, and now she's probably halfway to Bali on a catamaran!"

"Becky, who the fuck *is* he?"

I could hear her breathing heavily on the other end and for the first time, her dramatics were pissing me off.

"He's an extreme sport vlogger. He's got a channel even bigger than hers. Quiksilver sponsored his last surfing competition, the one where he got bitten by a shark and just kept going?

"If you're Jesus's Abs, Drake Lawless is Lucifer's Penis. He's like the final boss boyfriend that you have to fight in a video game once you've defeated all the lesser exes. He looks like Patrick Swayze in *Dirty Dancing*, only with blond hair and tribal tattoos. And sorry, but he's, like, way cooler than you. I mean, I hate to say it, but it's true. You won't even get on a plane, and Drake carried her down a mountain in Venezuela wrapped in a parachute. Oh my God, they're probably getting married by a shaman, right now. How could you let this happen?!"

I paced Vanessa's tiny living room. "Is he her ex or—"

"Yes, he's her ex! How can you not know this? The Drake-and-Vanessa saga was, like, the biggest YouTube romance of all time. There were T-shirts and everything! They were all crazy about each other and had tantric sex on, like, every beach in Barbados. And then she broke up with him because he had that coal-walking accident in Tibet and she told him he had to quit doing dangerous stunts, and he was all, 'I can't! I do it for the children!' Because he donates all his money to pediatric cancer research? So she left him and he was so devastated he spent two months in a tiki hut on his private island making sculptures of her out of driftwood." She paused. "He brought her up like three times during his TED Talk. We were all really worried about him."

I dragged a hand down my beard.

Vanessa never talked about him. Not *once*. I told her I'd watched her videos. Maybe she thought I knew already and it bothered her to bring him up so she just... *didn't?*

I felt like a popped balloon. I just stood there, staring into her kitchen, listening to Becky gasp and moan about what an idiot I was for letting this happen.

"I have to go," I mumbled, hanging up on her.

I put Grace in her swing and sat down heavily on the couch to google Drake—I got as far as typing in the first four letters of his name before Google suggested Drake Lawless and Vanessa Price. The other suggestions weren't much of a comfort. There was Drake and Vanessa pregnant. Drake and Vanessa secret wedding. Drake and Vanessa get back together…

I poked around and found the video of how they met. It was his. He was BASE jumping off a waterfall in Venezuela and Vanessa was there doing her own video blog. She sprained her ankle and he carried her down the fucking mountain, just like Becky said.

Apparently Vanessa wasn't initially interested, because the next three videos of his were him doing grand gestures to get her attention. He followed her to Brazil and rappelled onto her hotel balcony from the roof to ask her on a date. Then he flew her to a botanical garden in Cornwall to see the corpse flower bloom—and he actually piloted the plane. I was halfway through their romantic motorcycle ride through Peru when I decided I'd seen enough.

I knew Vanessa had another life, that her current situation wasn't what she normally did with her days. But I don't think I truly realized how exciting her other world was, how exotic her tastes were—both in travel *and* men. The guy lived in a yurt, for God's sake. And Becky was right. I didn't even fly.

Now what we did together looked boring and sad in

comparison. Hanging out with me was probably something she did just to pass the time until she got back to what she'd rather be doing.

And I thought she said she'd never touched a six-pack before. What the fuck???

I tossed my phone on the couch and sat there feeling completely blindsided. And jealous. Ridiculously, wildly jealous.

Why hadn't she talked to me about this? We talked about everything—except her channel. Maybe this was another topic she preferred didn't bleed into the rest of her life. After all, it was over between them.

At least it had been before today.

Now I half wondered if she said she didn't date because she was holding out for someone else. Holding out for *him*. Maybe he couldn't stand being away from her and he was quitting stunts. Maybe this was him coming to tell her. Sweep her off her feet.

And now I was sitting here, babysitting for a woman I was in love with while she went out on a date with her ex.

And that's truly what it was. I was in love with her.

The reality of this hit me like a gavel coming down. An instant call to attention. A hard stop.

I was in *love* with her.

But of course I was in love with her. Who *wasn't*?

She could have any man she wanted. Any man at all.

Women like Vanessa were muses for artists and musicians. They became famous paintings and love ballads. They danced in the rain and ran away with princes who would give up their thrones to have them. They were the sirens that sailors wrote about with voices that could lure a man to his death.

She was a beautiful migratory bird with her wings clipped. And the second she could, she'd fly again. Out of St. Paul, away from me...

And probably back to him.

# CHAPTER 20

# THE LUCRATIVE INVESTMENT THAT THE EXPERTS DON'T WANT YOU TO KNOW ABOUT!

## VANESSA

A crowd of fans had gathered outside of Vermilion. Someone must have leaked our location.

By myself, I was a draw. By himself, Drake was a *massive* draw. Together, we were a galaxy-level, defying-the-laws-of-physics, magnetic force. People were probably feeling the pull and getting into buses to drive in from out of state and they didn't even know why.

Laird was getting his camera ready and Malcolm was putting new batteries in my mic.

Drake was drinking some banana flip thing with a sprig of pine in it across from me. "You're doing a great job with Grace," he said, taking out the garnish and setting it on a plate. "But you should really use cloth diapers. Reduce your carbon footprint."

"I don't have a washing machine, remember?" I said. "I use Adrian's and I seriously doubt he wants me washing dirty diapers in it."

Malcolm snorted. "That guy would let you eat crackers in his bed."

I laughed dryly. "Oh yeah? I kissed him last night and he pushed me off him. So riddle me that."

"He pushed you off him?" Malcolm asked, clipping the tiny mic to the front of my dress.

"Yeah. Like you know how you act when you look down and you see a spider on you? And you're like, 'Oh my God! A spider!' and you hop off the sofa and do a little freak-out dance and then run from the room? It was like that."

"Come on, it was not," Drake said with his amused smile.

"Okay, it wasn't quite that dramatic. But the sentiment was the same." I scoffed. "Why does everyone keep telling me this guy is into me? Like, literally everyone I know in the last twenty-four hours had sworn that he can't keep his eyes off me. Honestly, if it wasn't for that, and liquor, and the super sweet 'you are the breeze' thing he said to me on my sofa last night, I might not have made a total ass of myself. I blame all of you for this."

Drake smiled. "You're blaming us? I hadn't even met him until today. We weren't even there."

I put a hand on my chest. "Well, it's not *my* fault. I wasn't there either. It was Drunk Vanessa, who is a totally different person and shouldn't be held accountable for her actions."

Drake laughed.

I sighed. "Do I catch him checking me out sometimes? Sure. And does he like to spend time with me? Totally.

But thinking my ass looks nice in my jeans and enjoying my company are very different from wanting to date me and my fifty percent chance of dying by thirty. It's official," I mumbled. "I'm probably never having sex again. My last sexual encounter will probably be with TSA."

Malcolm laughed.

"He seems good with the baby," Drake offered.

"He's great with the baby. You know, just not interested in *me*."

Malcolm turned on my mic. "Why don't you just go over there and ask him why he didn't want to kiss you?"

I shook my head. "Nope. I need to start putting boundaries between us. I just threw myself at a guy who didn't want to make out. I totally humiliated myself. I think it's time to exit this situation while I still have some dignity left."

Like I even had a choice in the matter. Adrian was probably ready to go back to the noncommittal head nods in the hallways. He texted me saying he wanted to talk, but what was there to say? It would always be awkward between us now. He probably came to watch Grace today because he said he would and then he'd start making excuses and find someone else to hang out with. Someone datable who didn't pounce him on the sofa after one too many martinis.

Drake reached across the table and put a hand on my wrist. "Enough about him."

I raised my eyes to his. A woman outside the window behind him pressed a naked boob to the glass. It was negative five outside. I applauded her commitment. "Whatever you do, don't turn around," I said.

"Why would I turn around when I have *you* to look at?" He grinned at me.

And now we were in character. Malcolm and Laird were already filming.

I arched an eyebrow. "You know, there's a reason we broke up, Drake. It was a good one."

He leaned across the table and pressed the top of my hand to his lips. "Yes. It was."

I gave him a long lingering look. "I miss you," I whispered.

He stared at me for a moment. Then he sat back in his chair and took something from his jacket pocket. When he pulled out the gorgeous engagement ring and held it between us, I gasped. It was a band with inlaid pearl.

"I found the pearl myself," he said. "I spent half my life looking for it, just like I did for the one who's going to wear it."

"Drake..." I breathed, a hand on my chest. I wasn't even faking it. It was beautiful. The ring *and* the sentiment.

We let the moment sit for a few seconds.

"Aaand we got it," Malcolm said, lowering the camera. "One-take wonders, both of you."

"Phew." I sat back in my chair. "Drake, I appreciate this more than you know."

"Enough to entertain a brief sales pitch for a startup I'm interested in?"

I tilted my head. "You need me to invest?"

That was weird. Drake was a gazillionaire or something. He hardly needed *my* money.

"I think you might want to get in on the ground floor for this one." He made a come-here motion to someone behind me. I twisted in my seat to see who he was calling over.

*Brent* was making his way to the table.

"No. Are you fucking serious, Brent? You called *Drake*?"

Brent sucked air through his teeth. "He's the only other rich person I know," he said, arriving at the table with his hands balled in front of his mouth.

I shook my head. "No. You're not sucking Drake into one of your get-rich-quick schemes—"

"Butterfly, that's not what this is," Drake said. "Hear him out. Trust me."

I looked back and forth between them. Drake was giving me his easy smile, and Brent looked like a puppy dog who wanted to be let back into the house.

I crossed my arms. "*Fine.* But only because it's *you* asking," I said to Drake.

Brent grinned and did a little happy dance. "Can someone get the lights?" He whirled back in the direction he came from and Laird and Malcolm took their seats next to us at the table.

Joel appeared and started placing professional-looking bound catalogs of some sort in front of us, and Brent turned on a small projector on a tripod.

A PowerPoint presentation popped up on the wall.

Okay...So far this was all a little more than I expected. I had to admit I was already slightly, if not cautiously, impressed.

Brent took his place in front of our table and cleared his throat. "Women's clothing doesn't have pockets." He let this hang in the air for a moment. "I'm here to speak to you about an exclusive, innovative new product that was inspired by my sister Vanessa, and her life hack for the fact that none of her cute clothes have places to put her lip balm."

Drake looked over his shoulder and smiled at me.

Brent clicked to a picture of us making a snowman circa five years ago. "Growing up in Minnesota, my older sister Vanessa loved spending time outside. And anyone who knows my sister knows that she's obsessed with Carmex. You know, those little yellow lip balm tubes with the red caps?" He clicked through to a picture of a tube of Carmex. "Great product, tastes like shit. Sorry, Vanessa—but it does."

The audience gave a little titter and the corner of my mouth twitched.

"In addition to its questionable flavor, Carmex gets hard when it's cold outside and it won't squeeze from the bottle. So to combat this problem while wearing her pocketless clothes, my sister would put it in her bra to keep it warm. Unfortunately, you could see the pokey end of the tube through her shirt. Not sexy." He clicked to a picture of me. Eighteen years old in gloves and a hat smiling in the driveway, with a red arrow pointing to my boob, where the end of my Carmex poked out.

"This gave me an idea," he went on. "What if we made a lip balm that doesn't taste like shit? Formulated to soften with the heat from your body. It's got a soft tube so it lays flat on your skin and you can't see it through your clothes. All natural, organic, sustainable ingredients with SPF. *And* the tube is bio-degradable with a seed in it, so if you bury it, it breaks down and then grows a flower. Giftable, Earth friendly, edgy, super millennial." He clicked to a picture of a tube of lip balm. "Ladies and gentlemen, I introduce to you BoobStick."

Joel was walking around with a tray, placing prototypes in front of us. I picked one up and turned it around in my fingers.

It was cute. Instagramable cute. Pink with a delicate teal floral filigree on the front.

Everyone started taking off the caps and trying it. I put some on my lips and licked it. It tasted like guava. It tasted good. *Really* good.

Brent went on. "In front of you are sales forecasts and return projections, a market analysis, and full marketing, manufacturing, and operational plans. As you can see, our production costs are low and we feel due to the novelty nature of the product, we can sell it at a higher price point than comp items. Our website is already up and functional." He clicked through to a professional-looking website that matched the artwork on the lip balm.

"We offer different flavors. We roll out additional products over the next eighteen months. Hand creams, bath bombs. We offer a gender-neutral DipStick on a rope, perfect for the active customer who doesn't have pockets or bras." He winked at Drake. "We target retailers like Anthropologie, Trader Joe's, Whole Foods. We launch the brand at Drake's next sporting event as welcome gifts in the guest rooms, where we can get the product in front of a VIP list of influencers."

I opened the professional-looking packet in front of me and flipped through the graphs and numbers. This was not Brent's MO at *all*. He was always so instant gratification when it came to his business pursuits, but this? This must have taken him months. Longer. All this work…

"This is amazing," I breathed, looking up at him.

He broke into a grin.

"No, I'm serious, Brent. This is incredible. You thought this up? You put all this together by yourself?"

He smiled. "I did. You sent me to business school, remember? You just didn't think I was paying attention."

I laughed and looked down at the tube of lip balm. I would buy this. It was like something you'd see by the register at Sephora.

"I had some help with the graphic design," Brent said. "Annabel did it, actually. You know. Before."

I looked up at him. "Annabel did this?"

"All her. The website too. She's good at it. And I got the idea for the seed from Dad. Remember that time a Chia Pet broke in the living room and he just left it there and the carpet started growing a lawn?"

I snorted. "God, yes."

"Oh, and my first investor is someone you know," he said. "I hope you're not mad. I asked him not to tell you. Adrian gave me a small loan for the materials for the pitch meeting."

My heart did a little flutter. "He *did*?"

Brent nodded. "I pitched him at the hospital in the men's room."

My face fell. "Ugh, are you serious?"

"He wasn't mad," he said quickly. "He agreed to let me send him my business plan. He liked it. He sent me the money the next day. Also, I heard you talk about the spider thing." He sucked air through his teeth. "I'm sorry. That's super weird he didn't kiss you back. Joel and I both thought he was into you."

I scoffed. "Wouldn't be the first time this week I've

misjudged a situation," I mumbled, looking at the packet again.

Brent took another step toward me. "Vanessa, Adrian believes in this. So does Drake."

I didn't blame them. I believed in this too.

I nodded. "My answer is yes. I'll give you as much as you need."

Brent yelped and Joel crashed into him. They hugged and hooted, spinning around the restaurant.

Drake tipped his head at me. "You can't give him *all* of it. What about me? I want to invest too."

I shook my head, watching Brent and Joel celebrate. "I'm surprised you even let him pitch me. You could have just backed him and had the whole thing to yourself."

Drake laughed good-naturedly. "I wanted to. I offered it. But it was important to him that you do it."

I wrinkled my forehead. "Me? Why? I don't think he cares as long as he gets his money."

Drake looked amused. "He wants your approval, Vanessa. He wants you to be proud of him. He wants that more than anything. More than the money."

My smile fell a little.

Did he?

Brent looked over his shoulder at me. His smile was enormous.

Maybe he *did* want my approval. I couldn't imagine Dad's meant much to him.

And I *was* proud of him. So, so proud. And I decided right there in that moment that I'd always make sure he knew that, as long as I was around to do it.

# CHAPTER 21

# THE ULTIMATE GUIDE TO ESCAPING THE FRIEND ZONE

## ADRIAN

When Vanessa texted that she'd be back in five minutes, it was a full hour later than she said she'd be home. I'd been through a symphony of emotions over the last four hours, none of them good. I'd landed solidly on bad mood and wasn't planning on changing.

I was hurt that Vanessa said she regretted kissing me and that it was a mistake. I was pissed that she didn't tell me about Drake. I was jealous, frustrated, and scared I was going to lose her to this guy.

The fucking medicine-woman swaddling...

Grace seemed to like it. I don't know why this pissed me off more than anything else that had happened today, but it did.

Grace smelled like him—I had to give her a bath. She smelled like incense.

I was at the dining room table on my laptop with a baby monitor next to me trying to get through emails when Vanessa finally let herself into my apartment. I had Harry next to the table in his little dog bed and he raised his head at the sound of her coming in and growled like he was mad at her too.

"Sorry I'm late," she said, closing the door behind her. "There was a mob outside the restaurant. I had to autograph, like, two hundred sponges. And I think someone cut a piece of my hair off…"

I didn't look up at her. "I changed her diaper about an hour ago. She was a little fussy. I gave her some gas drops and she seems fine now. She's in the playpen in the office, sleeping."

Then I slid my chair out, got up, and went to the bar.

"Well, you're in a mood," she said from behind me.

I pulled the stopper off the bourbon. "So does your ex own any damn shirts or did he get frostbite on his nipples?" I mumbled.

"Drake? He should own a shirt. He wore one on the cover of *People* when he got Sexiest Man Alive."

I scoffed.

I heard her set down her purse. "What's wrong with you?"

"Why didn't you ever talk to me about him?" I said, not looking at her.

She laughed. "Uh, why would I?"

"He's obviously someone who's important to you." I dropped ice into a tumbler. "We talk. I thought we didn't keep things from each other."

"Yeah, I thought that too. But I didn't see you running to tell me that you loaned money to *Brent*."

I twisted to look at her and she stood with her arms crossed.

"He asked me not to," I said. "It was between me and him, and you had to wait all of forty-eight hours to find out about it. It's not the same thing as hiding an entire relationship."

"I *didn't* hide Drake."

"Well, you didn't exactly volunteer the information."

She rolled her eyes. "You'd have to live under a rock to not know about Drake. And I've never talked about him because he wasn't worth mentioning."

"Right." I went back to my drink, putting the stopper back in the decanter. "I thought you weren't dating anyone."

She laughed at my back. "Are you serious? You're crabby because I went on a date? You want me miserable and alone with you in solidarity? Is that it?"

I set my drink down, turned around, and crossed my arms. "Are you getting back with him?"

She threw her hands up. "And what does it matter? It's not like *you* want me."

I stared at her, incredulous. "You have made it exceedingly clear to me, since day one, that you don't have any interest in me beyond friendship." I gestured between us. "This is what *you* wanted. *You* wanted friends only, you set that boundary. *I* respected it. Then you kissed me, declared it a huge mistake, and *I'm* the bad guy?"

She put a hand to her chest. "*I* set the boundary?"

"Are you getting back with him?" I asked again.

She laughed. "No. I prefer my men a lot less gay."

My arms dropped. "He's gay? Since when?"

She snorted. "Birth?"

I gawked at her. "Well—what the hell was all that shit about online?"

"Adrian, there's a certain level of theater that goes into what I do. Drake and I hung out so much because he was dating my cameraman, Laird. He wasn't ready to come out yet. People assumed what they wanted to assume. That dinner today was a collab. He's announcing their engagement, and he teased it with a video entitled 'He Proposed!' with clip of us in a restaurant and him showing me a giant ring. It's clickbait. Then when you play the whole video, he's inviting me to the wedding. It gets both of us views and new subscribers. He was doing me a favor."

I blinked at her. "So you're not seeing him."

"No! I'm not seeing anyone. And I probably never will, ever again, if that makes you feel better." Then her chin started to quiver. "And don't worry, I won't ever try to kiss you again. Gross, right?" Her voice cracked on the last word.

I shook my head. "I don't get you. Did you *want* me to kiss you back? You wanted me to cheapen our friendship with something that didn't mean anything to you? You wanted a fling? This isn't some game for me, Vanessa. Kissing you *means* something to me."

She blinked at me through tears. "It...it does?"

"Of *course* it does. How can you even ask me that?"

She sniffled. "But...but you didn't kiss me back."

"You were *drunk*," I said. "You were so drunk I had to carry you home. I don't kiss intoxicated women. Even if I want to. And then you said it was a mistake, that you..." I didn't finish. I couldn't.

I paused for a long moment, turning away from her. I dragged a hand down my beard and then looked her in the eye. "I've wanted to kiss you almost every single day since the day I met you."

And there it was. Out in the universe.

She stared at me, speechless. Shocked.

Nothing was going to be the same after this.

I wondered how much damage was done, if we'd even be friends now. We might have moved past her drunken misstep. But not this. My one-sided feelings would be too much.

I waited for the letdown that I knew was coming. The gentle "I don't see you that way" or "It's me, not you."

She looked at me with wide apologetic eyes and licked her lips. "Adrian, I've wanted to kiss you almost every single day since the day I met you too."

It hit me like a storm throwing a door open. Everything inside me burst into chaos. My heart launched into pounding as hope ripped through me.

A small smile tugged at the corners of her lips. "And I'm not drunk now…"

I broke into a grin and was clearing the distance between us before she took another breath.

# CHAPTER 22

# LEARN THE NUMBER ONE SECRET TRICK FOR PERFECT ABS!

## VANESSA

He crashed into me.

And I do mean he crashed. The impact knocked the emotional breath out of me and butterflies dove right from my stomach directly to my crotch.

His hands raked into my hair, his beard scratched my face, and his lips pressed warm against my mouth...

*This.*

This was the kiss he didn't give me last night. This was the kiss that felt like a thousand kisses built up and funneled into one. He'd been holding this back for weeks. And I knew because so had I.

"I can't believe you went to Vermilion without me," he breathed against my mouth, smiling.

"I didn't like it," I whispered.

He bit my bottom lip gently. "Liar." He grinned against my lips and then he devoured me again.

Oh my *God*, he was a good kisser.

He trailed his mouth along my jaw, down my neck, and over the bare skin of my collar bone and I gasped, tipping my head back. I still wore my jacket, and he peeled it off my shoulders until it caught around my back in the crook of my elbows. I shed it and it dropped to the floor behind me.

His breathing was ragged. He was already hard. A boner was pressing through his pants into the front of my dress.

"Let's go to your room," I breathed.

He nodded and then threw me over his shoulder. I shrieked and he turned us for his bedroom door.

"Wait, wait! The baby monitor!" I said, giggling, tapping his shoulder.

He backed up and leaned me over the table so I could grab it, laughing. Then he hauled me straight to his bedroom.

I'd never been in there before. It felt like he'd just carried me off to his lair, some inner sanctum that I'd never been invited to explore.

It smelled like him and looked exactly like the rest of the apartment. Dark furniture and a gray bedspread, neat and orderly. I wanted to look around, but I had more pressing activities to see to.

He sat me down on the edge of the bed and stood between my legs while he kissed me, reaching around my back to undo my zipper.

I tugged at his belt buckle and he peeled off his shirt. Then he backed up to take his pants down as I wiggled out of my dress. When he pulled his underwear off and his penis sprang free, I froze in the middle of slipping an arm out of my bra. "What the fuck…" I breathed.

It was amazing.

Breathtaking.

It was that moment at a hibachi restaurant when the chef does some crazy thing with the rice and you realize you're in for a good show.

I twisted onto my side and reached for the phone on his nightstand.

"What are you doing?" he asked.

"Calling Kristen. I have to tell her the prophecy is true."

He snorted. "Well, can you wait until after?"

I turned back to him. "But what if I need tips? Best practices? I am not prepared for this, Adrian." I stared at it. "My God, no wonder you have those abs. You're doing a crunch every time you stand up. It's like a twenty-five-pound dumbbell hanging there."

He laughed and climbed onto the bed, sliding over me. He finished taking off my bra and started kissing his way between my breasts, down my stomach.

Heat radiated off this thing like a lightsaber. I watched his head dropping farther down my body. "I mean, what if I can't lift it?" I breathed.

Fingers wrapped around the waistband of my underwear and dragged them down my thighs. "I'll do the heavy lifting," he said, throwing my panties over his shoulder. He reached to the drawer of the nightstand and pulled out a condom. He tore the wrapper with his teeth. It was a Magnum. I was afraid it still wouldn't fit.

I sat up on my elbows to watch him put it on. His eyes

raked down my body as he did it, taking me all in. I could see how much he wanted me. He looked like he was about to fuck me into the headboard and I was totally here for it.

I needed to savor every second. Press my lips to every surface that I'd been shamelessly ogling for the past few weeks. I was going to treat his body like a decadent dessert at the end of a great meal—because really, that's what he was. He was the grandest of finales to a life well lived. The cherry on top of the cake.

He was very likely the last man I'd ever sleep with.

And it occurred to me that this would have been true even if I *wasn't* probably dying.

# CHAPTER 23

# SEE WHICH CELEBRITY IS YOUR SOUL MATE!

## ADRIAN

I'd *never* had sex like this. To say it was fun was the understatement of a lifetime. She was as playful in bed as she was outside of it and she had no problem asking me for what she wanted. We couldn't get enough of each other. We woke each other up in the middle of the night. I was on about three hours of sleep.

I loved the unique language of her affection. She climbed and explored me. Hung from my neck and kissed my Adam's apple, hugged me from behind while I cooked a midnight snack for us, bounced off me and boomeranged back. She beamed at me, nestled into me, perched on my lap, peppered me with kisses. I wish I'd been able to unlock this level sooner. I wish I'd met her years ago. High school. Grade school. A previous life. It all felt like lost time.

It was Tuesday morning and I was getting ready to head into the office. I'd dealt with Annabel's arraignment over the weekend. She was getting released from the hospital today straight into a rehab facility in Iowa. Sonja and Gerald were taking her.

She'd specifically requested that Vanessa not come. She didn't want to see her. She was mad at her sister, probably for cutting off her credit cards and phone. Vanessa seemed hurt, but she was just glad Annabel was getting help.

I stood over the bed, putting on my tie, smiling down at the sleeping woman curled up in my comforter.

I loved having Vanessa in my bed. I loved waking up and being able to pull her in instead of staring at a wall between us or waiting for her to wake up and text me back. I loved the smell of her hair on my pillows and the things she'd say when she was half asleep. I loved when I got to get up with Grace and bring her back to give her a bottle in between us in the bed and we felt like a little family.

The corners of my lips fell.

*Grace.*

The best possible scenario was that Annabel would get clean and take her daughter back. Then I could still see her. And with Annabel heading to rehab, the chances of that were good.

It was the other thing that bothered me. The reason Vanessa couldn't adopt Grace herself.

She'd be going back to work soon.

In fact, the sooner Grace was gone, the sooner Vanessa would be too. And I didn't like what that would look like. On any level.

Vanessa was usually gone so much she didn't even keep a place here. All her stuff had been in a storage unit for the last two years. She'd rented an apartment because she'd planned to be home for a few months to help her sister with the baby. Then she'd ended up with Grace altogether and got stuck here. But when that was over...how did I—*us*—fit into that?

I didn't fly. And even if I did, I couldn't leave work for weeks at a time to travel the world with her. And she couldn't stay here and make videos. Not in the long-term. She was already clutching at straws trying to come up with content as it was...

But I was trying not to look at the sun.

Annabel was months away from completing her ninety-day program. After that she'd move into sober living. She wouldn't be able to have Grace there. That meant Vanessa was still months away from leaving. We had some time to figure it all out.

Vanessa stirred, and I smiled down at her. She peered up at me sleepily. "Where are you going?" she asked, rubbing her eyes.

"I have to go to work."

She put her lip into a pout. "Awwww. Stay with me."

"I can't." I smiled, knotting my tie. "I changed Grace and gave her a bottle. I gave Harry his meds and put some wet food down. Satan has been fed."

She laughed. She threw the blankets off her and stretched like a cat.

She was naked.

My hands froze on my tie.

She looked at me over her shoulder and gave me a

mischievous grin—and then grabbed her T-shirt, pulled it over her head, and went to the bathroom to brush her teeth. When she came out, she started jumping into her pajama pants.

"Where are you going?" I asked.

She shrugged. "You're leaving. I have to go home." She climbed onto the mattress and stood on her knees on the edge of my bed and wrapped her arms around me, squeezing my waist.

"You're not going home." I smiled. "I don't *ever* want you to go home. In fact, I think we should cut a door between our apartments. Use yours as a closet."

She laughed and smiled up at me with her chin on my chest. "So I get to stay here while you go to work?"

"I'll give you a key."

"I'm gonna snoop through your medicine cabinet."

"Let me know if anything's expired."

She grinned. "So, what? Does this mean I'm your girlfriend now?" She bit her bottom lip and bounced her eyebrows.

I smoothed the hair down on the top of her head and looked at her seriously. "That title doesn't even feel worthy of what this is."

And I meant it. It didn't. It felt wildly inadequate.

She beamed up at me. "Hey, since we're exclusive now, we can stop using condoms if you want. But we both have to get STD testing first," she said, looking at me sternly.

"Okay." It wasn't a bad idea. I always used protection, but you could never be too safe. "But what about birth control?"

She shrugged. "My tubes are tied."

I jerked my face back. "What? *Why?*"

"Because I don't ever want to accidentally get pregnant and pass down my shitty genes."

I snorted. "Okay…"

Her smile fell a little. "Does that bother you?"

I shook my head. "No. Not really. There's more than one way to have kids if you want them. And I'm good either way if you do or you don't. It's just that it's such a permanent procedure."

"Well, I needed a permanent solution. Took forever to find a doctor to do it. Heaven forbid a woman in her twenties knows what she wants to do with her fallopian tubes." She nipped at my bottom lip. "I got you a Christmas present," she whispered against my mouth.

I made a dismissive noise in the back of my throat and went to kiss her again, but she shook her head and draped her arms around my neck. "I have to give it to you now so you can think about it."

I smiled. "Okay. Give it to me now, then."

She bit her lip and beamed up at me. "I got us into Badger Den."

I pulled my face back and grinned at her. "You did? When?"

"Tomorrow."

Ahhhhhhh. *Fuck.*

"I know what you're gonna say, and I already have a plan."

I shook my head. "I can't fly. You know that." And Lord knows I couldn't afford to miss any more work.

"I know you *think* you can't fly. But hear me out," she said. "I put a lot of thought into this. We have dinner at the airport tonight. We get there three hours before our flight.

There's a place I love to eat in the terminal and we can get nice and sloshed and watch the planes on the tarmac like a little dose of immersion therapy. It's only a three-hour flight and I got us first-class tickets. We'll be in our seats with drinks in our hands and plenty of time to get comfortable and used to the plane before it even taxis from the gate. I downloaded season five of *The Office* to watch while we're in the air and I had Yoga Lady make you a lavender-and-eucalyptus essential oil roller for your anxiety. And then, when we get there, we're staying in an amazing five-star hotel on the beach and having dinner at *Badger Den*. It's the ultimate motivation to overcome your fear."

I dragged a hand down my mouth. "And if I can't get on the plane?"

She shrugged. "Then you can't get on the plane. All I'm asking is that you *try*."

I blew a breath out through my nose. I guess I'd have to figure this shit out eventually. My girlfriend was a travel vlogger. We'd need to fly to places. If I couldn't fly, it meant I couldn't come to her even when I *could* get away for a few days. And she was right, Badger Den was a pretty amazing reward—even if it *was* for three hours of what I was sure would be pure hell.

"Who's watching Grace?" I asked grimly.

She smiled in that bubbly excited way she had. "Dad and Sonja. Sonja says it's good for him to see that his efforts reap rewards."

"And Harry Puppins?"

"Becky. I already texted her."

I arched an eyebrow. "You text my assistant?"

"I text your everyone. All your people are my people now, remember?"

I snorted.

"Come on. Pleeeeease?" She wiggled.

I took another moment. "All right. Let's try it."

She clapped animatedly. "Okay, so I have a tip for you. A little life coaching."

I let out a grim breath. "What?"

"Don't think about it yet. Don't think about it until it's happening."

I rubbed my forehead. "Yeah, I have a feeling that's not going to be possible."

"You know how when you're running late, you're all stressed? I don't do that. Ever. If I'm supposed to be somewhere at two and I know I'm not getting there until two fifteen, I don't let myself be stressed until two. Because until then, I'm not actually late yet. All I'm doing is feeling the stress of a thing that hasn't even happened."

"Yeah, but you know it's coming. You know it's going to happen."

"That's just looking at the sun, Adrian. Fuck what's coming. Don't focus on what's going to happen. Or in this case, what *might* happen. Because who knows, you might get there and realize that you've built this whole thing up in your head. You might get on that plane and find out that you're stronger than you think and you're capable of anything." She smiled at me. "And you are. I've never known anyone as capable as you."

She kissed me gently. Then she leapt off the bed and went to the bathroom. I watched her go and waited for the door to click closed before I clutched a hand over my racing heart. The fact that I felt like I couldn't catch my breath and we hadn't even left the apartment yet should have been an indication.

My day didn't go well. I couldn't focus at work. I kept thinking about the plane ride. It was ridiculous, and I was getting pissed off at myself.

What was the big deal? It was three hours. That's it. I could do anything for three hours. I'd sat in a prison for a week interviewing a client who'd chopped his neighbor up with an ax. I couldn't get on a fucking airplane?

I tried to push it from my mind like she said. She was right. Maybe if I didn't let myself dwell on it, I could just show up and tear the Band-Aid off. I'd walk onto that plane and just do it.

Ten hours later we were in the airport parking lot. Grace had been dropped off. Our bags were in the trunk. We'd checked in online and Vanessa had rolled essential oils on my pressure points and held my hand the whole way there.

I had a panic attack before I even got out of the car.

# CHAPTER 24

# 7 SMALL TOWNS YOU *MUST* VISIT IN YOUR LIFETIME (YOU'LL *LOVE* #1)

## VANESSA

We drove down a tiny main street with an enormous MERRY CHRISTMAS garland draped over the entrance. It was Christmas Eve and we'd just arrived in Nebraska to spend the holiday with Adrian's mom and dad.

All the businesses were decked out for the holiday with Christmas lights and wreaths. It was snowing gently and people in parkas were bustling up and down the sidewalks with bags on their arms.

"This town looks like a Hallmark movie," I said, petting Harry Puppins in my lap. "I feel like a big-city girl who's about to learn the spirit of Christmas from a handsome local bachelor in a chunky reindeer sweater."

Adrian laughed. "I hope not, since I don't own that

sweater." Then his smile fell a little. "I'm sorry," he said again. "I wish we could have flown here."

The airport panic attack had been four days ago, and he was still apologizing for it. He didn't have to.

"It's okay," I said again. "I told you I appreciated you even trying."

His jaw flexed. "It's not okay."

"When I have to do overseas stuff, I'll just go without you," I said. "I'll come back as fast as I can."

The lines in his forehead got deeper. This suggestion obviously wasn't helping.

I put a hand on his arm. "*Or*, we can do local stuff so I can stay with you. We can do a weekend series on the best bed-and-breakfasts in Minnesota. And then when you get time off we'll do cruise ships and road trips like this one. Rent an RV and explore all the cool campgrounds. We'll figure it out. It's not a big deal."

But I could see in the set of his body that it was.

He was disappointed in himself. This wasn't a man who was used to failing. At *anything*.

"I kinda thought it might happen," I admitted. "I have a backup Christmas gift for you and everything."

He glanced at me with a weak smile.

I think on top of this, he was stressed out about this weekend, about seeing his dad again. I fully planned on greasing this entire situation. I was going to make sure he had a good time no matter what. I'd pull him into broom closets for blow jobs if the circumstances required it.

I sorta hoped the circumstances required it.

We drove another two minutes and then turned down a

tree-lined drive to a beautiful Victorian house. Adrian pulled up behind an old beater truck and put the car in park. He didn't move to get out.

"Is this it?" I asked, looking over at him.

He sat there, staring at the house. "I haven't been here in almost two decades," he said quietly.

"How's it look?"

"Good. It looks really good. He's been taking care of it."

I peered back out through the windshield. It looked like the kind of house that smelled like cinnamon inside. There were white Christmas lights along the eaves and a huge wreath on the front door. It reminded me of the inside of a Christmas snow globe or something.

"Why haven't you been here?" I asked.

He put an elbow on the ledge of his window and rubbed his forehead. "I used to come every summer. We all did. All the cousins. It was my grandparents' house. I stopped coming when my dad left."

"Why?"

He shook his head a little, still staring out the windshield. "I didn't want to run the risk of seeing him. And Mom fell apart. I couldn't leave her."

I scoffed. "Yup. I know what *that's* like. Being the only one who has their shit together," I mumbled. I looked back at the front door. It was flanked by small lighted pine trees. Very tasteful. All the windows were lit and warm. "It's a cool house."

"It's been in the family for as long as I can remember. My uncle bought it when my granddad died. Then he retired to Florida. Sold it to Richard earlier this year." He paused a few heartbeats. "I'm glad Mom gets to live in it. She likes houses like this. She always loved coming here."

I narrowed my eyes. "Is that a snowplow on the front of his truck?" I asked, squinting at the old Ford parked in front of us between the house and the garage.

"If you live here, you have to help out. They don't have much infrastructure. Mom said he's on the town council too."

"Wow. And here you are with only one job and no political aspirations. I'm sorta disappointed in you."

He smiled, but he didn't make any move to get out of the car. We sat there, silently looking at the house.

"I used to tell everyone I hated coming here," he said quietly.

"Why?"

"Because I couldn't. It was easier to pretend that I didn't want to. I didn't want Mom to feel bad that I was staying to take care of her. And I didn't want to even admit to myself how much I missed this house." He paused. "I guess if the decision not to come was mine, it made it something I was in control of. Even if I wasn't."

I sighed. "Coping mechanisms. Isn't it amazing the things we do to be okay? At least you get to come home again," I said. "And hey, maybe your old room won't be filled with rusting bikes."

He laughed.

Grace made a noise from the back seat and it was our cue to get out. She'd need a diaper change and a bottle soon.

Adrian took a deep breath and pushed open his car door. The second he did, the door to the house opened too and a man jogged down the steps to greet us. It had to be Adrian's dad because he looked exactly like him. And any worries I had about weirdness between these two was instantly put to rest. His dad went right in for a hug.

It took Adrian a second. Like old reflexes were still at work. But then he hugged his dad back and within a few moments, both men were crying.

Adrian's mom stood at the top of the steps watching this with her hands over her mouth. She was crying too.

"I missed you, son," Richard rasped.

Adrian paused. "I missed you too."

When we made it inside the house, Adrian set Grace down in her car seat and hugged his mom. When he let go, he turned to me, beaming. "Mom, this is Vanessa. Vanessa this is my mom, Robin, and my dad, Richard."

Richard was hanging up our jackets on a coat hook as an old woman in a pink housecoat shuffled around the corner.

"Adrian! You're home!" she said, lifting her thin arms to hug him.

Adrian kissed her cheek and then turned her to me by the shoulders. "Grandma, this is my girlfriend, Vanessa. Vanessa, this is Audrey."

The small woman lit up like a Christmas tree. "Adrian! A girlfriend?" She put her hands over her mouth and looked up at her tall grandson, her green eyes almost childlike. "Are you going to marry her?" The question was so innocent and sweet.

"I promised I'd marry her on her thirtieth birthday." Adrian winked.

She inched forward and hugged me. "Oh, bless your heart." She let me go and patted my cheek. "She's a beauty, a real catch. Robin, he's getting married! It's a Christmas miracle!"

She padded back into the living room and I had to cover my laugh with a hand.

Adrian leaned over and whispered, "I think she likes you."

"Are we just going to ignore the Christmas miracle thing or...?"

He laughed. "I've never introduced her to anyone before."

Adrian was looking around the entryway. "The place looks amazing. Wood floors!" he laughed, looking down.

Robin smiled. "They were under the shag." She shuddered.

The house looked like a photo in *Good Housekeeping*. And yes, it did smell like cinnamon.

There was a gorgeous dark wood staircase off the entryway with a fresh pine garland wrapped around it. The living room had a huge fireplace with a blazing fire in it and a glittering Christmas tree decorated like one in the lobby of a five-star hotel.

Every inch of the house looked meticulously restored.

"I can't tell you how happy I am that you're here," Robin said.

Richard smiled. "We picked up a special bottle of wine just for you. Boone's Farm."

Adrian blanched and Richard laughed. "I'm kidding."

Richard grabbed our bags, smiling. "Come on, let me show you to your room. You kids can get situated. We'll have dinner when you're ready."

Our room had a mahogany four-poster bed and private

bathroom with a claw-foot tub. There was already a fire burning in our fireplace, logs shifting. It was super romantic. This weekend was going to be epic.

We had dinner and then drinks in the living room. Both Robin and Richard were great, and Adrian spent a good hour just catching up with his dad. Adrian's grandma got tired and went to bed early. She took a liking to Harry Puppins and brought him to her room with her when she left. Adrian and I stayed chatting with Richard and Robin a little longer. At midnight we called it and went to bed.

Back in our room, Adrian set Grace in her Pack 'n Play.

As soon as his hands were free, he cleared the space between us and pulled me into a kiss. It was more passionate than usual, and I didn't expect it.

"Wow," I said against his lips.

"Thank you," he whispered.

"For what?" I said breathlessly.

"For coming. For making me come. For making me see things differently." His eyes moved back and forth between mine. "The holidays never meant much to me. But this one does."

"Why?" I smiled.

"Because it's our first one. Because everything with you is better. Because I've found the person I can't live without."

My lips fell a little. "Don't say that."

"Don't say what?" he whispered.

"That you can't live without me."

He shook his head. "Why?"

"Because it's a fucked-up thing to say. I don't want to

know that you won't want to live if I'm not here. That's not a compliment. That's sort of my worst nightmare, actually."

He smiled at me. "Okay. I've found the person I want to share everything with. Better?"

I nodded. "Yes. Better."

He grinned.

I nodded up at him. "Hey, what do you think of giving Harry Puppins to your grandma?"

He pulled his face back. "You want to give our dog away?"

I shrugged. "Well, he's not actually *our* dog. We're fostering him. And our lifestyles aren't conducive to long-term dog ownership when you really think about it. Your grandma really likes him. And you notice how he hasn't bitten her?"

He scoffed. "God, can you imagine that dog with teeth?"

"Can you imagine that dog as a dragon?"

Adrian barked out a laugh.

"I'll bet your grandma reminds him of his previous owner or something. We could arrange it with the rescue, pay the adoption fee for her as a gift."

He seemed to mull this over. "I guess you're right. He probably *would* be happier here. There's always someone home. I'm going to miss that little asshole."

I laughed. "We could foster another dog if you miss having one. Save another life."

He smiled at me. "I like that you're such a good person. You make me want to be a better person too."

I rubbed my nose on his. "You already *are* a better person."

His eyes moved to my lips and then came back up. "Are you ready for your Christmas gift?"

I cocked my head. "You don't want to wait until tomorrow?"

"It's midnight. It's Christmas."

"Is it your dick in a box? Because if it is, I'm very excited to open it."

He laughed. "No. Though feel free to open that gift as often as you'd like."

I snorted.

He pulled something out of his pocket and put it in my hand. A small, flat package wrapped in candy cane wrapping paper.

"Is it a gift card?" I asked, prying the paper open.

It was an Altoids tin.

"I didn't want you to have any idea what's in it until you saw it," he said.

I smiled and shook it next to my ear and it made a rattling sound. Then I opened the lid and sucked in a gulp of air. I blinked at it a moment, not believing what I was seeing.

It was Mom's ring.

I put a shaking hand out to touch it like it might not be real. "How did you...?" I breathed.

"I started looking for it right after you told me it was stolen."

A choking sob burst from my mouth.

"Adrian...this is..." I shook my head and looked up at him with tears in my eyes. "This is the best Christmas gift anyone has ever given me," I whispered.

He smiled. Then he took the ring out of the tin, slid it onto my finger, and bent to kiss me. When he came back up, I stood there, looking at my hand, blinking back tears.

"Thank you," I breathed, peering up at him.

His green eyes held mine. "I would give you the whole world if I could." He studied me for a moment. "You had all of this planned, didn't you?"

"What?" I sniffed.

"You knew I was going to fall for you. That I didn't stand a chance."

I smiled. "I'd like to take more credit. But to be honest, with all my problems, I didn't think you'd even want me."

He shook his head. "Did you know my grandparents lived their whole life in this house? They were the happiest couple I've ever known. My grandma married my grandpa a month after they met. I never understood it. I never imagined that I'd ever feel that sure about anyone that soon. Or ever. Until you."

He put his warm hands on my cheeks.

"You are the flood, Vanessa. You pour into me, washing away everything that I used to think mattered and then filling me up to the top until I'm drowned in nothing but you."

My mouth fell open and I couldn't even breathe. No one had ever said anything so beautiful to me. Ever.

"Adrian..."

He shook his head. "You don't have to say anything. It's just true. And I never had any choice in the matter."

The welling tears broke free and slid down my cheeks.

I felt so lucky to be cared for by him. And to be different for him than anyone else had ever been.

He was different for me too.

I was in love with this man. There was no other way to put it. I was in love with him. And he wasn't even *trying* to make me love him. He was just being who he was.

I'd seen so much of the world. But I'd *never* see enough of Adrian. Even if I got a lifetime on this Earth, to be married to him and grow old with him, it wouldn't be enough.

A sudden, bottomless, aching sadness overcame me. Invisible fingers reached up and choked me from the inside.

I was probably going to die. Soon.

This realization hit me in a way that it never had. In all my years of living with this unknown, I'd never felt it this deep in my bones. It had never been this savage.

I'd always suspected I would die young. Then my hand started acting up and I knew I would. I was at peace with it, for the most part. I'd lived a great life. I had no regrets. But now everything was different.

I wanted to stay. I wanted to stay with *him*.

And the fact that I couldn't, that I couldn't get all of him that I wanted, was devastating.

I didn't want to leave him.

How could the universe show me how pure, how perfect, love could be, and then kill me?

A wave of grief poured over me. That forbidden emotion that I never let in. I looked right at the sun and it exploded, crashed into me, and seared me alive.

I started to cry. Racking, choking sobs.

His arms wrapped around me. "What's wrong?"

I shook my head into his chest. "I'm so afraid of losing you."

"You won't," he whispered. "You will *never* lose me."

No.

It would be the other way around.

He would lose *me*.

# CHAPTER 25

# 10 SIGNS THAT YOUR PERFECT RELATIONSHIP IS TOO GOOD TO BE TRUE

## ADRIAN

I woke up on Christmas morning, my arms wrapped around her warm body. She was in nothing but a baggy T-shirt. Her hair was pulled over one shoulder and I kissed the bare skin on her neck and she tipped her head to one side.

She smelled like vanilla. She smelled like *home*.

I couldn't even understand how I had lived without her once. How I'd gone through my days not knowing her. I was turned to her now the way a house plant leaned toward a sunny window. I felt like the luckiest man in the world.

Christmas was one of the best I'd ever had. We ate breakfast and opened presents. I got Richard and Mom an espresso maker. A smaller, less vulgar (as Vanessa called it) version of the one in my own kitchen. We'd gotten the approval from the rescue and we talked to Richard and Mom about Harry. Grandma was already holding him when we told her, and she was *very* excited.

Vanessa's mother's ring was my main gift to her. When all was said and done, I could have bought five rings for the price of what it cost me to find this one, but I wouldn't have changed it for the world. The look on her face when she saw it was priceless.

I also got her an *Office* shirt with Jim's face and BEARS, BEETS, BATTLESTAR GALACTICA on the front. She loved it.

Since Badger Den hadn't panned out, she got me a bottle of 2010 Château Lafite Rothschild Pauillac. She said it was "a Bordeaux with a strong sense of its own self-importance"—a lot like her dad. Her words, not mine. She also bought me an ant farm, which was ironic since my last gift to her, still en route to her apartment, was a butterfly habitat.

After presents and lunch, Dad offered to take Vanessa ice fishing with him. I opted to stay back and spend some time with Mom and Grandma. Grandma went to take a nap about thirty minutes in, and Mom and I moved to the four-season porch on the back of the house overlooking the pond. It had a little fireplace in it, and we were on the couch. We could see Richard and Vanessa like two little dark specks out on the white frozen tundra.

"She's exceptional," Mom said, putting her teacup down on the coffee table. "And she's perfect for you. I *never* liked Rachel."

I laughed. "You only met her once."

"She couldn't look me in the eye!"

Well, I guess *that* made sense.

"Thank you for coming," Mom said. "It meant the world to me." She nodded to the pond. "And to him."

I gazed out the window at Vanessa and Dad.

Vanessa was right. I needed to forgive.

I didn't realize the weight I'd been carrying around on my back all these years until it was gone.

It seemed so pointless now, all the time I'd hated him. I felt like if I'd ever given him another chance, I would have realized that I never really did.

I'd gotten something back today that I'd lost a long time ago. Maybe it was him—or maybe it was just the place I used to keep my feelings about him. Either way, there was room inside of me for other things now. Better things.

And I was looking forward to them.

"I'm glad you're happy, Mom. You've got a nice life here. I can see why you wanted to make the move."

She smiled. "I am happy. I really am." Then she seemed to remember something. "Vanessa says she wants to talk to me about joining a club she and Kristen are in?"

I started choking on my coffee. "Don't join." I cough-laughed. "Trust me. You'll learn more about me and Josh than you'll ever care to know."

Mom smiled. She nudged my arm. "I like her. You know, I think it's destiny that you met this girl."

And then I had to laugh, because I think it was the first time in my life that I actually believed that. But what other explanation could there be?

If I hadn't met Rachel, I wouldn't have gone to Vanessa's apartment that morning. If Becky had taken the studio when it was available or if Vanessa had moved into a different building—or even into a different unit—we wouldn't have met. I'd have never known her or Grace.

It had to be destiny. Stars aligning. Some master plan.

I wasn't ready to have Becky drop my horoscope into my email every morning, but I was open to considering that there might be more to all this than I'd given it credit.

Mom nodded at the baby sleeping in her swing. "I have to be honest, I never thought you'd be like this." She shook her head. "And to be with someone like Vanessa, even knowing that she might be sick?" She smiled at me. "You've grown into a good man, Adrian. I'm so proud of you."

I wrinkled my forehead at her. "What do you mean? She's not sick."

"No, I know." She waved me off. "But with the ALS always being a possibility for her. God, Richard and I must have watched half her videos after you told us you were bringing her. She is *so* brave."

I stared at her. "What are you talking about? ALS is random."

She scrunched up her eyebrows. "Well, yes, most of the time. But it runs in her family. She has a fifty-fifty chance of getting it."

I felt the color drain from my face. *What?*

"You saw this on her channel?" I asked, trying to keep my voice level.

"She talks about it in almost every video she does." She waved me off again. "But you knew that."

I blinked at her for a long moment.

"I have to go change the baby," I said, getting up, trying to keep calm. I grabbed Grace and made a beeline for my room.

As soon as I got there, I locked the door and pulled out my laptop. I googled "Vanessa Price First Video" and hit Search. When I saw the one I was looking for, dated three years ago, I played it, my heartbeat pounding in my ears.

A younger Vanessa came onto the screen. "Hi," she said, waving at the camera. "My name is Vanessa Price."

She held up a glass with something dark sloshing around in it.

"My sister died yesterday. I just poured myself a glass of Sambuca and decided that it was too gross to drink straight so I poured some grape juice in it, which only managed to make it worse. And I sat there staring at this and I asked myself, 'Vanessa, do you really want to be the kind of person who deals with loss by drinking shitty cocktails?' And I decided no. I don't want to take the edge off my sister's tragic and untimely death with disgusting alcoholic beverages because, one, she wouldn't want that. And secondly, I don't want that either. You see, I might be dying too. And dying changes things. I'll get to all that in a minute.

"If I know my days might be numbered, I want to savor each day. I want to enjoy every single thing I eat and drink, and all the people I meet, and every last second on this Earth. I want to laugh. I want to explore. I want to live my life, what's left of my life, like a butterfly in the wind and go where the world takes me. I *definitely* don't want to sit around in my dead-end job and wait for the next installment from the creepy old guy in Monett, Missouri, who met me in an online support group once and now sends me handwritten love letters in cursive." She leaned into the camera. "Let me just tell you, as someone who might have a fatal health condition, there's still nothing more terrifying than a handwritten letter in cursive. Especially when it's accompanied by a Ziploc bag of his slightly-moist-for-some-reason homemade beef jerky. Trust me on this.

"So, I cashed in my 401(k), all $1,023 of it. Oh, and by the way, Patrick, I quit. Sorry you had to find out like this. And I'm leaving today. Now. Right after I upload this video. Actually, no. Right after I have a yard sale, sell my hair, and pawn my jewelry. Then I'm leaving. So, like, maybe tomorrow.

"Probably nobody will watch this. I don't even know who I'm making this for. But I figure if it leads to even one dollar donated to research or one person deciding to live their best life, then I guess it's worth it, right? Now, about my sister.

"My sister died of a rare fatal disease called amyotrophic lateral sclerosis. ALS. You probably know about it because a few years ago everyone was doing that Ice Bucket Challenge and dumping ice water on themselves in support of ALS research.

"*I* know about this disease because it's been a part of my earliest memory. It is my family curse. My family has what's called familial ALS, meaning it's hereditary. The strain my family suffers from starts earlier and kills faster than the sporadic kind and the limited treatments available will only extend your life about three months. The particular mutated gene that causes it in my family hasn't been identified yet. Meaning I can't even test for it." She paused. "I might have a ticking time bomb in my DNA.

"My grandmother had it. My aunt had it. My mom had it, though she died in a car accident before ALS took her life. My sister Melanie had it. And there's a fifty percent chance I have it too…"

What she said after that, I don't know, because my ears started to ring.

I'd been pacing, but now I had to sit. I had to sit or my knees were going to give out.

A 50 percent chance?

I mean, I knew about Melanie, but I didn't know about the rest of them. She never told me, I didn't know, it wasn't in Drake's videos or... She probably thought I knew because—

Her hand...

I started to wheeze.

Her *hand*...

She had *told* me. She told me and I didn't fucking listen. I didn't fucking *hear* her.

Information came flying back to me in patches, each bit sticking until it pieced together into some black, macabre obituary.

Hand weakness.

Her reasons for not dating.

Her tubes were tied, her saying she couldn't adopt Grace because she wouldn't be here in a year...

No...no no no no no.

I couldn't breathe.

It was a wrecking ball to my universe. The shattering of everything. A beautiful stained-glass window in a thousand pieces at my feet.

She might be dying. The love of my life might be dying.

And I was going to have to *watch*.

# CHAPTER 26

# YOUR WORST
# NIGHTMARES RANKED!

## VANESSA

After ice fishing, I jogged up the steps and let myself into our room. Adrian was standing in front of the fireplace facing the door when I came in.

"Hey," I said, pulling off my beanie. "God, I love your family. Your dad's like a mountain man or something. Do you know he—"

"Are you sick?"

I unraveled my scarf. "What?"

"Sick," he said again. "Are you sick? Do you have ALS?"

I wrinkled my forehead. "I don't know…" I stared at him, confused. "Why are you asking me this?"

"I didn't know…" he breathed.

I blinked at him. "You didn't know *what*?"

He shook his head, and I realized how pale he looked. "I didn't know it was hereditary."

I felt my face fall. "What do you mean you didn't know it was hereditary?" I said carefully.

He let out a shuddering breath. "I didn't watch all your videos. I just...I just watched that one where you talked about meeting me and then ghost peppers—"

"Ghost peppers? That's not even my channel. That's Willow Shea's channel. It was a collab." My stomach dropped. "Adrian, what are you saying? Are you saying...you actually didn't know about this?"

"I didn't know," he said again.

And then he started to wheeze.

I darted over to him. "Adrian!"

He was doubled over with his hands on his knees, gasping for air.

"You're having a panic attack. Sit down. *Sit.*" My heart was thrumming in my ears.

It took me a moment to get him moving, but I finally led him to the edge of the bed.

I crouched in front of him. "Slow down your breathing. You're hyperventilating. Breathe through your nose. In through your nose, out through pursed lips."

He took a few labored breaths.

"You need to go to the doctor," he rasped.

"What?"

"Go to the doctor. I'll go with you. We need to know if that's what this is."

"I...Adrian, you don't just walk into a doctor's office and come out with an ALS diagnosis. There's no test for it."

He looked me in the eye, breathing shakily through his nose. "There has to be a test for it. People get diagnosed with it."

"It's diagnosed by excluding other diseases and monitoring your deterioration. It's months and months of testing to rule out other things. It can take a year to get a diagnosis—"

"Then go do that."

I scoffed. "No."

He stared at me.

"No. I won't. HIV, human T-cell leukemia, polio, West Nile virus, multiple sclerosis, multifocal motor neuropathy, Kennedy's disease—they *all* mimic ALS. I'll be tested for all of it, poked and prodded in the hospital for months and for what? I either have it or I *don't*. And if I do, it's fatal. There's nothing they can do about it."

He blinked at me. "But...but what if that's not what it is? What if it *is* something else?"

I shrugged. "Then it won't progress, and it won't be a problem. If it's still around in six months, but nothing else has changed, I'll have my hand looked at again. But the most likely contender was carpal tunnel, and they've already ruled that out."

He stared at me like I'd gone mad. "How can you live like this?" he said incredulously.

I shook my head. "What choice do I have, Adrian? What choice do I have but to live like this? I've *always* lived like this."

His breathing was ragged. He looked like he was going to be sick. I felt like I was going to be sick too.

I sat next to him. "Look, let's just calm down. Okay?"

I rubbed his back. "We can talk about this when you're calmer."

"No. We talk about it now." He was so out of breath it took him a minute to say the next thing. "If you don't have a diagnosis, how can they get you on the right medications?"

I felt my heart shattering.

He knew nothing. None of it. None of the things that I thought he did.

How had this happened? How did something so big slip through the cracks?

"Adrian," I said gently. "I won't be taking any medications."

He froze to stare at me. "What?" he breathed. "What do you mean?"

"I'm not seeking treatment."

"What do you—you *need* medications, there's clinical trials—"

"So I can spend the rest of my short life getting spinal taps and dealing with side effects worse than the disease? In exchange for maybe a couple of extra months of life expectancy? And that's if they don't give me a placebo. And treatments?" I scoffed. "Do you know how few medications there are to treat what I might have? Do you know what they do? They give me three months, Adrian. That's it. Three extra months. Melanie took them. She had headaches and vomiting and was so dizzy and tired she could barely keep her eyes open. She was hooked up to an IV every single day, they had to constantly monitor her blood and her liver function. I don't want to live like that. I'll be tied to whatever hospital is treating me, I won't be able to travel—"

The look on his face could only be described as horror.

"But…what if there's a breakthrough?" he said. "What if it's happening right now? What if they find a cure and you're not in the trial? Vanessa, you have to get treatment—"

I shook my head. "No. I won't. I'll do physical and speech therapy virtually so I can travel. And when I need help breathing and eating and moving, I'll take those steps. I'll do what I need to do to stay comfortable and independent for as long as possible. But I won't take the medications and I won't enter a trial. If I have this, it's already too late. My family's strain progresses too fast. Not any of the promising research they're doing in those trials reverses the damage of the disease. It only slows the deterioration. By the time I got a diagnosis and got in a trial, there wouldn't be any fixing what it had already done to me—and then what? I get to be a guinea pig? That's it? That's the rest of my time here?"

He didn't reply. He just looked at me, breathing heavily through his nose.

I licked my lips. "Adrian, I want to live my best life. I want to travel and have adventures and drink all the wine while I'm still able and laugh and have fun for as long as I possibly can. I don't want to give this disease one more minute. And neither should you."

He got up and my hand fell away from his shoulder. He started to pace. "No." He shook his head. "No, you can't. You have to hang on for as long as possible. You don't know what might happen. You don't know what developments they might come up with—"

I let out a long breath. "There's no clinical trial I haven't read about or study I haven't followed. There's not going to be a miracle. At least not in time for me. If I have this, I'm dying. And all I'm asking is for you to understand how I want to continue to *live*. Believe me. This isn't some spur-of-the-moment decision. I know what I want. And I *won't* change my mind."

He shook his head at me, tears in his eyes. "No. I won't let you do it."

I blinked at him. "Won't let me do what?"

"I won't let you give up."

"I'm *not* giving up. I'm just choosing to live and die on my own terms."

He closed the space between us and put his hands on my arms. "We're a couple. We decide things together, Vanessa. You have to fight this. Let me help you fight it. We'll find the best doctors in the world, we'll go anywhere. I'll fly—" He choked on the last word and my heart broke all over again.

"You can't fix this," I whispered. "I know it's hard for you not to be able to control this. But Adrian, please. I need your support."

His anguished eyes searched mine. Then he dropped his palms from my arms. He turned away and dragged a hand through his hair.

"No. I won't support it." He shook his head and looked back at me. "I won't let you abandon hope. What if there's a breakthrough? What if you could live another twenty years?"

"And what if I *can't*?" I snapped. "What if I only have one more year before I can't swallow or breathe without equipment? One more year before I'm *dead*. I want to keep living my life, Adrian. I'm not wasting precious time hooked up to IVs, trapped in hospitals chasing rainbows."

We stood there staring at each other, breathing hard.

"I'm doing this with or without you," I said, tears welling in my eyes. "Please don't make me do it without."

We stood there in a standoff of silence. I saw his heart breaking. It cracked and tore across his face. A strong deep-rooted tree, struck by lightning, split right down the middle. He looked instantly worn. I'd never seen him look this tired. Like some sort of vitality had left his body since I saw him last.

"I just want none of this to be happening," he whispered.

I swiped a tear off my cheek. "Okay. Then let's forget it's happening. Let's go do something fun. Let's rent snowmobiles or go tubing. Let's stay up late trying some acrobatic sex move in the bathroom. Get an injury we don't want to explain to the paramedics."

This garnered me a tiny smile—but it didn't last. "I need to have a say in this, Vanessa."

I blinked at him. "A say in *my* life?"

"It isn't just your life. This doesn't just affect you."

I set my jaw.

His eyes begged me. "Please. People fight this. They try everything possible—"

I nodded. "Yes. Many choose to try everything. That's *their* choice. That was Melanie's choice. This is *mine*. And the only person who should be making it is *me*."

He stared at me bleakly from across the room. Then he sat on the damask chair and put his face into his hands, squeezing his fingers into his scalp.

"I won't be a captive to this illness, Adrian. I won't spend my life catering to its what-ifs. It's already taken enough from me."

He didn't look up.

I couldn't be sure, but I thought he might be crying.

I wanted to tell him that everything would be okay, like he'd told me once. But I couldn't. I didn't want to give him false hope.

Then I realized that day in his office when he said that to me, he hadn't meant it. How could he? He didn't have any idea what he was talking about.

It wasn't until just now that he realized how hopeless it all really was.

# CHAPTER 27

# THEY THOUGHT THEY HAD EVERYTHING, THEN DISASTER STRUCK!

## ADRIAN

We went around in circles about it all night. Me begging her, her digging in. We somehow faked our way through dinner and then went back to our room and picked up where we left off. Finally, we fell asleep out of sheer exhaustion.

I'd been in the same tornado she was this whole time. I'd been in the eye, in the calm, while it built up all around me without me knowing, and now I was sucked into the vortex, spinning in the howling black, grasping for something to hold on to, and there was *nothing*. She wouldn't give me anything to cling to. Nothing to give me hope.

Yesterday I'd driven us home. We barely talked the whole six hours.

We weren't fighting. We weren't mad at each other. We were just at odds, and there was nothing to say.

As we'd passed a billboard for Minnesota's Largest Candy Store, she waved a white flag and asked me if I wanted to go. I didn't. I just wanted to get home. I wasn't up for any adventures or side trips. I wanted to be back in our space, where I didn't have to pretend to be okay because we were in public—because I was not okay. At *all*.

I didn't begin to know how to accept the situation.

I understood Vanessa's reasoning, but I still couldn't support it.

She didn't know whether she'd have the same reaction to the drugs that Melanie did. What if she tolerated them without side effects? She wouldn't know unless she tried them. Three months wasn't much—but it was something. It was better than nothing. How could she throw away three months of life without even trying?

What if the next clinical trial brought the cure? Or halted the disease in its tracks? Or reversed it altogether? What if that trial was happening now, and she wasn't there to participate in it?

It was unacceptable to me. *Unfathomable.*

How could she just give up?

Waves of anxiety and panic had been rolling over me for two days. I'd never been this tired. It was an emotional weariness that settled in my bones. I felt hopeless. Powerless. I wanted to save her, do *something*, but my hands were tied because she wouldn't even give me one thing. Not *one* thing.

If she'd agreed to see someone about her hand, at least I could busy myself with looking for specialists, making appointments for her. There'd be an actionable plan, there'd be something *happening*. But there was nothing to do. She wanted me to just forget about it. To sit here and go to candy stores with her and pretend like my entire universe hadn't just imploded.

When my alarm clock went off Monday morning for work, I was already up, reading ALS case studies and pouring over medical journals in my office. I'd been up for hours. There was a manic energy to it, a frantic need to educate myself, to be able to present every angle to her, counter every point.

I argued for a living. I convinced juries of twelve that guilty men were innocent. And I couldn't convince one woman to take life-extending medications or agree to a clinical trial to save herself. There had never been anything more important, and I'd never felt so incompetent. I felt like I was riding the edge of a mental breakdown, like I was living in a nightmare that I couldn't wake up from, running to exhaustion because if I stopped moving, it would knock me down so hard I'd never get up.

Nothing would ever be as good again...

From this point on, I'd always be living in the shattered afterward of this disease. Even if by some miracle this thing with her hand *wasn't* ALS, she could still get sick at any time, and if she did, she wouldn't fight then either. We would never be free of it. And if she wouldn't agree to fight it, then we'd never even have hope.

I wanted to go back to being blissfully ignorant. I wanted to forget.

I dragged myself to the bathroom and took a shower to

go to work and then stood next to the bed, knotting my tie, looking down on her sleeping like I'd done last week.

So much had happened in seven days.

Last week my whole life had been perfect. Our future was bright and endless and there was nothing but possibility. I had everything. I had *her*. And I thought I'd *always* have her.

And this week she might be dying.

She'd asked me if she was my girlfriend, and I'd said that word didn't do her justice. It still didn't.

I wanted her with me for the rest of my life, not just the rest of hers. I never wanted to wake up another day without her next to me. And looking at her lying there, knowing that in a year she might be in the ground...

My throat got tight and that wave of helplessness crashed over me again, that thick shallow breathing that came with a panic attack fluttered at the edges.

My happiest moments might be measured in months, not years. And I knew that I should be cherishing every second with her, but I couldn't stop looking at the sun. I *couldn't*. It was careening toward the Earth, and I was angry because she wouldn't try to stop it.

I turned and sat on the edge of the bed and put my face in my hands.

I didn't realize she was awake until she spoke from behind me. "Are you okay?" she whispered.

I dragged a hand down my beard and stared wearily ahead. I didn't answer her.

"Adrian, you won't have to take care of me, if that's what you're worried about. I'll have nurses and aides and we can—"

I shook my head. "I don't care if I have to take care of you, Vanessa. That's not even the fucking..." I couldn't finish.

It didn't matter to me if I had to spend the rest of my life in service to her. I didn't give a shit. I just wanted her *here*.

I put my face back into my hands.

"Do you regret me?" she said into the darkness.

I turned around and looked down at her deep brown eyes peering up at me. "What?"

"Do you wish you never met me?"

I shook my head at her, my voice thick. "How can you ask me that?"

"I didn't mean to mislead you. I didn't mean for you to have feelings for me under false pretenses and have the rug pulled out from underneath you. I thought you knew..."

Her voice cracked. She draped an arm over her face and then she started to cry.

I climbed into the bed in my suit and tie, and pulled her to me. I wrapped her in my body and held her like she might vanish.

She gasped through tears, and I kissed her.

It was desperate. Frantic. Like this kiss could somehow make her change her mind, give me more time or just make me fucking forget. And she must have wanted that too because she kissed me back.

I wanted to overwhelm my senses. I wanted to overwhelm *hers*. I wanted to scream that I loved her, beg her to give me something, some say in what was going to happen. I would make a deal with the devil, sell my soul, if it could save her. But nothing I could do would heal her broken genes. Nothing could undo it or turn back the clock. Time was the only thing that would give us the answers, and it was our enemy.

Her kisses got more urgent. She reached for my zipper and I tugged down her underwear. Her hands fumbled to undo my shirt, but her fingers couldn't do it. I sat up and ripped it open, buttons raining over her and bouncing from the headboard. I whipped off my belt and she grabbed my tie and yanked me back on top of her, pushing my pants down, wrapping her legs around my waist.

The sex was frenzied. Raw. I felt tears squeeze from my eyes as I thrust inside her and she pulled me in like I couldn't get deep enough.

She was everything. *Everything.* I'd found the one thing that was limitless. I'd found the love that poets wrote about.

Only it was a tragedy.

She gasped under me and her back arched and I was right behind her. Then we just lay there, panting at the ceiling, tangled in each other.

"Don't you ever think I regret you," I whispered. "I could *never* regret you. I would trade fates with you if I could. I'd give *anything.*"

I moved to look down at her. "Please, Vanessa. Just say you'll try. Take the medications, do the clinical trials…"

Her eyes went sadder than they already were. "Adrian, maybe you should see someone. A grief counselor. I could go with you…"

I squeezed my eyes shut. "It's not going to help."

*Nothing* was going to help.

"It *will.* They can help you deal with how you're feeling."

I shook my head.

"I just don't know how to do this," I whispered.

She looked up at me, beautiful, her hair on my pillow like a halo. "*Nobody* knows how to do this, Adrian. You need help to get through it. *Please.*"

I shook my head again. "I can't do what you do," I said, my voice thick. "I can't act like none of this is happening. I can't pretend to be happy."

"I don't pretend to be happy. I just refuse to be sad."

If she knew how much I loved her, she'd know this was never going to be possible. My despair was multiplying like cancer. It was consuming me and eating me whole. It put shadows on everything. It stuck to the windows and light bulbs. It blocked the vents, sucked the air out of the room.

And I didn't know how to forgive her for not making any effort to stay.

~

I lay there holding her until she fell asleep again. Then I went to work without waking her up. I was late, but I didn't give a shit. Becky had been blowing up my phone, probably wondering where I was.

I didn't even know how I was going to get through the day. All I knew was that I looked forward to the distraction. I wanted to think about something else, even just for a little while.

When the elevator doors opened on my office floor, Becky pounced on me from out of nowhere. "Adrian—"

"Whatever it is, can it wait until later?" I asked tiredly. "I can't right now."

"No!" she whispered, jogging next to me. "Marcus is, like, *super* pissed."

I pushed open the glass doors into our office. "Pissed about what?"

"The cops didn't give Bueller a sobriety test until three hours after his arrest and—"

She didn't get to finish. Marcus's voice boomed across the office. "How nice of you to finally join us."

I stopped and stared at him with bleary eyes over the desks. He looked furious. His cheeks were ruddy and he had a sheen of sweat on his brow. I registered almost absentmindedly that he looked the human version of a heart attack.

Just like I probably looked like the human version of a broken heart.

I kept walking. I ignored him and everyone's eyes on me, and I made my way to my office and shut the door with Becky standing outside. If he wanted to give me a dressing down, fine. But he could do it in the privacy of my office, not in front of our team.

Marcus came charging in behind me. "The Breathalyzer blow on the Bueller case was invalid. You would have seen this had you bothered to watch the bodycam footage yourself instead of passing it off to John. This whole damn case could have been thrown out weeks ago. You missed the call from the police station when Keller was rearrested so he was interrogated without counsel, you didn't get the medical records for the Garcia trial and now we have to file for another extension. I should fire you right now."

It was almost shocking to know that I had anything left to feel, but my stomach dropped.

He glared at me. "You've had your head up your ass for weeks. I don't know what your problem is, but it's not going to be this firm's problem."

I shook my head. "I'm sorry. I—"

"Don't be sorry. Do your fucking job. Or pack your shit and get out of here. These are people's lives."

He stormed out of the office, and I felt the hushed quiet outside my door that meant everyone had been listening.

I sat heavily in my chair.

Becky came tiptoeing in a few moments later. She clicked the door gently behind her and stood quietly, looking at me with pity.

"So what does my horoscope say about today?" I asked tiredly.

"It says it's gonna be shitty."

I laughed dryly and stared back at her with what I knew were red, grief-stricken eyes.

"What's wrong with you?"

I rubbed my forehead. "I just found out Vanessa might have the gene that carries ALS."

Becky looked confused. "Didn't you know that?"

"No. I didn't know."

She blinked at me a second. "*How?* It's, like, the cornerstone of everything she does. She talks about it like twenty-four seven."

"I know," I said wearily.

She studied me. "Well...does it matter to you?"

"It matters to me that she might die, yeah."

She rolled her eyes. "No, I mean would it have changed things. Would you have not fallen all in love with her if you knew?"

I scoffed. Like I ever had any choice.

"I was done for the minute I laid eyes on her," I said.

I meant it. And losing her was going to kill me. And if she wasn't willing to fight, the countdown for my end had already begun.

Everything I loved was coming undone. My universe was unraveling, one strand at a time.

I couldn't save Vanessa. I couldn't even convince her to reconsider her options. Grace would be gone in a few months. I'd managed to fuck up my job. I'd lost control. All of it. The tornado was flinging bits and pieces of my life in every direction and the mess was getting larger by the minute, too big to clean up.

A frantic, primal self-preservation instinct clawed around inside of me. An urge to fix it, make it right. Stabilize *something*.

But there was only one thing I could fix. I could backpedal the damage I'd done here. At least *this* I could put back in order. This was in my control.

"What do you need, boss?" Becky asked like she could sense my shift in resolve.

"I need you to make a discovery request from the Minneapolis PD. I want the bodycam footage for the Bueller case."

I sat up and clicked open my briefcase. "I need you to call everyone in here. Order takeout for dinner and get me the Keller, Bueller, and Garcia files. We're pulling an all-nighter."

## CHAPTER 28

# TAKE THIS QUIZ TO SEE IF HE'S GHOSTING YOU!

## VANESSA

Adrian didn't come home last night. Or the night before that or the night before that. I mean, he *did*—sort of. He crawled into bed at 2:00 a.m. Then he'd get up and leave again at 6:00. He'd reply to my texts with one word.

Sometimes he didn't reply at all.

I'd shown up with lunch yesterday to surprise him and found him in the conference room with a dozen other people, already eating sandwiches. He'd smiled up at me almost professionally. Like I was a client.

He kissed me swiftly, promised to eat what I brought for dinner, and apologized for needing to go back to work. Then he led me out with a hand on my lower back, and I found myself in the lobby outside the elevators wondering what had just happened.

I kept telling myself it was temporary. He was slammed with a big case—he'd gotten behind the last few weeks.

But another part of me knew it wasn't.

I felt like he was trying to distance himself from me. It was like I was watching his life after I'd died. Like he was working himself to the bone to fill the void, mourning me, and I wasn't even gone yet.

I understood why he was struggling with my decision. He was pragmatic, a man of action. When presented with a problem, he researched it, looked at all the angles, and then argued his way out of it—and he wasn't used to losing.

He wanted to exhaust every avenue. Take me to every specialist, read about every case study, and enroll me in every clinical trial. But none of it would save me. *None of it.* The sooner he understood that, the sooner we could get back to living our lives—because right now we weren't.

I missed him. I missed him *so* much.

Something had fractured between us, and I didn't know how to fix it because I couldn't give him what he wanted. So I just spent the days wandering around his apartment like a ghost, hoping he'd come back to me.

Brent had thrown himself headfirst into BoobStick production, so he was busy. Dad got the job he interviewed for and was gone during the days now, which meant I couldn't take Grace over there for lunch. Dinner was out of the question because I wanted to be here if Adrian came home at a decent hour. So I was alone. All the time.

Just me and Grace.

I was lying on the bed with her yesterday, her little hand wrapped around my finger. I wondered if she would remember me when I was gone, some tiny, internalized recollection of a brown-eyed woman who loved her once. I felt myself willing her to look at my face and keep it somewhere safe inside her. Then I realized that she'd have to put it the same place she'd put Adrian—because she'd be losing him too.

I'd always thought of Adrian as a sentinel. A lighthouse in a storm. Safe and grounding and orienting. Constant. But he was crumbling under the weight of this. And I had the sad realization that if Grace was ours and he lost me like Dad lost Mom, Adrian would have disappeared on Grace too, back into his work, to cope with my loss.

Dad, even with all his faults, had kept us all together after Mom's death. We'd lost her, but we never lost each other.

It was funny to think that Dad was stronger in this way than Adrian. *Dad.*

Dad's coping mechanism hadn't been much healthier. But at least he was there.

I needed something to do, so I completed my end-of-life checklist. Today I went to the funeral home and made my arrangements.

I didn't want an urn. I didn't want to be part of the hoarded clutter in Dad's house if he went back to it, but I fully rejected spending $7,000 on a casket and a burial plot when that money could go to ALS research.

So I bought a cremation and opted for the cardboard box for my remains. I didn't trust that Dad would spread them someplace meaningful, even if I spelled out exactly where I wanted to be laid to rest. I'd probably end up in the pantry next to the cans of expired corned beef hash and fruit cocktail. My guess was that Adrian would be too upset to carry this out. So I entrusted this final task to Drake and told him to sprinkle my ashes in the ocean.

Instead of an end-of-life celebration, I put money down with my travel agent to book Dad, Annabel, Brent, Joel, and Grace on a round-the-world cruise. They could celebrate my life while celebrating the beauty that living has to offer.

And then I was done.

I'd planned it all. Set everything up. The only thing left was to make sure I had a plan for Grace.

Annabel still wouldn't take my calls at the rehab center. But at least she was *at* rehab.

It was New Year's Eve and I'd booked a room for Adrian and me at a bed-and-breakfast in Stillwater for the weekend. When I'd surprised him with it two days ago, he'd seemed excited—well, as excited as he *could* be at 1:15 in the morning after a nineteen-hour day at the office.

I had high hopes for this weekend.

Maybe he needed the space over the last week to process what had happened. Maybe by now the initial shock had worn off and he'd be ready to move forward. This weekend we'd relax, get some sleep. Get some time without the baby, reconnect.

I'd made us dinner reservations at Ladeyra, my favorite wine bar. My plan was for us to ring in the New Year naked with a bottle of Dom Pérignon I'd brought, in the king-size bed in our room.

I dropped off Grace with Dad and checked in at 4:00.

Adrian said he'd leave the office around 5:00 to meet me here, but he hadn't texted me yet for the address. I hadn't told him where we were going because I didn't want him to google it. I wanted him to be surprised when he saw this place.

I'd booked us into the Agatha Christie suite at the Rivertown Inn in Stillwater. I'd stayed at bed-and-breakfasts all over the world, and none paralleled this one. Our room was decked out like an old-fashioned first-class train car inspired by the novel *Murder on the Orient Express*. There was a King Tut sarcophagus in the bathroom next to a huge hot tub for two. It had a private steam room and a rainfall shower. It was opulent and gorgeous and totally the escape we needed.

There was a quote on the wall that I especially liked.

*I like living. I have sometimes been wildly, despairingly, acutely miserable, racked with sorrow, but through it all, I still know quite certainly, that just to be alive, is a grand thing.*
*Agatha Christie, 1890–1976*

It seemed very fitting.

At 6:00 Adrian still hadn't texted. He didn't answer my call either. I went to the inn's cocktail hour without him.

When I got back to our room at 6:45, he hadn't called me back. But dinner wasn't until 9:00, and I knew he had a jury trial starting on Monday and he was probably trying to wrap things up so he could relax this weekend. I decided to take a bath while I waited for him.

A half hour passed.

Then a full hour. I added more hot water to the tub.

When he finally called, I could hear the wind in his car.

"Hey, you on your way?" I asked, putting my toe into the

dripping faucet. "You missed the cocktail hour. There's a golf pro staying here with this girl. They're married, but I don't think to each other—"

"Vanessa, something's come up."

I dropped my foot away from the faucet. "What do you mean?"

"I'm on my way to La Crosse."

My stomach plummeted.

"Wisconsin? *Why?*"

"Garcia got arrested. I have to go down there."

I sat up in the tub. "Wh—*what?*"

"I'm sorry. I'm not going to make it tonight."

The disappointment lingered for only a moment before it turned into hot, boiling anger. Something inside me snapped.

"If you want to break up with me, then just fucking break up with me," I said.

"What?"

I shook my head. "You can't even stand to be in the same room with me, can you? You can't even *look* at me."

"It's not— Vanessa, I don't have a choice. I'm his attorney. I *have* to go down there."

"The only reason you have to go down there is so you won't have to face a night alone with *me*. He's got a whole firm of attorneys. You said it yourself, anyone can go, it doesn't have to be you."

I could almost see him dragging his hand down his mouth, looking anywhere but at me.

I squeezed my eyes shut. "Don't pretend this isn't *exactly* what we both know it is, Adrian. You're *running*. Even when you're *with* me, you're not here. Stop ghosting me and calling it work. Please. *Please.* Turn around. Come back. And *stop* doing this to me."

There was a long pause on the other end.

"And then what? I watch you let yourself die?"

And there it was.

So I was right.

My chin quivered. "I can't give you what you're asking, Adrian."

"And I can't give you what you're asking either. I *need* this job. Right now it's the only thing making me feel halfway sane."

"So being away from me twenty hours a day is what's making you sane?"

"I didn't mean it like that—"

"Yeah, you did." I forced down the tears. "I get it. You're still whiplashed and trying to figure it out, and you're doing what you do when you feel out of control—you work. But you're wasting precious time." I shook my head. "It's just an illusion, Adrian. The control is an illusion. No one can promise you forever. People die unexpectedly every day. They have car accidents and heart attacks and strokes and if all you do is live your life fixated on how it ends, you're just living the end twice. We still have time and all these things that you think will save me *won't*. Stop chasing it and just be happy. Be happy with *me* while you can."

He didn't answer, but the wind in the background had stopped, like he'd pulled over.

"This might be my last New Year's," I whispered. "Don't you get that? Don't you get that every single holiday might be my last one? That every day with me is a gift? Doesn't that mean something to you?"

"Of *course* it does."

"Then treat it like a gift! Come back to me. If not tonight, fine. If you have to work, I get it. Go do what you have to do. But then *be* in this relationship. Your knee-jerk response to finding out that I might be dying should be to spend every waking moment with me, not disappear."

He was quiet for so long I thought I'd dropped the call.

"I can't be helpless, Vanessa." His voice was thick. "I can't sit here and watch you die without knowing we did *everything* we could to prevent it."

I shook my head, and the tears that had been welling in my eyes spilled down my cheeks. "I can't wait months for you to come to terms with this, Adrian. I don't have months to spare. Especially if you're not going to do anything to help you work through it. You won't go to therapy, you won't join a support group, you won't even talk to me. And I'm not willing to be unhappy and alone while you act like I'm already dead. I'm just not."

There was a long, quiet pause.

"I need you to tell me that you'll seek treatment," he said into the silence. "That you'll get diagnosed, that you'll do clinical trials, take the medications available. I need answers. I need a plan." He paused. "This is my bottom line."

The words hung between us.

"Your bottom line?" I whispered. "Your bottom *line*? You're giving me an ultimatum?"

He didn't reply.

I shook my head. "And what if I say no?"

He waited a long beat. "Vanessa...I need to know you're going to give us more time."

My heart shattered and disintegrated into a thousand tiny pieces.

"Fuck you, Adrian. You don't even want the time you have."

And I hung up on him.

# CHAPTER 29

# THIS GOODBYE WILL LEAVE YOU IN TEARS

## VANESSA

Annabel's rehab facility was a nice one. It should be. It was costing me enough.

After I hung up on Adrian, I left the bed-and-breakfast and drove to Iowa.

I spent New Year's Eve at a Motel 6 a mile from where Annabel was staying. I checked the rehab's visitors' hours, set an alarm for the morning, and then downed half the bottle of champagne I brought out of a paper cup and went to sleep before the countdown.

Adrian had called me back almost as soon as I hung up on him. I turned off my phone. There was absolutely nothing left to say.

He'd given me an ultimatum. An *ultimatum* about how I'd live the rest of *my* life.

He wouldn't have even dated me if he'd known I might be sick. It was something I had been afraid to think about. It was something he'd vehemently denied. But now I knew that all of this, all his love, had been given in ignorance.

I was clickbait.

I was a deception. An enticing promise of worthy content. But when you really looked, it was nothing but false advertising. Not at all what you thought it was going to be. I'd sold Adrian on something that didn't exist. I hadn't done it on purpose, but he'd been misled nonetheless.

I should have known he was too good to be true. I should have looked for the reason a man like that would be willing to love someone like me. It was because he didn't know any better.

And now he did.

The implications were too enormous to think about. So I didn't. I showered, grabbed a shitty coffee at the gas station, and went to see my sister.

Annabel wasn't expecting me, and I didn't know if she'd see me. I checked in at the front desk and they buzzed me in.

When she came out into the visitors' area and saw me, she paused for a moment. Then she pressed her lips into a line and dropped into the chair across from mine.

"Hey," I said.

She crossed her arms. "Hey."

We sat there in a tense silence.

She seemed tired, but her eyes were clear. She wore a clunky sweatshirt and gray sweatpants. Her blond hair was up in a messy ponytail. She looked thin. Almost gaunt.

"Are you eating?" I asked.

"The food here is shit," she mumbled.

"Do you want me to get you some protein bars or something?"

She shrugged and looked away, picking at a small tear in the arm of her recliner.

"How's your shoulder?" I asked.

"Fine, I guess," she muttered. "They won't give me anything so…"

"Well, no. You're in rehab," I said sarcastically.

She ignored me.

"Grace is doing well," I offered.

She didn't reply.

"I called you," I said. "A lot."

She pursed her lips. "I didn't want to talk to you."

"And why?"

"Because you're a liar."

I scoffed. "And how's that exactly? Because I refused to unconditionally fund your bender?"

She leveled her eyes on me. Sharp blue eyes. Grace's eyes.

"So where's your brace?" she asked.

I blinked at her. "What?"

She glared at me. "Your brace. For your *hand*."

I shifted in my seat. I'd never worn it in front of her. I'd never worn it in front of anyone except for Adrian.

"I saw it when I came to see your apartment. Before I had the baby." She sat there, daring me to deny it. "So when were you gonna tell us? Were you just gonna, like, die and let us find out after?"

A flash of hurt flickered on her face. A microsecond of

vulnerability that she covered up with the hard expression she used for a mask.

She knew. This whole time she *knew.*

"Did you tell Dad and Brent?" I whispered.

She shook her head. "No. But they know. We're not idiots. We can see when you can't even open a ketchup bottle."

I sat back in my chair.

So this was why Dad had gotten worse. Why they both had. No wonder she went off the rails. No wonder she lost her shit.

Defeat bolted into my throat and choked me.

ALS's grip would never let go. It just kept wrapping its tendrils around our ankles and pulling us down.

And now it had Adrian as well.

It had anyone who got close enough.

I swallowed. "I'm not sure if that's what it is," I said.

She scoffed. "Right."

We fell into silence again.

She tugged at the ripped fabric on her chair. "Almost took a whole bottle the day I found out," she said quietly. "Went right to the clinic. Got a script and everything. Didn't fill it though. Kept telling myself that Mel would be disappointed in me if I took it while I was pregnant. It was the only thing that kept me from doing it, thinking Mel could see me."

I leaned forward with my elbows on my knees. "Annabel, if this is what...what it *might* be—I can't keep Grace. I can keep her while you finish this program. But when you get out, you have to take her."

She looked back at me, and all I could think was how

young she was. She didn't look nineteen. She looked like a kid. She didn't even look old enough to drive.

"Give her to Dad."

I stared at her. "Give her to *Dad*?"

"Or Brent and Joel."

"Wha…Brent will bail the second she has a diaper blowout! He's not ready to have a kid." I shook my head. "You have to take care of her, Annabel. She's *yours*."

"I don't want to. I can't."

I licked my lips. "Yes, you can. You *can*. I'll help you. I'll help you with money, you won't have to work—"

"I won't stay clean."

She said it matter-of-factly. It wasn't a threat. It was just a statement.

"I won't. I want to, but if I have to take care of her, I won't. It's too hard. I'm just being honest. They tell me in here to speak my truth and that's what it is. I never wanted her. I don't want to be a mom. I can't do it."

"You know Dad can't do this," I breathed. "If something happens to me, he'll be a mess. He's *already* a mess. You can't leave Grace with him—"

"Then find somebody else. People always want babies. She's good. Somebody will want her."

Tears pricked my eyes. "You can't mean that," I whispered. "She's your daughter."

She shrugged again. "Least I'm honest."

We sat there in silence.

I studied her. Her baby face with its deep forehead lines and wear beyond her years.

She was damaged. So, so damaged.

And why wouldn't she be?

She was only fourteen when Mel got sick. She was a child, living in a trash heap, watching her oldest sister, the one who had been the only mom she ever knew, wither and die.

And now she knew I might be dying too.

How much did I expect her to endure? She wasn't even old enough to drink and she'd already lived through more tragedy than most people three times her age.

Her own mother had abandoned her. Then Mel died, and I left her alone with her grief and traveled the world while Dad descended further into his mental illness. She got pregnant by accident, her body taken hostage by a baby she didn't plan and didn't want and wasn't emotionally capable of caring for. She was an addict. She had her own demons to deal with—and at least she was self-aware enough to recognize it.

Was I doing to her what Adrian had done to me? Insisting I knew what was best for Annabel when she was the one who had to live with her choices?

Maybe listening to her was doing what was best for her *and* Grace.

Even if it didn't feel that way.

"Okay," I whispered. "I'll make sure she ends up with a good family."

For the first time in a long time, her face went soft.

Probably because for the first time in a long time, I decided to hear her.

Two hours later I sat in the parking lot of the wellness center, typing the address to my apartment building into my phone to navigate home.

Annabel had given me a long hug before I left.

I saw a spark of who she could be today. It took a while to bring it out, but it was in there. She talked about the future, about going to college and getting her degree. She wanted to do graphic design, make websites for people. I told her how impressed I was with what she did for BoobStick and her eyes lit up. She reminded me of Grace when she looks up at Adrian, that same pure happiness that I'd been afraid my sister was no longer capable of.

I'd told her it was a great idea. I liked that she was looking ahead.

I knew she could stay clean. She was strong. And she had access to all the resources she needed now. I think it freed her to admit that she needed to let Grace go. I guess it freed me too in a way. Hoping never was my favorite strategy. There was no more what-if now. I didn't have to worry if Annabel's addiction would ruin Grace's life after I was gone. It wouldn't—because Grace would be gone too.

I finished typing in the address and went to hit Send on the search bar...

And then I just stopped.

What was the point in going back to St. Paul? What was there for me?

Adrian had said his piece, and I'd said mine. He'd given me an ultimatum, and I'd given him my answer. It was over. And now everyone had what they needed. So what was the point in continuing to be there?

Annabel was getting help. Grace had Dad for now, and Dad had Sonja to support him. They'd be able to take care of Grace until I got her placed with a family. Brent was on the right track.

Adrian had his work and his bottom line.

And for the first time in a long time, I had the prospect that my family might be okay. That was more than I'd ever hoped for.

But would they still be okay if I stuck around? If they had to watch me slowly decline like they watched Melanie?

They wouldn't. Because looking at me now was nothing but looking at the sun.

They were a fragile house of cards by an open window...and I was the breeze. I had to go.

I wouldn't get to say goodbye to Grace...

I couldn't go back. I'd lose my nerve.

This punched me right in the heart, made me feel like I couldn't breathe.

My baby...

I'd seen her for the last time and I didn't even know it. I'd kissed her face and snuggled her and smelled her head and I didn't savor it, I didn't hold it in...

She was more mine than she ever was Annabel's. She'd always be mine, even when she didn't remember a thing about me.

And that would have to be good enough.

I had to hope that the tiny pieces she'd gotten of me would be enough to last a lifetime.

I'd call her case worker and my lawyer and make sure they knew where she was.

I wiped the tears off my cheeks, looked down at my phone, and cleared the address from the search bar. And suddenly the road ahead was a giant question mark.

I'd set off all those years ago to live my life. To be a butterfly in the wind. I'd left on my quest alone. No cameraman to mic me up and follow me and edit my footage. No production assistant to book hotel rooms and plan agendas. Nothing but a single suitcase and the clothes on my back. I had that in the car now. I even had my passport. I'd embarked with a goal to laugh and see the world and live like I had one year left. And now maybe I actually did.

I wasn't ready to give up my love for life. And I wasn't going to spend one more day looking at the sun. I'd never do it again. I chose living—because anything else was just waiting to die.

I started the engine and pulled out of the parking lot. When I had to make a turn, I went wherever the wind took me.

# CHAPTER 30

# THE ULTIMATE GUIDE TO SURVIVING A BREAKUP (THAT'S YOUR FAULT)

## ADRIAN

Nothing had changed about my place. The tree was still up and lit, Grace's swing was still next to the sofa. Even Vanessa's throw blanket was where she'd left it, balled up on the couch, smelling like her. But everything was different now. Like the lights had gone on in a nightclub.

I hadn't heard from Vanessa in two days. Since she hung up on me on New Year's Eve.

The second it happened, I knew I'd fucked up.

I'd turned my car around, called Lenny and asked him to go in my place, and drove straight to Stillwater. But Vanessa wouldn't answer my calls or texts and I didn't know where to go. I googled bed-and-breakfasts in the area and drove to each one, looking for her car, but I couldn't find it.

That was the last time I spoke to her.

I betrayed her. I made her choose: me or *herself.*
And she'd called my bluff.

That ultimatum was an act of desperation from a despondent, sleep-deprived man who was descending into madness at the thought of losing her. It was manipulative and wrong, and I could have never in a million years acted on it. I knew that now more than ever. I wasn't capable of leaving her, no matter what her position on the end of her life continued to be.

Everything in my universe had been forcefully ranked all of a sudden. My shortcomings laid out with the clarity of hindsight—I was so afraid of being left again by someone I loved I couldn't even wrap my brain around what was right and wrong.

I should have done what she said. Gone to grief counseling, joined a support group, found a therapist, talked to someone. *Anything* other than what I did. Anything other than shutting down and giving her an ultimatum because *I* couldn't handle the choice she made—and it was *her* choice to make. She was an expert witness on ALS, giving her testimony, and I'd refused to listen because I wasn't emotionally capable of accepting it. I was as damaged as they came and I'd never done a fucking thing about it, I'd never dealt with any of it, my abandonment issues, my need for control.

I was no different from Richard. Only *I* left my family without going anywhere.

I didn't think things could possibly get worse than they already were.

I'd been wrong.

This was my rock bottom. *This.*

I couldn't eat, I couldn't sleep. It felt like my family had disintegrated. Like I'd failed them and my wife had left me and taken our kid. I didn't know what to do with myself. I was afraid to leave. I kept everything quiet so I'd hear her next door if she came home, but she didn't.

I'd given away the time we had left.

She was right. I should have cherished every second with her.

I wanted to go back in time and talk to her on the car ride back to Minnesota from Nebraska. I wanted to take her to the candy store she asked to see and have lunch with her that day she came to my office and kiss her as the ball dropped on New Year's Eve. Instead I'd spent those last days just staring at the sun.

And now I was living the worst possible thing twice.

I hoped she just needed some space. Maybe she just needed to calm down. Then she'd come back, give me the chance to apologize. I was clinging to that hope.

It was almost 2:00. I was in the living room with my head in my hands when my cell phone rang. I jumped for it, but it was only Becky.

I dragged a hand down my mouth and slid the phone to my ear. "Hey—"

"Adrian, what have you done?"

Her voice was shaking.

I sat up. "What are you talking about?"

"Vanessa just uploaded a video."

I hung up on her and bolted to my laptop to bring up her channel.

The video opened with Vanessa sitting in a Delta lounge. Her eyes were red and puffy. It was entitled "Goodbye Forever."

My stomach dropped.

"Hey, everyone." She did her wave at the camera. But she didn't have the usual light around her eyes. She was in a hoodie and her hair was in a messy braid. She looked the way I felt. Heartbroken.

"I wish I were here to give you better news, but like you see from the title of this, this is going to be my last video. I haven't been honest with all of you, and I want to be honest now because I think you deserve that." She paused. "For the last few months, I've been having what I'm afraid might be the early-onset symptoms of ALS.

"I've been giving my life a lot of thought and knowing that I might only have a little time left, I've decided how I want to spend it. And that's in privacy.

"I'll still be out there in the world. And I'll make videos of my final time here, if that's what I'm staring down at. But they won't be released until after my death. Why?" She shrugged. "Because they'll be worth more when I'm gone, and I'd like to give my charity one final push after I go. My last middle finger to this disease—while I can still lift one." She gave the camera a weak smile.

"You guys have been the wind beneath my wings. Truly. I couldn't have done any of this without you. We've raised millions for ALS research and done more for awareness than I could have ever hoped for. You gave me a legacy I can be proud of and one day all of this will save lives. Thank you for that. For giving me a platform and for making a difference." Then she took a deep breath, and her face went sadder than it already was. "Jesus's Abs—*Adrian*." She looked right at me. "I never told you thank you. I never told you a lot of things.

You gave me so much over the last month. You were a friend and a support. You made me feel safe and still. You gave me the chance to have a family of my own for a little while, and though I know I wasn't, I felt like I got to be a wife." Her chin quivered, and my heart shattered. "You are the love of my life—and not because my life is probably going to end a lot sooner than I hoped. I want you to know that I don't blame you for not being able to do this. I hope you find someone who can give you the lifetime of memories that I can't, because you deserve it." She pressed her lips together like she was trying not to cry. "Don't ever forget the things I taught you. Life's too short, Adrian. It is too fucking short. Eat the cake, take the vacation, dance in the rain. And don't do anything that's going to break your heart. I'm just sorry that in this case, that thing was me."

She looked at me through the screen for another moment. Then the video ended.

It hadn't even been over a full second when something banged on the adjoining wall to our apartments. I jumped to my feet and ran to the door, gasping for air, thinking maybe she had come back for her clothes or Grace's things. Maybe it wasn't too late.

But when I opened the door, a couch drifted out of Vanessa's apartment down the hallway, carried by two men in blue mover's shirts.

Gerald's voice came from inside. "Be careful with those, they're collector's items! And I'm watching you, so don't think you're going to slip something into a pocket!"

He saw me come into the doorway and stopped his delegating. "Ah, the lawyer!" He smiled at me.

I looked around the small studio, my heart pounding against my rib cage. A team of people were packing things into boxes. Someone in white gloves was pulling Vanessa's Banksy down and wrapping it in paper. Her mattress was propped against a wall, and a man was disassembling her bed. Someone was in the kitchen, boxing up Grace's bottles. A woman was on a ladder scraping the glow-in-the-dark stars off the ceiling.

"What are you doing?" I breathed, looking back at Gerald, though it was obvious.

He rocked back on his heels with his hands in his pockets in that unaffected way of his. "Moving my daughter's possessions, per her request." He held up a hand. "Don't worry. You'll have the unit back in a couple of hours. Broom clean, just like the lease says."

I stared around at the activity in disbelief. I couldn't breathe. It felt like she was being erased. In an hour this place would be like she had never been here at all.

"Where is she?" I asked, looking back at him, standing in the middle of the chaos.

His smile fell, and for a moment he looked almost sorry for me. "Son, you know I can't tell you that."

I looked at him desperately. "You *can*. You have to tell me where to find her. Please," I begged.

His bushy eyebrows drew down. "Maybe we should go have a chat. I'd say your apartment is probably better suited. Shall we?"

I blinked for another moment at the impossible scene in her studio. Her life disappearing before my eyes. "Yes."

When we got back to my place, he nodded to the bar on

the way to the dining room table. "Pour me a stiff one, will you? It's been a bit of a day."

I poured him a bourbon with shaking hands and slid it to him before sitting down.

There was a fog of disbelief over all of this so thick it almost didn't feel real. I looked at him sitting there like he was an extension of a strange dream I was having.

He put his nose into the tumbler and breathed in. Then he gave me a nod of approval and took a swallow. "Ahhh, that's nice. Very, very nice. You have good taste." He raised his glass to me. "In bourbon *and* women."

"You have to tell me how to find her. Now. I need to go now," I said, too desperate for tact.

He chuckled. "You know, you remind me a little of myself when I was your age. And Vanessa is a carbon copy of her mother. Same energy. Luminous." He swayed his glass at me. "You know what I'm talking about. They have that inner light. And stubborn! My God, are they ever." He laughed dryly into his tumbler. "My wife, Samantha, had been symptomatic for a year when she got in the car accident. They said she lost control of the wheel. Shouldn't have been driving, truth be told, but nobody ever could tell Samantha what to do." He smiled to himself, his eyes distant, like he was remembering. Then the corners of his lips dropped and he looked up at me from under his bushy eyebrows.

"You know, she wouldn't do the trials either. Couldn't wrap my brain around it. Was angry—for *years*. How could she leave us like that? Why didn't she try? Took me a long time to realize that just because you don't recognize the fight they choose doesn't mean they're not fighting."

He leaned forward. "This isn't even the hard part, son. Loving her isn't the hard part. Neither is just shutting up and supporting her, even if you don't believe in how she's doing it. The hard part's on its way and it's going to last the rest of your life once that light you've been living under dims and goes out. Even if this thing ends up being nothing, you'll just be waiting for the shoe to drop, driving yourself mad. It'll eat you from the inside out. If you can't handle it now, believe me, you're not cut out for what's coming." He paused. "But I think you knew that."

He looked at me levelly. "You knew what you were doing when you gave her that ultimatum. You knew you weren't built for this. Don't chase her. You have your whole life ahead of you. Take the gift she's given you, go back to work, love another woman. Move *on*. Let her go."

I studied him. He couldn't be more than fifty-five. But he looked ten years older. Hard lines. The wear of decades of grief.

He took a final swig of his drink and pushed up on his knees. "I have custody of Grace. Annabel's waiving her rights. Feel free to stop by and say hello." He paused in my doorway and looked at me a long moment. "You always had my blessing, Fancy Hall Cop. I liked having a lawyer in the family."

And he let himself out.

## CHAPTER 31

# ARE YOU BROKENHEARTED? TAKE THIS TEST TO SEE!

*Two months later*

## VANESSA

We should probably hurry up if we want to catch the light," Laird said.

We were standing on the beach at an empty tiki bar. I was leaning on the bamboo railing overlooking the water. The sun was setting and a warm salty ocean breeze blew my hair back over my shoulders.

Brent was in the surf with his pant legs rolled up, watching the waves.

I was on Drake's private island. Brent had been in the country almost as long as I'd been on the road. Part of Drake's condition in backing BoobStick was that production of the lip balms take place on the neighboring mainland to bring jobs to the locals. Brent and Joel came out to oversee training and do quality control.

Drake and Laird's wedding was tomorrow, so Brent had taken a boat over to be my date. It was fucking depressing. Not only was my date gay and in another relationship, but he was also my brother. I'd achieved the crying emoji wedding date trifecta.

Brent and I had our come-to-Jesus on the phone a few days after I left. He'd known the whole time I might be sick, and he'd respected my wishes not to tell anyone about it, so he never brought it up. But it hurt him that I didn't confide in him.

We'd gotten a lot closer over the last few months. I stopped being his big sister and started being his friend—and I liked it better that way. I needed a friend. And he needed me to know he could take care of himself.

And he could.

There was a raging pig roast going on in front of the dock. I could see the glow of the tiki lamps from between the palm trees, and music was pulsing in the distance. It was an interesting crowd over there. You were as likely to be sitting next to a Sherpa at dinner as you were Brad Pitt.

"You should get back," I said to Laird. "You're missing your own party."

He smiled as he clipped my mic to my lei. "Eh, I'd rather be here. That's Drake's thing, not mine. I hate crowds."

I smiled. "Well, I'm happy to have the company—and the help. It'll be nice to have a video for this series that wasn't made in selfie mode."

I'd spent the last two months lying low, trying not to get recognized. I backpacked for a few weeks in the UK. Spent a week in Amsterdam in random hostels.

Then I'd sort of lost my way. Like a windup toy that ran out of up, I just stopped. I couldn't move forward anymore.

There was nothing I wanted to see. No places I wanted to go. I always enjoyed Ireland, so I went there thinking it would cheer me up.

It didn't.

I rented a cottage near Dublin and I just sat. For three solid weeks, binging romance novels. I didn't go check out the quaint village nearby, I didn't make any friends. The only thing that got me out of that little house was the wedding, and I'd probably squat here on this island until I died for no other reason than I simply couldn't go anymore.

Drake didn't care if I stayed. I don't think he had any idea how many people lived on his island. It was sort of a living, breathing entity, gathering and losing inhabitants with the tide. Yesterday I asked him who the dreadlocked man living in the hammock out by the gardens was and he legitimately didn't know. He said he thought it was, and I quote, "The llama guy maybe?"

If there was a random hammock llama guy, there could be an eccentric vlogger chick who drank all the wine and lived in the hut by the banana trees.

My hand hadn't gotten any better.

I had good days and I had bad ones. On the good days I could feel my fingers. I could lightly grip things. On the bad days I had almost no use of my hand at all.

It wasn't unusual for ALS's progression to stop for a time, or even regress a little. But eventually it would progress. It *always* progressed. And now it had started to move up my arm. I'd lost strength in my bicep. The change was noticeable now compared to the other side. Skinny.

*Atrophied.*

It was scary to look in the mirror and see the differences. So scary that I'd taken the full-length mirror out of my hut. It was even worse seeing everyone else notice. To turn around and catch Brent's eyes darting away from me like he hadn't been staring at it.

It made me even more certain that I'd done the right thing leaving when I did. Annabel and Dad couldn't have handled this.

It was official. There was a tiny, toothless, ancient Chihuahua in Nebraska that was probably going to outlive me.

Drake's acupuncturist took a shot at helping. It worked a little. The good days were usually right after a visit. But my apathy, my lack of drive and enthusiasm and love for life— nothing could improve that.

I lost something when I lost Adrian.

It took me a long time to come to terms with that. But I did. I'd lost the ability to decide not to be sad. That was officially out of my hands.

There are people you can know for a lifetime and they never get into your heart. And then there are those who are already inside it, before you ever even lay eyes on them. Adrian was a part of me always, I realized. It didn't matter that I'd only known him for a minute in the day of my life, or a second in the day of his. He was eternal for me, immortalized in my soul, before, after, and forever. And forgetting him wasn't any more possible than changing my DNA.

I missed him. Sometimes I woke up in the middle of the

night and it took me a minute to realize I was alone. That Adrian wasn't next to me or just on the other side of a wall. Sometimes I'd see the back of someone's head and I was sure it was him. But of course it never was.

It never would be.

I imagined he'd thrown himself fully back into his work. Maybe he'd started training for a new marathon.

Maybe he'd started dating again…

Hopefully everyone was getting back to their lives. I wouldn't know.

I'd been radio silent with Dad and Annabel. I changed my number and canceled my email. It was better that way, at least for now. I was a crutch for them—and maybe they were a crutch for me too.

I had to acknowledge that there was some codependency between me and my family, and all of us needed to learn to live a different way. They needed to make decisions on their own, and I needed to accept being okay with them failing. They'd never be independent if I kept being one phone call away from bailing them out. It was better if they learned to stand without me, that they practiced that now before they had to do it in earnest.

If Dad or Annabel needed to reach me for anything that wasn't money, Brent knew how to find me. I put my adoption attorney in touch with Sonja. I knew between her and Dad, they'd find a perfect family for Grace. They didn't need me to micromanage it. Dad was a smart guy—and way too paranoid to let her go to anyone who didn't pass muster.

And Adrian…he'd move on. He'd be fine in another relationship, one that was more manageable and predictable.

I hoped he got that. I really did. I loved him enough to want him to be happy.

Aaaaand I was also petty enough to hope their sex wasn't as good as ours—but I digress.

Brent came up from the shoreline looking at his phone. "Hey, did you know #WheresVanessaPrice is trending on Twitter?"

I snorted. "Doesn't surprise me. I made a dramatic exit. And good. It means the videos will get more views when they finally get posted."

He gave me a sorry look. "You know, if you want, I could come with you somewhere after the wedding. We could go on an adventure. Maybe someplace exotic that has those really aggressive monkeys that snatch your food and shit everywhere?"

I laughed dryly.

"I'm serious, Vanessa. This funk you're in is gross. You need something to look forward to."

I shook my head. "Nope. I'm gearing up to be the hermit who lives on Drake's island. The crazy braless American who day drinks and kidnaps all the baby goats."

Laird made a face. "I think we already have one of those." He hoisted his camera. "Ready?"

Brent sat on a barstool and went back to looking at his phone.

I nodded. "Ready."

I put my fake smile on first. Then I turned to face the camera. "Hi, all! Well, I made it! I'm at the wedding. You guys would *not* believe this guest list. The Weeknd showed up on a Jet Ski this morning and Anthony Hopkins is over there." I leaned in. "I'm gonna see if I can get him to do the fava bean line from *The Silence of the Lambs* later. It's been an amazing couple of—"

"Vanessa! Oh my God! Chrissy Teigen just mentioned you on Twitter!"

I paused in my monologue to look at Brent. "Really? For what?"

Getting mentioned by a celebrity wasn't exactly unheard of for me, but I didn't know her.

Brent was staring at his phone and he didn't answer.

"Well? What did she say?"

"Oh my God. Oh my God oh my God oh my God."

He jumped off his stool and shoved his phone into my hand. "LOOK!"

I read the tweet.

> Can someone please put this poor man out of his misery and tell him where to find Vanessa Price?

She'd used the Where's Vanessa Price hashtag and retweeted an article titled "This Man Is Searching the Globe for His Lost Love and You Won't Believe Why!"

My soul. Left. My *body*.

I clicked on the article and held my breath, hoping to God it wasn't Monett Missouri Guy.

It wasn't.

> Adrian Copeland is on a worldwide quest to find the woman who got away—and chances are you know who she is.

For weeks famous YouTuber Vanessa Price had been teasing her viewers with stories of a handsome, mysterious love interest. We now know this man is a prestigious St. Paul attorney who won't stop until he finds her.

Price is known for her passionate pursuit for a cure to amyotrophic lateral sclerosis, also known as ALS, the disease that inspired the Ice Bucket Challenge of 2014.

Price lost her sister to the illness and in a recent final farewell video, Price revealed she may have the early-onset symptoms of the disease. She announced that she was shutting down her popular channel, Social Butterfly, and in a heart-wrenching goodbye, alluded that her potential diagnosis was too much for her beau, Adrian, and that she was leaving him.

According to Copeland, they had a disagreement about her choosing to not seek treatment and the couple broke up.

"I made a horrible mistake, and I lost the love of my life," Copeland said in a viral video he made three weeks ago, pleading for information on her whereabouts.

Copeland, who is in the process of adopting Price's infant niece, said he struggled with a lifelong fear of flying and had to spend a month in intensive therapy to overcome his phobia and deal with the feelings about Price's potential diagnosis. He's since followed leads all over the globe, baby in tow, in his attempt to locate Price, who has gone underground. We can't say if she knows he's looking, but Copeland has made one thing very clear:

"I'll never stop looking. And when I find her, I'm spending the rest of her life letting her know how much I love her."

"Oh my God..." I breathed.

"How the *fuck* did you not know about this until just now?" Brent said to the side of my face.

I looked at him wide-eyed. "I'm on a social media hiatus, and when I'm not, I get like two million notifications a day! It's like a flock of seagulls squawking at me constantly over half a dozen different social media networks! I ignore it!! Why didn't he call you to look for me? You knew where I was!"

"I blocked him in solidarity! He's been dead to me since New Year's!"

"Didn't Dad call you?"

"Well, yeah, but I didn't answer! Who answers when *Dad* calls???"

Grace. Adrian was adopting *Grace*.

I did a laugh-cry as I felt around my dress for nonexistent

pockets, searching frantically for a phone that I hadn't even charged in a week. "My phone. I need my phone!"

Brent gestured dramatically to my hand. "You're holding mine! Use mine!"

I fumbled to the call screen. "His number. I don't know his number!" I typed his name into Brent's contacts and it didn't come up. "How do you not have his number?! He's one of your investors!"

"It's under Jesus's Abs! No! Wait! It's under Fancy Hall Cop! Type in Fancy Hall Cop!"

I pulled up the contact and hit Send, pacing along the bamboo railing.

The call wouldn't connect.

I made a guttural shrieking noise and whirled to run to beg Drake for his satellite phone.

I was going to miss the wedding. I was going to get on The Weeknd's Jet Ski and take it right to the nearest airport. I wouldn't stop moving until Adrian was in front of me.

"Vanessa!" A faraway voice drifted from somewhere in the distance.

I slid to a halt in the sand, panting. "Did you guys hear that?" I asked, looking back at Laird and Brent, who'd followed me. Laird was still filming.

"Vanessaaa!"

I twisted around. "Okay, that was definitely closer. Who is calling me?"

Laird was looking around now too. Panning the shoreline with the camera.

I think we saw him at the same time, because Laird's camera stopped moving and focused on a man running up the beach from the direction of the pig roast. It looked like a wedding guest. He was in a white linen outfit, kicking up sand at a full run.

"Vanessa!"

I narrowed my eyes.

And then I put a hand over my mouth.

It was him.

*Adrian.*

I only had a moment to register it before I broke into a run toward him down the beach and we crashed into each other.

I was instantly whole.

He gathered me up like I'd seen Drake gather a parachute after landing a BASE jump. Hand over hand, tucking it all into your belly to carry it off in your arms. My thighs were lifted around his waist, my dress hiked up, hands under my ass, warm lips on my mouth, and I wondered briefly if I'd finally died and this was heaven.

I broke away from his kiss. "Wait. Wait wait wait, what are you doing here?" I breathed. "How? How did you find me?"

He pulled away just enough to look at me. He was crying. He looked like a man who had cried every single day for months. Like he'd gotten good at it and it was easier to cry now than it was to stop.

"I knew you'd be here. You wouldn't miss Drake's wedding. I knew I only had one shot at knowing exactly where you were. Vanessa, I'm so sorry. I was wrong. I was wrong to ask you what I did. I had no right."

I shook my head. "You were just being honest about what you need—"

"Fuck what I need. I should have kept you still. It was my *job* to keep you still. I've worked really hard to deal with the things inside of me that made it difficult to be strong for you. That was my own shit, and I had to work through that and I'm sorry."

I swallowed down the knot in my throat.

His eyes bored into mine. "I love you. I never said it and I should have said it every fucking day. I love you."

My chin trembled. "You got on a plane..."

He shook his head. "I got on dozens of planes. I quit my job. I woke up every day with no idea where I was going or what I was doing. I didn't even know whether you'd talk to me if I found you."

"You adopted Grace?" I said, my voice cracking.

"I went to get her from Gerald the day you had him clear out your apartment."

"You...you did?" I breathed.

A small smile played at the corners of his lips. "He gave me a long speech about how I should let you go. Then he made a dramatic exit and I didn't even let him get down the hallway before I went after him and told him I'd never give up on you and I wanted my daughter back. He said he wanted to see if I'd fight to keep my family together. I must have passed his test."

I laughed through tears.

He smiled. "It was the negotiation of a lifetime. He made me promise to let him see her and to only give her gender-neutral toys. Then he went on a rant about the patriarchy and subliminal messages in children's movies. I've been taking your dad to Perkins with Grace once a week since you left."

I didn't think it was possible to love Adrian more, to be prouder of him. But I was.

He nodded over his shoulder. "She's here, actually. She's with Drake—who still doesn't have a shirt, by the way."

I laughed and the welling tears spilled over.

His green eyes held mine and he wiped off my cheek with his thumb. "Please," he whispered. "Tell me it's not too late. Tell me you'll give me another chance. I don't want to waste another minute. I've wasted enough time as it is."

I nodded. "Yes," I whispered.

"Yes?"

I laughed through tears. "Yes."

His smile was enormous. It radiated. He kissed me again and I melted into it.

There was nothing nostalgic about him, not in his familiar smell or the shape of his body, because nostalgia would have suggested that he was a memory. He wasn't. My heart had never left him, had never forgotten a thing about him. It just started right back up from where we left off, like an on-going conversation. The inhale to the long exhale of the last two months.

He pulled away to look at me. "Let's make this the best time of our lives. Live every day like it's your last."

I sniffed. "And when one of them *is* my last?" I asked, looking at him.

"You're my soul mate. I'll find you in the next life. Like I found you in this one."

# THESE CELEBRITIES HAVE FALLEN OFF THE MAP, SEE WHERE THEY ARE NOW!

*Ten months later*

## ADRIAN

Come on. Put your elbow around my neck."

Vanessa pressed her lips into a line. She hated this. "I can do it myself."

"No, you can't." I scooped her into my arms. "You're not strong enough. You'll fall and hurt yourself. Besides, you let Drake do it on that mountain in Venezuela." I smiled, carrying her to the living room of my—*our*—apartment and setting her on the couch.

I tucked her throw blanket around her and kissed her forehead. "There. Was that so bad?"

She crossed her arms defiantly. Grace had started to do this too. I was outnumbered, two to one.

Grace stood at my feet, opening and closing her little fists. "Dada."

I picked up our daughter. "Do you see how stubborn Mommy is?" I said, tickling her tummy, and she giggled, little blond curls bouncing.

"I am not stubborn," Vanessa huffed, trying not to let me see her smile.

"Don't even get me started with you," I said, grinning. "You could have had this done months ago and you wouldn't have nerve damage in your hand."

The issue hadn't been ALS.

Six months after I'd come to find her at Drake's, Vanessa was still struggling with tingling fingers and weakness—but it never progressed past her arm. She'd finally agreed to some doctor's visits and they found a benign cyst had been pressing on a nerve. She'd just had it removed this morning. It was an outpatient procedure and she was still loopy from the anesthesia.

Since she hadn't been using her hand, she'd lost muscle tone in her arm, but a little physical therapy and she'd get that back.

She got a lot of things back when she got this diagnosis.

She was thirty now. She'd officially outlived her grand-mother, her aunt, her mom, and her older sister.

That didn't mean we were out of the woods. We'd never be out of the woods. ALS could always strike, at any time. She would always be a potential carrier of the gene. But every day that passed without the onset of symptoms, we felt more hopeful. And every day that passed we treated like a gift.

It was Christmas Eve tomorrow. We were home for the holidays—among other things. Namely her surgery, her birthday, and the big one—our wedding.

Our apartment was decorated for the holiday. The tree was up. Vanessa's artwork hung on our walls, plus a few new pieces we'd picked up on our travels. Our bedroom ceiling had glow-in-the-dark stars and our junk drawer was chaos. My office had been turned into a nursery—not that we were here very often to use it. At the age of one year old, Grace had visited more countries than most people do in their lifetime.

I grabbed my laptop and settled on the couch next to my wife.

She peered up at me as I attached a file to an email to Malcolm. "Are you sure you want to do this?" she asked. "There's a lot of private stuff in there."

I leaned in and kissed her. "I'm sure."

Our entire life was in this file. Videos of the last ten months. Our emotional first week back together, reconnecting on Drake's island. Our trip to India, our cruise on the Baltic Sea, me kissing her in front of the Eiffel Tower. Grace saying mama for the first time, Grace saying dada for the first time. An emotional freak out by Vanessa at a resort in Hawaii after she couldn't paddle board with her bad arm. I'd calmed her down and kept her still. Bushwhacking in Colombia, slow dancing on a promenade in Rio de Janeiro, Grace's first steps. Back to the United States to see Mom and Grandma and Richard. Thanksgiving with Gerald and Annabel and Brent. Then my surprise wedding proposal in the hallway of our apartment building on the one-year anniversary of the day we met. Our engagement photo, our feet with a chalkboard between us with SHE SAID YES (TO TAPAS).

We made the last video in the series last week. It was our

wedding, on Vanessa's thirtieth birthday, a private affair at the Sunken Garden in Como Park in St. Paul.

Drake had officiated—he even put on a shirt for the occasion. My cousin Josh was my best man, and Gerald gave her away.

Vanessa's dad was doing well. Staying in therapy, holding down his job, and keeping the house clean. Vanessa was really proud of him.

Brent and Joel were engaged. BoobStick was a huge success—as we knew it would be. It helped to fund most of our travels.

Annabel...

She left rehab early and relapsed. She had a hard couple of months after that. When she eventually returned to treatment, she was finally ready to get clean. She'd been sober since May and she was doing really well, working for Brent doing graphic design and taking classes online. She Skyped with Grace now and then and had spent lots of time with her since we'd been back in town.

We'd decided that we'd tell Grace about her birth parents as soon as she was old enough to understand, but Annabel made it clear she only wanted to be an aunt. So even though our daughter would always know the truth about where she came from, Vanessa would always be Grace's mommy.

Annabel was Vanessa's maid of honor at our wedding.

This whole year had been our honeymoon, even if we weren't officially married until a few days ago. And now we were going to share us with the world.

There hadn't been any updates on my wife or her condition

since our reunion video. Laird had gotten the whole thing on camera. We'd posted it in response to the Where's Vanessa Price hashtag that was trending on Twitter. Then we went back underground.

There were rumors and sightings, but nothing that would take away what would likely be a thunderous roar for the fight against ALS by the release of this series. We'd be donating all the proceeds to research. If it would bring us closer to a cure, then I was perfectly happy to give the world our most intimate moments.

I'd given up a lot of things for Vanessa, and I did not regret any of them.

I still practiced law, but I focused my efforts exclusively on fighting for disability rights. It was something I'd become very passionate about over the last year.

I saw the world through a different lens now. I noticed how hard it was to get wheelchair-accessible taxis and hotels. How rare it was in some places to find things I'd always taken for granted, like sidewalks. How so many restaurants and souvenir shops didn't have ramps. On our last trip to New York, I saw blatant violations of the Americans with Disabilities Act with subways lacking elevators in most of their stations.

If Vanessa ever did get sick, I wanted her world to stay as big as possible. I didn't want there to be anywhere she, or others like her, couldn't go and I'd spend the rest of my life fighting to make that a reality. It was rewarding and fulfilling—and I finally had my balance.

I kept up with my therapy sessions and I was in an online support group for people living with terminal loved ones. I took care of my mental well-being with the same commitment that I took care of my family—because I couldn't do one unless I did the other.

Vanessa snuggled up to me and I put an arm around her. Grace leaned into me on the other side, holding her favorite stuffed bear.

I told them I loved them every day. I never took tomorrow for granted. Aaaaand I read the horoscopes Becky texted me without exception.

"Are you ready?" I asked, hovering my finger over the button that would send the file through. "We can't get it back once it's gone."

Vanessa grinned. "I don't think ALS will know what hit it."

My lips twisted up into a smile. "Good."

{Send}.

# READING GROUP GUIDE

# AUTHOR'S NOTE

While Vanessa's character is fiction, I went into this book in awe of the inspirational real-life activist and YouTuber Claire Wineland.

Claire lived with cystic fibrosis, an illness she refused to let define her. She used her platform to inspire and educate, traveling the world to speak to others about her life and encouraging those with chronic illnesses to find fulfillment and live proudly. A documentary about her life titled *Claire* can be found exclusively on YouTube.

Claire passed away in 2018 at twenty-one from complications after a lung transplant. She donated her organs to those in need.

She was a beautiful soul.

# DISCUSSION QUESTIONS:

1. Would you have given your baby to a strange man at 4:00 a.m.?

2. Would you help friends and family suffering from addiction? At what point is it enabling, and when should you stop?

3. How difficult is it for you to live in the moment and enjoy life to the fullest today versus saving and investing for the future? Can you do both?

4. How do you feel about Vanessa's decision not to seek treatment?

5. Do you believe that couples in a relationship should make decisions about end of life and medical care together? Or is that for the dying person to decide?

6. Could you enter a relationship knowing your partner might have only a year to live? Is it better not to know?

7. If you had the platform, what issue or cause would you raise awareness for? What can you do now to make a difference today?

# ADRIAN'S CHICKEN AND WILD RICE SOUP

- 3½ 32-ounce cartons chicken broth (or 112 ounces)
- 14 ounces mirepoix mix (or 2 carrots, 1 stalk of celery, 1 large white onion—chopped)
- 2 cups sliced mushrooms (optional)
- Fresh poultry bouquet (two stems each of rosemary, sage, thyme)
- 1 pound cooked shredded chicken
- 2 boxes of Rice-A-Roni Long Grain & Wild Rice with seasoning
- Salt to taste

**Roux:**

- ¾ cup butter
- 1 cup flour
- 3 cloves minced garlic
- ¼ cup cooking sherry
- 1 pint heavy whipping cream

**Directions:**

Put broth, onions, carrots, celery, mushrooms (if using), herbs (on the stems), chicken, and rice and seasoning packets into a large stock pot and simmer until the rice is cooked and the carrots are soft, approximately 20 minutes. Remove the herb stems and any loose sage leaves. Add salt to taste.

**Make the roux:**

In a medium saucepan, melt the butter over medium heat. Add the flour and garlic, whisking constantly until the mixture boils. Boil for one minute. Slowly pour in the sherry and cream, mixing constantly until thick. Add the roux to the soup and serve.

Note: If soup is too thick, it can be thinned with more broth or milk.

*Makes 12 servings*

Tastes extra yummy in bread bowls. Can be frozen up to three months for later.

# VANESSA'S HORSERADISH
# MASHED POTATOES

- 3 pounds quartered russet potatoes, skins on
- 8 ounces cream cheese
- ¼ cup butter
- 4 tablespoons creamy horseradish or horseradish sauce, plus more to taste
- Salt to taste

**Directions:**

Bring water to boil in a large stockpot. Add potatoes. Boil the potatoes until soft, approximately 15 to 25 minutes. Drain.

Use a handheld mixer to combine all ingredients, adding the horseradish 1 tablespoon at a time until you reach the desired flavor.

# ACKNOWLEDGMENTS

Thank you to pharmacist Tracy Nelson for helping me get the narcotics and the details surrounding addiction in this book right.

A big thank-you to attorneys Lisa and Katie Tuntigian-Ringer and attorney Larry Hales for your legal prowess. Thank you, Terri Saenz and Dan Schoonover, and as always a huge thank-you to my group admins, who make so much of what I do possible. Jeanette Jett, Terri Puffer Burrell, Lindsay Van Horn, and Dawn Cooper, you guys rock.

Thank you to beta readers Kim Kao, Lyndse Kay, Amy Edwards Norman, Trish Gee, Lisa Stremmel, and Leigh Kramer. To my agent, Stacey Graham; my editor, Leah Hultenschmidt; my publicist, Estelle Hallick; cover designer Sarah Congdon; production editor Mari Okuda; production coordinator Marie Mundaca; and the whole Forever Romance team. I can't believe I suckered you guys into another three-book deal—haha!

Additional thanks to these fabulous supporters!

Kristina Aadland
Dara Abraham
Kristin Abraham
Cime Adili
Erin Alexander
Aubrey Algar
Karla Aliperto
Lacy Allaire
Jamilah Allen
Terri Allen
Victoria Allen
Kristol Allshouse

Diana Alonzo
Nicole Altherr
Amy Amundson
Ashlee Anderson
Bridget Anderson
Caitlin Anderson
Carrie Anderson
Elizabeth Anderson
Lindsey Anderson
Tamara Anderson
Laura Andert
Ariadnae Andrews
Kristie Andrews
Margaret Angstadt
Alyssa Anttila
Nicole Aquilina
Angela Arandela
Anastasia Artayet
    Shepherd
Lisa Ashburn
Carol Au
Katie Ault
Megan Ausborn
Elena Austin
Cheyenne Baca
Kaylee Backen
Nicole Backen
Cathy Bailey
Sarah Bailey
Danielle Bailleu
Janean Baird
Marci Baker
Emily Bakken
Jenny Ballman
Gina Barboni
Kristen Barker
Kimberly Barkoff
Dulce Barraza
Sofia Barraza
Lindsay Bartels
Mies Bastille
Kristie Basting
Kelly Bates

Jennifer Battan
Lydia Baugh
Elizabeth Baumann
Ashley Baylor
Janelle Beal
Jessica Bearak
Justin Beaudry
Dawn Beavers
Heather Beedy
Sara Behnejad
Kristine Bemboom
Jessica Bennett
Michelle Bennett
Rose Bentley
Cassie Berdahl
Lucinda Bergen
Maria Berry
Stefany Besse
Betty Best
Angelina Beuadry
Hope Biersach
Brittany Bikkie
Dolly Bina
Courtney Birdsall
Lori Bishop
Betsy Bissen
Melissa Bjerke
Erin Blair
Lisa Blanchar
Corrie Block
Susan Block
Nicole Blomgren
Rachel Blust
Kim Blythe
Sarah Bock
Helen Boettner
Allie Bohlman
Carrie Bollig
Krystal Bollinger
Daryl Bondeson
Micaela Boney
Tyler Bonneville
Shana Borgen

Katie Borgstahl
Christine
    Borkenhagen
Ann Borysowski
Emily Bosch
Breanna Bouley
Agapi Bountouri
Andriana
    Bourboulia
Hannah Bowers
Maggi Bowers
Kathryn Boyer
Heidi Bradish
Josie Bragg
Amelia Brant
Marjorie Branum
Ashley Brassard
Sheryl Braun
Crystal Bremer
Elizabeth Brimeyer
Elizabeth Brimeyer
Kathryn Brimeyer
Cheryl Briol
Whitney Brionez
Robyn Bristow
Erin Broadbent
Danielle Brochu
Rachel D. Brock
Jenni Brooks
Kelly Brooks
Amanda Brown
Jessica Brown
Kim Brown
Melody Bruen
Shelly Budz
Jennifer Buechele
Sara Buffie
Justine Burke
Stephanie Burkey
Liesl Burnes
Terri Burrell
Lien Busby
Melissa Bussell

Megan Butler
Alexis Buxton
Kristin Cafarelli
Danielle Calderoni
Yvette Cano
Acacia Caraballo
Lindsey Cardinal
Meghan Carlisle
Julie Carlson
Melissa Carlton
Lindsay Carson
Paige Carter
Carlita Cartwright
Creya Casale
Christine
    Castellanos
Laura Castro
Ashley Cavazos
Shelly Caveney
Sarah Caverly
Marissa Cazares
Dori Cedillo
Serene Chamberlin
Kristen Chasey
Sylvia Chavarin
Vanessa Chavez
Shari Chim
Cara Ching
Liz Christiansen
Mingy Chung
Michelle Church
Alyssa Cihak
LiAnna Clement
Kristen Climes
Jamie Cluff
Sheree Cluff
Robyn Cody
Jenny Coker
Anna Cole
Sarah Colford
    Russell
Paula Colon
Leanne Colton

Kylie Combs
Michelle Comstock
Heather Cone
Kari Cone
Kerry Conneely
Katie Connnors
Michelle Conrad
Abby Cook
Heather Cook
Emily Cooper
Jenn Cooper
Megan Cooper
Patty Cooper
Peggy Coover
Kimmy Corey Jr
Cirsten Cornetta
Robyn Corson
Sylvia Costa
Liz Cote
Heather Cottrell
Andi Cowan
Nicole Cowling
Carissa Crabb
Deana Crabb
Becky Cramer
Mallory Credeur
Cholie Crom
Kristina Cromwell
Caitlin Cross
Sara Cross
Kathryn Crotty
Katrina Crouse
Grace Cuda
Lisa Cullen
Whitney
    Cunningham
Kristin Curran
Susan Czeterko
    Jordan
Kelli Dade
Anna Dale
Lynn Dale
Ruth Dano

Anna Davenport
Holly Daymude
Laura DeBouche
Kimberly Decur
Ashley DeFrank
Jennifer DeGarmo
Denise Delamore
Angela Denardo
Julie Dengerud
Elise Dennis
Bridget DeRoo
Jayme DeSotel
Jami DeVoe
Kate DeVries
Robin Diamond
Katrina Diaz
Nicole Dirden
Leandreea Divito
Carissa Dixon
Elle Dobosenski
Wendy Dodson
Colleen Dols
Rhonda Dominick
Alyssa Douglass
Elizabeth Dowell
Tricia Downey
Shelby Doyle
Heather Dryer
Melissa Dubois
Danielle Duerr
Stacey Duitsman
Elizabeth Duncan
Meggan Duncan
Lindsay Dupic
Leslie Dupont
Kathleen Duppler
Jo Ebersole
Sarah Edie
Precious Edmonds
Jennifer Edney
Sarah Edstrom
    Smith
Gabrielle Edwards

Erin Egan
Larayne Egbert
Joanne Ehrmantraut
Ashley Eisenberg
Michele Eisenberg
Elaina Eiser
Angie Elliott
Tiffanie
   Elliott-Stelter
Tamarae Ellis
Casey Ellsworth
Korissa Emerson
Nancy Emmerich
Jessica Engel
Carly Engels
   Johnston
Shelley English
Lindsey Engrav
Helen "Nana" Ennis
Kayla Ercolano
Amanda Erickson
Corrine Erickson
Elizabeth Erratchu
Jenna Ervin
Tara Escue
Lisa Eskelson
Megan Eskew
Breanna Essoi
Madeleine Estherby
Lydia Eubanks
Jennevieve Evers
Krissy Fairfield
Rebecca Falk
Danielle Fantillo
Ashley Faria
Nicole Feigl
Nicole Fellrath
Cindy Femling
Christina Ferdous
Krystina Ferrari
Melinda Fierro
Laurel Fike
Afton Finley

Anna Fisk
Dianthe Fleming
Selina Fleshman
Kristine "Goo"
   Flores
Emily Foltz
Jessica Fontana
Shawn Ford
April Forse
Taylor Forsyth
Stephanie Foster
Larice Fournier
Devin Fox
Jennifer Fox
Julie Frazzini
Ashley Freburg
Janel Freel
Becky Freer
Shelley Friedrich
Holly Friker
Heather Fullam
Katie Fulton
Ashley Fultz
Sharon Funkhouser
Jennifer Furr
Samantha Furrer
Goldie G
Tamara Gaglioti
Sheila Gagnon
Lauren Galante
Emma Galligan
Rena Galvez
Christina Gamboa
Nicole Garand
Melissa Garcia
Sara Gardner
Melissa Garrity
Allie Garza
April Gassler
Pamela Gedalia
Samantha Geissler
Amy Gelwick
Leia Georgeopolus

Annie Gerlach
Bridget Gibbons
Bonnie Gidzak
Julie Giese
Amanda Gilbert
Amanda L. Gilbert
Heidi Gilbert
Kourtney Gillan
Karla Glass
Sarah Gleason
Amanda Glueck
Sarah Gocken
Jennifer Godsey
Anna-Lee Goethe
Virginia Gonzalez
Zoe Gonzalez
Amy Goodrow
Buack Gordon
Julie Gordon
Anna Gorna
Rebecca Gossard
Jaimie Gosselin
Alex Jo Goulet
Michelle Gour
Nichole Graham
Christina Granados
Brianna Rache'
   Granberry
Kirsten Grayson
Chelsea Green
Michelle Green
Julia Greenham
Nikki Greer
Meghan Greyeyes
Deanna Griese
Debra Grodin
Katey Grof
Christina Grubbs
Rachell Gualpa
Tammy Guccione
Alicia Guerrero
Catherine
   Guilbeault

Elizabeth Gustafson
Norma Gutierrez
Sonia Gutierrez
Gina Haars
Tina Hackley
Christina Hager
Becci Haifley
Stacy Haight
Maddie Hake
Jennifer Hallett
Casey Hambleton
Trista Hammer
Alyssa Handevidt
Jenny Hanen
Lisa Hannawa
Kristin Hannon
Kristyna Hanson
Lauren Hanson
Mackenzie Hanson
Nicole Harbour Lau
Mackenzie Harrison
Susan Hart
Shannon Harte
Kelsey Haukos
Kylie Havner
Dana Hawley
Dana Hayes
Melinda Haynie
Stephanie Heinz
Lauren Heinze
Michelle Helgeson
Angela Helland
Jessica Hendricks
Joanie Hendricks
Amber
    Hendrickson
Haley Hendrickson
Angie Hendrickx
Stephanie Henigin
David Henkhaus
Lisa Henkhaus
Amy Henley
Melinda Hennies

Carmen Henning
Kimberly Her
Brielle Herbst
Natalie Hering
Jennifer Herlick
Dalia Hernandez-
    Hermann
Bridget Heroff
Stephanie Heseltine
Ashley Hester
Kim Hildebrand
Stephanie Hill
Tressa Hills
Rhonda Hinkel
Becky Hochstein
Amanda Hoeger
Faith Hoenstine
Kim Hoff
Amber Hoffman
Julie Hoffman
Shanna Hofland
Tiffany Hokanson
Emily Holien
Elizabeth
    Hollingshead
Sarah Holmes
Toni Holmes
Amber Holtz
Jamie Holwerda
Cassandra Hornsby
Jennifer Hoshowski
Elizabeth Housman
Becca Houston
Kelli Houts
Kendra Hovingh
Corissa Howard
Jennifer Howell
Lacey Howell
Alyssa Hudson
Kristi Huntley
Whitney
    Hutcheson
Joli Huynh

Samantha Nicole
    Ibanez
Jonathan Icasas
Danielle Inagaki
Tiffanie Ing
Kayla Innis
Viktoriya
    Ivanova-Piram
Ashley Ivey
Colantha
    Izzard-Amo
Nicole Jackson
Raelyn Jackson
Gabrielle Jendro
Michelle Jenkins
Brigette Jennings
Angie Jensen
Brianna Jensen
Jeanette Jett
Adrienne Johnson
Amy Johnson
Bailey Johnson
Brittany Johnson
Bryana Johnson
Crystal Johnson
Janine Johnson
Kim Johnson
Morgan Johnson
Paige Johnson
Rachel Johnson
Shawna Jokinen
Cassie Jolley
Mary Joslyn
Amanda Jules
Daryl Jul-ul
Jean Jurek
Dhanushka
    Kadawatharatchie
Olivia Kägel
Kim Kao
Julia Kautz
Debbie Kearschner
Irene Kedrowski

Kelly Keefe
Haley Keegan
Linda Keeler
Devon Keenan
Shekenah Keith
Tara Kekahuna
Andrea Kelly
Stephanie Kelly
Krista Kemper
Megan Kennedy
Kelly Kent
Noël
   Kepler-Gageby
Bridget Kersey
Bex Kettner
Judy Keyes
Sharon Kill
Andrea King
Kris King
Shannon King
Victoria King
Donna Kiolbassa
Leslie Kissinger
Liv Kittelson
Kelle Klocke
Nicki Kobaly
Clare Koch
Monica Kocon
Joy Kokolus
Melissa Kolyer
Julie Kornmann
Kelly Kornmann
Dawn Kosobud
   Johnson
Kristiina Kovala
Tricia Kovely
Amy Krajec
Holly Kramer
Emily Kremer
Nichole Krueger
Traci Kruse
Marta Krzemien
Jessica Kudulis

Anne Kuffel
Katie Laban
Alexa Lach
Kelly Laferriere
Kimberley Laimonis
Annette Laird
Jennifer Lalos
Naomi LaMarr
Sue Lammert
Patty Langasek
Jennifer Langlois
Amy Langowski
Brenda Lanners
Annie Lanning
Victoria Larsen
Becky Larson
Jaimie Larson
Andrea Leaf
Bethany Lee
Eunhea Grace Lee
Kayla Lee
Michelle Lee
Jackie Leibowitz
Dana Lenertz
Stephanie Leslie
Rebecca Levitan
Teresa Limtiaco
Martha Lindhorst
Samantha Lindner
Stacy Link
Rebecca Linscott
Amanda Little
Rochelle Livingston
Kristin Lockwood
Monica Logan
LeeAnn Longmore
Christina Lopez
Carly Lorio
Melissa Lotz
Jamie Lotzer
Ashley Lubrant
Krissy Luce
Kelsey Lucero

Natalie Lucindo
Jessica Ludwig
Sarah Ludwig
Megan Lundberg
Jackie Lynch
Linda Lynch
Brian Lyon-Garnett
Rhonda Lyte
Jillian Mabee
Kelsey MacDonald
Megan MacDonald
Megan MacDonald
Kristin Macklin
Amanda Madden
Jen Maddigan
Katrina Madriz
Michele Magnuson
Leigh Ann Mahaffie
Amy Mahan
Kelley Majdik
Cynthia E
   Maldonado
Karleen Malmgren
Marcella Malone
Savannah Mankoci
Alicia Manley
Sean Maple
Debby Margolis
Mim Markey
Heidi Markland
Jessica Marsden
Mary Anna Martell
Michelle Martin
Samantha Martin
Julie Martineau
Catalina Martinez
Marie Martinez
Lucinda
   Martinez-Carter
Melissa Martius
Tracy Mastel
Marcia Matchett
Cecelia Mattos

Amanda Mattson
Colleen Mawby
Melissa Mayorga
Krystal McBride
Bobbin
    McCullough
Kim McDermid
Katie McDonald
Carly McEathron
Callie McGinn
Jaime Lee McHale
Brooke McKenna
Tamara McNelis
Elissa McPherson
Joann McQuaid
Priscilla McRae
Stephanie Means
Laurie Mease
Karen Meier
Mylissa Merten
Chynna Mesich
Steph Meyer
Jodi Michaelis
Chandelle
    Michaelson
Julie Miedtke
Kristy Miller
Meridith Miller
Pam Million
Deborah Mills
Kimberly Mills
Jessica Minor
Aayanna Minott
Maribel Minott
Debbie Miranda
Errin Mitchell
Megan Miura
Elise Mock
Samantha Modi
Jessica Modriskey
Rachel Modrow
Trista Moffitt
Katie Monaghan

Jaime Monson
Meagan
    Montgomery
Mikhaiel
    Moody-VanDuyne
Kate Moon
Megan Moore
Julie Morales
Jami Morgan
Laurel Morgan
Sue Morgan
Jana Morimoto
Kelsey Morin
Lauren Morris
Michelle Morrisette
Emily Morrison
Liz Morrison-Thron
Ginny Mosier
Jenni Mueller
Alice Munoz
Rebecca Munro
Bethanne Murphy
Cassandra Murphy
Claire Murphy
Laura Murray
Stephanie Murry
Ginny Muse
Katy Myllykangas
Michele Myran
Cheryl Myrum
Sheryl Nall
Lynn Nalupta
Elizabeth Narolis
Sarah Naumann
Cookie Navarro
Dwon Nave
Kristin Nelsen
Antonia Nelson
Joan Nelson
Shanna Nemitz
Wendy Nenner
Shastine Neptune
Annie Ngo

Christine Nichols
Nicki Nidelkoff
Jennifer Niehoff
Kayla Niekrasz
Carrie Niezgocki
Jeanne Nihart
Courtney Nino
Astoria Niverson
Dannah Niverson
Heather Noeker
Adeline Noland
Karen Noland
Taylor Noland
Jacque Nordahl
Danielle Norkunas
Amy Norman
Jen Nystrom
Andrew Oakes
    Champagne
Danielle Oakes
Danielle Ochoa
Sarah O'Connor
Kathleen O'Dell
Liz O'Donnell
Adrienne Oeschger
Elaina O'Grady
Christina Oien
Nicole Ojakian
Ewa Okla
Molly Okoroafo
Denise Oleary
Hillary Oliver
Jeni Oliver
Cori Olson
Kristina Olson
Mariette Olson
Mary Olson
Lindsey Orick
Stacey Osland
Anna Ostendorf
Kristin
    Osuna-Larson
Kate O'Toole

Megan O'Toole
Hall
Alyssa Overfield
Olana Owen
Mary Catherine
Ozcelik
Sidney Pacheco
Jody Packard
Kristyn Packard
Noelle Parenteau
Christina Parker
Sarah Parkos
Ashley Parks
Sue Paron
Elaine Patch
Roberta Patch
Merrisa Patel
Sonia Patel
Crystal Paul
Fiona Payne
Marisa Peck
Justine Pederson
Amanda Pedulla
Way-Way Pee
Cynthia Peloquin
Shelby Perkins
Colleen Peterson
Crystal Peterson
Jasie Peterson
Kamisha Peterson
Tyra Peterson
Emily Petrich
Jennifer Petska
Hilary Peyton
Julia Phillips
Katherine Phillips
Melissa Phillips
Chelsea Phipps
Shelley Pierce
Nicole Pilarski
Jaime Pint
Nicki Pipes
Anne Pitre

Courtnie Pollard
Ashley Polomchak
Carrie Pons
Melissa Porter
Danielle Portillo
Marilyn Possin
Michelle Possin
Jennifer Presley
Mary Prichard
Rachel Prince
Melanie Probasco
Lorraine Purcell
Lana Purdie
Amanda Pusateri
Morgan Qin
Pam Quist
Danielle Rabe
Keytelynne Radde
Sarah Raines
Abby Rainville
Fay Raisanen
Deanne Ramirez
Carey Raph
Dawn Rask
Randi Rasmussen
Laura Rausch
Kristin Raymond
EC Raymundo
Shauna Reardon
Megan Reed
Missy Reed
Myria Reed
Lisa Reeves
Amaza Reitmeier
Kris Reynolds
Cheryl Richardson
Jenelle Ries
Janine Rife
Jessica Ringelsten
Emily Rios
Liza Ritchie
Kyree Ritter
Sherry Ritter

Abbe Roberts
Richelle Robinson
Sherri Robinson
Stephanie Robinson
Angie Robson
Caitlin Rock
Samira Rockler
Isadora Rocourt
Kristin Rohde
Sara Roman
Summer Romero
Tiffany "Fattness"
Romero
Kendra Romig
Susan Rooney
Michelle Roop
Laura Rosenberger
Sara Rosenberry
Amber Rosin
Angie Ross
Heather Ross
Jen Ross
Jennifer Roth
Lindsay Routh
Joanne Rubinsohn
Tasha Runyon
Sarah Rushford
Liz Rust
Kylie Ryan
Michael & Shannan
Sabby
Sarah Saeed
Natalie Gianna
Saenz
Ilene Sago
Natalie S. Samples
Megan Sanchez
Caitlin Sand
Rhonda Sandberg
Tiffany Sanders
Barb Sanford
Allison Santaella
Bernadette Santana

Jackie Saval
Aundrea Saville
Emily Saylor
Chloe Scalici
Trisha Schable
Ailiah Schafer
Briana Schalow
Jen Schildknecht
Tammy Schilling
Ashley Schleif
Brooke Schlottke
Alisyn Schmelzer
Jodi Schmidt
Adrianne Schneider
Andrea Schneider
Jill Schneider
Michelle Schroeder
Kayla
    Schroeder-Kessler
Brittney Schultz
Melissa Schulz
Sonja Schultz
Wendy Schuster
Samantha Schwartz
Kelly Scott
Mindi Sechser
Anne Seeley
Kelsey Seeley
Amanda Seibert
Kristen Selinsky
Brianne Sellman
Brittani Sepko
Cassandra Sepko
Tami Serna
Jean Shaffer
Rebecca Shamblin
Jamie Shaull
Laura Shiff
Amanda Sichmeller
Catalina Sierra
Bridget Sigman
Amy Simmons
Tracye Simmons

Lisa Simms
Dawn Sitter
Ashley Sitz
Stephanee
    Skaradzinski
Cindy Slabich
Kristen Sloan
Alicia Smith
Ashley L. Smith
Cheryl Smith
Devin Smith
Jennifer Smith
Julie Smith
Katie Smith
Lauren Smith
Megan Smith
Melissa Smith
Nan Smith
Olive Smith
Kelly Snow
Michele Snyder
Elizabeth Soares
Elisabeth Solchik
Lauren Solmonson
Laura Sonnee
Melissa Sonnek
Therese Sonnek
BananaBlue Soriana
Britta Soronen
Andi Soule
Julianna Spilker
Marlana
    Splettstosser
Laura Sprandel
Jane St John
Amanda St. George
Melissa St. Pierre
Tarah Stafford
Angel Stagi
Kristin Stai
Kerry Stallings
Amanda Stamm
Amanda Stamm

Diane Stansbury
Brittany Steffen
Patricia Steffen
Maile Steffy
Amy Steger
Martha Stellmach
Martha Stering
Lindsey Stevens
Tracy Stevens
Christina Stewart
Renee Stine
Shawna Stolp
JoAnn Stoltman
Kristin Stormer
Melissa Stream
Katie Stryker
Krystina Stuber
Kasey Sullivan
Julia Sumrall
Stephanie Sweat
Wendy Swerdlow
Sarah Symonds
Kristen Szeto
Jynell Tackett
Cindi Tagg
Jenifer Talbot
    Nicolson
Marianne Talukdar
Shandrea Tanglao
Stacey Tarr
Amber Taylor
Ashley Taylor
Casey Taylor
Jennifer Taylor
Angie Thaxton
Annette Theel
Katie Then
Christine Thiel
Robyn Thogmartin
Michelle Thomas
Lynnae Thompson
Mandy Thurmes
    Pung

Crystal Thurow
Emilee Thursby
Sara Thurston
Allison Thyng
Shay Tibbs
Rhonda Tinch
Nicole Todd
Rae Toledo Latsch
Pritika Tolento
Shelby Tomlinson
Megan Tonn
Rose Tonn
Jacqueline Torfin
Emily Torrance
Jessica Tounzen
Sara Towne
Christa Treptow
Arleen Trevino
Bianca Trevino
Miranda Tsai
Jennifer Turner
Stephanie Turner
Rebecca Upshaw
Kathleen
    Uttenweiler
Kristin Uzzi
Ash-Leigh Vagle
Jennifer Van Dusen
Charlene
    VanWinkle
Eileen Vazquez
Christine Verrill
Heather Vetsch
Danielle Via
Linden Vimislik
Erica Viola
Kristie Viscasillas
Allison Vogel
Karen Vollmer

Megan
    VonDeLinde
Nina Vopni
Michele Voss
Kimberly Walker
Michelle Walker
Taylor
    Walkky-Byington
Nadine Walz
Ted Wanken
Laura Warcholek
Brandy Warner
Jenna Warner
Deena Warren
Erica Weaver
Leah Weaver
Carli Weber
Rebecca Weber
Deana Wegner
Andrea Wehrung
Alexis Weidoff
Marie Weisbrod
Amanda
    Weissman
Marina Weissman
Lesli Weldy
Jenny Weller
Jessica Weller
Ashli Wells
Theresa Welsh
Jennifer Welter
Larissa Wenszell
Megan Wentz
Alison Werner
Jennifer Westberg
Danielle Wettrick
Danielle Whitmore
Jenna Wild
Mindy Wilkinson

Deanne Wilkinson
    Deneke
Rhonda Williams
Rylee Williams
Cheryl Wilson
Jo Wilson
Ruth Wilson
Amanda Wilson TX
Sara Witkowski
Emma Witthuhn
Cait Wodarski
Ariel Wolf
Mandy Wolfe
Julie Wood
Mariah Woodrum
Christina Woolsey
Kelli Worley
Rachel Wornica
Amy Wroblewski
Meghann Wyss
Katie Xiong
Helen Yang
Diane Yeager
Shannon Yockey
Jennifer Yuen
Tracy Zachow
Michele Zalak
Krista Zaleski
Kathy Zavala
Zoë Zellers
Allison Zellman
Michelle Zilisch
Pamela Zimmer
Jessica Ziolko
Mara Zotz
Lisa Zuhlsdorf
Abby Zuis
Stephanie Zwirn

DON'T MISS ABBY'S
NEXT NOVEL, *PART OF YOUR WORLD,*
COMING IN SPRING 2022!

# ABOUT THE AUTHOR

Abby Jimenez is a Food Network champion and *USA Today* bestselling contemporary romance novelist living in Minnesota. Abby founded Nadia Cakes out of her home kitchen in 2007. The bakery has since expanded to multiple locations in two states, won numerous Food Network competitions, and amassed an international cult following. Abby's wry literary wit was spotlighted as the admin behind the hilarious viral comments on the now famous Nadia Cakes Vageode® cake.

She loves a good book, coffee, doglets, and not leaving the house.

You can learn more at:

AuthorAbbyJimenez.com
Twitter @AuthorAbbyJim
Facebook.com/AuthorAbbyJimenez
Instagram @AuthorAbbyJimenez